LETHAL IN LAGUNA

A Ruby Ray Mystery
(Book 2)

Debra L. Brunner

Debra L. Brunner

Cover design and art by Debra L. Brunner

Illustrations by Debra L. Brunner

Published by **Coral Cloche Press**
Orange County, CA

Paperback edition ISBN: 9798992297607

Printed in the United States of America

FOR CHARLES

My dear son, who loves Laguna Beach
as much as I do. You are that treasured piece of
my heart moving through the world,
making it a better place.

Ruby's Laguna Beach

Map not to scale

PACIFIC OCEAN

KEY

1. Crystal Cove	2. Dos Rocas	3. Shaw's Cove
4. Pier	5. Cabrillo Ballroom	6. Main Beach
7. Downtown	8. La Casa Del Camino	9. Coast Inn
10. Aliso Auto Camp	11. Table Rock	12. Three Arch Bay

Downtown Detail

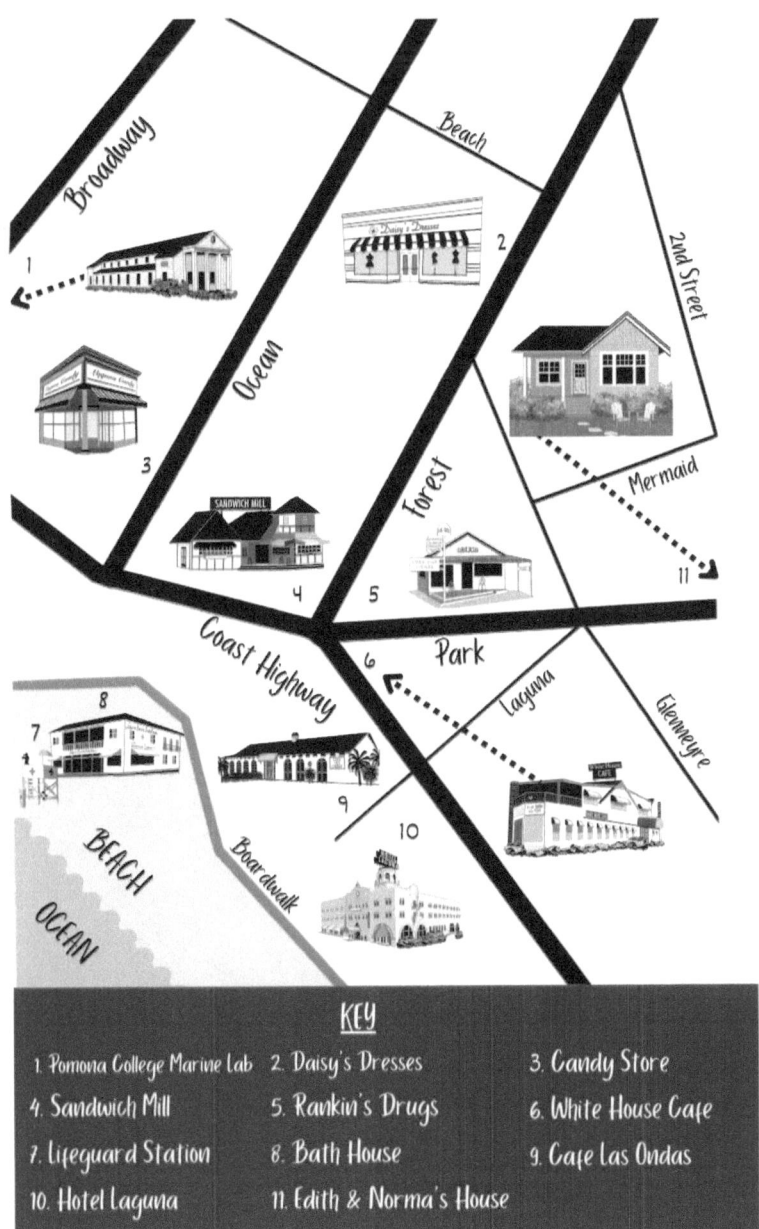

KEY

1. Pomona College Marine Lab
2. Daisy's Dresses
3. Candy Store
4. Sandwich Mill
5. Rankin's Drugs
6. White House Cafe
7. Lifeguard Station
8. Bath House
9. Cafe Las Ondas
10. Hotel Laguna
11. Edith & Norma's House

Debra L. Brunner

PROLOGUE

SUNDAY, AUGUST 24, 1930
LAGUNA BEACH, CALIFORNIA

"Hand me my knife, will ya?"

"Aye, Captain Sal." The deckhand's eyes, wide with astonishment, reflect the general demeanor of the rest of the crew as he retrieves the tool from a canvas bag of diving gear.

Captain Sally Mackay impatiently grabs the blade from the youth and gives it a twist, securing the knife within its sheath. After removing the weights from her diving belt, she attaches the sheath and tightens the belt around her waist.

"Is that a child?" The first mate passes Sal the binoculars. Peering through the eyecups, Sal adjusts the focusing wheel to sharpen the image of the drowning victim who's flailing in the water about 100 yards away.

"Nah. It's a lady," Sal replies. While petite, the figure is definitely that of a woman—her bathing cap has slipped off to reveal unnaturally blonde hair. Closer to shore, a lifeguard furiously swims toward the victim while pulling a towline attached to a floating container. Onshore, a group of junior lifeguards uncoil the other end of the line. Sal refocuses on the struggling woman who's become entangled in the kelp, despite the slime that's coating the lengthy ribbons.

If she'd just relax, the fronds would help her float, Sal thinks to herself.

"I'm goin' in," she calls over her shoulder and passes the binoculars to a crew member. With the fluid motion of an experienced diver, she raises her muscular arms overhead and launches herself into the dark sapphire water.

The motley gang aboard the *Bonnie Boat* gawk, open-mouthed, as their captain races toward the drowning woman with powerful strokes.

"Well, I'll be damned," one exclaims.

"Why didn't we take the boat closer?" the young deckhand inquires.

"Too risky." The first mate points over the starboard side of the boat. "There's a rocky reef between us and that kelp bed."

"That current ain't helpin' her none either!" A geriatric crew member monitors his captain's progress with the binoculars.

In the distance, the lifeguard reaches the drowning victim first, but her writhing obstructs his attempts to secure the towline under her arms.

"Hold still," his voice carries across the water, but the woman doesn't appear to hear him.

Meanwhile, Sal paddles toward them at an angle, trying to break free of the current that's slowing her progress.

She was born to the sea.

Sal recalls her old man's proud words. In truth, her father taught her everything she knows about the ocean and navigating its waters in the *Bonnie Boat.*

"*Speed, bonnie boat, like a bird on the wing.*"

Her father used to sing "The Skye Boat Song" as they sailed up and down the Southern California coastline. Now, Sal paces her strokes to the song's cadence.

"*Onward the sailors cry.*"

Having spent the first light of morning searching the deep blue in a heavy diving suit, the muscles in Sal's arms burn fiercely. She lowers her head into the water and, swimming submerged for several lengths, spies the brilliant orange of a garibaldi, the foot-long damselfish that prefers the safety of the kelp forests.

Nearly there.

Sal surfaces about 5 yards from the lifeguard, who is desperately trying to extricate the woman from the dense stems.

"Hold still. I have a knife," she calls, then dives beneath the pair. With a firm grasp on the handle, she untwists the blade from its sheath and begins hacking at the vegetation around the woman who, thankfully, has finally stopped struggling.

"She's free now," the lifeguard declares when Sal comes up for air. "Help me get the rope around her."

The wide-eyed woman's body is rigid, but she's no longer thrashing, which makes the task of securing the towline much easier. Further, the metal canister attached to the line gives it some buoyancy.

Sal pats her arm. "Relax. You'll be fine. They're gonna pull you in." But the woman groans, her body stiff as a plank.

"Why don't you swim along the other side of her," the lifeguard suggests, and they accompany the victim to shore.

As soon as they've navigated the small breakers, two of the junior lifeguards wade out and help them carry the woman to the dry sand.

Sal kneels next to her and watches her torso. "She's not breathing."

"Flip her over," the senior lifeguard instructs the teens. When they begin to roll the woman onto her belly, he barks, "Turn her head, for Pete's sake, and fold her arms so her face rests on her hands. Did you forget your training?"

"But, sir," one youth exclaims, "Her arms won't bend."

The lifeguard rolls her onto her back "What the—"

"It's too late. She's dead." Sal gazes into the woman's blank eyes.

The entire rescue crew is speechless.

Time seems to stand still until—several yards away—a diminutive young lady with platinum blonde hair emerges from the shelter of a beach umbrella and releases an ear-piercing scream.

The junior lifeguards snap up their heads—mouths agape—as the young woman sobs uncontrollably.

Then someone nearby shrieks, "It's that movie star! Corvi Styles!"

CHAPTER 1

SUNDAY, AUGUST 10, 1930
NEW YORK PASSENGER SHIP TERMINAL

Gulls circle over the Hudson River releasing high-pitched calls that resemble laughter. A group of young men, the targets of their mockery, attempt to fish from a nearby pier. One glances up and notices the birds then pulls his creel closer to prevent the vexing fowl from raiding his haul of striped bass. I return my attention to the dock below and scan the throng.

"Do you see them?" Miss Violet inquires.

"Not yet," I shake my head. "I can't make out one face from another."

When we sailed away two months ago, a few hundred family and friends gathered on the dock to wish their loved ones bon voyage. But today, more than a thousand spirited folks wave and cheer as the gangway is lowered.

"It's like finding a needle in a haystack," I observe, unable to locate my family.

"You'll find them," Miss Mabel gives my shoulder a gentle squeeze.

I recall standing at this very same deck the morning we departed, barely able to take in the chaos through my tears. Immune to the exhilarated shouts and optimistic chatter of my fellow passengers, my heart and mind were awash with fear and regret, not to mention loneliness—a feeling I hadn't truly experienced since being orphaned a dozen years ago. In fact, it was at that very moment—crying into a soiled handkerchief on the Promenade Deck of the *SS Statendam*—that I first met the Tenbrook sisters.

"So, what's his name?"

Stunned, I turned toward the speaker, a tall, willowy matron who simultaneously projected the dignity of her advancing years with the innocence of a schoolgirl.

"What? Who?" I quickly dabbed away my tears.

She must have mistaken me for someone else.

"Sister, you should be ashamed of yourself." A stout senior, the antithesis of her sibling, reached into her handbag and withdrew a freshly laundered hankie. "Here you go, dear. Don't mind her."

"Thank you," I accepted her kind gesture and finished drying my eyes.

"We should introduce ourselves," the maternal woman suggested. "I'm Mabel Tenbrook, and this is my younger sister, Violet Tenbrook."

"Nice to meet you." I returned the kerchief and extended a gloved hand to both women. "I'm Ruby. Ruby Ray."

"Please, call us Violet and Mabel," the younger sister encouraged.

"How about Miss Violet and Miss Mabel," I proposed, uncomfortable with addressing two women of their age and standing so informally.

"She's been raised properly," Miss Mabel observed knowingly to her sister.

Miss Violet gestured towards an empty pair of deck chairs behind us. "We were watching you, speculating as to why a beautiful young woman would be so distressed and alone at the beginning of a grand adventure."

"YOU were speculating," Miss Mabel interjected. "I was telling you to mind your own business."

Ignoring the interruption, Miss Violet continued dramatically, "I said that your groom left you at the altar, and you vowed to sail off on your honeymoon without him, brokenhearted as you may be."

"You're incorrigible, Sister!" Miss Mabel's cheeks reddened with exasperation.

Their banter broke the spell of my melancholy, and I began to laugh...heartily. This startled both women, who then eyed me warily. Perhaps they thought I was unhinged.

"Please excuse me," I apologized while attempting to restrain my amusement. "Your romantic hypothesis—while completely off the mark—reminded me how much worse things could actually be and that I am, in fact, heading off on a 'grand adventure,' as you so charmingly put it."

At that, Misses Violet and Mabel Tenbrook began to giggle. I released a snort, which was meant to be a chuckle. That set us off into peals of merriment, which alarmed the father next to us who'd been trying to prevent his young offspring from climbing over the railing. His annoyed expression was all it took to induce a round of full-bellied, eye-watering laughter.

"We shall get along splendidly!" Miss Violet declared while drying her eyes.

Conscious that we'd created something of a ruckus, we stepped away from the other passengers, and Miss Mabel suggested, "Let's chat over a cup of coffee."

The Palm Court—an impressive room on the Upper Promenade Deck—served as a lounge for the leisure activities of First-Class travelers. Rows of windows facing the bow and starboard sides offered pleasing views of the Hudson River and Manhattan. An attentive waiter in a starched uniform promptly approached us as we stepped into the lounge.

"Welcome, ladies. Can I help you find a table?"

"Hmm…I don't think that will be a problem," Miss Mabel mused, scanning the lounge, empty except for a pair of elderly men playing backgammon at a round table across the room. Most of the passengers were still outside tossing paper streamers to their loved ones as the ship began to pull away from the port.

"How about over here?" Miss Violet gestured toward a table situated in the center of the forward-facing windows.

"A perfect choice, madam," he pulled out a chair for Miss Violet then lightly draped a napkin across her lap.

Flattered, she blushed. "Thank you, young man,"

Once we were settled, the waiter asked, "Would you like menus?"

"That won't be necessary," Miss Mabel answered. "We'll share a pot of coffee with cream and sugar. We'll have plenty of tea once we reach England," she directed the last comment to Miss Violet and me.

"But I am rather peckish, Sister," Miss Violet announced.

"Oh, me too," I agreed.

In my haste to arrive at the terminal on time today, I forgot to eat lunch. However, hours later, I didn't wish to spoil my appetite for dinner. So, I turned toward the waiter and asked, "I don't suppose you have black and white cookies?" It's been many years since I enjoyed one of these frosted treats from Glaser's Bake Shop in Manhattan.

"As a matter of fact, we do," he winked at me. "Will that be all?"

"Yes, for now. We'll let you know if we change our minds." Miss Mabel gently dismissed him.

"You certainly know your way around the ship," I told her. "I became hopelessly lost trying to get from my cabin to the Purser's desk, which was on the same deck."

"This is our second trip aboard the *Statendam*," Miss Violet disclosed. "We sailed on her maiden voyage in April last year. Have you ever traveled abroad?"

"No, this is my first sea voyage of any sort," I confessed. "But I've longed to visit Europe since I was a little girl."

"Oh, my dear! You are going to absolutely love it!" Miss Violet insisted.

Miss Mabel explained, "Southampton will be our first port of call. It'll take us about a week to get there, weather permitting. From there, we can reach London in about two hours." Her eyes darted toward the passengers on the deck outside. "Will you and your party be staying over in London?"

"I plan to." I opted for the excursions coordinated by Holland America since the task of planning an itinerary seemed daunting. Plus, I figured it would be safer to travel with a familiar group from our ship rather than go it alone, Baedeker's guide aside. Truthfully, I felt terrified as soon as I handed over my passport during passenger embarkation a couple of hours ago.

What am I doing? Am I intrepid or insane?

"It's just me. No one else," I revealed hesitantly, knowing what their reaction would be. After all, they were bound to find out sooner or later.

"You're traveling alone?!" both sisters exclaimed at the same time.

"Oh, my!" Miss Violet muttered. "I assumed you at least had a maid with you."

"My dear, no! That will never do!" Miss Mabel urged, "You must be our companion."

"Yes, good idea," her sister agreed. "We can tell everyone that she's our niece."

"Really, that's not necessary. I'll be—"

"Not another word," Miss Mabel asserted. "We'll make sure you're safe from the sort of scoundrels and cads who prey on unsuspecting young ladies left unattended."

I nearly chuckled.

If only they knew.

In my role as an inquiry agent, I've had many encounters with scoundrels and cads over the years. In fact, my most recent case landed me in the emergency room with a concussion after being whacked on the head by a bootlegging arsonist who left me unconscious in a burning orange grove.

"I will be fine," I insisted and held up a hand to stop Miss Mabel from interrupting. "However, I would be delighted to join you for adventures on the high seas."

"Hear, hear!" Miss Violet swung out her arm as though she was holding a glass of champagne and nearly thumped our waiter in the belly. He adroitly regained control of the serving tray he was holding before resting it on the table beside us.

"Oh, I am so sorry! Are you alright?" She apologized with concern.

"Not to worry, madam," he replied calmly. Sidestepping near calamities must be a daily occurrence on a ship this size.

After cups had been filled, cream and sugar had been offered, and nibbles of cookies had been savored, Miss Mabel revisited her narrative about our journey to come. Although I had become quite familiar with our ship's route while preparing for the trip over the prior few weeks, I appreciated her experience and enthusiasm.

"After Southampton, we'll dock at Boulogne-sur-Mer, and then board a train for Pair-ee!" Miss Violet added.

"I am, without a doubt, most looking forward to Paris." I imagined strolling on the Seine and taking in the Eiffel Tower and Arc de Triomphe.

"My dear, the shopping on the Champs-Élysées can't be matched anywhere else in the world, and that includes Fifth Avenue," Miss Mabel commented.

"I'd adore a Jeanne Lanvin tea gown," I replied dreamily. I reasoned that I'd get more use out of that than a Schiaparelli.

"Paris will be difficult to leave, but I think you'll like Holland," Miss Violet informed me.

"Rotterdam will be our port of call there," Miss Mabel continued seamlessly. "While we're in Holland, you'll want to visit Leiden. Our ancestors left Leiden for New Amsterdam three hundred years ago," she proudly proclaimed. "It's absolutely lovely. Windmills...quaint bridges...unfortunately the tulips will no longer be in bloom."

"I look forward to seeing it," I remarked.

"I heard they've added Hamburg this year. I'm not sure how comfortable I'll feel in Germany after what they did in the war," Miss Violet admitted nervously.

"We will be fine, Sister," Miss Mabel assured her. "But since we've never visited before, we'll sign on for excursions organized by the ship."

"Of course, on our return stop at Plymouth, Mabel and I will be staying with our sister, Edna Adley, Marchioness of Barnstaple," Miss Violet emphasized the noble title.

"Your sister married an English marquess?" I set down my coffee and leaned forward with interest. I've long been fascinated by the British peerage.

"Indeed," Miss Mabel picked up the chronicle. "For her society debut in 1905, I told Papa that, in no uncertain terms, Edna would be presented at Court in England."

"Were you also been presented at Court as a debutante?" I asked.

"Alas, such was not my fate," Miss Mabel sighed. "Our dear Mama, God rest her soul, left this world while giving birth to Edna. I was fifteen, and Papa made it very clear that my role was to take care of him and my two younger sisters."

"I was seven at the time," Miss Violet added.

"Were you presented at Court, Miss Violet?"

"By the time I turned eighteen, I was already engaged."

"It's true," Miss Mabel sighed. "She was never a debutante."

"So, you were married?" I asked, puzzled that she and Miss Mabel still shared the same surname.

"He died in the Spanish American War." Miss Violet murmured quietly, "And not even in battle. He died of yellow fever."

"They were never married," Miss Mabel reached across the table to squeeze her sister's hand.

"How devastating! I'm so sorry for your loss." My heart ached for her.

"He was my one great love, and I vowed to never love again."

I sympathized with Miss Violet. Three years ago, betrayed by Eddie—my only serious boyfriend—my broken heart left me wary of romance. However, just two weeks before boarding the ship, I started to open myself up to the possibility of a relationship with Sam, a medical resident I met at our local hospital.

"Enough about us," Miss Mabel discretely swiped away a tear with her napkin. "What do your parents think about your travel plans?"

"Well," I hesitated for a moment to collect myself. "My parents died in a car accident when I was sixteen."

"Oh, Ruby. How tragic!" Miss Violet patted my hand in return.

Whenever I mention this loss—no matter how many years have passed—I am emotionally transported to that time and the feelings of shock and terror I experienced. I had no idea what was to become of me. As an only child with deceased grandparents, my closest living relative was my father's brother—the sole parent of two young children, having recently lost his wife to the Spanish Flu. Further, my uncle and cousins lived on the other side of the country in California.

After a moment, Miss Mabel gingerly asked, "What became of you? Surely, a relative took you in…"

"Yes," I smiled, remembering the moment my hero arrived at our doorstep. "My Uncle Charles immediately caught a train from California to New York and welcomed me into his family. My cousins Dottie and Jack were quite young, but they insist they remember the day I arrived."

"Well, that's a happy ending," Miss Violet remarked with a grin.

But Miss Mabel's expression did not change. "Ruby, pardon me for asking—and please don't feel as though you must answer—but why were you crying out on the deck? I should think you'd be thrilled to finally fulfill your girlhood dream of traveling to Europe."

"I don't mind answering," I replied truthfully. It's fascinating to me how, when we are away from our familiar surroundings, we sometimes find it easier to confide in strangers than in those we know best.

Both sisters watched me expectantly.

"This morning, I signed the paperwork to sell the house where I was raised."

It was all so rushed. Dottie's high school graduation had been three days earlier, which left me little time to travel east via a combination of rail and air transport. I arrived in Manhattan the night before I needed to embark on the ship and met the real estate agent at his office that very morning.

It was not as though I suddenly decided to sell my childhood home. The property was transferred to me when I reached the age of majority seven years ago on my twenty-first birthday. At that time, I visited the grand house but hardly recognized the interior, which had been modernized to attract potential renters. And although I mourned the loss of my home as I knew it, I was unable to let it go. Since then, I wrestled with the fear of losing the last tangible thread that connected me to my parents, so I chose to lease the house until recently.

"It's understandable that you'd feel distraught," Miss Mabel said kindly.

"Where was your home," Miss Violet inquired.

"Upper West Side. Riverside Drive."

Miss Violet whistled. "I was wondering how an unmarried young woman could afford a trip to Europe."

"Don't be vulgar, Violet," Miss Mabel scolded.

That broke the emotional tension, and I released a laugh— thankfully not a snort.

"So, since you were already in New York making arrangements for the house, you decided to board a ship," Miss Violet rephrased her earlier comment. "That makes a great deal of sense to me."

"I think I also needed to get away for a bit," I confessed.

"How so?" Miss Mabel looked up from her coffee cup.

"First, I should probably tell you about the work I do."

"You have a career? How very modern," Miss Violet enthused, and I had to assume that, despite her travels, she lived a rather sheltered life.

"Please continue," Miss Mabel shot her sister a warning glance.

"I'm an inquiry agent."

"Inquiry agent…" Miss Violet echoed as though saying the term aloud would render its meaning.

"Yes. In a nutshell, it's rather like being a private investigator, but 'inquiry agent' more accurately describes the delicate nature of my work."

"Which is?"

"Helping women in difficult circumstances," I clarified.

"Could you give us an example?" Miss Mabel requested.

"Absolutely. I've helped many battered women find safe lives elsewhere, and I've also done a bit of sleuthing and covert observation. My most recent cases involved theft and the disappearance of a group of teenagers." I didn't mention that one of the teens was my cousin

Dottie, and that they had been recruited into a cult by their math teacher. Long story.

The sisters were stunned, a common reaction when strangers hear about my occupation.

"Your work sounds…intense," Miss Mabel uttered.

"Which is precisely why I need to get away," I remarked. "Those last two cases left me exhausted and in dire need of a break."

"I can only imagine," Miss Violet commented with awe.

"Of course, I did have to make arrangements for the reading parlor," I added, recalling the flurry of activity as I prepared for my trip.

"Reading parlor?!" Miss Mabel exclaimed.

"Yes, my career as an inquiry agent actually grew out of my work as a tutor for women who never learned to read."

"Ruby Ray, you are, without a doubt, one of the most interesting women we've ever met!" Miss Mabel proclaimed.

"And that's saying something," Miss Violet added. "Our sister is a marchioness, after all."

Waiting to disembark, my mind is drawn back to the present moment by a collective chant that has erupted from the energetic crowd on the dock below.

"Corvi! Corvi! Corvi!"

"Here we go again," Miss Mabel groans.

CHAPTER 2

"So, Corvi, where are you off to next?" an eager reporter inquires.

"Why, Hollywood, of course," the enchanting actress replies with a melodic voice.

Corvi Styles smiles fetchingly for the photographers, as they fire off a volley of photos. With her Marcelled blonde bob and Chanel travel suit, she embodies movie star glamor. The journalists can't get enough of her and press in for a closer shot.

Panic flashes across Corvi's petite face. At barely five feet tall with delicate, angelic features, it's no wonder she's become the bright-eyed darling of the big screen. I feel compelled to protect her, having already witnessed just how rapidly these situations can spiral out of control.

"Okay, that's it, fellas." Her burly manager, Ike Bronson, abruptly ends the press gig. "Thanks for coming out. Miss Styles will be back in California soon to start shooting her next film."

"Can ya tell us what it'll be about?"

"Where's it bein' filmed?"

"What's it called?"

Ike plugs a cigar into his mouth and—with a massive hand on Corvi's back—firmly guides her inside but not before she blows kisses to her adoring fans over the ship's railing—thus inciting another round of cheers on the dock below.

"We should stay aboard until the hullabaloo dies down," Miss Mabel recommends.

"Let's go inside though," I suggest. The afternoon temperature has reached the mid-eighties and, despite the breeze coming off the river, I'm beginning to feel overheated.

"Good idea," Miss Violet agrees, fanning her face with a travel brochure for next summer's trip.

A little while later in the cab ride to the hotel, Dottie declares irritably, "Ruby, I can't believe you never once mentioned in your postcards that Corvi Styles was sailing with you!"

"Hardly sailing WITH me." I chuckle and crane my neck out the window to catch a glimpse of the Chrysler Building.

"You can't see it," Jack says gloomily. "I tried."

"That's okay, sport." Uncle Charles reaches back from the front seat of the taxicab to ruffle Jack's golden-brown curls. "I've arranged for a visit while we're here."

"No joke?!" Jack's eyes widen. How I've missed my thirteen-year-old cousin with his spirited and—at times—mischievous personality.

"No joke." his father smiles, pleased by Jack's delight.

"Say, Jack." I lean forward to look past Dottie, who is seated between us. "It was clever of you to bring your harmonica to the dock."

"See, Dad," he says pointedly.

I continue, "With so many people in the crowd, I couldn't find you anywhere, even after folks started to disperse. But when Miss Violet heard your shanty, she said, 'Ruby, I think they're nearby.'"

"How'd she know it was me?"

"I may have mentioned your fascination with sea shanties to the Misses Tenbrook at some point."

In fact, I shared so much about my family that Miss Mabel and Miss Violet felt they'd known them for years and were thrilled to meet them in person. As we were parting, we made arrangements to see one another again before my family and I return home to Southern California.

"I'm glad his music helped, but I could've done without that particular song." Uncle Charles smirks over his shoulder, at which point Jack retrieves his mouthpiece and begins to play "What Shall We Do with a Drunken Sailor."

I stifle a laugh after noticing the driver's scowl in the rearview mirror.

"Back to Corvi—" Dottie redirects our attention.

"Polka Dot, perhaps Ruby doesn't want to talk about Miss Styles right now," my uncle interrupts her. "I'm sure she's exhausted."

I appreciate the gesture. From the moment I went to live with Uncle Charles and his children, he has offered me nothing but kindness and respect. Over the years he has become not only a father figure, but also a cherished confidante. It's challenging for some of my friends to understand why, as a twenty-eight-year-old woman, I still live with them, but my family means the world to me, and I haven't yet had the desire to move out.

"It's no problem, Uncle Charles," I grin. "I might as well answer her questions now, or she'll be at me all day."

More like a younger sister than a cousin, Dottie shares my enjoyment of films and Hollywood facts, so I understand her enthusiasm. And, thank heavens, she seems to be back to her lively self, despite the trauma she suffered when she and her friends were trapped in an underground tunnel for days. I'll check in with her later to make sure.

"What do you want to know?" I ask.

"When did you first meet her? How did you meet her? Did you become friends?"

"Hold on there," I chuckle. "One question at a time. First…how we met. Even though I'd seen Corvi around the ship, I didn't actually meet her until midway across the Atlantic. I guess that was about five days after we sailed."

Dottie leans her head on my shoulder as I continue.

"It all started with a missing necklace…"

Holland America Line is known to make a big production of the first formal dinner on all their ships. So, naturally, I was filled with an anxious anticipation while getting ready that first evening. I'd brought a lovely pale blue chiffon gown to wear. However, much to my dismay, I realized I was unable to fasten the eye hooks that ran along the back. So, out of desperation, I slipped my robe over the unfastened garment and darted to the Tenbrook's cabin which, luckily, was on the same deck.

"Just a moment," Miss Violet called through the closed door when I knocked.

I peered nervously up and down the lengthy hall. The last thing I wanted was to meet my new neighbors while wearing a bathrobe and slippers.

After a moment, Miss Violet opened the door. "Oh, Ruby. We weren't expecting to see you until dinner."

"I'm so sorry," I apologized while entering the room. "I have a bit of a problem." I turned around and slid the robe off my shoulders.

Miss Violet giggled, "You can't reach the fasteners."

"Precisely," I shrugged.

"Not to worry," she swiftly closed the hooks and turned me around. "What a lovely dress. It's been years since I attempted to wear something so elegant.

"You look lovely yourself, Miss Violet." And she did. The cinched waist of her long-sleeved emerald gown revealed the figure of a woman decades younger. Her black and silver hair twisted up the back of her head and ended in a mass of curls at her crown.

"You're too kind," she blushed. "You know, that's a benefit of traveling with a sister…another pair of hands to help with hard-to-reach fasteners."

"Yes, I didn't think about that," I admitted. "Dottie usually helps me."

"Sister, have you seen my jade pendant?" Miss Mabel entered the sitting room through the connecting door from the bedroom. Their suite was much grander than my cabin. That being said, my smaller cabin had all the amenities I would need, including a private washroom.

"Is it still in the safe deposit box? You didn't hesitate to remind me about locking up my jewelry," Miss Violet replied somewhat acerbically.

While waiting to board, I read an article in the ship's newspaper, *The Ocean Post*, urging guests to secure their valuables at the Purser's office. So, I too dropped off my jewelry before we set sail, knowing that this trip would give me the rare opportunity to wear the jewels left to me by my mother and grandmothers. I'd have felt devastated if something happened to them.

"No, I intentionally left the jade and diamond pendant here in the room after we unpacked. I knew I'd wear it this evening," Miss Mabel insisted while smoothing a few stray hairs into the chignon at the nape of her neck.

"I was going to pay a visit to my box on the way to the dining room," Miss Violet said.

I had the same idea.

"This is quite distressing, Sister," Miss Mabel lamented. "Papa brought it back for me from Guatemala on my eighteenth birthday."

"Our Papa owned a railroad expansion business," Miss Violet informed me. "He mainly worked out west and even ventured down to Central America."

"Can we help you search for it?" I offered.

"Thank you, Ruby, that's very kind of you. But I've looked everywhere, and we don't want to be late for dinner," Miss Mabel sighed. "Besides, you need to finish getting ready."

I looked into a mirror on the wall and realized that I hadn't removed the hair clips I'd used to tame my strawberry blonde curls into loose waves. "Oh, I guess you're right. Well, I'll see you soon in the dining room."

I stealthily sneaked back to my room, narrowly avoiding a doting husband helping his expectant wife into their cabin.

Later that evening we learned that another passenger had experienced a similar loss. The thefts continued over the course of the next few days, despite warnings in *The Ocean Post*. Of course, people assumed that one of the ship's crew members was responsible, such as a housekeeper. But I knew that these hard-working folks wouldn't jeopardize their jobs and were probably more trustworthy than many travelers onboard. Some people suggested that a third-class passenger had crept up to the first-class cabins, but I found this just as improbable.

Meanwhile, a massive storm struck three days after we departed. With the exception of a sailing expedition to Catalina Island during my college days, my experience on the high seas was limited. Were it not for Miss Mabel and her motherly ministrations, I'd have been confined to my quarters.

"Here you go, my dear." She placed an envelope in my hands and cautioned, "Take one every six hours."

I opened the packet and poured a few white tablets into the palm of my hand, "But they're so small."

"Don't let that fool you," she replied solemnly. "Hyoscine hydrobromide is quite potent."

"Duly noted." I carefully returned the tablets to the paper sleeve.

She laughed, "It's not as bad as all that. My sister and I depend on these little pills. Neither of us has experienced sea sickness since we began taking them a couple of years ago. Before that, we spent the duration of our yearly transatlantic crossings in our suite."

The medication worked like a charm, and in no time, I was swimming in the indoor Venetian-themed pool and enjoying bridge games in the Palm Court. A long queue outside the infirmary suggested that others had heard about this "miracle cure," as Miss Violet put it, and were procuring the tablets for themselves. Before long the dining room was once again full for the evening table service.

On our fifth evening at sea, we had just finished dinner, a satiating meal of striped sea bass, roasted asparagus, and chocolate gâteaux, when a commotion started in the center of the room under the ornate Italian ceiling mural.

"Are you sure they were stolen?" An imposing, broad-chested man removed a mottled brown cigar from his mouth.

"Yes! I searched my cabin from top to bottom. They're both gone!"

19

At the time, I recognized his diminutive dining companion as Corvi Styles, the young actress whose innocent, wide-set eyes and heart-shaped face recently catapulted her from background extra to starlet.

"Well, you better find that necklace before Mr. Lake catches wind of this." Seated to Corvi's left was actor Rex Langdon, well known for making young ladies swoon with his staggering good looks and thick wavy hair.

"What an attractive young man!" Miss Violet exclaimed.

"Shush," Miss Mabel silenced her. "I think the bandit's been at it again."

A suave Black fellow with a thin, wispy mustache sank into the empty chair at the celebrity table. "Mr. Lake knows. He's on his way."

Everyone at the table groaned in unison.

"What I don't understand is why you kept the real deal in your room," Rex complained to Corvi.

"That was my doing." The other young man buries his dark brown face in his hands. "I swapped it out with the paste copy so Corvi could wear it for photos later tonight. I never dreamed anyone would swipe it in such a short period of time."

"Well, Archie, Mr. Lake's going to blame me for it." She swiped away the tear rolling down her cheek.

At that moment, Lewis Lake—the famous film director—strode across the dining room with a fierce scowl directed at Corvi.

"It wasn't me," she cried out.

Mr. Lake couldn't have been taller than five-three and was one of the thinnest men I'd ever seen, but he towered over the cowering Corvi.

Miss Mabel *tsked* beside me.

"Let me explain." Archie stepped between Mr. Lake and Corvi, then described the events leading up to Corvi's discovery that the jewelry was missing.

"That was a CARTIER DIAMOND AND PLATINUM NECKLACE! Do you have any idea how much it's worth?!"

The room instantly fell silent. Conversations abruptly ended, the serving staff froze mid-step, and the pianist stopped playing "Für Elise" on the Steinway.

Archie quietly pleaded, "Sir, perhaps we can talk about this private—"

"In my suite! Now!" Mr. Lake adjusted his ascot and stormed out the doors, muttering, "I can't believe I have to miss steak and lobster in the captain's dining room for this!"

"You guys stay put. I can sort this out." Archie motioned for his companions to sit back down then hastened after Mr. Lake.

"Well, I'll be!" Miss Mabel exclaimed.

"Ruby," Miss Violet grasped my arm. "You're an investigator. I bet you could figure out who's behind these thefts."

Before I realized what she was doing, Miss Violet pulled me up and dragged me toward Corvi Styles' table.

I tried to resist and hissed, "Miss Violet, no..." But she only tightened her grip on my wrist.

"Miss Styles," she called as we reached their table.

Corvi looked up, perplexed at our sudden appearance, but very politely said, "I'm sorry. This isn't a good time."

The beefy man beside her began to stand, but Miss Violet held up a hand. "It'll only take a moment. I think Miss Ray here can help."

By the time she finished describing my occupation and experience, the occupants at the table looked intrigued. Corvi blinked slowly and took a deep breath, as though arriving at a decision, then motioned to the empty chair across from her.

"Miss Ray, would mind joining us?"

I hesitated and looked around. Everyone else in the dining room had returned to their own private conversations, the drama having passed. So, I accepted and sat down.

"I'm sure the ship's security officer is investigating these burglaries..." I started to suggest.

"Well, he's doing a shoddy job." The man to my left extended a large paw. "Ike Bronson. I'm Miss Styles' manager."

His grip was firm but, fortunately, not bone-crushing. "Nice to meet you. Please call me Ruby." I directed the last comment to everyone in the group.

Corvi leaned across the table and placed a pale, dainty hand on mine. "I do hope you can help, and not just because of the necklace."

"Is something else missing?"

She released my hand and retrieved a lace-trimmed handkerchief which, I couldn't help but notice, was embroidered with thread matching her fitted satin gown.

"Yes, an amethyst brooch." Her shoulders slowly slumped forward, and she twisted the kerchief forlornly.

"Is it also from Cartier?"

"No," she smiled wistfully. "It's not expensive…but my older brother gave it to me before he headed off to war. The Forest of Argonne."

"Aah," I murmured.

"Exactly," she sniffed. "He left in September and never returned. His last letter arrived in October."

While the Meuse-Argonne Offensive helped end the war, it cost tens of thousands of lives and was considered to be the bloodiest operation during the Great War.

"I understand why the brooch is so important to you."

She nodded. "I don't usually travel with it, but I plan to visit his grave when we arrive in France."

"And the other piece that's missing. The necklace…"

"A publicity stunt," Rex interjected with a huff.

"Now, see here, Langdon," Ike interrupted. "I don't like it either, but as far as the public is concerned, you two are a couple."

"Rex gave it to me at the sail away on the dock," Corvi explained.

"For the cameras," Rex added. "It was only borrowed for this trip and has to be returned when we get back to New York. Corvi was only supposed to wear the paste copy around the ship."

"I see." Despite my skills, I could tell right away that I didn't want to get involved in this affair. Above all else, this trip was meant to be relaxing. That being said, my heart went out to Corvi, and I felt compelled to help.

"Alright. I'll see what I can do," I said reluctantly. After all, we were in the middle of the Atlantic. The stolen items had to be hidden somewhere onboard the ship.

How hard could it be to find them?

Corvi beamed. "Oh, thank you, Ruby! I know you'll crack the case!"

"And you did!" Jack declares with keen interest.

"Let her finish!" Dottie commands.

"I'm just saying that I'm sure she figured it out!" he argues

"We'll find out if you pipe down!" she admonishes.

"Well, who dunnit?" The taxicab driver interrupts. "We're almost to the hotel, and I gotta know how it ends."

I chuckle. "After interviewing the victims, I realized that all their cabins were located on the same side of the same deck. However, the burglaries took place at different times of the day."

"Ya know, this is like one of them 'True Detective Mysteries' on the radio," the driver comments.

"Shh," Dottie reprimands him.

The driver looks over his shoulder and frowns.

"I asked one of the housekeepers about the keys they used to access the cabins," I continue. "She told me there was a master key for each wing of passenger rooms."

"Someone stole a master key!" Jack shouts excitedly.

"Exactly! Only, no keys had been reported stolen."

"So, it WAS one of the housekeepers!" Dottie exclaims.

"Shhhhhh!" Jack and the driver quiet her sarcastically.

"No, I interviewed all the staff responsible for that deck, and I was quite confident they were as eager as the passengers to find the culprit. So, I decided to set a trap."

"Good thinking," Uncle Charles joins our conversation.

"On the seventh night at sea, Miss Violet wore a pair of sapphire and diamond dangle earrings and styled her hair to ensure they were visible. During dinner, she loudly complained that the screw was loose on one of the earrings and excused herself to return them to her room. While she was gone, I claimed to have a headache and excused myself to lie down in my cabin."

The taxicab slows down in front of the newly opened New Yorker Hotel. I peer up at its majestic forty-three floors and see why it's referred to as a "Vertical Village" in newspaper and magazine ads.

"Tell ya what," the driver says, "I'll turn off the meter but take ya around the block so you can finish the story."

"Deal." Uncle Charles shakes his hand with a friendly grin,

Just then, a porter walks toward the cab to help with the baggage, but we've already begun to pull away from the curb. Uncle Charles cranks down the window and shouts, "Sorry. We forgot something, but we'll be right back."

"Now, where was I?"

"You went to lie down," Dottie reminds me.

"Yes, I went back to my room while Miss Violet pretended to deposit her earrings in their suite."

"But she didn't, did she?" Jack asks.

"Nope. She put them in her handbag and returned to the dining room, giving a light scratch at my door when she passed. I then peeked out my door and, finding the hallway clear, rushed down to the Tenbrook's room and let myself in."

"Wait, why didn't you just pretend that the earrings were yours and hide in your own room?" Uncle Charles asks.

"Great question. The thief had already stolen Miss Mabel's pendant. We reasoned that they might find Miss Violet an easier target than me. Plus, there was much more space in their suite for me to hide than in my small cabin."

"Did the bandit show up?" the driver inquires.

"Would you believe that they didn't? I waited over an hour, and no one appeared."

Uncle Charles, Dottie, Jack, and the driver all moan with disappointment

"Hang on. You haven't heard the rest. I was about to leave and return to the dining room when I heard a door close in one of the rooms nearby. I quickly peeked out, and who do you think I saw?"

"A masked bandit?"

"One of the housekeepers?"

"A pirate with an eye patch and a sack of loot?"

We all laugh at Jack's suggestion.

"Enough sea shanties for you, young man," Uncle Charles teases.

"No, no, and definitely no," I laugh. "I saw a very expectant young woman…"

"Rats!" Jack blurts.

"With a belly full of stolen goods," I finish.

"What?! I never saw that coming," Dottie replies with astonishment.

"It turns out that the woman wasn't pregnant at all. She'd break into rooms while her husband made sure the target was occupied elsewhere on the ship. Then she'd hide the stolen items in a pocket within a pillow she wore under her clothes. That explained how she'd gotten away with several bulkier items, including a 300-year-old ruby encrusted dagger and five thousand dollars in cash."

The cab driver whistles.

"But if none of the master keys were stolen? How'd she get into the rooms?" Dottie asks.

"This part was rather ingenious."

I describe how the couple came up with the idea while on a Caribbean cruise for their honeymoon—a gift paid for by the bride's parents who believed that the duo had finally settled down after a series of juvenile pranks. Still wild and reckless, however, they managed to steal—not only a four-carat diamond ring—but also a master room key. After returning home, they sold the diamond ring and booked a cruise on the same ship for the following year when it sailed to Europe, where they used the master key to break into passenger's cabins. Continuing this cycle of stealing and selling, they'd worked their way around several different ships over the past five years.

"How on Earth did you find out of all that?" Uncle Charles asks.

"When the security officer found all the stolen items hidden in their room behind a wall panel, the husband came clean but claimed that his wife coerced him to go along with the scheme."

"Do you believe that?" Dottie inquires skeptically.

"To be honest, I just don't know," I confess.

The taxicab returns to the front entrance of the hotel, this time coming to a complete stop. My Uncle apologizes to the porter for the confusion and helps him shift my luggage from the trunk to a trolley.

As I close the cab door and start to walk away, the driver leans across the passenger seat to the open window "Say lady, I don't suppose you could find my cousin Jimmy for me?"

"Is he missing?"

"Yeah, I lent him some dough for his old lady, but he lost it at the racetrack, and the next thing I knew, twenty-three skidoo."

I smile, amused at his use of local slang. "I'm sorry that happened to you, but I'm afraid I won't be able to help."

"Well, it was worth a try," he grins sheepishly and pulls away from the curb.

CHAPTER 3

~ 🪷 ~

SUNDAY, AUGUST 10, 1930
SARDI'S RESTAURANT, MANHATTAN

"Look at that, Ruby!" Dottie points toward the colorful caricature hanging above our red leather booth then snaps a photo with the Brownie camera she received for graduation.

"Douglas Fairbanks!" The drawing has perfectly captured his heavy eyebrows and pencil mustache, a feature he shares with my uncle.

"I spotted Lawrence Olivier on the way in," Uncle Charles comments while hanging his fedora on the wall hook just below Mr. Fairbanks' profile. He smooths his dark, Brilliantined hair and scoots onto the bench next to Jack.

"This place is swell!" Jack's eyes are saucers. "I wonder if they have a drawing of Pancho somewhere?"

"Who's Pancho?" I inquire.

"Pancho Barnes," Dottie answers. "She won't be up there. She's a pilot, not an actress."

"Jack's been obsessed with Pancho since we saw her in Los Angeles last week," my uncle explains.

"You shoulda seen her, Ruby," Jack gushes. "One hundred and ninety-six miles per hour! She broke Amelia Earhart's record for the fastest woman on Earth."

"And how did you happen to be there?" I inquire while snapping a breadstick. I'm famished.

"Union Oil sponsored her." Uncle Charles reaches for a breadstick of his own.

My uncle is an oilman in Fullerton, a rapidly growing community in Southern California known for its oil and oranges. While Union Oil is, without a doubt, his stiffest competition in our area, he has cultivated friendships with a few of their employees. "Keep your friends close, and your rivals closer," my uncle frequently says.

"Speaking of airplanes, what did you think of your flight to New York?" he asks.

"I rather enjoyed it," I admit.

This really surprised me. Since I had such a tight window between Dottie's graduation and boarding the *Statendam*, air travel was the only option during the daytime. But as the date for my first flight approached, I became increasingly uneasy with the thought of soaring thousands of feet above the ground in a metal tube. In fact, I was tempted to cancel my vacation the day before leaving. Ultimately, though, the sale of the house was dependent on my signature, and once I decided to sell, I wished to expedite the process. Plus, I'd put down a hefty non-refundable deposit on the cruise. Needless to say, I was quite unprepared for the thrill and wonder I experienced while seeing the world below as a miniature display laid out before me. Still, I found the seats cramped and uncomfortable and by nightfall was ready for the gentle rocking of the train cabin, where our nighttime journey by rail provided a welcome respite.

"I liked the stewardesses," Jack comments with a lopsided grin.

"That's only because they gave you extra snacks," Dottie rolls her violet eyes.

"You know," my uncle informs us, "This was the first airplane trip I've had where the stewards were female. Boeing Air Transport was the first airline to make the change just this year."

"Is that so?" The women on each of my flights, in their smart double-breasted jackets and chic berets, seemed so comfortable and experienced. I figured they'd been on the job far longer.

"Well, I couldn't wait to be done with those cold, shaky tin cans," Dottie complains. "And on eight of the nine flights, the same man smoked cigarillos. Disgusting!"

Our waiter appears wearing a wine-colored coat and black bowtie. "Can I take your order?"

"So, what's good here?" Jack asks.

The waiter proceeds with a passionate and detailed description of nearly all of the Italian entrees on the menu.

"What? No hot dogs?"

"Oh, Jack…" Uncle Charles places a hand over his face.

The waiter, on the other hand, raises an eyebrow and glares at my cousin.

Abashed, Jack politely opts for zuppa di tartaruga. "Cuz it's fun to say," he adds.

However, when the server brings the dish and explains that the meat is, in fact, turtle, Jack decides he'd rather eat breadsticks.

"I miss Bob," he solemnly sighs.

Jack was quite fond of the spiky, sharp-beaked "alligator snapper" tortoise that he released at a small watering hole a few months ago.

"I'm sure he's much happier in the lake," I reassure him with a smile, relieved I won't be sharing a bathtub with the beast when we get home.

Jack frowns and shrugs, so I change the subject. "How's Nan?"

"She said to tell you she's 'missin' ya somethin' fierce!'" Uncle Charles replies, perfectly imitating her "Missoura" dialect.

"She's planning a special lunch for you when we get back," Jack informs me.

"That's supposed to be a surprise!" Dottie scolds him.

"I could never be surprised by Nan's thoughtfulness, especially where food is concerned," I reply.

If you ask Nan, she'll tell you she's our housekeeper, but to us, she's a surrogate grandmother and beloved member of our family. Whenever I felt homesick during my cruise, I'd think about her warm hugs and words of encouragement. She's been my cheerleader since the moment I arrived in California, and I love her dearly.

"Nan also wanted me to tell you that there's a stack of letters for you from a certain dashing physician," Uncle Charles raises his eyebrows and smiles.

My heart skips a beat.

He did write!

I think back to the first time I met Dr. Sam Armstrong late last year. I'd taken Jack to the emergency room at Fullerton General Hospital following an explosive and painful accident involving his chemistry set. Yet, despite my worry over Jack's injured hands, I was taken aback by the handsome medical resident who pulled the curtain aside and sauntered toward Jack's gurney with an easy stride, his stethoscope casually draped over one shoulder. Thanks to Sam's good humor and infectious smile, Jack calmly weathered the uncomfortable treatment that ensued. After that, I encountered Sam a few times while working on a case, all very professional. But when he stopped by for a house call following my assault—even though he wasn't really my doctor—I knew that he too was interested.

We last saw each other in May when Sam suddenly appeared at my cottage bearing a tall, potted rosebush—I should mention that Sam's an amateur horticulturist. He then swept me off my feet as we danced to "I'm in the Market for You," which was playing on the radio. The energy between us was palpable, and I still feel weak in the knees every time I recall that day. Yet even though we both wanted to get to know each other better, the timing was terrible. I was about to leave for my trip, and he was off to Arizona for a rural medicine rotation. Now that I think about it, Sam should be back in Southern California by now. I'm curious where he ended up after leaving Arizona. When we last spoke, he still hadn't heard about his next placement.

"Hello…Ruby…" Jack waves.

"Oh…sorry." I clear my throat. "I was just remembering something."

"Daydreaming is more like it," Dottie nudges me playfully.

Snap out of it, Ruby.

I refocus my attention on my family.

"So, Dottie, how's Polly?" I ask.

Jack blushes and becomes preoccupied with the salt and pepper shakers. If I'm not mistaken, Dottie's best friend is his first crush.

"Peeved," she replies while tucking her chocolate bob behind one ear.

"How so?"

"Well, Leo broke it off when he left for college a few weeks ago, not that she'd seen him much after graduation. Would you believe that her parents sent her to Idyllwild to be a counselor at a Bible camp...for the whole summer?!"

"I absolutely believe it."

When the kids went missing, Polly's parents were convinced that she'd eloped with Leo, someone they considered unsuitable as an Italian and a Catholic. So, while the other families were beside themselves, begging the police to search for the missing students, Mr. and Mrs. Baker refused to involve the police and pretended that nothing had happened. However, they changed their tune when their daughter nearly died of blood loss.

"And what's Earl up to?"

"Oh, you know...playing gigs with his band and helping his mom with the little ones. He'll be taking classes at the junior college, though, in a few weeks."

"I'm glad." Hopefully the women who attend my reading parlor have already welcomed Earl's mother into their babysitting collective. Six little ones and a seventh on the way—it's just too much for one woman to manage alone.

I inquire, "Have you decided when you're leaving for Berkeley?" Dottie was accepted into their chemistry program, something she's dreamt about for years.

"Polka Dot and I will be driving up after Labor Day," Uncle Charles beams proudly.

Dottie returns his smile, but I sense apprehension. She's undoubtedly nervous about leaving home and living in a boarding house. Unfortunately, the only dormitory on campus, Bowles Hall, is for male students, and the university has no immediate plans to build a dormitory for co-eds. I asked Dottie about pledging, thinking that a sorority house may be a safer living environment, but she just scoffed. "Those girls are only interested in finding husbands."

I hope that's all it is.

The manipulation and control that Dottie's teacher had over her and the other students was insidious, and I'm sure she's still coming to terms with the subterranean nightmare she and her friends experienced.

I lean against her and speak in a low voice, so we're not overheard. "You know, Dottie, I'm here if you'd like to talk…about anything."

"Everything's great, Ruby," Dottie fakes a bright grin then takes a big bite of veal piccata.

So much for that. I'll try again when we're alone.

SATURDAY, AUGUST 16, 1930
L'AIGLON RESTAURANT, MANHATTAN

"There we were, front row seats in right field. Bottom of the third. Two outs with one man on base. Babe Ruth comes up to bat. He swings and WHAM, knocks it over the fence in right field!" Jack nearly tips over his water goblet while waving his arms.

"Did you catch it?" Miss Mabel asks.

"No!" he shouts, startling a baby at the table beside us, who begins to cry. "It was coming right at us, but some guy two rows behind jumped out of his seat, over the lady in front of him, and snatched it before it landed in my glove!"

"No!" the sisters exclaim loudly.

Miss Mabel immediately mouths "sorry" to the baby's mother.

"It was maddening." My uncle shakes his head. "I really thought he had it."

"Was that the game on Tuesday afternoon against the Detroit Tigers? When they were tied going into the bottom of the ninth with two outs—"

"And Babe hit a double to left field, sending Combs home for the winning run?" Miss Violet excitedly interrupts her sister.

"Yes!" Jack nods energetically.

"Sister and I listened to the game on the radio," Miss Violet proclaims. "We love baseball."

"How lucky you were in town to see the game," Miss Mabel comments. "Do you see much baseball in California?"

"Sometimes." Uncle Charles informs her, "We have the Los Angeles Angels and Hollywood Stars, which are part of the Pacific Coast League, but it's not quite the same as major league baseball."

"Doesn't William Wrigley, Jr. own the Angels?" Miss Mabel inquires.

"That's correct."

"The Chewing Gum King?" Miss Violet cocks her head.

"He's made quite a fortune. In fact, he built a second Wrigley Field in Los Angeles, albeit smaller than the one in Chicago."

"Then there's everything he's built on Catalina Island, including the new Avalon Casino that opened last year," I add.

"I wish we had a major league team in Southern California. You have three!" Jack bemoans. "Any chance the Yankees would move to California? Heck, I'd even be okay with the Dodgers or Giants."

"I don't think so, dear," Miss Violet laughs. "Ruby, what did you think of the game?"

"Well, I've never been much of a fan, myself, but I must admit, the game the other day was quite thrilling. I'm sure that had everything to do with the Sultan of Swat."

Until this week, I hadn't been to a ballpark since I was fifteen or so. My father used to drag me to Yankee games as a child and teenager. Despite grumbling when I was young, being back at the stadium the other day brought back fond memories.

"Yeah, Babe wasn't around back when I attended games," My uncle smiles wistfully.

"Dad used to live in Manhattan," Dottie discloses. "That was before he moved to San Francisco to work for Standard Oil."

"San Francisco? Before or after the big earthquake?" Violet inquires with a frown.

"Just after," Uncle Charles replies. "But some of the buildings were still smoldering."

"Disasters terrify me!" Miss Violet admits.

"Then let's change the subject." Miss Mabel pronounces and asks us, "What else have you done over the past week?"

"Where to begin?" I muse.

"Let me answer." Jack straightens and begins his synopsis. "Central Park, the Zoo, the Chrysler Building...did you know it's the tallest building in the world?"

"Now, that depends on who you ask," Miss Mabel cuts in. "The Manhattan Company claims their building on Wall Street is the tallest."

"I doubt Dad would've let me spit off the roof of that building either," Jack shoots an annoyed glance at his father.

To be clear, the Chrysler Building exceeds the Manhattan Company Building by 119 feet due to its spire, but I choose not to point that out. Nor do I mention that there's no way Jack would be allowed on the roof of either building.

"How about you, Dottie? What did you enjoy seeing?" Miss Violet queries.

"Well, Ruby and I saw *Dancing Partner* at the Belasco Theater."

"Ooh, is that the one with Suzanne Caubet, Sarah Bernhardt's goddaughter?" Miss Violet inquires, "How was it?"

"Yes, that's the one. We really enjoyed it," Dottie smiles.

"The interior was lovely, especially the Tiffany lamps." I close the immense French menu I've been examining.

"That makes me think of the play we saw in London, Ruby. *Black Coffee*. Do you remember?" Miss Violet recalls.

"How could I forget? Although Manhattan's Belasco is much grander than the British Embassy Theater." I turn and apologize to Miss Mabel, "I'm so sorry I couldn't invite you as well."

"As I said at the time, you only had two tickets, and my sister is the Agatha Christie enthusiast in our family. Further, this was Mrs. Christie's first play. I would never have deprived Violet."

"Agatha Christie wrote a play?" My uncle sets down his open menu.

"Yes, we were quite fortunate to be there for opening night. Mr. Lake, the director I mentioned—"

"From the burglaries on the boat?" Jack brightens.

"Yes. Believe it or not, Mr. Lake was so thankful after the return of the Cartier necklace, he gave me a pair of tickets to the play."

Dottie leans forward, "Was Corvi there?"

"Indeed. Not only that, her striking co-star, Mr. Langdon, was also there," Miss Violet enthuses.

"Apparently, Mr. Lake had arranged a photo session with Corvi, Rex, and Mrs. Christie," I add.

"You met Agatha Christie?!" Dottie squeals.

"Not quite," I chuckle. "Only the film people got to meet her. But I did get to see her, and she's taller than I imagined. And younger." For some reason, I always pictured her as a short, elderly spinster.

"And what a fuss was made!" Miss Violet complains. "Somehow word got out that Corvi would be at the performance. There were more than a hundred people waiting outside the theater, all trying to catch a glimpse of her."

"That's how it was the entire trip," Miss Mabel criticizes. "I find it remarkable that the fans and press always happened to show up when Corvi arrived."

"Archie Duval told me it was intentional," I say. "After all, the purpose for the entire trip was publicity."

According to Archie, the tour was to garner interest among continental moviegoers for Corvi and Rex's latest film, which had just been released with subtitles. Intertitles in movies have been used for years, but the French and German subtitles for this latest film were quite novel and, thus, stretched the studio's budget.

"You and Archie certainly seemed chummy," Miss Violet remarks.

I start to lecture, "If I've told you once—"

"WHO'S ARCHIE?" Dottie demands.

"Settle down," I hold up both hands. "Archie was the assistant director traveling with Mr. Lake. We were on friendly terms. That's it."

"How friendly?"

"Friends—as in he'd ask me to dance so the cads on the boat would leave me alone."

"I was concerned about that," Uncle Charles mutters.

"We made sure she was safe from unwanted advances the entire time," Miss Mabel assures him.

Uncle Charles winks at me.

An attractive man, Archie Duval's black mustache was meticulously trimmed, and he always sported a bow tie. More than anything, I found his affable personality delightful—not that I was looking for a shipboard romance, nor was I his type. I'll never forget how our friendship began. Late one night, after the thieves had been caught, I was awakened by a commotion outside in the hall. At first, I suspected someone was trying to get into my cabin. Miss Mabel had warned me about the bed-hopping that goes on at night and encouraged me to prop up a chair against my doorknob. Until that moment, I hadn't given it much thought. So, I waited a bit until the hallway was quiet. Then I cracked open the door for a quick look. To my surprise, I saw Archie with his arm around Rex several doors down. I assumed that Rex had imbibed too much—a fate shared by many passengers as soon as we cleared the U.S. territorial waters. I thought Archie must be helping him to his room. But then Rex caressed Archie's cheek, and I realized the nature of their relationship. As Rex entered his room, Archie turned and noticed me, panic in his eyes. I smiled and pretended to zip my lip. He sighed with relief and nodded his thanks, then he joined Rex inside the cabin. After that, Archie kept my dance card full whenever we were on the boat.

"I'm starved, and this menu is huge!" Dottie says with frustration. "What do you recommend?"

"If you like seafood, I suggest you order the Sole Meuniere." Miss Mabel points to the entree on her own menu.

"Or the Bouillabaisse de Marseille," her sister proposes. "It's as good as the one we had in France. Remember that, Ruby?"

"I do. Although, I think I'll have the lobster thermidor. It just isn't the same out west."

Once we've ordered and are waiting for our food, Jack urges, "Ruby, tell them about the psychic."

"Psychic? Please don't tell me you visited Coney Island." Miss Mabel *tuts*.

"Oh, Sister, Coney Island is delightful!" Miss Violet grins.

"The heat was unbearable yesterday, so we thought a trip to the shore would be just the thing," my uncle clarifies.

"What's this about a psychic?" Miss Violet asks.

"Well, we hadn't planned on stopping by her booth, but she called to Dottie and me as we passed by."

"She didn't just call. She stepped out in front of us," Dottie corrects.

"That's right. Then I told her we were in a hurry to meet our family, but she grabbed my hand and ran a finger down my palm."

"How unnerving!" Miss Mabel recoils.

"Yes, it was."

"Did she say anything?" Miss Violet's props her chin on her knuckles.

"Yes, she said, 'Beware or forces beneath the surface may sweep you away!'"

"That's rather vague," Miss Mabel frowns.

"And utter baloney." Dottie rolls her eyes.

Miss Violet shakes her head, "I wouldn't be so dismissive. What do you suppose she meant by 'forces beneath the surface.'"

"*All art is at once surface and symbol. Those who go beneath the surface do so at their peril,*" Miss Mabel recites.

"Oscar Wilde," I comment. "*The Picture of Dorian Gray.*"

"That's correct," she smiles.

Jack looks puzzled. "So, she should beware of art?"

"To be honest, I thought the psychic was referring to water," Dottie confesses.

"Well, it's a good thing we were heading back to the hotel." The beach was packed when we got there, and we spent limited time in the waves.

"You know, Ruby, you would be surrounded by water if you take that undercover detective job," Miss Violet comments.

"Undercover detective job?" Uncle Charles raises his eyebrows.

Miss Mabel casts a proud glance in my direction. "After Ruby so brilliantly solved the mysterious thefts aboard our ship, the Ship Security Officer offered her a position to join their crew."

"Imagine that!" Miss Violet muses. "Sailing around the world for months at a time among the first-class passengers, all the while keeping an eye out for nefarious miscreants. No one would ever suspect that she's part of the ship's security."

"No joke, Ruby? Are you leaving us again?" Jack asks nervously.

I ruffle his hair. "Not a chance. I turned down the offer as soon as the SSO approached me."

Our discussion is interrupted when the family behind us stands to leave. While trying to gather blankets and bottles, the young mother fails to notice that her baby has just spit up…on Jack.

"Eww!" Jack grabs his napkin and furiously rubs at his coat.

"Serves you right," Dottie teases.

"Well, you did startle the poor thing earlier," Uncle Charles observes.

"Oh my! I am so sorry!" The baby's mother tries to help clean the mess with one of the blankets.

"That's okay," Jack reddens, embarrassed by the young woman's attention. "No biggie."

"It's really no problem," my uncle assures her.

The mother nods, "Well, I am sorry. It's been one of those nights."

After they're gone, Miss Violet asks me, "Did you have a chance to visit your childhood home this week? It's a shame you had to sign the papers at the real estate agent's office."

"Thankfully, we were able to stop by two days ago," I answer.

"And?"

"Well, from what I could tell, it looked exactly the same."

I was filled with fond memories as soon as I spotted the light Elizabethan Renaissance house. From the sidewalk, I looked up toward the rooftop garden that I'd adored as a child. Then I peered across the street at the waterfront park, where I'd played with my friends. I'd expected to see a construction crew bustling in and out of the house. The agent told me the buyer planned to partition the grand rooms into small apartments—such was the need for inexpensive housing. Instead, the curtains were drawn on all the windows, and the door was firmly closed. It felt eerie, as though I was standing before a ghost.

"Miss Violet, did Ruby tell you that Marion Davies was her neighbor?" Dottie inquires.

"Not really my neighbor," I remind her. "She lived several blocks away."

"Mr. Hearst bought the house for Marion and her family," Dottie continues.

"After I moved out!" I laugh. "I never even saw her."

It's funny she should mention Marion Davies. Just a few months ago at the Fox Theater, we spotted a movie poster for *The Floradora Girl*—Marion's new movie—and Dottie insisted I looked just like her. I suppose, at a glance, I may bear some resemblance, but that's where the similarity ends. I'd never be mistaken for such a glamorous film star.

"Is that so?" Miss Violet states, "Well I'm not surprised that Mr. Hearst bought her that house. As I recall, he also had a home on Riverside Drive…with his wife."

"I remember reading that they sold the house after that terrible business on William Hearst's yacht. Something about him shooting that movie producer, Thomas Ince, because he thought Marion was having relations with Charlie Chaplin. None of it made a bit of sense." I'm surprised to hear this tidbit from Miss Mabel. She usually eschews Hollywood gossip.

"I don't think that's correct, sister. They later said that the man died of indigestion."

"Nobody dies of indigestion, Violet," Miss Mable says dismissively.

"Ince…wasn't he the guy who was gassed at the California Hotel?" Jack references the bizarre incident involving the "Chloroform Burglars," who terrorized our hometown a few years ago by pumping chloroform into people's windows then robbing them while they were unconscious.

"No, that was Ralph Ince, his brother," Dottie answers.

"Your dinner, mesdames et messieurs." Our waiter and a server appear with four large trays laden with food.

"Is that my hot dog?" Jack jokes, and we all groan.

CHAPTER 4

~ ❦ ~

TUESDAY, AUGUST 19, 1930
FULLERTON, CALIFORNIA

There's no place like home.

I'm not sure who coined the phrase, but those very words come to mind as we approach our two-story Craftsman house. The muscles in my head, neck, and shoulders relax, while a pleasant coolness tingles from my head to my toes. Until this moment, I hadn't realized I was so tense, despite our grueling travel over the past two days. Tornado warnings in the Midwest ground three of our flights, and we spent the better part of yesterday on buses and trains. Early this morning, we assumed that our flight to Los Angeles from Clovis, New Mexico would also be canceled, but thankfully the weather cleared, and our plane took off. Both the passengers and stewardesses applauded as we pulled next to the newly built terminal at United Airport in Burbank.

"Now that's a sight for sore eyes," I comment as we pull into the driveway.

"I can't believe it's only 11:00 in the morning," Dottie remarks while looking at her wristwatch.

"It feels like 11:00 at night!" Jack complains. "My body can't tell what time it is."

"Say, it looks like Nan arranged for someone to mow the lawn while we were away," Uncle Charles observes.

Neat horizontal lines extend evenly across the lawn.

"Very orderly...but not quite up to your standards, Jack." I reach back and give him a nudge. My cousin's mowing skills can best be described as "creative"—so much so that Uncle Charles and I have yet to figure out how he managed a perfect spiral one weekend.

"Boy, am I glad! I thought Dad would want me out there this afternoon."

"Come on, now! As exhausted as we all are, do you honestly think I'd force you to mow the lawn today?" My uncle pretends to be offended.

"Nah, I guess not."

"I'd have waited until first thing tomorrow morning," Uncle Charles adds.

"Da-ad!" Jack whines lightheartedly.

When we step out of the car, Dottie pronounces, "I used to hate the summer heat, but after the New York humidity, the weather here feels positively chilly."

When we landed in Burbank, the pilot announced that the temperature was eighty-two degrees. It feels a bit warmer than that now, but the dry air is a welcome change. Overhead, the cerulean sky is cloudless, yet in the distance, a towering plume of thunder clouds gathers over the desert. Even so, these sporadic storms rarely travel past the mountains this time of year to drop rain in our area.

"Welcome home!" The screen door slams as Nan rushes down the steps, strands of salt-and-pepper hair bouncing around her plump face.

I drop my bags and dash toward her, immediately throwing my arms around her when we meet in the center of the pathway to the house. "Oh, how I've missed you!"

"It ain't been the same without you, Ruby." Nan pulls a kerchief from the pocket of her apron and wipes the tears flowing from her soft blue eyes. "And I been worried sick! You—all by yerself halfway round the world."

"Trust me. I would have called you every day, if I could."

"And I'da answered too!" Nan has long held a deep mistrust of telephones.

"Did you get my postcards?" I sent one from each city I visited, knowing Nan would appreciate the postmarks from different countries.

"Yep. And I saved each one. After showin' 'em to my family, I tied 'em up with the white ribbon from the corsage ya gave me fer Mother's Day," Nan says affectionately.

"I'm glad." I take her hands in mine and notice the swollen knuckles—a sure sign that her arthritis is acting up. Despite her pain, however, a huge smile spreads across her freckled face. She's never been one to let ailments of any kind stand in her way.

"Ahem," Jack clears his throat. "Didn't you miss us?"

Nan drops my hands and pulls him into a tight hug. "Well, a course I did!"

Uncle Charles drapes an arm across her shoulders, "Nan, thank you so much for taking care of things while we were away. I see you recruited someone to cut the lawn."

"Sure did! Gabe was glad ta do it," Nan nods.

"Once we get settled inside, I'll give you a little something to pass on to Gabe," my uncle promises.

"That's mighty kind a ya. He'd a dunnit fer nothin', but I'm sure he'll be glad to send extra money home to his folks."

Gabe arrived on our sleeping porch during a hailstorm and startled Addie, one of Nan's great nieces, when she went out back to dump a pail of wastewater. Since Nan's gotten older, Addie and her twin sister, May, stop by each week to help with the housework. My uncle pays generously, so the young ladies don't seem to mind. According to Nan, Gabe had just "rolled in" on the Santa Fe railroad when the storm intensified. He rushed up Balcom—our street—from the tracks and sought shelter on our porch. When Addie found him, Nan immediately brought him inside, sat him down at the kitchen nook, and proceeded to feed him until he was full. Evidently, Gabe's parents sent him out west from Kansas to find work when his family lost all their crops.

"How is the hobo?" Jack jokes.

"Not funny, Jack," Uncle Charles scolds. The one thing he won't tolerate is unkindness.

"I'm gonna ignore that," Nan sniffs. "As a matter a fact, he's doin' good. He's learnin' at Coleman's Machine Shop and livin' with the boss and his wife."

"And May?" I inquire. She had developed quite an attachment to Gabe when I left in June.

"Two peas in a pod," Nan grins.

"As much as I love catching up," Dottie interrupts, "I'd like to wash off the airplane filth and change my clothes."

"Why a course you would!" Nan blushes. "Lemme help with the bags. You go right in."

"Absolutely not!" Uncle Charles declares. "Dottie, you can bring in your own suitcase, and Jack, you help me with the others."

"Well, lemme do somethin'," Nan insists.

"Tell you what. If you take my handbag, I can manage my suitcases," I suggest.

She reluctantly agrees.

Entering the house a moment later, I'm overwhelmed by the rich aroma of comforting foods. "Bacon gravy and biscuits!"

"And all the fixin's," Nan informs me proudly.

"You made my favorite breakfast! But it's lunchtime!"

"Breakfast, lunch, what's the difference? I'm starved!" Uncle Charles stacks three cases by the stairs.

"Me too!" Jack bolts toward the dining room.

"Now, hang on there!" Nan holds up an arm to bar his way. "You gotta warsh up first."

"Dibs!" Dottie bellows while racing up the stairs with Jack close behind.

We hear a door slam, followed by, "Hey, that's not fair!"

"When will she realize she can't outrun him anymore," my uncle rolls his eyes. "I'll wash up in the kitchen."

"Don't you go samplin' the food," Nan warns.

"I wouldn't dare," he winks.

"I think I'll head over to the cottage to freshen up." I drop my suitcases next to the others and exit through the front door.

I venture around the side of the house, past the carport, and gaze upon a single-story periwinkle cottage. The hydrangea bushes, still pink I notice, are in full bloom, and the rosebush Sam gave me is covered with delicate champagne blossoms. The upper half of the Dutch door is open. *Nan's been here.* My heart warms as I enter my beloved haven.

Uncle Charles built the cottage as an art studio for his wife when they moved to Fullerton many years ago. Aunt Beatrice was a talented painter who loved impressionism more than anything. In fact, one of her seascapes is hanging in the cottage. When I came to live in Fullerton, Uncle Charles realized that, as a high school student, I'd need a hideaway from my two little cousins in order to study. He offered me the space, which over the years has become my office and a meeting place for the reading parlor.

A vase of lilies and an envelope rest on a side table beside an armchair. I open the envelope and find a note of thanks from my reading group. A couple of the women I tutored years ago have become voracious readers and offered to keep the parlor going while I was away. In addition to the flowers and note, Nan has deposited a package of coffee, a pitcher of iced lemonade, and a plate of freshly baked cookies on the counter in the nearby kitchenette. I smile to myself. Nan is the reason I started tutoring in the first place.

When Jack was learning to read, he'd sometimes ask Nan for help. Watching her struggle, I soon realized that she was illiterate. A college friend who was studying education at the time taught me how to help Nan unlock the written word. Then, through word of mouth, women in our community began contacting me for lessons. After a while, I started to notice friendships developing among the women who met in passing at my cottage, and it occurred to me that the support of women with similar life circumstances was just as important to my clients as the reading instruction itself. Thus, the reading parlor was created.

After washing my hands in the tiny lavatory, I head toward the front door to leave but pause in my tracks. Somehow, I failed to notice the stack of letters on the coffee table in front of the divan. A tingling warmth radiates outward from the center of my chest.

I snatch up the first envelope. "Sam Armstrong" and an Arizona address have been written on the upper left-hand corner. I'd love to tear them open and take my time reading each one, but my stomach is growling and—if I'm not careful—both Jack and Dottie will polish off the food before I get there.

Entering the dining room, I hear my uncle declare, "Nan, the place looks wonderful!"

"Thanks fer noticin," she beams. "We cleaned every nook and cranny. The girls even straightened the linen closet and polished the silver."

"Well, we appreciate it, don't we kids?" Uncle Charles prompts.

"Mm-mm," my cousins mutter around mouthfuls of food.

Nan notices me. "Well, there ya are. Dontcha worry none. I set yers aside."

She darts back into the kitchen and returns with a plate laden with eggs fried in bacon grease, roasted potatoes, and slices of bacon alongside biscuits and gravy. Her thoughtfulness moves me, but there's no way I'll be able to get through even a fraction of this feast, despite my hunger. I'll pass some along to Jack when Nan isn't looking.

Uncle Charles places his napkin on an empty plate and examines the front cover of today's *Los Angeles Daily News*, which he picked up at the airport.

"Jack, listen to this. 'New Speed Mark to Coast Established by Boy Flyer.'"

"What?!" My cousin grabs for the paper.

"Hold your horses!" Uncle Charles shifts the paper out of Jack's reach and separates the page containing the front and back covers. "Here. If I give you the entire paper, I'll never get it back."

"Haven't you all had enough with airplanes? I, for one, will never fly again," Dottie vows.

"I'm sorry to tell you this, Polka Dot, but I suspect that air travel will be the way we get around the country in the future," my uncle predicts. "Maybe even the world."

Dottie grumbles and breaks open a biscuit.

Jack looks up from the paper and proclaims, "I don't know why they call him a boy. He's as old as Dottie!"

"Gee, thanks," she grunts.

"That's okay. It's still pretty swell!" Jack explains how an eighteen-year-old young man from New Jersey broke the junior record for flying from east to west coasts. "He woulda gotten here sooner, but he got lost over Los Angeles. The airport attendants at Long Beach Airport had to tell him how to get to Burbank where he was supposed to land. How embarrassing!"

"Still, though. That's quite an accomplishment for someone who was probably sitting behind a school desk a couple of months ago," I say.

"Speaking of planes." Uncle Charles lowers the paper. "Howard Hughes is raking it in with his new movie, *Hell's Angels*."

"That came out just before I left on my trip," I comment.

"It was crackerjack!" my cousin enthuses. "Dottie took me to see it at the Fox Theater during the first day of summer recess."

"That was kind of you," I praise. "What did you think?"

Dottie shrugs. "It was loud."

"You shoulda seen the dogfights, Ruby!" Jack interjects.

I think I'll pass.

I nudge my plate toward Jack. "Are you interested in helping me finish this?"

He needs no encouragement before scraping the remains onto his own plate. "Gee, thanks."

"I'm going upstairs to unpack," Dottie announces.

I should probably do the same, but instead I excuse myself and pass through the kitchen toward the back door. From the porch, I examine the jacaranda tree, whose canopy shades a large corner of the backyard. There are just as many purple blooms on the ground as on the limbs above. I glance at the little wishing well my uncle built years ago but, having no coin at the moment, turn left toward the avocado tree. I'll be back later with a penny for the well, a ritual I started many years ago and one that Jack, in particular, has profited from.

A few steps away, the dark green avocado tree is heavy with fruit— I grab several. An "alligator pear" mask and a warm bath sound heavenly, and I'll no doubt wish to snack on one, as well, later this afternoon. Discovering avocados was one of my greatest delights after moving to California.

Settling back into the cottage, I pour myself a glass of watered-down lemonade—the ice having already melted—and set a peanut butter cookie on a plate. Even though they're not Mallomars, my personal favorite, I can't resist a bite or two of the chewy treat. Placing the glass and plate on the coffee table, I retrieve the letters and sink into the soft cushions of the divan. The first letter was posted the day before I left on my trip.

June 5th
San Carlos Apache Reservation
Dear Ruby,
Apologies for not writing sooner. You probably won't receive this letter until you're back from Europe. In that case, I hope you had a wonderful trip, free of onerous circumstances.

About six months after first meeting Sam, I ran into him again at the hospital while working on a case. When we parted, he told me, "I hope, at some point, we run into each other under less onerous circumstances." Since that time, the phrase has become a good-natured quip between us. In this very room, the day before he left for Arizona, Sam held up a Mallomar and proposed a toast "to less onerous circumstances." This memory unleashes a cascade of feelings, both emotional and physical. The last words he said to me were, "I'll miss you," and I realize at this very moment how much I miss him. Sam has been present, just below the surface of my conscious awareness, during every moment since we parted. I can't say that I've ever felt that way about a man before. It's all rather overwhelming…and frightening. After all, we haven't even had a proper date yet. I roll my head from side to side and shake my shoulders. Back to the letters.

Unfortunately, I can't say the same for my trip to Arizona. I rode the Santa Fe from Los Angeles to Phoenix, which went smoothly. However, things went haywire after that. The letter I received from the Bureau of Indian Affairs instructed me to take a bus from the railroad station to the San Carlos Apache Reservation. When I asked a station porter for directions to the bus stop, he said that I was just in time, as the bus only comes once daily. But after waiting for three hours under the beating sun, I walked back to the station and was informed that the bus broke down and would not make it for at least another day. Thankfully, I'd brought enough cash to get a room for the night. However, when I asked about the bus at the train station the next morning, I was told that the mechanic on the reservation was waiting for a part and that the bus wouldn't be repaired for two more days. So, I went back to the motel and called the San Carlos Agency Hospital to explain the situation. The doctor I spoke with was abrupt and said he was dealing with an outbreak of trachoma at the local boarding school. Furthermore, two doctors were out sick with a summer flu. He suggested I arrange alternative transportation, since he could really use my help. The woman at the motel desk overheard my conversation and said that her husband, Alfred, could drive me but that I'd have to ride in the back because he only allowed Toby to ride up front. I told her I was grateful and assured her that I wouldn't mind and that I would, of course, pay for the gasoline. You can imagine my surprise when I learned that Toby was a two-hundred-pound Mastiff, and "the back" referred to the bed of a stake body truck. Just imagine bouncing around in that on a dusty road for nearly four hours…in 100-degree heat. When we finally arrived, I shook Alfred's hand and told him how thankful I was that he spent his entire day driving through the desert to help a stranger. He said, "No bother. It was that or go to church."

Every day since arriving, I've been tasked with visiting isolated communities—on horseback. Most of these people haven't had medical care in months. That's a whole other story for another letter. Anyway, I know I promised to write

immediately so you'd have my mailing address before you left for your trip, and I'm
sorry. I vow to be a better pen pal from here on out.

> *Fondly,*
> *Sam*
> *P.S. Is it too soon to tell you that I miss you?*

I return the letter to its envelope and examine the return address. I admit, part of me felt slighted when I didn't hear back from him. I wondered if I'd misread his intentions or worse—his character. After all, I'd once been so enamored with my ex, Eddie, that I'd overlooked his controlling and dishonest nature. Relieved, I read and then re-read the other letters, each describing entertaining narratives about his work and the varied landscape of southeastern Arizona. I find one letter, in particular, quite charming.

A part of me wants to tell you everything about myself—my childhood, where I grew up, my college years, my likes and dislikes, why in the world I went into medicine in the first place—but that sort of discussion should be a dialogue, preferably in person. These letters feel more like a one-sided conversation where the speaker yammers on and on, completely ignoring cues that the other person is bored to tears. Have you ever been on the receiving end of a conversation like that? I sure have. Ask me about my college roommate someday. Anyway, getting to know another person should be reciprocal. And I am VERY interested in getting to know you, Ruby Ray.

"Ruby, are you in there?" Dottie hollers through the opened top of the Dutch door.

I quickly stack the letters and hop up from the divan. "Sure am. Come on in."

"You've been here for hours," she remarks.

I look down at the delicate gold face of my new wristwatch. For years I'd relied upon the silver Elgin pocket watch that had belonged to my mother, but I didn't dare take the treasured timepiece with me to Europe for fear that I might lose it. After weeks of asking other people for the time, I finally picked up this watch in France.

It's 3:17. "Oh, I hadn't realized."

"Here you go," she hands me an envelope. "Nan said she forgot to put it with the others. It arrived yesterday."

I immediately notice that the return address is in Laguna Beach.

"So-oo...Sam Armstrong..." She raises and lowers her eyebrows.

"Oh, that's right. You haven't met Sam," I reply and plop back onto the divan to open the letter.

"Nope, but Jack seems to like him." Dottie sits beside me and openly gapes at Sam's note.

I turn the page away and read the brief message, so unlike his other correspondence.

August 16th
Laguna Beach
Dear Ruby,

Welcome home! I hope your travel wasn't remotely onerous. I'm counting the days until I see you again. While I'd hoped my next placement would be closer to Fullerton, at least we are now in the same country. I need to make this one short but sweet, as I'm heading off to my night job doing autopsies. That's right. In the wee small hours, I play Dr. Frankenstein at the coroner's office. My daytime post is with Dr. Carroll, a fantastic GP in Laguna Beach. Let me know when you're back.

Fondly,
Sam

"Are you gonna see him?" Dottie cranes her neck to sneak a peek.

"I'd like to," I quickly fold the letter and shove it back into the envelope.

Dottie says kindly, "I'm really glad, Ruby. You deserve a nice guy for a change."

Her earnestness touches me. "Thank you. I'm glad too."

"So, what now?"

"I guess I'll write him a letter letting him know I'm back."

"Write to him? Just call him!"

"I don't know…"

She marches across the room to my desk and points. "Call him!"

"When did I get a phone?" I'm astounded. In June, we only had one line in the house. "How did I not notice that?"

"I'd say you were preoccupied," she smirks. "Dad had it put in while you were away."

"I can't believe it! How thoughtful!" This was going to radically improve my investigative work…not to mention my social life.

"Well, don't just stare at it. Call him, or I'll call for you."

"You'll do no such thing," I grab the receiver from her hand and return it to the cradle. Truthfully, I'm not comfortable calling him, which is absurd. If I had a medical question regarding a case, I wouldn't hesitate. But I feel so uncertain and don't want to bungle things with him. I'll write and let him make the first phone call.

"O-kay," she huffs.

"Tell you what—let's go unpack my cruise suitcase," I suggest.

Her eyes widen, "That's right! I completely forgot about it."

"I find that hard to believe. From the moment I returned to New York, you've been pestering me about whether I got you anything in Europe."

It had taken me hours to securely pack the fragile items I'd picked up on my cruise, including gifts for my family, and I had no desire to repeat the process. So, I'd insisted that Jack and Dottie would have to wait until we got home.

"I know you got us something." She heads for the door. "Let's go."

After dinner, notes from Jack's new Seydel mouth organ float down the hall from his room. Considering that the harmonica was first invented in Germany, there was really no other option. And through my open bedroom door, I can smell spicy smoke wafting up the stairs from the Ben Wade pipe I bought in England for Uncle Charles. He particularly appreciated the amber stem and sterling silver detail.

Dottie knocks. "Nan just left cradling the Delft cake plate you got her."

"I knew she'd love it," I smile thinking about its darling blue and white windmill. "But I'm not so sure she'll actually use it."

"She said she's putting it in her hope chest," Dottie chuckles and sits on my bed. "Wrapped up in the quilt her grandma made."

"Where did you put your perfume tray?" I bought Dottie a French silver tray engraved with a lace pattern around the edge.

"On my nightstand," she grins. "It's perfect for Mama's brush and mirror." She's lovingly cared for the silver-backed set since her father gave them to her for her eighth birthday.

"I figured you'd like to take it with you to Berkeley."

She passes a finger over my chenille bedspread. "Mm-mm."

"Is everything alright? It's barely been three months since everything—"

"I'm fine," she stands and walks toward the door. "Honestly, Ruby. Everything's fine. Why do you have to bring that up?"

"I'm sorry I've upset you, Dottie. That wasn't my intention."

"I'm not upset," she replies flippantly. The phone starts ringing downstairs. "I'll get it. That might be Polly."

During our entire stay in New York, I sensed that Dottie was struggling with something, but she clammed up every time I broached the topic. Before this past year, Dottie and I were so close. She'd come to me with everything. She'll be leaving for Berkeley in no time, and I'm concerned about her being so far away from home and feeling she has no one to confide in.

A moment later she shouts up the steps, "Ruby, it's for you."

My stomach flutters. *Maybe it's Sam.*

"Hello, this is Ruby." I take a seat at the telephone desk.

"Ruby, welcome home," the familiar voice intones through the receiver.

"Edith, how lovely to hear your voice," I reply, only slightly disappointed. "I just got back today."

"Oh, you must be exhausted. I'm so sorry to bother you this evening."

"It's no bother at all. How are you? How's Norma?" I got to know the couple in May while working on a case. They'd asked me to locate Norma's brother, Frank, who had stolen their savings. As high school teachers, it had taken them years to save enough to buy their own home, and they were devastated by the loss and betrayal. Thankfully, I located Frank, who ultimately told them where he'd stashed the money.

"Norma's doing very well. She's been happy as a clam since Puck arrived."

"Puck? Who's Puck?" I'd remember if they'd mentioned that name before.

Edith laughs, "Puck's our new kitten. Norma is besotted."

"Oh," I laugh as well. "That makes more sense. Have you settled into your new home? Is Laguna Beach treating you well?"

"We absolutely love it here! The people are nice, and the friends we've made through the art colony have helped us get settled."

"I'm so pleased to hear that. Will you be teaching there in town?"

"We will, but not high school. Laguna Beach students attend high school in Tustin, since they haven't built one here yet."

"So, you'll be teaching younger students?" I inquire. I can picture Norma working with elementary children, but I can't imagine Edith in a grammar school classroom.

"For now," she answers. "It's my hope to become more involved with the art community and maybe teach art education at some point."

"I can see that."

I pause—wondering about the status of Frank's case but feeling reluctant to bring up the subject. When I left, he had recovered from methanol poisoning and left the hospital only to go directly to jail. The charges were larceny, bootlegging, and child endangerment, since he was responsible for locking the kids in the tunnels. On the one hand, I feel furious about what he did to my cousin, but on the other hand, I feel pity for his brokenness following years of child abuse.

Sensing my hesitation, Edith says, "You'd like to ask about Frank but are trying to decide the best way to go about it."

"Yes, that's correct. You know, if you ever decide to change careers and become an inquiry agent, let me know. You're quite good."

"Thank you," she chuckles. "Norma is here and would actually like to tell you about Frank."

She passes the telephone.

"Hello, Ruby," Norma's gentle voice greets me.

"Norma, hello there. It sounds like everything's going well at your new home, including your little friend."

She giggles, "Yes, Puck's a sweet boy."

"What's the latest news about Frank?"

"Well, he's doing as well as can be expected. Since he cooperated with the district attorney's investigation of Floyd Phillips, they've lessened his charges. The larceny count was reduced to a misdemeanor, as Floyd was the mastermind behind the whole thing, and the bootlegging charges were dropped. There was no evidence that Frank was producing or transporting the moonshine. Everything pointed to Floyd. But Frank was convicted of felony child endangerment. Even though he was suffering from alcohol poisoning at the time, four minors were involved, and Polly's father demanded the maximum penalty."

"I'm sure he did," I roll my eyes.

"Frank's attorney persuaded him to plead guilty to all charges. He'll be in jail for five years," Norma sighs.

"I'm sorry about that."

He's lucky it wasn't twenty years.

Norma quickly changes the subject, "On another note, you'll never guess who we ran into at the grocery store—Dr. Armstrong from Fullerton General Hospital. Remember him? He was Frank's doctor."

"Yes," I choke. "I'd heard he was doing a rotation in Laguna."

"What's that, Edith?" Norma asks. "Excuse me, Ruby."

I hear muffled voices for a few seconds.

"I'm sorry, Ruby. I need to hand the phone to Edith. That's the whole reason we're calling."

"Oh…alright. Goodbye, Norma."

"Ruby?" Edith is back on the line. "I know you just returned, but we have a favor to ask you."

I wonder what's come up. "Of course. How can I help?"

"Well, my aunt passed away," she begins.

"I'm so sorry to hear that."

"Here's the situation. She lived in Nebraska and, as her only living relative, I need to settle her estate—as small as that may be."

"I really don't know anything about that sort of—"

"So, Norma and I were wondering if you'd come stay at our home for several days while we're away," Edith continues.

"To care for Puck," I hear Norma shout in the background.

"We hesitated to ask but thought perhaps you might like a short stay at the beach," Edith explains.

My initial reaction is to politely decline, but then I reconsider. Several days at the beach with Dottie might be just the thing to help her open up to me. And then there's Sam…how can I even consider declining?

"Edith, I think that would be fine. How soon do you need me?" Hopefully not tomorrow. I don't know how I could possibly catch up on things here before heading down.

"Oh, Ruby. Thank you! What a relief! We're leaving Thursday, but our neighbor can look after Puck until Friday. Would that work for you? We'll return the day before Labor Day"

That leaves me two full days to tidy up everything here at home and more than a week to enjoy Laguna Beach. "Yes, I believe I can make that work."

"Thank you so much!" Then Edith gives me their address and phone number.

I wander into the living room where Uncle Charles asks, "Another case already?"

"Not exactly."

CHAPTER 5

~ 🪷 ~

FRIDAY, AUGUST 22, 1930
LAGUNA BEACH, CALIFORNIA

Sloping walls of rock and sagebrush rise on either side of the narrow gorge that has become Laguna Canyon over the millennia. As we drive through the canyon, oak and eucalyptus trees sporadically line the road, while the occasional post and rail fence prevents inattentive drivers from drifting off the shoulder.

"Where do we go next?" I ask Dottie, my navigator.

She examines the strip map we picked up at the Automobile Club in Fullerton yesterday. "This road will fork into Broadway and Third. We'll want to turn left onto Third Street, but that's several miles from here."

We both stare at the back of the slow-moving dump truck in front of us.

"We'll be here a while," she grumbles.

"That's okay. In no time we'll be relaxing at the beach."

And hopefully she'll feel comfortable opening up to me sometime over the next week.

"Thanks for inviting me. It sounds like a lot of fun, but boy was Jack sore."

When he overheard my discussion with Uncle Charles about the getaway, Jack bellyached about how unfair it was that "Dottie gets to do everything."

His father reminded him that he'd been gone for more than a week already and that he needed to collect his pets from his friend's house. Evidently the boy's mother left several messages while we were away. She had not agreed to having Jack's lizards and tarantula under her roof, and she wanted them gone as soon as possible. In the end, Uncle Charles softened the blow by promising he'd bring Jack to Laguna Beach on Thursday to stay through Labor Day.

"I'll arrange for a room at one of the new hotels down there," he assured his wounded son.

"Take your pick," I remarked. "Hotel Laguna, La Casa del Camino, and the Coast Inn all opened over the last year."

The truck ahead suddenly stops, and I grip the steering wheel of my 1925 Balboa. I'm regularly asked by strangers about my car, as it's one of only a handful that were ever built. The Balboa Motor Corporation had plans to manufacture the car in Fullerton but went belly up before that could happen. My uncle, who'd invested heavily in the company, persuaded them to part with one of the prototypes, and I've been driving it ever since.

"Did you call him," Dottie asks coyly.

"Did I call who?" I lift my foot from the brake as the truck begins to roll forward.

"You know who!" She needles. "Sam!"

I really don't want to have this conversation, but she'll never let it rest. "I mailed him a quick note on Wednesday telling about our stay."

"Oh, Ruby," she derides. "I hope you gave him the phone number at Miss Holmes' and Miss Graham's house."

"Of course I did," I answer tartly.

Thankfully, the behemoth turns left onto a dirt road, and I'm able to accelerate. We ride in silence through the canyon for a couple of miles when Dottie suddenly shouts, "Watch out!"

Several yards ahead of us, a large, black bird perches atop the remains of a mottled gray and brown animal. The scavenger ignores our approach until the last possible second, when it casually takes wing and settles in the upper branches of a willow on the side of the road.

"That's one big crow!" Dottie exclaims.

"It's probably a raven," I remark.

"Either way, it's not very bright."

"I wouldn't underestimate it. That bird seemed to know exactly how much time it had before it was in any danger. Do you remember the story Nan told us about the henhouse?"

Nan lives in Fullerton with her sister and her great-nieces. Earlier in the year, Addie decided they should raise chickens, reasoning that they would save money in the long run by selling the eggs they couldn't use. However, this venture was short-lived due to coyotes raiding the henhouse. After losing half of their brood, Nan's nephew installed a hasp latch with a sturdy cotter pin on the coop door. But one evening, Nan heard frantic squawks and went outside to investigate. To her astonishment, a raven had pulled out the pin and swung open the latch with its beak.

"I still don't get it. The raven didn't attack the chickens," Dottie reasons.

"No, but once the coyotes made off with the hens, the raven had access to the eggs."

"Oh, I see," she reflects. "Clever bird."

"Precisely!"

At the end of the canyon, a salty breeze drifts through our open windows, and the temperature seems to drop by twenty degrees. We both sigh audibly.

"I'm so glad to be here." Dottie beams.

"Me too. You know, your mother loved Laguna Beach," I remind her.

She nods. "Dad says she used to take me to the tidepools, but that's probably the last time I visited Laguna."

"I've never been."

We ordinarily head to Huntington Beach for family seaside excursions. I assume that's because Huntington is closer, but I have to wonder if, perhaps, Laguna Beach brings back too many memories for Uncle Charles. He adored Aunt Beatrice, and he's never shown any interest in remarrying or even dating, for that matter.

"Ruby, turn left," Dottie says quickly.

I merge onto Third Street.

"Sorry about that." Dottie's finger traces over our route on the map.

"That's alright. When is our next turn?"

"It looks like we're almost there. In about a quarter of a mile we need to turn left onto Park Ave."

I chuckle. "It's rather ironic—after a week in New York, we come to Laguna to stay on Park Avenue."

"Here it is," Dottie points to a shingled cottage on our left just after the turn.

I swing around and pull up to the curb in front of the house. A sycamore tree shades the tiny front lawn where a pair of cedar Adirondack chairs rest on either side of a squat stool serving as a table. Stepping stones on the grass lead to the light turquoise dwelling from which a desperate mewling carries through one of the open windows.

"Oh no!" Dottie bolts across the grass and jiggles the doorknob.

"Check under the potted fern," I direct her.

She's already inside before I can open the trunk. I grab my two cases and rush to join her. A modest living room with sea green furniture conveys a cozy warmth. One of Edith's paintings is hanging above the mantle—a beautiful seascape with a woman, who bears a striking resemblance to Norma, walking barefoot across the sand. Straight ahead, a door leads into the kitchen, but I enter a hallway on the left that is lined with rooms on either side. The first is a small study containing a cramped desk, a narrow filing cabinet, and a camp bed tucked into the corner with a blanket and pillow. The next room, clearly a bedroom, belongs to Norma and Edith. I place my suitcases on the bed.

Dottie walks in with a black kitten, about the size of a loaf of bread, clinging to her knit blouse and whimpering.

"It's alright," she comforts him. "We're here now."

"You found Puck. Where was he?"

"In the bathroom." She scratches between his ears, and he begins to settle.

I walk toward the door, but Dottie lifts her hand. "You might not want to go in there yet."

"Why not?" I ignore her warning and head down the hall.

Shredded bathroom tissue litters the floor, and wet sand has been kicked out of an enamel tray. The odor is atrocious. I crank the window fully open and close the door before returning to the bedroom.

"Ugh!"

"I warned you." Dottie cuddles the kitten and stares into his large golden eyes. "I'm sure he felt abandoned. Weren't you, Puck?"

"Why is there sand?"

"I think he's meant to do his business in the pan." Dottie smoothes Puck's fur.

I'm confused. "Don't they go outside for that?"

Dottie just shrugs.

"Well, it looks like they set up an extra bed in their office," I remark. "Do you want to take that or sleep here with me?"

That's when Dottie notices the double bed. "Oh! So…"

"Yes," I answer.

"I had no idea," Dottie confesses.

"They've tried to keep it that way. They were afraid they'd lose their jobs."

"I can imagine," she frowns. "People like Polly's parents…"

"Exactly."

"Well, I'm happy for them. They were both really nice teachers."

"So am I. They've waited a long time to have a home of their own—together."

We wander into the living room, where I discover an envelope lying on the coffee table. Inside is a letter in Norma's handwriting.

Dear Ruby and Dottie,

How do we begin to express our gratitude for your help with our darling Puck while we are away? You'll no doubt find him to be a delightful kitten, and we're sure that you will enjoy his company. Here are a few things you'll need to know.

1. *His favorite dish for food is the small bowl with the yellow daisy. Feed him half of a can of tuna twice a day.*
2. *His favorite dish for water is the slightly larger bowl with an orange pansy.*

61

3. *He prefers to drink his milk from the mint green teacup (½ full), but the matching saucer frightens him. Also, please warm the milk, but be sure it's not too hot.*

4. *Puck likes to nibble grass, which is good for his digestion. So, the shallow terracotta pot of alfalfa in the living room should be watered twice while we are away. Please be careful not to overfill it, or tiny flies will breed in the damp soil.*

5. *The sanitary pan in the bathroom should be emptied and washed twice a day. You'll find a large can with sand just outside the back door. Please use this sand (and not sand collected from the beach) as filler for the pan.*

6. *Under no circumstance should Puck be allowed outside.*

7. *Puck's favorite toy is one of Edith's old bath slippers. If you can't find it for him, check under the bed. He often forgets that he's left it there.*

8. *He loves to be scratched between his ears and on his tummy but not when his pupils are dilated.*

9. *If he begins kneading the furniture, gently pick him up and relocate him to his scratch post which is behind the sofa.*

10. *Puck loathes being alone, so try to be available for him as much as possible.*

Hopefully, these instructions cover everything you'll need to know. Again, from the bottom of our hearts, thank you for looking after our precious pet.

Sincerely yours,

Norma and Edith

"Sanitary pan? Digestive grass? If they'd allow Puck to go outside, they wouldn't need any of that." I've never heard of people keeping cats indoors.

Dottie tickles the white heart-shaped spot on his chest. "They probably don't want him to run away."

"He can be supervised. Who knew that cats are so much work?" I murmur.

"That's okay, Ruby. I don't mind taking care of Puck."

Then I spot the additional lines that have been scrawled across the back of the note.

P.S. Apologies in advance—Edith

P.P.S. He's a menace. Good luck!—Tilly from next door

"Great!" I mutter.

Dottie laughs. "He can't be that bad. Tell you what—if you bring in my bags, I'll clean up the bathroom."

"Deal!"

After I've unpacked, I wander into the office and find Dottie resting on the cot with the kitten on her chest. Dottie's suitcase is open on the desk, but the clothes remain neatly folded inside.

"I thought we'd go into town for lunch and then pick up some groceries afterward. Do you want to unpack first?"

"No, I'll just leave everything in the suitcase and iron if I need to." Dottie sits up, and the tag on the kitten's collar jingles as he stretches. "What should we do about Puck?"

"I'm not so sure we should leave him free to roam around the house while we're away." I imagine all the damage that might result. "Let's put him back in the bathroom."

"O-kay," she says reluctantly. "I suppose we should remove the bathroom tissue."

"Most definitely!"

We slowly cruise down Forest Avenue looking for parking. Dozens of automobiles fill the angled spaces along both sides of the street.

"Wow! I never thought we'd have trouble finding a spot," I comment.

"Up ahead on the right—someone's backing out." Dottie points excitedly.

When the car pulls away, I quickly glide into the space—much to the annoyance of a driver on the other side of the street who noticed the spot just after we did.

"I don't suppose we'll have much use for the car this week, but today I'd prefer to drive than walk the quarter of a mile uphill with an armful of groceries." I adjust my wide-brimmed sun hat in the rear-view mirror. We get out of the car.

"Let's go this way," Dottie suggests.

I follow, all the while envying her choice of full shorts that skim just above the knee. My wide-legged jersey trousers, while comfortable, already feel rather warm, and the temperature will only rise as the afternoon unfolds. When we reach the intersection with Coast Highway, a large "Laguna Beach" sign welcomes visitors. Next door, a striped awning shades the front of the Sandwich Mill Restaurant.

"This looks good," I decide. "Let's stop here for lunch."

"Not a moment too soon! I'm starved!" she declares.

I laugh, "When aren't you hungry?"

Inside, about a dozen people wait in line for a table. Dottie plucks a menu from the pile on the hostess stand then joins me at the back of the line.

"Popular place."

"You're not kidding." I gaze over her shoulder. "What looks good to you?"

"I might order the chili beans," she muses. "How about you?"

"Club sandwich and half an avocado."

"Ruby, you always order that!" She shakes her head. "What about chicken salad? You can still add avocado."

"Maybe. Say, what's this here?" I direct her attention to an item that's been handwritten at the bottom of the menu. "The Pancho?"

Unexpectedly, the man ahead of us turns around and answers, "Pancho Barnes. It's her favorite sandwich."

"Pancho Barnes? The aviatrix?" I inquire.

"Yeah, but she hates that word. She always says, 'I'm just a pilot.'"

"You know her?" Dottie asks incredulously.

"I've seen her around. She has a house here called Dos Rocas," he explains. "Just south of Emerald Bay."

"I can seat you now, sir," the hostess addresses the fellow.

"Have a nice lunch," I call after him as he walks away.

"Jack's going to flip when he hears about this," Dottie exclaims.

"Thankfully, he'll be here at the end of the week. Until then, let's keep this under wraps."

"Good idea. Otherwise, Dad will never hear the end of it."

We step forward to request a table but are taken aback when a hearty middle-aged woman with an Eton crop hairstyle rushes toward the hostess.

"Sorry, Mary, I'm in a rush. I got one of those lifeguard kids watching my rowboat by the tower." She turns, an apologetic grin on her tanned face.

"Hey there, Sal. The usual?" Mary begins scribbling on a pad.

"Yeah, except for Willy's bacon and tomato. He left early."

The hostess hands the page to a passing busboy then asks Sal, "Where've you been? I haven't seen you in a while."

"Lately, there's been a big tuna run off Newport, so we've been takin' out fishermen, but we'll be here in Laguna all week."

"Were you hauling anglers this morning?"

"Nah, we took out some divers...movie folk, you know."

"How'd that go?"

Sal scowls, "When they showed up with their own gear, I figured they were experienced. Turns out they were first-timers. Kept arguin' they knew what they were doin'. Malarkey!"

"Oh, brother!" Mary commiserates.

"Well, what can you do? That's where the big bucks are." She rubs her thumb and index finger.

"Can you hang on a sec, Sal? I wanna get these ladies seated."

"Of course, Mary."

"Sorry about that." Mary walks us to a table in the back. "Thanks for your patience. The waitress will be with you shortly."

After we place our order, a heated discussion breaks out at the table next to us.

"I tell you, Clarence, they have no right! I only needed thirty minutes more before the sun was too high. The shadows this morning were perfect." The woman places a hand over her lovely ebony face

"I don't disagree, Lilian, but what can we do? The city council approved their permit."

"If it happens again I'm going to plant my easel directly behind those actors and refuse to move until my painting's dry." Her dark eyes flash mischievously.

Clarence snickers. "I'd like to see you try."

"Actors?" Dottie smiles at me with glee.

"Shh! They'll know you're listening," I whisper.

"I bet they're filming a movie!" she posits hopefully. "Wouldn't that be something!"

"I've had my fill of Hollywood hoopla for now. All I want is a week of peace and quiet."

Why do I feel like that's never going to happen?

After a satiating lunch, we cross the street and stare up at a white gate hanging on a tall pole with words printed across its slats.

THIS GATE HANGS WELL AND HINDERS NONE. REFRESH AND REST. THEN TRAVEL ON.

"Curious," I comment. "I'm sure there's a story behind that."

"Look, Ruby! They sell ice cream!"

"We just shared a slice of peach pie." I chuckle. "Maybe next time."

"Well, it's a pharmacy too, and I'm out of film." She charges ahead and pushes open the door.

I reluctantly follow and nearly collide with a tall gentleman in an apron, bearing a box full of cigars.

"I'm so sorry!" I exclaim and pick up a few stogies from the floor.

"There's no need for that," he accepts the items. "I was preoccupied and didn't notice." A badge on his smock identifies him as the owner.

"I have a question for you, Mr. Rankin." I glance over my shoulder.

He rests the box on a nearby counter and chortles. "Let me guess...the gate."

"Yes!"

"Well, it's like this..." He paws at his chin. "Carl Hofer used to own this place. Only, it was further up the road. Anyway, he told everyone in town that he was having a contest to name the store. A little girl suggested 'The Gate.' She even included a poem with her submission. Not only did she win, but her poem was inscribed on the gate you see hanging outside."

"What a sweet story!" I profess. "Thank you for taking the time to share it with me."

"My pleasure." Mr. Rankin smiles then turns as a customer taps him on the shoulder.

"What was that all about?" Dottie approaches.

"I'll tell you later. Did they have your film?"

She shakes a small brown bag. "I bought three rolls."

"Good idea. Given all the photos you took in New York, I'm sure you'll be back for more in no time."

A few doors down from Rankin's Drugs, we find a grocery store. It seems to be well-stocked with a fine selection of fresh meat and produce. We take a hand basket and wander up the first aisle.

"It's a shame neither of us can cook," Dottie mentions casually.

"Speak for yourself. I help Nan in the kitchen all the time."

"Helping her cut vegetables or mash potatoes isn't the same," she argues. "When have you ever made an entire meal by yourself?"

I reflect on my culinary experience and realize that I can really only manage boiling eggs, toasting bread, and heating soup in a pan. Humbled, I admit, "I guess you're right."

"What are we gonna do this week?" Dottie looks around at the shelves.

"Let's keep it simple." I grab a jar of peanut butter and a smaller jar of strawberry jam. "We can eat out once a day for lunch or dinner. I think I can manage eggs and toast for breakfast. Sandwiches the rest of the time?"

The front door swings open. In saunters a buxom woman wearing a daring dress, her decolletage barely covered by the nearly transparent fichu draped around her shoulders. She lowers her tortoise shell sunglasses and scans the store to make sure everyone has noticed her. A teenage girl, not quite as old as Dottie, hesitantly steps forward.

"Excuse me," the teen gulps. "Are you Bebe Gish?"

Bebe's red-stained lips part to reveal white teeth, too perfect to be real. She pats her jet-black curls. "And what if I am?"

The poor girl is tongue-tied. "I-I-I…"

"You'd like an autograph." Bebe extends her hand, palm up.

"I-I don't have anything to sign."

"Well…that's alright." Bebe pats the teen on the head. "I really don't have the time anyway."

"She's younger than I thought," Dottie observes in a hushed tone.

"I was thinking the same thing."

I've seen Bebe Gish in a handful of movies, usually playing the older vixen who tries to seduce the young hero. This woman, however, appears to be around my age.

The other customers quickly finish their shopping so they can line up behind Bebe, and one asks her a question about Corvi.

"Don't mention that name to me!" Bebe snaps and huffs out of the store.

When the crowd has cleared, Dottie and I approach the cashier, a mature woman with a ruddy complexion. We've hardly placed our baskets on the counter when Dottie blurts, "Is it true? Are they filming a movie in town?"

"Yes! And it's a doozy," the cashier gushes enthusiastically. "Would you believe Corvi Styles and Rex Langdon are here too?"

I sigh heavily, and the woman cocks her head, bemused.

"My cousin, Ruby, just finished a month-long cruise. Corvi and Rex were on the ship," Dottie explains.

"Well, that sounds like a dream come true!" the cashier proclaims.

"You'd think so," I answer. "But with the press and fans, it was quite disruptive."

She nods her head knowingly. "I understand. It's always the same here when a film crew is in town."

"Have other movies been filmed in Laguna?" Dottie leans her chin on her palms, her elbows resting on the counter.

"Oh my, yes. I think the first was *False Colors*. That was filmed around 1914—I know it was before we joined the war."

"I've never heard of that one," Dottie confesses.

"Well, I don't suppose you would have—you're too young. But you must have heard of *Captain January* or *The Lighthouse by the Sea*. They were both filmed here around '23 or '24."

"Definitely!" Dottie looks at me with a smile.

She was twelve when we saw *Captain January* and were both taken with the little actress, known as "Baby Peggy." Then there's *The Lighthouse by the Sea*—she absolutely adored the German Shepherd.

"I've seen all the Rin Tin Tin movies! Is the lighthouse really here?"

"Sadly, no. The studio built that for the movie then tore it down."

Dottie frowns.

The cashier suggests, "Maybe you'd like to see the tower instead."

"What tower?" Dottie brightens.

The woman lowers her voice conspiratorially, "A senator from Los Angeles built a tower next to the bluff where his mansion sits. It looks like something out of a fairytale. And there's a staircase inside so he can privately go down to the beach and enjoy his swimming pool whenever he wants. The pool fills with ocean water during high tide, and when the water recedes, it's perfect for splashing around...or so I've heard."

"We have to see it!" Dottie demands.

"Isn't it private property?" I don't want to trespass.

"Yes, but people sneak over there at night all the time," the cashier discloses.

Dottie shoots me a hopeful smile.

"No."

Disappointed, my cousin asks, "Were any other movies filmed in Laguna Beach?"

"Sure! The most recent was *Tanned Legs*. Did you see it last year?"

I nudge Dottie. "If I'm not mistaken, you were quite fond of the dashing young man who played the lead."

She blushes.

"There's always folk from Hollywood stopping by for one reason or another. Mary Pickford and Douglas Fairbanks were here a few years ago for the ceremony when Coast Highway was opened between Newport Beach and Dana Point. Rumor has it, they had a little hideaway nearby." The cashier packs the last of our groceries into the string bags I found in Edith and Norma's kitchen.

"I suppose when you live in a home like Pickfair, you need someplace else to get away from it all," I joke. Pickfair is the four-story, twenty-five-room mansion that the couple built in Beverly Hills when they were first married.

"And, of course, I have to tell you about the rumrunners," the cashier continues. "That's a good one."

"Rumrunners?" I sway. I've had quite enough with bootleggers after my last case.

"Yes. Several years ago, a film crew rolled into town with cameras, megaphones, the whole works. The directors spoke with a few locals and said they'd need extras for one of the scenes. Well, you can imagine the excitement! People would be able to see themselves on the big screen, and they would be paid three dollars a day, to boot!"

"What'd they have to do?" Dottie urges, captivated.

"The movie was about rumrunners, and a dummy ship was anchored just offshore. The extras were asked to row boats back and forth to retrieve cases of fake liquor, then load them into trucks. The camera rolled all day, and the directors kept shouting instructions."

"Did you go to watch?"

"I strolled out on my lunch break. It was quite a spectacle."

"What was the movie called? Maybe we saw it," Dottie asks.

"That's the kicker. When the trucks drove away, the extras went to collect their money. But everyone had cleared out, including the directors. Turns out, they weren't making a film at all—they were actual rumrunners who'd conned the whole group into unloading their cargo."

I snort. "You've got to be kidding?!"

The cashier holds up a hand, "I swear on the Bible!"

CHAPTER 6

Brrring...Brrring...

"Can you get that, Dottie?"

Somehow Puck has tangled his back paws into the woven edging of a cotton bath towel. I gently loosen the final ensnared claw.

"There you go, Puck."

I start to stroke the fur along his back, but he hops out of my lap and scampers out of the confined room. Rising from the edge of the bathtub, I grasp the broom handle and reach for the dustpan.

Dottie pokes her head into the room, waggling her eyebrows. "Ruby, the phone is for you."

Tossing her the broom, pan, and towel, I call over my shoulder, "Can you make sure every towel is out of Puck's reach? I'll explain later."

When I reach the telephone, I find the kitten playing with the cord attached to the wall outlet.

"Oh, no you don't!" I scoop him up, securing the little imp under my left arm and—after taking a deep breath—answer the phone.

"Hello, this is Ruby."

"Ruby! Gosh, it's great to hear your voice!" Sam's tenor conveys affection.

My entire body tingles with joy. "You too! I can't believe we're finally in the same town again."

"That's the truth! I have to confess...I tried to call you on my lunch break, but the phone just rang on and on."

"We went out for a bit."

I hand Dottie the cat as she passes by—no doubt to eavesdrop—and place my hand over the receiver.

"Keep him away from the phone cord, please. And how about some privacy?" I add.

She giggles and retreats to the office, closing the door behind her.

"Sorry about that," I apologize. "The kitten we're watching for Norma and Edith has been a handful."

"I can imagine," he chuckles. "I'm more of a dog person, myself."

"Really? I'd have pegged you as a man with a parrot. One of those chatty birds that sings jaunty tunes and lives to be eighty or so," I tease.

He releases a loud guffaw. "What do you think I am? A pirate?"

"Well, how am I to know? We've spent a total of maybe three hours together since we first met. The night job at the morgue could be a cover for something far more nefarious."

"Like piracy?" He exaggerates the "R."

"Yes—or money laundering," I reply with mock seriousness.

"You clearly don't know me at all," he says indignantly. "We need to remedy this at once."

"Well, Doctor, what do you suggest?"

"I prescribe a double dose of vitamin D."

"Discussing and divulging?" I retort, enjoying our repartee.

"I was thinking of dining and dancing," he banters. "Although, discussing and divulging would not be contraindicated."

"That doesn't sound particularly onerous."

"I'm glad to hear it," Sam laughs. "As much as I'd like to begin treatment immediately, I'm off to my night shift on the Jolly Roger."

"Sounds dangerous."

"You have no idea. Why don't I pick you up tomorrow at six? The Cabrillo Ballroom is on the boardwalk."

"That sounds perfect. And the dining?"

"How about Mexican food? Cafe Las Ondas is near the ballroom and serves the best guacamole."

"Have I mentioned that I adore avocados?" I can't recall whether I brought it up.

"No, but I'm glad to hear it. I can tell I'm going to enjoy the discussing and divulging part of the evening."

"I agree." Why was I so worried about this? How many hours have I wasted indulging my fears?

"It's five-thirty. I should be off. I'm really looking forward to seeing you tomorrow," he says earnestly.

"Me too, Sam. Bye."

The office door flies open. "A parrot? Money laundering? You said he was a doctor,"

"Were you eavesdropping?"

"Shamelessly." Dottie shifts Puck from one arm to the other. "So, what next? Is he taking you out?"

"As a matter of fact, he's taking me to dinner tomorrow evening." I reach for Puck and carry him toward the bathroom.

"That's a good start." She follows.

"And dancing afterward," I casually mention.

"That's more like it." She watches me clear the bathroom of anything that might be remotely interesting to a kitten. "Are we going someplace?"

"How about a walk to the beach?"

"Yes! I've been dying to explore. Let me grab my camera."

"No rush. I need to make sandwiches first. I thought we'd have dinner on the sand."

"I wonder if you can go up there." Dottie gestures toward the eight-sided cupola that sits atop the Hotel Laguna.

"I wouldn't know, but I imagine the view is stunning."

The Spanish arches and red awnings give the three-story hotel a Mediterranean feel. Uncle Charles called the hotel earlier in the week to reserve a room for Labor Day weekend, but he was told that they were fully booked through mid-September. The front desk clerk he spoke with said they've been at maximum capacity since they opened their doors this past Tuesday.

"Get a load of that!" Dottie exclaims as a Duesenberg pulls in front of the hotel. A well-heeled couple emerges from the lobby, and a doorman escorts them to their vehicle.

"Let's peek inside the hotel," I suggest, so we cross Coast Highway.

As soon as we approach the main entrance, a security guard steps before us and asks, "Are you hotel guests?"

"No…we thought we'd dine at the restaurant inside," Dottie fibs. I elbow her.

"I'm sorry, ladies. The entire restaurant is in use this evening. If you're not hotel guests, I cannot allow you to enter," the guard firmly informs us.

Before turning to leave, I recognize an emblem on the guard's uniform—a four-pointed star with a spray of smaller stars underneath.

"Stardust Productions," I tell Dottie.

"What?" She furrows her brow with confusion.

"The movie studio…Stardust Productions. That's who he's working for," I explain.

"Do you suppose they're filming at the Hotel Laguna?"

"That's exactly what I think—and staying there, as well."

No wonder they're fully booked. I'd hoped that the filming in town would be limited to this weekend only. Instead, it sounds as though they'll be here throughout our entire visit.

"Something smells good!" Dottie declares. A spicy aroma emanates from the open courtyard of the mission-style restaurant across Laguna Avenue, a small street running alongside the hotel.

"I'll tell you how it is after tomorrow evening." I grin.

"Is Sam taking you here? You should sample the food ahead of time, so you know what to order," she advises.

"Nice try," I laugh. "We've already eaten out today. Not only that, I've made sandwiches for dinner. Speaking of which, it's your turn to carry this. My arm is sore."

I saddle her with the weighty basket. In addition to sandwiches, it contains a small blanket, a thermos of lemonade, and a couple of peaches.

"Let's move closer to the shore." Dottie walks toward the boardwalk.

The film crew has cordoned off the beach behind the hotel, and studio security won't let anyone past. Several cameras are trained on a pair of actresses lounging under a large umbrella. A young man in immaculate white shorts carries a serving tray laden with beverages toward the women. Meanwhile, the crew members stare intently through their camera lenses. A few moments later, we hear, "Cut!" I look for its source and immediately recognize the slender director.

"I should have known. Stardust produced the film that Lewis Lake and the others were promoting in Europe."

"There's Corvi!" Dottie grips my arm.

Both Corvi and Bebe rise from their lounge chairs and stroll with Mr. Lake, while he gives them instructions. At first, I don't recognize Bebe. She's wearing a frizzled gray wig and matronly robe. Bebe shakes her head and leaves her coworkers, all the while walking in the direction of the onlookers standing near us. She removes her wig, shakes out her raven locks, and smiles broadly at the fans.

From the set, Corvi calls to her, "Don't be away too long, auntie!"

Bebe turns and, through a clenched grin, mumbles, "Just die!"

Dottie raises her eyebrows at me, and we decide to head further up the beach.

"What was that about?" She chuckles.

"I haven't the foggiest."

Although she does seem to have it in for Corvi.

Dottie smooths out our blanket near the lifeguard tower. Behind us is the Bath House building which includes a cafe called Fountain Lunch. We share the cup attached to the thermos flask and unwrap our sandwiches. It's after six, and my stomach is grumbling. I've just unwrapped my sandwich when a lifeguard carrying a round wooden board over his head runs toward the water and inadvertently kicks sand on our blanket. Mesmerized, I watch him approach the advancing wave, throw down the board and jump on, only to skim along the top of the shallow water for a dozen or more yards. He repeats this process until he reaches the shoreline near the hotel, where a security guard stops him. Jogging back to the tower, he shrugs good-naturedly to another lifeguard who is closing up.

"It was worth a try," he comments, amused.

"Did you get a picture of him?" I ask Dottie, who unfastened her camera as he started to slide.

"It'll be blurry, but I took one anyway." She brushes sand off our blanket.

While eating dinner, we watch a small group of children at the shore. Each time the water recedes, the tykes race toward a line of bubbles in the sand and dig furiously. Occasionally, a child shouts, "I got one," and drops a sandy blob into their pail. They continue their search until another wave crashes upon the shore—at which time they scurry away from its tug.

"What do you think they're doing?" I wonder.

"Beats me." Dottie removes a peach from our basket. "Say, are you gonna eat this?"

"It's yours," I laugh and walk over to the children.

"That's the biggest one yet!" A boy with missing teeth grins proudly.

I squint into their bucket, only to find about three inches of sand. "What do you have in there?"

"Sand crabs," a much younger child enlightens me. "D'ya wanna see 'em?"

"Sure!" I lean in to get a closer look.

The older boy scoops up a handful from the pail and lets the sand pass through his fingers. What remains are a few gray oval-shaped shells, which I assume are empty. A second later, however, pale legs and antennae protrude from the shells, and the creatures scoot backwards on the boy's palm. He returns them to the bucket, where they swim down and burrow into the sand.

"Here's another one!" A small girl plops a fistful of sand into the pail.

"That's twenty-nine!" The older boy exclaims.

"What will you do with them?" I query.

"Mom won't let us keep 'em," the boy complains.

"So, we gotta toss 'em back when we go," the smallest child sulks.

Having packed up our basket, Dottie joins us. "What's all this?"

"They're showing me their sand crabs." I point toward the bucket.

"D'ya wanna see 'em?" The younger child asks, and the show-and-tell process repeats until a wave crashes upon the shore.

"That one was huge!" The boy drops the bucket on the sand and dashes toward the retreating whitewash. His siblings race behind.

"So, where to next?" I inquire.

Dottie points up the coast. "I think there are tidepools under the pier. I have a hazy memory of going there with my mama."

"Sounds good to me."

Wet sand is far easier to walk on—and cooler too—than hot dry sand, so we remove our sandals. Dottie wore a bathing suit underneath her shorts but, so far, has shown no interest in swimming. Along the way, we pass thick mounds of dark green and brown plants. Upon closer inspection, they're slimy and contain water-filled bulbs. Dottie kneels to touch one of the bulbs, but a swarm of tiny flies rises from the briny mound, compelling us to press on toward the pier. When we reach the tidepools, we notice a toddler whining and dragging his feet through the sand.

"No wanna go!"

"If we stay here, we can't get ice cream," his mother reasons. The youngster instantly picks up the pace and follows her toward the boardwalk.

Leaving our shoes and basket on the sand, Dottie and I scramble up the uneven rocks, careful not to tread on the slippery algae or prickly bits of crushed seashell. At the top, we find a young woman—about Dottie's age—with bushy cropped hair that tangles around the temple of her round spectacles. She's squatting next to one of the pools and appears to be writing notes on a clipboard. Occasionally, she reaches into the pool but doesn't bring anything above the surface of the water. When she sees us, the young lady rises, however her shoulders remain stooped, as though she wants to appear shorter than her tall, lanky frame will permit.

"Sorry. We didn't mean to disturb you," I apologize.

She slides the bridge of her glasses up her button nose. "Oh, you didn't disturb me."

"What are you writing?" Dottie tilts her head.

"This?" She turns the clipboard, and we see a rough drawing with circles and numbers. "I'm surveying sea anemones. But I'm about to throw in the towel."

"Why?" Dottie sweeps her gaze across the numerous pools.

"I tried to reach the low intertidal pools earlier, but the film crew chased me away. I don't have any data for those yet." She references several empty circles at the top of the drawing. "Now the tide has covered them."

"We were driven away from the hotel by studio security a little while ago," Dottie replies.

She nods sympathetically. "I'm Iris, by the way."

"I'm Dottie, and this is my cousin, Ruby."

"What's the survey for?" I inquire.

"I'm a student at the Pomona College Marine Laboratory." She nods toward Coast Highway, but our view is blocked by the bluff behind us. "My professor is studying the relationship between hermit crabs and sea anemones in local tidepools. I've become interested in the anemone-crab mutualism that's been observed in the Mediterranean and Eastern Atlantic. Of course, those are different species than ones we have here, but I'm curious if any of these crabs scamper around with anemones on their shells."

"Why would they do that?" Dottie asks.

Iris explains, "The anemones eat the food that the crabs drop, and the crabs benefit from the security that the anemones provide."

Dottie listens intently. "Have you had any success?"

Iris' shoulders slump. "No, nothing so far. All I've accomplished is collecting data for my advisor's project, and my project ends next weekend. Then it's back to classes at the main campus."

"Excuse me," I interrupt. "What exactly is a sea anemone?" I've heard of them, but I can't recall ever seeing a photograph or drawing of one.

Iris' face lights up, and she invites me to kneel by the pool she's been surveying. "Look there, off to the right side. Do you see something that looks like a bright green flower?"

"I see it!" Reaching into the pool, I glide my index finger along one of the petals. "It feels sticky. Not at all what I was expecting."

"That'll be the nematocysts," Iris explains.

"Pardon?"

"Stinging cells," she clarifies. "Sea anemones aren't plants. They're actually animals related to jellyfish. Those 'petals' are its tentacles, each containing nematocysts which can release venom when touched."

I jerk my hand from the pool and examine my finger. "It doesn't hurt though."

"The venom from these species won't harm humans, but it will paralyze or even kill smaller creatures. The stickiness you felt were the barbs at the end of each stinging cell."

"So, that's how an anemone protects a crab," Dottie remarks.

"Exactly!"

"Do you know anything about the chemical composition of their venom?" My cousin queries.

"Not personally, but I'm sure my professor does. Do you want to come by the lab tomorrow?" Iris invites.

"I'd love to!"

"Great! If you're interested, I'll be surveying the tidepools by the Coast Inn. You could meet me there at three, then we can go back to the lab afterward. Do you know how to get to the inn?"

"No, but we have a city map. I'm sure I can find it," Dottie answers.

"Fantastic!" Iris smiles warmly. "I can't do much here now that the tide has risen. I better head back and turn this in." She waves her clipboard then carefully clambers down the rocks.

We peek into pools for a little while and spot sea snails, small striped crabs, and mussels. Dottie snaps the occasional photo, even though the sea life is too small to capture on film.

"What's that?" Dottie points toward a dark purple sphere with sharp spines resting in one of the pools.

"Some sort of sea cactus?" I shrug.

"I didn't know there was such a thing. I'll ask Iris tomorrow."

Just then, an impressive wave crashes over the pools sending a salty spray toward the bluff behind us. We're far enough away to avoid being pulled into the water, but our legs and feet are drenched.

"Let's head back," I suggest while squeezing water out the legs of my trousers.

"You should've worn a bathing suit—or at least shorts."

She has a point.

Dottie pouts, "Besides, I really wanted to see the sun set over the water."

I tilt my head to examine the wooden pier above us. Supported by thick beams, the pier extends about a thousand feet to a platform built upon a massive rock. "I bet the view is great up there, but I'm not sure where the entrance is."

"Is that a set of stairs?" Dottie points toward the bluff and frowns. "They're quite steep, though. Maybe we should stay here."

"Nonsense!"

My cousin bites her lower lip and nods. "Okay. If you really want to."

I'm puzzled by her reluctance but head for the stairs, nonetheless. Moments later I have second thoughts as we ascend the precipitous steps—it's quite a climb. My thighs are burning by the time we reach the top, where dozens of like-minded beachgoers make their way toward the end of the pier. Orange and gold tones emblazon the horizon as the sun descends behind a distant isle.

"Dottie, I think that's Catalina," I gesture toward the long island.

An archipelago of eight islands extends all the way up to Santa Barbara. However, Santa Catalina and San Clemente Islands are the only two that are visible from Orange County beaches. Today, a distant haze clouds our view of San Clemente Island, but the hills and bays of Catalina are quite clear.

Dottie relaxes and sighs, "I'd love to visit Catalina someday."

"It's beautiful," I reply contentedly. "I'd love to go back."

The glowing orb slowly descends behind the highest peak of the island, while all around me, excited shouts suddenly burst from both children and adults alike.

"Ruby, look!" Dottie cries and steps back to position her Brownie camera.

About two hundred feet from the pier, five or six dorsal fins slowly appear and disappear in a rolling fashion.

"Ow they shawks?" a little girl with sand encrusted braids asks her father.

"No, sweetheart. They're dolphins." He wraps an arm around her tiny shoulders.

"But there are sharks in the water," the girl's older brother informs her eliciting an immediate whimper which, I assume, was his intention.

"That's enough," the father scolds.

"But Dad! There ARE! Leopard sharks are probably swimming under us right now!"

The little girl explodes into full blown hysterics.

Engrossed with her camera, Dottie misses the entire saga. "I wish we could take pictures that show color," she complains.

"I wouldn't be surprised if that happens someday." From the corner of my eye, I spot a line of pelicans skimming just above the water.

"Quick!"

I turn Dottie's body so that she's facing the majestic procession. She looks through the viewfinder and presses the shutter lever.

"Thanks, Ruby! I think I got them."

We're the last to remain on the pier, but I'm glad we waited. About fifteen minutes after the sun vanishes from view, the sky above the horizon bursts into bands of saffron, scarlet, and heliotrope. I shiver from my damp clothing but refuse to budge. Dottie retrieves the blanket from our dinner basket and wraps it around me.

"Thank you."

"This is perfect." She murmurs and rests her head on my shoulder.

I try to imagine what's going on in that beautiful brain of hers but am reluctant to disrupt this idyllic moment by asking questions. I kiss the top of her head and smooth her hair. Closing my eyes, I deeply inhale the fresh breeze that carries brine from the tidepools below and cedarwood from a nearby fire pit. The rhythmic rumbling of the waves lulls me into a deep sense of calm.

This is exactly what I needed.

Lost in serenity, I have no idea how much time has passed when Dottie raises her head. "Do you want to head back?"

I open my eyes and realize that the sky has darkened. "I suppose so."

A couple of hours later, Dottie turns in for the night, but I feel restless. I write a letter to Miss Mabel and Miss Violet, apprising them of our unexpected trip and describing our evening at the beach. Miss Violet, in particular, would be taken with the charm and vitality of this seaside community. After that, I attempt to read *Murder at the Vicarage*, Agatha Christie's latest novel. To my understanding, it has not yet been released in the United States, but I was able to pick up a copy in England. Violet told me that many others aboard our ship did the same thing. Unfortunately, I've found the protagonist to be somewhat unsympathetic and, consequently, have been unable to settle into the narrative. To me, Miss Marple is the most intriguing character, but after the first couple of chapters, she hasn't been mentioned again. Granted, I'm only on chapter five…

Oh, this is no good.

I set the book aside and opt for a cup of chamomile tea. While waiting for the kettle to boil, I root around in the pantry and find a round tin of shortbread cookies. The colorful tin reminds me of the one Nan uses for old buttons. "You can never be too sure when you may need 'em." Behind another cabinet door, I find a slender taper and candlestick which, along with the cup of tea and small plate of cookies, I carry outside. Since Dottie insisted that Puck sleep with her, I don't have to worry about him sneaking up behind me. Once seated under the sycamore, I light the candle and rest the teacup and plate on the wide arm of the Adirondack chair. The neighborhood is silent, except for a radio playing through an open window nearby. After a while, I begin to feel drowsy and contemplate heading inside, but instead I just close my eyes.

"No-o-o-o!" A scream pierces the silence.

My eyes fly open. The candle has burned down halfway, so I must have been asleep for a while. Disoriented, I can't tell where the sound came from, but I know it was nearby. I blow out the candle and race inside, leaving it behind with the cup and plate. My heart begins to slow once I've locked the door, and I wonder if I should telephone the police. This seems like a safe community, but as I know from past experience, that rarely means a thing. I've just lifted the receiver when a terrified cry, louder than the first, issues from the next room.

CHAPTER 7

~ ❦ ~

SATURDAY, AUGUST 23, 1930

"I give up."

Throughout the night, my sleep was disrupted by phantom screams that, at the time, seemed quite real. Thank goodness I didn't call the police when I first heard Dottie's cries. Now, despite my fatigue, I'm unable to fall back asleep, so I shuffle my weary body into the kitchen where a fuchsia and carmine sky brightens the windows. Keeping a drowsy eye on the percolator, I uncork the quart-size Stanley vacuum bottle I found tucked behind a nested stack of mixing bowls. It's larger than I need, but it'll be easier to carry than the thermos we toted to the beach last night. Once I've tucked the coffee, a banana, and house keys into a cloth tote, I peek into Dottie's room and find that both she and the kitten are sound asleep. I won't be gone long, nevertheless, I leave Dottie a note.

The dawn air is cool but comfortable on my bare arms. I opted for a pair of beach pajamas with a sleeveless blouse but tossed a long silk scarf into the bag just in case. August in Southern California, even along the coast, is typically quite warm. In fact, I can already feel the temperature rising as I meander downhill along Park Avenue. Distracted by the sunlight bouncing off the windows, I fail to notice that I'm not alone on the sidewalk.

"Excuse us," tuts a petite elderly man walking a miniature poodle with pom-pom legs.

"Oh, pardon me," I exclaim, startled.

"Have a nice day." The gentleman continues, as though the near collision never happened.

With greater caution, I proceed toward the beach and see several other people out for an early morning stroll. When I reach the boardwalk, I slip off my sandals and hop down onto the sand which has cooled overnight. Just past the Bath House, something in the water catches my eye. Curious, I approach the shore, where a dark brown animal twists and dives in the breakers then retreats just before the waves crash upon the sand. At first, I assume that a dog has jumped in for a swim, but looking around, I don't see the owner. I briefly wonder if a baby dolphin has become separated from its pod, but the face has whiskers, and there's no dorsal fin.

"That's Skipper."

I turn around and notice the short-haired woman who picked up an order yesterday when Dottie and I were waiting for lunch. She's about five feet one, but her muscular physique and stalwart bearing suggest a formidable personality. She's holding a rusty pail that reeks of fish.

"Oh, hello there. Is Skipper a seal?"

"Close—she's a sea lion. I'm Sal by the way." She offers a hearty handshake.

"Nice to meet you, Sal. I'm Ruby." My gaze returns to Skipper. "I thought seals and sea lions were the same thing."

"Most people do," she remarks. "Sea lions have a flap over their ears. Harbor seals just have ear holes—no flaps. There are other differences too, but they're hard to see unless yer close."

"So, Skipper's a female?"

"Yep. Still pretty young, though. She's about four feet nose to tail right now. Her mama was about six feet long."

"I didn't realize they were so large." I've already learned so much on this trip.

"Aw, that's nothin'. You should see the bulls. Some of 'em are eight to nine feet long and can weigh a thousand pounds during breeding season."

"I had no idea!" I always thought that dolphins, whales, and sharks were the only large animals along the coast. "Is Skipper safe this close to shore?"

"She's fine! Watch this."

Sal reaches into her pail and pulls out a chunk of pink flesh, which she then waves in the air. After riding a small breaker onto the shore,

Skipper uses her flippers to wobble toward us. A crescent shaped scar runs across her forehead.

Sal tosses the fish when Skipper's about ten feet away. "Here ya go."

I marvel as the sea lion expertly catches the treat with four sharp canine teeth.

"She loves albacore!" Sal comments. "Do you wanna try?"

I reach into the pail and grasp a cold, squishy handful. Having swallowed the first mouthful, Skipper scoots closer. I panic and toss the tuna onto the sand in front of her.

"Don't want her eatin' from yer hand?" Sal laughs. "I don't blame ya."

I watch Sal feed Skipper the rest of the fish and ask, "Did you teach her to do that?"

"Sort of," Sal tosses the bucket onto the sand. "Her mama came ashore several weeks ago cuz she was sick. Skipper followed her and stayed with her till she died."

"How awful!"

She nods sadly. "Poor lil thing. When I found her early that mornin', she was cryin' somethin' fierce."

"What did you do?"

"Well, I knew someone would be at the Sandwich Mill bakin' bread. So, I went over and told 'em to call the head lifeguard. He'd know what to do with the body. Then I asked 'em for a pail of tuna. I figured it'd be best to get Skipper back out into the water where the others could care for her."

"So, you lured her with the fish?"

"Yep. Got in my boat and started tossin' chunks so she'd follow."

"Did it work?"

"Eventually. But ever since, she's remembered me and shows up here most mornin's."

I scan the water for signs of other sea lions. "Where does she go the rest of the time?"

"She'll swim out to the kelp beds a little later or loll around on Seal Rock with the others."

I'm confused. "If they're sea lions, why is it called Seal Rock?"

"I dunno. That's what it's been called my whole life. But, from time to time, we spot harbor seals out there too."

"I'd love to see Seal Rock while I'm here," I confess.

"Best view from the shore is at Crescent Bay." Sal points northwest. "About a mile past the pier. But if you're really interested, I can take you out sometime this week."

That's when I notice the tiny rowboat behind us. A wide flat path in the sand marks the trail Sal left while dragging the boat from the lifeguard station, where a larger dory still rests beside the tower.

"Um…do you think your boat's big enough?"

Sal stares at me blankly, then bends forward and cackles. I chuckle along because I'm not sure what else to do. After what feels like several minutes, Sal wipes the tears from her eyes.

"Not the dinghy!" She declares. "I'm talkin' about the *Bonnie Boat.*"

"*Bonnie Boat?*"

"Sure! My diving boat." Sal fingers the corner of her eye to remove one last tear. "Her berth's in Newport Harbor, but I've always lived here."

"It must take a while for you to row there."

"About an hour…so I don't do it too often. I usually take my truck. But this week, the *Bonnie Boat* will be offshore here." She points into the distance toward a large two-masted ship. "My first mate brought her out a little while ago. We'll tow this dinghy astern until I need her later." She taps the rowboat.

"I'd love to go out on your ship. It must be thrilling to dive." I picture the illustrations from *20,000 Leagues Under the Sea* that my parents read to me when I was young.

"Aye, that it is. My old man taught me to sail and dive."

"Do you look for something specific when you're down there?"

"Like treasure?" I can't tell if she's joking.

"Yes—or sea life."

"Both actually. The Marine Lab hires us to collect specimens. But my favorite part is searchin' for loot that rumrunners and mobsters dumped overboard before getting' caught."

"So, it's true…about the rumrunners."

"Definitely. They were really active here several years ago. They'd bring down booze from Canada and try to unload it in one of our coves. If they spotted Prohibition agents, they'd drop the crates through a trapdoor in their hull, and there—on the ocean floor—the crates would sit until someone like me comes along."

"Is this still a problem?"

"Haven't seen 'em here in a while, but last spring, they snuck into a cove in Sunset Beach early one foggy morning. Two feds were patrolling the beach near the chowder house there and spotted several men runnin' away. They investigated the bay and found over a hundred cases of liquor, a truck, two cars, and a dory." Sal shakes her head. "Didn't catch the rumrunners, though."

"Do they smuggle anything else?"

"Aye! We found a duffel full of Tommys one time."

"Guns?!" She wasn't kidding about the mobsters.

"Yep. You'd be surprised what we've found over the years." Sal starts pushing the dinghy across the damp sand at the shorebreak. "Sorry to rush off, but my crew's waitin' for me."

"Of course! Thank you for sharing your stories with me," I wave.

"I was serious about takin' you out on the *Bonnie Boat*. Just let me know."

"I'll do that," I smile. "Thanks."

I watch Sal deftly maneuver her dinghy into the water and paddle out between the breakers. She waves and sets off toward the schooner.

For some reason, Sal's stories about diving trigger a memory of the psychic in Coney Island and her warning about "forces beneath the surface." Then my thoughts shift to the detective position I was offered on the *Statendam*. At the time, I didn't give it a second thought. I could never tolerate being away from my family for most of the year. But now, I feel a deep yearning for something more than the life I've so carefully crafted. Don't get me wrong, I love my career as an inquiry agent. Yet, I have to wonder what's behind the restlessness that started stirring as soon as I returned home.

A colony of seagulls resting on the sand simultaneously takes wing and heads toward the pier. My rumination disrupted, I decide to follow them. Thankfully this time, my legs aren't burning as I ascend the bluff. At this rate, by the end of the week I should be as fit as I was in college when I cycled everywhere because I didn't have a car.

Men line both sides of the pier with fishing rods extended into the water. The tide has come in further than last night, so the tidepools are completely covered. The pungent stench of chum drives me toward the end of the pier where fewer people are fishing. From the wide platform, I gaze out at the horizon toward Catalina, but a layer of clouds block my view of the island. A bird, about the size of an eagle or hawk, perches at the edge of the rock below me and rolls its black and white head back and forth, while occasionally fluffing its mottled brown wings. The raptor's screech becomes increasingly louder and higher pitched, reminding me of the screams that startled me last night.

As soon as I realized they were coming from Dottie's room, I threw open the door and sprinted to her bedside. The moon outside was nearly full and shined brightly through the window, illuminating Dottie's posture. She was sitting bolt upright, her eyes wide with terror. I reached for her hand, but she didn't move a muscle. Puck crouched next to her on the cot with flattened ears and fur standing up along his back. He released a pitiful "Meow."

"What did you do now?" I asked him.

Dottie closed her eyes and lay back down. I couldn't see anything wrong with her physically...no scratches from the cat...no blood. When I gently shook her shoulder, she grumbled and turned away from me onto her side. Puck settled in close to her chest and closed his eyes as well. I haven't a clue what caused her distress, but when I was able to fall asleep, it was with one ear open.

The great bird's screech calls me back to the present moment. It weaves its head several times then swoops off the rock with its talons extended. A fisherman moans as the raptor brings up a round, flat fish that happens to be attached to the man's line. He and his neighbors wave their arms and bellow, trying to compel the bird to drop its prey. Instead, the fowl beats its mighty wings and soars away from the pier, snapping the line in the process.

"Tough break," someone says.

"Damned osprey! Got my corbina last week," someone else curses.

"It's not just the halibut—that was my last mullet." The fisherman turns his bait pail upside down. "Guess I'm done for the day."

Preoccupied with the mournful fisherman's lost catch, the others fail to notice that Skipper has pilfered a fish from someone else's line. I chuckle and head back to the house.

"Thank goodness you're here, Ruby!"

I look around but for the life of me cannot locate Dottie. The windows and front door of the house are closed, and no one else is in the front yard. While turning in a full circle, I hear a rustling above me in the sycamore tree.

"Dottie! What on Earth are you doing up there?"

Then I spot the saucer-eyed kitten in her arms.

Of course...Puck.

"Can you help us down?"

My cousin is wedged between two large branches about ten feet above me. From the ground I can see several footholds that should make it easy for her to climb back down, and I'm surprised by her reticence. As a child, we'd often find her in the backyard at the top of a pepper tree reading a book. Yet, she never fell or suffered scrapes and bruises from her arboreal escapades. I stand on the seat of a chair that's sitting beside the trunk.

"Hand me Puck. Then you'll have both hands free."

She tentatively leans forward and lowers the quivering kitten into my outstretched arms. When I've secured him, Dottie gingerly slides her foot into a notch, all the while clinging tightly to a smaller branch that bends from her weight.

"Honestly, Dottie, you could hop down from there."

She grimaces and releases her grip. When her sneakers thump the grass, a tattered slipper falls from her back pocket. Puck springs from my arms and pounces. Then he rolls onto his back and tears at the shabby footwear with his claws.

"I'm so embarrassed," Dottie blushes.

"No need to feel awkward with me. I didn't exactly scale the tree myself to give you a hand," I laugh. "There must be a good story behind all this, though. Let's go inside, and I'll make breakfast. You can fill me in."

Over poached eggs and toast, Dottie explains how she found a box of Wheaties in the pantry and decided to enjoy a bowl outside. After Puck whined and scratched at the door for several minutes, she figured he'd stay put if she brought him out with his food dish. After eating his tuna, Puck rolled around on the grass for a while. Dottie said he seemed quite content, and she was beginning to wonder what all the fuss was about.

"That's when he spotted the bird," she says ominously.

"The bird?" I wonder if perhaps it was the raptor I saw earlier.

"Yes. A mockingbird settled on a branch above us and began to run through its calls."

"Oh! And I suppose Puck bolted for it."

"Right up the tree! Of course, the bird immediately flew away, but Puck had climbed about fifteen feet before he realized it."

I'm puzzled. "With his sharp little claws, why didn't he just climb back down? Isn't that what cats do?"

"I thought so too, but he just cried and cried. I stood on the chair, like you did, and reached up for him, but he refused to even try."

Puck, who'd been grooming his foreleg on a sunny patch of kitchen flooring, suddenly looks up at us and meows. I shake my head.

"So, what was the slipper for?" I inquire

"I remembered the note and ran inside to find it."

Puck's favorite toy is one of Edith's old bath slippers.

"Was it under the bed?"

"The sofa." Dottie rolls her eyes. "I went back out and waved the ratty thing at him, but he just yowled even louder."

"Okay, I understand why you went up after him, but I'm confused as to how you got stuck there as well," I confess.

"I don't know, Ruby. I just froze." Dottie stares at her eggs.

"But you've never been afraid of heights before. Not too long ago, you and your friends managed to shinny up a tree to watch a meteor shower from our roof. That must have been twenty-five feet, at least."

Hearing footsteps on the roof that night, Jack was convinced that burglars were trying to break in through the chimney. He grabbed a baseball bat to guard the fireplace but fell asleep. When Dottie came in, she nearly tripped over him. The shouting match that ensued woke both Uncle Charles and me. Unsurprisingly, both of my cousins were put on restriction.

"Don't remind me. I had to miss Senior Ditch Day because of that!" Dottie refused to speak with her brother for two weeks after missing the snow day in the mountains with her friends.

"My point is that I'm surprised you couldn't get back down." I try to mollify her, "That's all."

"I'd like to see you climb down a tree with sharp claws digging into your chest," she retorts defensively.

"Okay, okay." I hold up my hands. "I get it. I'm sorry to upset you."

Dottie releases a breath, and her body softens. "It's okay. Sorry I'm so cross. I didn't sleep well last night."

"What happened?"

"Puck kept crawling around. At one point he was on my head." She looks over at the slumbering feline.

"Is that why you screamed in the night?" I query.

"Screamed?" Dottie's posture stiffens. "I never screamed. I just couldn't fall back asleep."

"I heard you scream a couple of times. Maybe you were having a nightmare," I say gently.

"I didn't have any nightmares, Ruby! Maybe you were the one having nightmares," Dottie snaps defensively before rising to carry her dishes to the sink.

Her overblown reaction takes me by surprise. She must be exhausted, so I put my plate and utensils in the basin with hers and lightly rest a hand on her shoulder.

"I'll clean up. Why don't you lie down for a while. When I'm done here, we can go to the beach. You can sleep under the sun for the whole day if you want."

Dottie nods and retires to her room.

I certainly bungled that.

"Look out!" I pull Dottie's arm, forcing her to duck. We're walking through town on our way to the shore, but she's preoccupied with something.

"What was all that about?" Dottie looks around.

"You were almost walloped by that pole." I point to a long rod with a microphone attached. The young man carrying it flashes an apologetic smile.

"What were you staring at, anyway?"

Dottie gestures toward a couple under the awning of a nearby shoe store. "It's Corvi," she says in hushed tones.

The actress appears flustered and is talking a mile a minute while waving her hands about. I examine her companion and realize that it's Ike Bronson, her manager. My interactions with him during our trip were limited, but one encounter in particular continues to disturb me.

Late one evening, midway through the cruise, I left the ballroom to get some fresh air out on the deck and overheard an outraged baritone. "You can't do this! I made you!" Ike's puce face glowered and his hooded black eyes bored into Corvi.

"You're hurting me!" She twisted and pulled her arm, trying to extricate herself from his unyielding grip.

Thinking on my toes, I opened my clutch purse and dropped it on the wooden deck. The clamor distracted Ike, and Corvi was able to wrench free from his hold.

"So clumsy of me!" I pretended to search the ground. "I don't suppose you've seen a tube of lipstick."

The scoundrel stepped away from Corvi and lit a cigar. Meanwhile, Corvi hurried to my side and mouthed the words "thank you" before assisting me with my hunt.

"What color is the case? If it's black, it'll be hard to find." She looked behind a deck chair.

"Yes, that's what I was thinking. The tube is black, but my compact is gold. And then there's my key..."

"Ike, why don't you go on ahead. I think I'll be here a while. After everything Ruby did to find my brooch, it's the least I can do." Corvi waved him on with her delicate hand.

"Sure, sure...you ladies and your face paint," he remarked with forced affability. But when he passed Corvi to go inside, he whispered, "This isn't over!"

At the time, Corvi laughed it off. "Ignore him. His bark is worse than his bite."

But now, here in Laguna, Ike's crimson face and Corvi's tears make me wonder if that's true. We can't hear what's being said, but Corvi's frantic gesturing and distressed expression arouse a protective instinct within me.

"You know, Dottie, I could use a pair of bathing shoes. Let's take a look inside."

She regards me with confusion but follows. "Sure, Ruby."

"Is that Corvi Styles? And Ike Bronson?" I declare as we draw closer to the awning.

Ike immediately puffs out his chest, ready to ward off our approach. "Miss Styles doesn't have time right now—"

Corvi's eyes widen with recognition, and she places a petite hand on his arm. "It's alright, Ike. Don't you remember Ruby from the *Statendam*?"

"Yes…Ruby…of course," he mumbles and withdraws a handkerchief to wipe the sweat from his brow. That's when I notice the damp rings under the arms of his shirt. I've never seen him without a coat.

"Warm day," I observe.

"What? Oh…yes," he grumbles.

While our attention is focused on Ike, Corvi discreetly dabs away her tears with a gloved finger. The red blotches around her cheeks and eyes begin to fade as she says, "Ruby, I cannot thank you enough for finding my brooch. That pin means the world to me."

"It was my pleasure. Truly." I smile sympathetically.

"Do you live here?" Corvi inquires politely, but her gaze shifts nervously from side to side.

"We're in town pet sitting for a friend," I explain. "Corvi, this is my cousin, Dottie."

The actress notices Dottie, and her face softens. "Pleased to meet you."

Dottie flushes but manages to choke out, "I'm so happy to meet you."

"I need to talk to someone," Ike informs us and walks away before we have an opportunity to reply.

I watch him approach a woman who could be Corvi's doppelgänger. Her height and build, not to mention her platinum bob, are nearly identical to the stunning actress. However, upon further inspection, their facial features are quite different. From the deep vertical line between her brows to the sharp angles of her cheeks and jaw, this woman appears older and more serious than Corvi, and it's clear that she doesn't care for Ike. She takes a step back and squares her shoulders.

Ike unplugs the cigar from his mouth. "We need to talk."

"There's nothing to talk about." The woman moves to walk around him.

He attempts to grip her wrist, but she twists her arm out of reach and tells him, "Lay off! You can't pull that crap with me!"

His nostrils flare, and he flexes the fingers on his right hand, but the woman bounds past him and joins two stagehands assembling a pair of tripods.

I lower my voice, "Corvi, I hope we weren't intruding, but I noticed how upset you were. Is everything alright?"

"Oh, yes. You know how it is." Corvi slips on her public persona and evades my question. "I suppose you've seen our film crew all over." She looks around at the bustling street as it's transformed into a movie set by dozens of stagehands.

I've overstepped.

"What are you filming?" Dottie asks shyly.

"The movie's called *Skin Deep*. It's a romantic musical comedy," Corvi explains in sweet tones.

"As in 'beauty is only skin deep?' What's it about?" Dottie asks.

Corvi smiles. "Do you want the movie tagline or the synopsis?"

"The synopsis, please, but only if you have time," my cousin starts to come out of her shell.

"Well, the story is about a socialite from San Francisco, that's me, who is vacationing with her aunt—are you familiar with Bebe Gish?"

"Yes, we saw her in town yesterday," Dottie informs her.

Given Bebe's vitriol toward Corvi, I watch her face for any sort of reaction, but she just smiles graciously and continues with her movie description.

"Well, my character gets caught in a riptide and is saved by a local skin diver who's out spearfishing. He's played by Rex Langdon."

"Rex Langdon?!" My cousin squeals the name.

Corvi chuckles with amusement. "That's right. As you can guess, romance blooms, but the aunt schemes to end things because my character is engaged to a prominent young gentleman from the Bay Area being groomed to take over his family's import business. The aunt even goes so far as to invite him down for a stay, insisting that my character would love a surprise visit. Like most romantic comedies, misunderstandings and hijinks ensue as the love story unfolds. In the end, we find out that the skin diver is not penniless but is, in fact, the son of a wealthy land developer in Southern California. The aunt is overjoyed by the match, and the couple live happily ever after."

"Ruby Ray! If I were a religious man, I'd say you're an answer to prayer!" a familiar voice announces.

"Archie! What a lovely surprise! I'm so glad you're here too!" I reply fondly.

"Mr. Lake wouldn't know what to do without him." Corvi's twin walks up behind me.

"Oh, Ruby, you haven't met Lena Young, have you? She wasn't on the boat," Archie remarks.

"No," I reply. "It's nice to meet you, Lena. I'm Ruby Ray." I extend my hand.

"You too." Lena's grip is firm.

"And who is this young lady?" Archie asks, his dark eyebrows raised.

"This is Dottie, my cousin," I answer. "Dottie, this is Archie Duval, the assistant director I told you about."

"Very nice to meet you." He greets her with a bow, which makes Dottie grin. "So, you were talking about me, were you?" He winks.

"I may have mentioned you in passing," I joke.

"I'm sorry to interrupt, but they need Corvi on the set," Lena delivers the message.

At that, both Lena and Corvi hurry to a restaurant across the street. Enormous stage lights project beams upon the covered patio, where bistro-style tables and chairs are arranged, reminding me of our time in Paris.

"Lena is Corvi's double," Archie explains. "She fills in during stunts and as a stand-in when the crew adjusts the lights and cameras before filming."

"Ah, that makes sense," I reply. "Archie, I'm so thrilled to see you."

"You too, my friend. You know, there's a ballroom in town. Maybe we can continue where we left off," he suggests playfully while straightening his bow tie, a deep orchid that complements his glowing skin.

Dottie stares with an amused smirk.

"Don't get any ideas," I chuckle. "Archie and I are just friends."

"If you say so," she answers skeptically.

Both Archie and I burst into laughter. "Oh, honey. You have no idea," he comments.

I quickly change the subject before Dottie starts demanding an explanation. "So, Archie, what did you mean when you said I'm an answer to prayer?"

He frowns and pinches his forehead with one hand. "Ugh. What a mess! We could use your professional expertise, Ruby."

"What's going on?" I ask. "Corvi seemed upset when we ran into her and Ike a moment ago."

He nods and blows out a breath. "Corvi's been receiving notes that are quite...unsettling."

"I'm sure she receives loads of fan mail—" I start to say.

"It's more than that. These notes are—how should I put it— cryptic."

"What do you mean? Can you give me an example?"

"I can do better than that." Archie reaches into the pocket of his plus fours and withdraws a postcard with a scribbled message in red ink.

"This was left at the front desk of the Hotel Laguna this morning when the clerk stepped away for a moment," he says while handing me the note.

An architectural line drawing of the Hotel Laguna has been printed on the front of the postcard. I flip it over and read, "*Of my darling, my darling, my life and my bride.*"

Archie watches as I reread the odd phrase.

I look up with confusion. "I don't understand. This isn't even a complete sentence."

"Corvi has the first three notes. There's definitely a pattern, and this one seems to fit with the one before it, but I can't recall the exact words."

"The red ink seems menacing," Dottie observes.

I was thinking the same thing. "How did Corvi receive the other notes? Were they mailed? Hand delivered?"

"The first was pushed under the door of her suite at the Plaza Hotel in New York."

"The Plaza? So, after we disembarked."

"That's right."

"Who knew she was staying there?"

"Everyone who reads *Photoplay*." Archie rolls his chestnut eyes. "I wanted to keep our trip quiet until after we got back, but Mr. Lake wouldn't hear of it. Our itinerary was printed as early as April."

"So, anyone could have left the note," Dottie remarks.

"What about the others?" I inquire. "How were they delivered?"

"She found the second note in her dressing room at the studio after filming a scene for *Skin Deep*. No one knows how it got there."

"When was that?" I'm trying to establish some sort of pattern in my mind.

"Just after we got back to California. The thirteenth, I think," Archie guesses.

"And the third note?"

"She found it in her mailbox this past Sunday. We needed to do a read through of the latest script edits before heading here for the location shoot. It was hot, so Corvi suggested we meet at her house." He lowers his voice, "She's got a place in Hamilton Park with a massive pool."

"When you say, 'we,' who exactly do you mean?" I ask.

"Well, the lead and supporting cast to start with—so, Corvi, Rex, Bebe, and Kit."

"Kit who?" Dottie interjects.

"Kit Morris. He plays Corvi's fiancé in the film," Archie clarifies.

Dottie looks at him blankly.

"He's had a few minor roles. I'm sure you'll recognize him when you see him," Archie goes on to say.

"Who else besides the cast and you, of course?" I probe.

"Ike—he rarely leaves Corvi's side—and Mr. Lake."

I mull this over. *Ike was in New York, at the studio, and at Corvi's house. But so were Archie and Mr. Lake.*

"I can see the wheels turning in your head, Ruby. But there's more you need to know."

"Please continue," I encourage.

"Well, Corvi believes she's being followed—and not just here in California."

My spine tingles. "Why didn't you just open with that?"

"No one else has seen him. It may just be a case of nerves."

"Not necessarily. Just because no one else has seen him—"

"Seen who?" Corvi walks up with Lena.

"We were just talking about the man you've seen lurking around," Archie explains.

"Does she know about the notes?" Corvi looks from Archie to me.

"Yes, I filled her in and showed her the one from this morning."

"Corvi, where exactly did you see this person?"

I retrieve a fountain pen from my beach bag and rummage around for something to write on—I never expected that I'd need my notebook today. Unfortunately, all I find are postcards from Europe that I haven't yet addressed. I choose one of the cards with a drawing of the Eiffel Tower—I have two more in the bag.

"The first time was in France—at the Meuse-Argonne American Cemetery. I went there to visit my brother's grave," she sniffs.

"You mentioned that visit on the ship," I recall.

She nods. "I also saw him on the *Statendam*."

"He was sailing with us?!" I look up from my notes.

"Yes! Although, he disappeared before I could notify security."

"How aggravating! Did you spot him in New York?"

"I saw him outside of the Plaza."

"The day we disembarked?"

"Yes, that's right. He was also at the studio, and then he had the gall to show up at my house." Her eyes fill with tears. "That was the most shocking thing of all. He knows where I live!"

"I can only imagine how terrifying that must feel." I give her a moment then ask, "When did you see him at your house?"

"The day I found the note in my mailbox," she wipes away a tear. "Archie arrived late, and when I opened the door, I saw the man across the street."

"Did you see him, Archie?" I query.

"I saw the back of him as he walked around the corner," he replies. "I tried to follow, but he disappeared. Then Corvi found the third note in her mailbox that evening after we all left."

"Corvi, do you feel like describing him to me?"

"That's just it," Corvi sighs with frustration. "He's very average. I couldn't even guess his age. He sort of blends in whenever I see him."

"Let's narrow it down to height and hair color," I suggest.

"About Archie's height, I suppose. And his hair is medium brown, but that really depends on the light. His clothing always seems to match what other men around him are wearing."

"Is there anything prominent about his facial features?"

"No, nothing at all."

"I'm wondering how you noticed him in the first place," I admit. "What made him stand out to you?"

"It was the look he gave me. I can't tell you anything more specific than that. But he stared at me with such intensity. It gave me goosebumps." She rubs her arms.

"And no one else has seen him?"

"No. Every time I try to point him out to someone, he disappears before they spot him."

"Have you seen him here in Laguna?" Dottie asks curiously.

A tear rolls down Corvi's cheek as she quickly nods. "This morning."

"That must have been frightening," I gently place a hand on her arm. "Was this before or after you received the note?"

"Before," she gulps.

"Corvi saw him out of her bedroom window. She said he was on the beach below," Archie discloses.

"Archie, you mentioned something about needing my expertise. What did you have in mind? I'm sure that security—"

"Security is hopeless," Corvi laments.

"I agree with you, Corvi," Archie interjects. "But their contract with the studio is for securing the sets. They weren't hired for personal security. That's why we put Lena in a room adjoining yours."

"When not performing stunts," Lena explains, "I do personal protection detail."

"It sounds like you have everything covered—" I begin.

"Ruby, when we first met, what impressed me most was how unobtrusive you were, all the while solving the thefts without anyone being the wiser," Archie compliments.

"Thank you, but I'm not sure what you'd like me to do. I'm here on vacation with my cousin." The last thing I want right now is to work on a case. Dottie and—hopefully—Sam should be the focus of my attention this week.

"Is this really necessary?" Lena questions. "I have everything in hand."

"Lena, we're so thankful you're watching out for Corvi, but you're part of our production. We need an outsider, someone who can inconspicuously keep an eye on things. Ruby would be perfect. She and Dottie blend right in with the beachgoing fans."

"I'm flattered, Archie, really I am. But I have other priorities this week. I'd like to spend time with Dottie before she heads off to Berkeley. Not to mention, the rest of my family will be joining us later in the week," I try to excuse myself.

"I'm not asking you to shadow Corvi around the clock. Do what you were already planning to do. Just keep your eyes and ears open for anything suspicious," Archie persists.

"Well..."

"Then there's the pay. The last thing the studio wants is to risk Corvi's safety. I assure you, the compensation will be substantial." Archie squeezes his hands together pleadingly.

I won't lie, the money is tempting. I hadn't even considered it from that perspective. A tidy sum from the studio would enable me to continue my pro bono work—as well as the reading parlor—for quite some time without dipping into my personal savings. And if I can get paid for going about with our vacation plans…well, how can I argue with that?

"Alright," I sigh. "Let's discuss how this will work."

Dottie smiles broadly.

At least someone's happy.

CHAPTER 8

"You should go soon," I suggest to Dottie while collapsing the striped beach umbrella. She agreed to meet Iris at three, and the Coast Inn is about a mile south of Main Beach. "Is there anything you'd like to leave with me?"

"Just my book." She waves a copy of *The Water Gipsies*, a British novel about a young woman with a romantic outlook on life who operates a river barge with her sister. I'm glad to see that Dottie has set aside the heavy tomes she's been reading to prepare for Berkeley.

"Drop that in my beach bag," I instruct. "And while you're at it, grab the sun-stick I picked up in Europe. Your shoulders are pink."

"Does this stuff really work?" She sniffs the aluminum tube suspiciously.

"According to *Vogue* it does." I fold up the sling chairs we rented along with the umbrella.

"Do you want a hand carrying those?" Dottie offers.

"Yeah, otherwise I'll have to make two trips."

After returning the rentals to the Bath House, Dottie asks, "Where are you off to this afternoon? It sounds like they won't need you to keep an eye on Corvi until later."

I was none too pleased earlier by Archie's request that I shadow Corvi this evening at the ballroom. I tried to politely decline, but when Archie persisted, I had to be direct.

"Look, I have a date tonight. Can't I start tomorrow?"

"Why, Ruby Ray! You haven't even been here a day, and you've already met someone." He playfully wagged a finger. "May I ask where he's taking you?"

"Dinner and dancing," I quickly murmured.

"Did I hear 'dancing?'" His vexing smile broadened. "Well, that's perfect!"

"Oh, Archie. I beg you—"

"No, there's nothing you can say to wiggle out of this, Ruby. All you need to do is occasionally divert your adoring gaze from the dashing…what's his name?"

"Sam."

"Dr. Sam Armstrong," Dottie added.

"A doc-tor! I'm impressed," he said approvingly. "As I was saying…all you need to do is look around every now and then. If it makes you feel better, I'll be there too."

"Alright," I conceded. "But promise me you'll be on your best behavior when you meet Sam."

"You have my word." Archie grinned mischievously.

My thoughts return to Dottie. "I suppose I'll poke around town for a while."

"Well, I'm off," Dottie says cheerfully.

"I'd say 'have fun,' but discussing anemone venom with a professor…"

"I know!" She laughs. "It may not be fun to you, but it's thrilling to me." Dottie kisses my cheek and bounces down Coast Highway, her Brownie swinging over her shoulder.

I turn around and head in the opposite direction for a bit of sightseeing. At the top of the hill, a two-story concrete building perches on the bluff. I nearly pass by the unassuming structure, but a sign reading "Art Gallery" draws my attention. Curious, I wander inside as a bell tinkles above the closing door. I am struck speechless by a large portrait—easily seven feet high—of a woman seated in a wicker chair. Her shoulders stoop forward, and she grips a collection of long-handled brushes in one hand. While her expression is serious, she gazes candidly at the viewer, as though she were about to begin painting a portrait herself.

"That's Anna Althea Hills," a feminine voice behind me draws my attention. "The artist drew inspiration from a photo taken by George Hurrell."

The name of the photographer sounds familiar. Then I recall the alluring photos last year of Norma Shearer that shocked her fans.

Instead of the sweet-faced innocent the public had grown accustomed to, the woman in Hurrell's photos was provocative and sensual.

I stand back to examine the totality of the painting. The loose style and soft hues are a marked contrast to Mr. Hurrell's dramatic photographs of intense light and dark shadows. Yet, while the rest of the painting is subtle, Miss Hill's eyes have been drawn in ink with sharp detail over the pale watercolor wash.

"This is stunning," I confess breathlessly.

"An exceptional tribute to the memory of our dear friend," the woman replies sadly behind me.

I turn around and recognize her as the painter from the Sandwich Mill yesterday who complained about being chased off the beach by studio security. The artist's black Marcel waves are pulled back into a low bun that she smoothes unconsciously while tears well in her sorrowful eyes.

"Her memory? Is Miss Hills deceased?" I inquire.

"Indeed. She died unexpectedly in June." She glances down at her smooth brown hands. "She was a founding member of the Laguna Beach Art Association more than a decade ago and a close friend to so many of us. It's because of her leadership that we have this gallery."

"I am deeply sorry for your loss. She must have been a remarkable person." I turn back to the painting to contemplate the woman who was so dearly loved. "This work captures a fierce intellect and passion."

"That was Anna. The artist really captured her essence, and the painting is even more impressive when you consider that she's just beginning her professional career as a painter."

"Who is the artist? I'd love to see more of her work," I inquire sincerely.

"Her name is Edith Holmes. So far, that's her only painting in our collection."

My mouth drops. "I should have known. There was something so familiar about it when I walked in."

"You know Miss Holmes?" The woman's expression brightens.

"Yes, in fact I'm cat sitting for her and Norma right now," I explain.

"Oh, that naughty Puck!" She chuckles.

"You've got that right!"

The front door swings open, setting the bell in motion, and an arresting man strides inside. He's more than six feet tall, with broad shoulders and a trim, athletic physique.

"Kit! I wondered when we'd see you!" The woman rushes toward him and wraps her arms around his torso.

"Hi, Lillian." His right cheek dimples with an infectious grin.

Lillian turns toward me. "I'm sorry, miss. I'll only be a moment. If you'd like to see some of Anna's work, several of her paintings are on that side of the gallery." She points toward the furthest aisle on the left.

"Take your time. I'm in no hurry."

So, that's Kit Morris!

I stroll along and examine the collection. Miss Hills' subjects range from deserts to canyons to seascapes. There's even a tiny painting— no bigger than three or four inches across—that looks like the courtyard outside Cafe Las Ondas, where Sam will be taking me this evening. But my favorite piece is an oil painting called *The Blue Pacific, Laguna Beach.* Azure waves crash upon sunlit rocks that resemble the tidepools we visited last night. As I meander, I cannot help but listen to Kit's conversation with Lillian.

"I heard you're covering set design for the Community Playhouse until they find someone more permanent," Kit confides.

Lillian exhales loudly. "Yes, but it's not my cup of tea. I'd rather be outside with my easel. I'm sure another artist will step up soon, though. But you—you're impossible to replace."

Kit dismisses her comment. "I know for a fact that there are plenty of actors in Laguna far more talented than me."

"You're too humble," she scolds. "So, tell me, Mr. Hollywood, how can I finish a painting at the shore without being chased away by those pretentious security guards?"

"Beats me!" he laughs. "Nobody ever asks my opinion. But I will tell you this—you're not the only friend or family member that thinks I can do something about it."

"Well, hooey! Promise me you'll at least try."

"I will do just that," Kit replies agreeably.

The bell jingles again, and heavy footsteps charge inside.

"Kit Morris! I was walkin' by and thought that was you!" The woman's contralto booms jovially.

"Pancho! I'd hoped to see you, but I thought you'd be off at some race or derby," Kit declares.

Pancho Barnes too? What a fortuitous afternoon!

No longer content to listen unseen, I return to the front entrance.

"Oh, I'm so sorry, miss. I forgot all about you," Lillian apologizes.

"It's no bother." I turn toward Kit and Pancho, both staring at me with curiosity. "I apologize for interrupting."

"You ain't interruptin' nothin', sweetie." Pancho's affable countenance puts me at ease. "I was just greetin' Kit here. I haven't seen him in what…two years?"

"Thereabouts," Kit glows. "Without you, I'd still be stocking shelves at the market."

"Don't forget the Playhouse," Lillian points out.

"I would never forget that," he responds earnestly.

"Nah, you're too beautiful for the stage," Pancho teases. "That's why I introduced you to Erich."

"And I'll be forever in your debt, Pancho. Mr. Von Stroheim gave me the break I needed."

"Well, he's good for somethin', I suppose," she says dryly about the famous director.

"Are you two at odds again?" Kit muses.

"He's miffed I agreed to fly for Howard's *Hell's Angels* instead of helpin' him with his latest film. He'll get over it." She runs a hand through her short mahogany bob.

Jack's going to go berserk when he hears about this!

The door flies open forcefully, knocking the bell against the casing. "There you are, Kit! I've looked everywhere for you. One of the extras just told me you were here," Lena pants.

"Oh, Lena. I'm sorry. I didn't think they'd need me so soon." Kit blushes.

"Hey ya, Lena," Pancho greets with a smirk.

"You!" the stuntwoman snaps testily.

"Me." Pancho feigns a curtsy.

"I don't have time for this." Lena scowls, then retreats. "Why they couldn't send a stagehand, I'll never..." her voice trails as the door closes.

"I'm so sorry, Lillian...Pancho...duty calls," Kit gives a cheery wave and follows Lena.

"Well, I gotta be goin' too," Pancho declares. "I promised my kid I'd take him for ice cream."

"Where is he now?" Lillian looks outside.

"Who knows...probably buggin' the lifeguards. I'll find him," she nods to us both. "I always do."

We watch Pancho casually traipse outside. Her shoulders are broad, but her waist and hips are quite narrow. She's wearing a pair of men's jodhpurs and a button-up shirt with the sleeves rolled above the elbows. Clearly well-liked by the locals, she can't take more than a dozen steps before someone stops to congratulate her on the new speed record. I'm impressed by her courtesy to each and every person she meets. She's larger than life but grounded as well.

"Whew," Lillian sighs. "I'm so sorry about all that. You'll find this hard to believe, but we don't usually have so many visitors at one time."

"There's no need to apologize. I enjoyed seeing them both. But what was that with Pancho and Lena? Everyone else seems to adore Pancho."

"Ah, well, who can tell with famous people," Lillian remarks. "After what our community went through several months ago, nothing surprises me."

"What happened?"

"I'm referring to the murder suicide in April. Didn't you hear about that?"

"Now that you mention it, I did read something about that in the *Times*." An actress living in Laguna Beach shot and killed her friend and then herself. "To be honest, I don't remember the details," I admit.

"Well, I knew both women—quite well in fact. They were involved with the Community Players. Adele Ritchie—she's the one who committed the murder—she was an actress in light opera and vaudeville. They once called her the 'Dresden China Doll.'"

"Was she from Laguna Beach?"

"No, she moved here last year after her divorce. Then there was Doris Palmer. Some said she was the most beautiful woman in Laguna. She was a lot younger than Adele, but they became close friends. Adele was the actress, and Doris was the set designer and decorator for the Playhouse."

"What could possibly compel someone to kill their close friend?"

"No one knows for sure. They had a falling out after some of the actors and actresses from our community grew weary of Adele. She approached our local theater productions as though they were Broadway shows and became quite controlling and bossy with everyone. Forgot that we're all volunteers. But everyone adored Doris."

"So, jealousy may have been the motive?" I find that hard to believe.

"Probably. But from what I heard, Adele became unhinged. She shot Doris, then drove around for two hours. When she returned, she moved Doris' body to another room, combed her hair, put makeup on her, and folded her arms across her chest." She lowers her voice, "My nephew's a police officer. He told me all that."

I'm appalled. "And she shot herself?"

"Yes, that's what happened. Then two months later Anna died…unrelated, mind you. It's been a difficult time for us."

"Well, I'm so sorry to dredge all of that up for you," I apologize.

"Please don't get the wrong idea about our community—"

"Of course not. All the residents I've encountered so far—including yourself—have been friendly and kind. I'm very glad to meet you."

"You as well. And good luck with Puck," she perks up.

"Thanks! I'll need it!" I snicker nervously.

"The bathroom was immaculate, Dottie! Not even a grain of sand had been kicked out of the pan."

"Good boy, Puck!" She bends to stroke the kitten as he weaves around her ankles. The pair follow me into the master bedroom.

"How was your afternoon with Iris? Dare I ask about anemone venom?" I open the closet to examine my options for the evening.

"I won't bore you with the specific neurotoxins, but it was fascinating."

"Hmm...which one?" I hold up two dresses. The first is a burgundy ankle-length gown with a scalloped hipline and matching sheer bolero. The other—a Lanvin gown I picked up in Paris—is pale pink and nearly backless, with filmy petal-like tiers dropping from the hips.

"Need you ask? The pink one, of course." Dottie sorts through the gloves I've arranged on the bed.

"But it's floor-length...and we'll be walking," I vacillate.

"Trust me. Wear the pink one," Dottie insists.

Puck attempts to leap onto the bed, but Dottie blocks him. "Oh, no you don't."

I move my gloves and stockings to the top of the dresser, then sit at the dressing table to apply my makeup. "Tell me about the tidepools."

"Oh, you'll appreciate this. Iris has a mystery on her hands." Dottie settles on the bed with Puck on her lap.

"A mystery? Do tell."

"Well, you know how she mentioned that she's surveying the anemones in the various pools."

"Yes—have they done something unexpected?" I can't imagine what that would be.

"It appears that the population near the Coast Inn has been declining. Even though the numbers at the other tidepools have remained stable."

"Is that unusual?" I apply just enough lash beautifier to give them a sheen.

"Yes, considering that these anemones usually stick to one place. And it's not just the anemone population. Even though Iris hasn't been tracking other species, she noticed that the crabs, starfish, and sea urchins are disappearing from those pools too."

"Huh. That does sound odd. What's she going to do about it?"

"Do you remember her mentioning that she hasn't found anything about crab-anemone mutualism—"

"Oh, you mean the crabs wandering around with anemones on their shells?"

Dottie laughs. "Yeah, exactly. Well, since she only has a week to finish a project, she's decided to solve the mystery of the disappearances instead."

"And you're going to help her, I suppose," I smile at her reflection in the mirror.

"If that's alright with you," Dottie says hesitantly. "I mean, it won't take up a lot of time. You and I can still do all the things we planned."

"Of course, it's alright. If you recall, just this morning I agreed to take on a job. We'll both be preoccupied, but we'll have plenty of time together."

"Great! Thanks for understanding."

Dottie rises to stand behind me and inspects the glass bottles on my vanity tray. She selects one that's shaped like a dressmaker's dummy with the letter *S* embossed on the attached diamond-shaped card.

"What's this?"

"That, my dear cousin, is the only Schiaparelli I could afford in Paris." I hold out my wrist. "Just a dab, please."

She splashes a drop onto her fingertip and smoothes it onto my wrist, then taps her own wrist. "Mmm...it smells like sweet roses."

"Another reason I picked it up." I think about the rosebush Sam gave me, and my stomach flips with nervous excitement.

This date is finally going to happen.

"Any guesses what I pulled from his nose?"

During our walk to dinner, Sam amuses me with anecdotes from his day at the doctor's office.

"A pinto bean?"

Stunned, Sam stops walking and remarks, "Navy bean. How in the world—"

"When Jack was a toddler, he shoved a pinto bean up his nose. We didn't realize anything was amiss until it sprouted." I'll never forget the tiny green stem and leaf that protruded from his nostril one morning.

"Now, why doesn't that surprise me?" Sam chortles while steering me around a man who's stopped to examine buckets of tiger lilies outside the florist.

"By the way, thanks again for the lovely roses this evening. What did you call them?"

With crimson-edged petals surrounding an ocher center, the fragrant blooms reminded me of the sunrise this morning.

"'Rosette Delizy.' First bred in France in the early twenties." The cleft in his chin becomes more pronounced when he smiles.

"Well, please thank your landlady for me. I'm sure her garden is divine."

"I'll do that." Merry lines crinkle at the corners of his eyes.

A few minutes later, we arrive at Cafe Las Ondas. Sam opens the heavy wooden door and lightly presses my lower back as I pass by him into the foyer. My skin tingles beneath the fleeting brush of his warm hand, and I'm glad I took Dottie's advice.

"Armstrong, party of two," he tells the hostess.

"Right this way, sir."

We follow her to an oceanfront table where, through an arched window, we see rolling breakers crash upon the sand. It's nearly six-thirty, so most families have cleared the shore. Nevertheless, a few daring bathers bob just beyond the waves.

"This is splendid," Sam tells the hostess while pushing in my chair.

"Absolutely perfect!" I agree.

She hands us each an open menu. "Someone will be right with you to take your order."

"I love the ambiance," I comment. "Do you come here often?"

"I've been here a couple of times with Dr. Carroll and his wife, but we sat on the patio."

"Well, thank you for arranging this incredible view."

"Anything for you, Ruby," he replies meaningfully.

Aware of his lingering gaze, I am struck, yet again, by his effortless good looks. Caramel blonde hair waves away from his face on either side of a slightly off-center part, and a remarkable shade of amber rings his gentle gray eyes.

Tongue-tied I blurt the first thing that pops into my head. "What do you recommend?"

"I usually order seafood tacos. The fish are caught locally."

"Fish it is, then—with extra guacamole," I close the leatherbound menu.

A waitress wearing a brightly embroidered dress takes our order. In addition to tacos and rice, we opt for colorful fruity beverages. Nearby, a boisterous group of college-aged young men hoot and cheer as two of their comrades race to finish multiple bowls of some sort of soup.

"Menudo…don't ask," Sam grins. "So, tell me about your day. I feel like I've been doing all the talking so far."

I describe my morning walk and finding Dottie and Puck in the tree, which Sam finds highly entertaining. Then I casually mention that I was roped into shadowing a film star for the week.

His eyebrows raise. "Does this have to do with the movie they're filming in town?"

"It's a long story." I briefly chronicle my interactions with Corvi during my trip and explain my role this week in keeping an eye out for anything suspicious.

Sam's face pales when I mention the bizarre notes and the man Corvi's seen following her. "I thought your stay here was meant to be less onerous."

"It'll be fine. Her stunt double is providing protection—not to mention the studio security on set and her manager the rest of the time."

Ike always seems to be around.

Sam nods. "I've never asked—how did you happen to get into this line of work in the first place?"

"Ah…so we've reached the discussing and divulging part of the evening," I joke.

"I did mention that I was very interested in getting to know you, Ruby," his eyes gleam.

Gulp.

My cheeks burn so I take a deep breath before recounting the circumstances that led me to my path as an inquiry agent.

"How about you? Did you always want to be a doctor?"

"Not in the least." Sam sips a pineapple and orange concoction that was placed in front of him.

"Now you must tell me," I insist, ignoring my own fizzy drink. "I have a nose for a great story."

"Well, I don't know about great, but it is rather involved."

"I'm all ears." I prop my elbows on the table and rest my chin against my clasped hands.

"First of all, I should tell you about the place where I grew up."

"You mentioned that your grandparents raised you," I prompt.

"That's right. My mother died when I was quite young, and my father was never in the picture. He split before I was born."

"I'm so sorry. That must have been hard for you." I reach across the table and lay a hand on his. "My parents died when I was sixteen," I share.

"So, you know what it's like…being taken in by family."

"I do. My Uncle Charles has been a saint, but it sets you apart from your peers when you're young."

"Exactly!" He relaxes. "My grandparents have been absolutely wonderful. But I grew up in a small town in the Sierra Nevada mountains—Twain Harte—I doubt you've heard of it."

"No, I can't say that I have." I wonder if Twain has anything to do with Mark Twain, but I don't want to interrupt.

"Tucked back away from the little village, our cabin is surrounded by redwoods and pine trees. Then there are the canals and flumes that run near our property—they were used for mining many years ago."

"Sounds idyllic," I comment.

"For an active kid like me, it was. So, logically, I decided early on that I wanted to be a forest ranger."

"I can see you doing that."

With his upbeat, easy-going personality, not to mention his love of plants, I can picture him traipsing through the forest in a sage green hat and uniform.

Sam continues, "I was admitted to Davis on a scholarship and studied biology for a while but dropped out after my sophomore year."

"Was it the yammering roommate?"

"What? Oh, right," he chuckles. "I forgot I mentioned him in my letter. No, it was actually my fiancé." He registers the shock on my face and quickly clarifies. "FORMER fiancé."

I sigh, relieved. "I take it you didn't get married."

"No. We were supposed to marry a couple of weeks after the end of term, but she got cold feet and moved back home to Eureka. After that, she refused to communicate with me. No letters. No phone calls. Granted, her parents were against the marriage from the beginning."

"That must have been devastating for you."

"It was. At the time, I was so confused that I couldn't return to school. Instead, I went home and worked for the Forest Service during the warm months and the Great Truckee Winter Carnival during the winter months."

"Winter Carnival? What did you do there?"

Here in Southern California, Big Pines Park has held a winter sports carnival since the mid-twenties, but I've never visited.

Sam replies, "I patrolled the area to make sure the runs were safe for skiing and tobogganing."

"How long did you do all that?"

A server rests our plates on the table. "Careful...they're hot."

"Thank you," I reply, but my thoughts are focused on Sam.

"About two years." He gives a nod of thanks to the server.

We pause our conversation to enjoy the food.

"What do you think of the tacos?" Sam asks.

"I wasn't expecting the fish to be fried, but I like it," I assure him. That said, I add another spoonful of guacamole to the crunchy shell.

Once I've had my fill, I lay my utensils face down on the plate. "What made you decide to switch to medicine? It sounds like you were doing exactly what you loved."

Sam swallows. "Helplessness."

I'm taken aback by his response. "Helplessness? How so?"

His eyes drift as though gazing into the past. "One of our tasks at the Winter Carnival was to ski the runs each day before the guests arrived. Early one morning, I was out with my buddy, Victor. We were inseparable growing up, and he also decided to work for the Forest Service. Anyway, it was snowing pretty hard, and we accidentally veered off the main trail."

"That doesn't sound good."

"It wasn't. At first, we weren't worried. We could still see our ski trail, so we turned around to backtrack. But then we heard a whump followed by a loud boom."

"Oh no!" I exclaim.

"Behind us we saw what looked like a massive cloud rolling downhill directly at us. We skied diagonally away from the avalanche, just as we'd been taught. I thought Victor was right behind me, but when I cleared the path of the avalanche and stopped, he was gone."

"How terrifying! Did you find him?"

"Eventually. He was about ten yards away. The tip of his pole was sticking out of the snow. I used one of my skis to dig him out."

"Was he alive?"

"I couldn't find a pulse, but it had been only a matter of minutes, and his body was still warm under his clothing. At that moment, I realized I didn't know what to do. I'd heard about resuscitating someone's heart, but I didn't know how to do it."

I squeeze his hand, "I'm so sorry."

He continues, "I draped my coat over Victor to keep him warm and blew puffs of air into his mouth. I don't know how long that went on. He just grew colder and colder, and I knew I was freezing as well. The shooting pain in my fingers and toes was worsening, and I was finding it hard to breathe. I realized that if I didn't get back, I'd die too."

"Oh, Sam."

"One of my skis was broken from digging him out. So, I strapped on the other one and half-skied, half-walked downhill. It turned out I wasn't far from the main trail, where other patrollers had heard the avalanche and were looking for us."

"I don't even know what to say."

"Yeah, there isn't much to say. It was shattering."

"What did you do after that?"

"I went home. My grandparents were incredibly supportive, of course. In the spring, I went back to work for the Forest Service, but my heart wasn't in it. Instead, I felt a burning desire to learn all I could so that if I was ever in a position where I could save someone's life, I'd know exactly what to do."

"Ah, now I see—Medicine."

"Medicine.

"Sam, I have to say…you are one of most resilient people I've ever met," I stare earnestly into his eyes.

"You're one to talk, Ruby Ray." He squeezes my hand.

"Will there be anything else?" our waitress asks.

"I think that's enough for now," Sam replies.

By the time we enter the Cabrillo Ballroom, the immense dance floor is crowded with couples bouncing energetically to the syncopated rhythm of a dozen musicians on stage. We survey the tables and chairs around the perimeter of the cavernous space, but they've all been claimed.

"Well, there's nothing for it," Sam declares. "Dancing it is."

"Let's wait for the next song. It'll be easier to squeeze in," I suggest.

"Good idea."

When the music ends, some couples retreat to their seats, but just as many leap from their chairs and rush to the floor.

"Now's our chance." Sam wraps an arm around my shoulders and maneuvers us toward the center, where slower dancers congregate. "If it's alright with you, I'd like to get my bearings before heading out into the throng."

"Fine by me. It's been a while."

Eddie and I were avid dancers and made the weekly rounds to local ballrooms during the years that we dated. We were always among the fastest dancers spinning and kicking at the outer edges of the dance floor. But after we split up, I couldn't bear the thought of running into him with his new girlfriend. I blamed myself for his betrayal and was sure I'd said or done something to make him stray. Eventually, I realized that he was a narcissistic liar and that I was lucky the relationship ended when it did. Even so, I've avoided ballrooms for the past three years. Thankfully though, the brief dance Sam and I shared last spring rekindled my passion for dancing.

The band leader steps up to the microphone and shouts, "Okay, dolls and daddies, who's up for a waltz?"

The crowd groans. Some dancers jeer and boo.

"Now, now. Don't cast a kitten. Here's one that'll tickle your toes—'Happy Feet!'"

A collective cheer explodes from the audience, as the band vaults into the brisk beats of the lively tune. With a huge grin, Sam swings his arms and begins kicking his feet. For someone so tall, his Charleston is impressively supple. He raises an eyebrow and extends his hand, which I gladly accept. In the closed position, I mirror his steps, then gasp as he pulls my waist toward his. A couple next to us begins to encroach on our space, so we take several traveling steps, all the while maintaining our synchronized dance. I throw my head back—dizzy with giddy laughter—when he begins a knee bounce, his arms crisscrossing while his knees open and close.

As the closing blasts from the trumpet squeal, Sam leans forward and asks, "How about a spin?"

I nod, and he takes me into his arms only to release me into an outside turn. From there he quickly dips me into a final pose. We're both panting, but I feel euphoric.

"I didn't know you could dance so well," I admit.

"There's a great deal you don't know about me," he winks, and my heart skips a beat.

The tempo changes dramatically as a honey-toned crooner begins singing "I'm Confessin' That I Love You."

"How about a foxtrot," Sam suggests. "I could use a breather."

"Me too." I follow his lead in a forward basic step. After a series of moves, I raise my eyes from his lapel and realize that he's tenderly watching me.

"You look radiant this evening, Ruby."

"Thank you." My skin shivers as he brushes my bare back with his fingers.

"I've been meaning to tell you all evening—" he begins sincerely.

"Ruby! I told Corvi that was you," Archie interrupts. They promenade closer to Sam and me.

"Hello, Archie." I scowl at him. "Hi, Corvi." I soften my tone.

"Sorry to interrupt, Ruby," Corvi says apologetically.

I introduce Sam to the pair, just as a man nearby shouts, "If you're gonna stand and gab, shove off."

"Let's wet our whistles," Archie nods toward the refreshment counter where they're selling sodas and punch. However, from the fumes I've inhaled so far, I'm sure quite a few fellows have concealed flasks in their coats.

Sam reluctantly nods and offers me his elbow. I mouth "Sorry" to him, but he shakes his head and smiles to signal that everything's fine.

Once we've settled with our drinks at the table Archie reserved, Kit and Bebe arrive. I notice that she deliberately sits as far from Corvi as possible, whereas Kit takes the chair immediately next to Corvi and tries to engage her in conversation. Corvi appears distracted and continuously averts her eyes toward the main doors while the young man speaks. Meanwhile, Bebe watches the exchange with undisguised indignation.

"Your doctor's hotcha-cha," Archie whispers to me. He's seated between Corvi and I.

I thwack him playfully and quietly reply, "Speaking of sweethearts, where's Rex this evening?"

"Surfing." He rolls his eyes.

"At night?"

"Who knows. One of the gaffers is from Balboa Island and volunteered to teach him. I suspect there may be more to that relationship than surfing," Archie discloses discreetly.

"Uh-oh. I'm sorry about that." I pat his arm.

Sam shifts uncomfortably beside me. "So, tell me Archie, how did you get into the film business?"

"To be honest, I wanted to be an actor, but there aren't many great roles for people with my skin tone—if you know what I mean. Thankfully, Mr. Lake took me under his wing when I was an intern."

"You never told me that," I interject.

"It sounds like you two spent a lot of time together during your trip," Sam says indifferently, but I can tell he's uneasy.

"It's not what you think," I assure him.

Archie snorts, "Not even close."

I pivot the conversation. "I've been meaning to ask you, Sam. Where did you learn to dance?"

He relaxes and places an arm on the back of my chair. "It's silly, but I'll tell you. During medical school in San Francisco, a few guys talked me into going with them to a taxi-dance hall."

"Oh, no! Like 'Ten Cents a Dance.' I thought only old men visited those places." I reference the new song that's become popular on the radio.

He chortles. "I suppose so, but there were young fellows there too who, like me, truly wanted to learn to dance. On my first visit, I had the good fortune of dancing with Opal. From then on, I always asked for her."

"Opal, huh? So how many lessons did the talented Opal give you?"

"About a dozen. We went every couple of months during our first two years."

"Well, I must thank Opal, if I ever meet her."

"You'd like her, Ruby. A remarkable woman who was just trying to feed her children. She lost her husband in the war."

"Are you still in touch with her?"

"No. Last I heard she married one of her clients."

"Speaking of dancing, have you ever been to the Casino Ballroom on Catalina?" I ask.

"I read all about it in the paper when it opened last year, but I've never been," Sam replies.

"Me neither, but I'd love to go."

Preferably with you.

"It's swell," Archie interrupts. "I'd love to shoot a picture there. Several silent movies have been filmed on the island but only one talkie so far—*Condemned* with Ronald Colman."

"I saw that. Quite dramatic," I point out.

"I'm trying to talk Mr. Lake into a project filmed entirely on the island."

I notice Corvi checking the doors, concern on her face.

"Is everything alright, Corvi?" I ask.

Her face brightens. "Of course. I'm just bored."

Kit jumps from his chair and offers his hand, "Shall we dance?"

"Sure," Corvi smiles politely but shoots a sidelong glance toward the entrance. As she passes, Bebe elbows her in the thigh.

"Play nice, Bebe," Archie scolds.

The irritable actress rises and stomps away from the table.

"What was that about?" I ask.

"She must've taken one of her vitamin pills. They tend to put her on edge."

"What sort of vitamin is she taking," Sam inquires.

"Amphetamines…Hollywood's dirty little secret," Archie answers nonchalantly.

"That wasn't at all what I expected," Sam declares while walking me back to the house.

"How so?" I stop to remove my shoes which are now pinching my toes. When I got ready earlier, I hadn't considered our uphill return to the house.

"I had no idea we'd be hobnobbing with celebrities." He offers his elbow.

"I'm sorry about that." I transfer the shoes to my right hand and slide my arm through his.

"I'm not complaining. It was just so surreal."

"Well, I for one had a lovely evening and am so glad we decided to go dancing. I had no idea you could samba." After our break with Archie and the others, Sam impressed me with other moves he'd learned under Opal's tutelage.

"It's easy to dance with you, Ruby," he compliments.

"Thank you." I lean my head on his shoulder.

"Ruby, look at that." He points skyward where three pelicans fly in front of the moon.

For a moment, I'm speechless. "There's something very special about this place."

"I feel the same way, but I think you have a great deal to do with that."

My heart warms. "Speaking of places, I forgot to tell you that I have postcards for you from each city I visited."

"I can't wait to read them. I feel like you have the advantage since you've read all my letters."

Read and reread.

"You know, it's been a long time since I've been on a date, but I don't recall ever feeling so joyful. Am I sharing too much?" I ask nervously.

"It's funny you should ask me that. When I told you about my ex and about the avalanche, I wondered if I was sharing too much," he confesses.

"You could never share too much."

"I feel the same about you," he wraps his arm around me. "I was about to tell you something earlier, but Archie and Corvi walked up."

"Yes. I remember," I say expectantly.

"We haven't spent much time together yet, but I want you to know how much I care for you."

We reach the front yard of Norma and Edith's house. The porch light is turned on, but it's dark under the sycamore tree where we've stopped. We turn to face one another.

"I feel the same way about you, Sam." I softly reply.

He places one hand on the side of my waist and lightly glides the other along my jawline. I tilt my head to look at him. He's watching me intensely. A flicker of uncertainty passes in his gaze, then he takes a determined breath before slowly leaning toward my willing lips.

The front door suddenly flies open, and Dottie cries, "Ruby! He's really done it now!"

CHAPTER 9

━ ✿ ━

"I'll never wear perfume again!" Dottie pronounces.

I nod silently and sprinkle more baking soda onto the drenched cushion.

"Look, Ruby, I don't blame you for being furious with me. I should have realized I'd left the door open when I grabbed an extra pillow from the bedroom," she says remorsefully.

Moments before Sam and I returned to the house, Dottie discovered that Puck had knocked all the glass bottles off of the dressing table. Most of the jars and atomizers hit the floor directly, but my cherished Schiaparelli shattered on the chair rail and doused the cushion. The dizzying cloud of floral fragrances is already giving me a headache, and I've only been cleaning for ten minutes.

"I'm not furious with you, Dottie," I reassure her. "However, I'm sorely tempted to leave Puck outside tonight."

"You wouldn't!" she cries.

"Of course not." I squeeze the sodden sponge over the bucket with more force than necessary. "But the timing of all this couldn't have been worse."

After our first kiss was abruptly thwarted, Sam and I rushed into the house to discover what had happened. Puck could be heard yowling through the closed bathroom door, and Dottie looked simultaneously panicked and penitent. Naturally, Sam was good-humored about the whole fiasco and offered to help clean up the mess. I, on the other hand, was disappointed and embarrassed and wanted nothing more than to distance him from the melodrama. I handed him the stack of postcards I'd prepared on my trip and, with a regretful farewell, sent him on his way. He promised to call me tomorrow.

"Dottie, there's nothing more you can do here. Why don't you turn in," I suggest.

"Are you sure, Ruby? I really am sorry." She tips the rest of the glass from the dustpan into the wastebasket.

"I know you are," I assure her. "Why don't you take the garbage out before lying down."

"Ok, Ruby." As she heads out the door, she mentions, "I'll keep Puck with me, so he doesn't cry all night."

"I'd appreciate that. Goodnight."

SUNDAY, AUGUST 24, 1930

"Ruby, it's for you."

For the second night in a row, I slept terribly. However, it had nothing to do with Dottie and night terrors. Cloying fumes kept me up, despite the open windows and copious amounts of baking soda scrubbed onto every surface that had been splattered. As soon as the sun rose this morning, I escaped the stench and spent the past few hours reading in the front yard. I close *Murder at the Vicarage*. Despite my initial misgivings, Miss Marple has become a key character, and I wouldn't be surprised if she solves the mystery of Colonel Protheroe's murder.

"Is it Sam?" I ask.

"No, it's Archie." She holds her hand over the receiver. "It sounds like something's wrong."

My stomach sinks. "Hello."

"Ruby, I hate to call you with bad news, but there's been a death."

I lean against the desk for support. "Was it Corvi?"

"No, thankfully. However, Lena drowned this morning." His voice shakes. "Can you come to the Hotel Laguna right now? Corvi's a mess."

"I'm on my way." My mind races with everything I need to do before leaving.

"What happened?" Dottie asks, as I sprint to the odiferous bedroom.

"Do you remember Lena? Corvi's stunt double?"

She perches on the bed while I hurriedly pack my handbag with a few necessities. "Yes. Why? Is she alright?"

I look up and meet her gaze. "She drowned this morning."

Dottie's mouth drops. "That's terrible!"

"I'm heading to the hotel right now." I toss an extra fountain pen into the bag. "I don't know when I'll be back. What are your plans today?"

"I'll be with Iris this afternoon," she scoops up Puck, who's attempting to climb the bedspread.

"Well, please make sure you lock him up before leaving." I stick out my tongue at the kitten.

I park at an angle and hop out of the car. Luckily, there are no studio security guards outside the hotel to slow me down. Noticing my brisk clip toward the arched entryway, the doorman quickly tips his hat and holds open the door. The front desk is conveniently situated a few steps inside the hotel. It's not yet nine-thirty, and the lobby is empty. A fresh-faced young man greets me with an open smile. It would seem that the tragic news has not yet reached the hotel staff.

"Excuse me. Can you direct me to Corvi Styles' room, please. I've been asked to see her."

The desk clerk's grin dissipates, and his eyebrows lower with suspicion. "And you are?"

"Ruby Ray. The studio's assistant director, Archie Duval, just called and asked me to meet him at Miss Style's room."

"One moment please." He jots a note on a small notepad and motions to an adolescent bellhop, who promptly scurries toward the desk. After handing the note to the youth, he directs me toward a pair of armchairs next to a potted palm. "This shouldn't take long."

I lower myself onto the padded seat and examine the wrought iron chandeliers and exposed beam ceiling overhead. Across the way, a staircase steeply rises next to a small elevator. To my left, a bank of windows and a pair of doors open onto a courtyard at the center of the hotel. And at the furthest end of the hall, a wide arch leads to a dining area with sweeping views of the ocean through immense windows. I no sooner complete my survey of the newly built interior, when the bellhop gallops down the stairs. The desk clerk approaches me while reading the reply.

"I apologize for the wait, madam. Mr. Duval requests that I send you right up. Vinny can escort you to Miss Styles' room."

"Thank you so much." I follow Vinny to the tiny elevator, reminiscent of those I encountered in Europe. Despite the cramped space, an attendant waits inside for Vinny to tell him our destination.

"Third floor," the bellhop proudly straightens his spine.

On the top floor, we traverse the long hallway, where Vinny knocks on the second of four widely spaced doors. He jumps back when the door flies open.

"How is she, Archie?" I enter a well-furnished living room with large windows overlooking the beach below.

"Shocked, as you can imagine," he rubs his face.

"Tell me everything." I sink onto the sofa.

"It's okay, Archie. I can do it." Corvi trudges through a connecting door which, I assume, leads to her bedroom. She collapses onto the sofa beside me.

"Corvi, I'm so sorry this has happened." I lay a hand on her limp arm. "Are you sure you feel like talking?"

She wearily nods her head. "You need to hear this."

I lock eyes with Archie, who warily shrugs his shoulders. "She was there. I wasn't."

"I didn't realize you saw it happen, Corvi. If you'd prefer to wait…"

"No, it's better that I tell you now." She stares at her smooth, ivory hands.

"Alright, but please stop at any point if this is too distressing."

Corvi's eyes close, and she takes a deep breath. "First, you should know that I can't swim. I never learned. So, Lena was hired to do the ocean stunts for me. Every day since we arrived, she's been going out for an early morning swim. She called it 'conditioning.'"

"What time did she go out today?"

"We left the hotel around six forty-five."

128

"So, you went with her." I retrieve a pen and tablet from my bag. "Do you mind if I take notes, Corvi?"

"Do what you need to." She waves languidly. "Yes, I went with her, but she usually went alone. I like to run through my lines here first thing in the morning."

"But not today," I comment.

Archie interjects, "There was an incident last night, and Corvi didn't feel comfortable staying here by herself this morning."

"Incident?" I straighten with alarm. "What happened?"

"I saw the man…the one who's been sending me the notes," Corvi shudders.

"Where? At the ballroom?"

"No. When we got back later, Ike was waiting outside the hotel," Archie explains. "He was telling me that Mr. Lake wanted to meet with the two of us before breakfast this morning when, all of a sudden, Corvi cried out, 'It's HIM!'"

"Did you see the man?" I ask Archie.

"It was dark, and he was on the other side of the highway. Ike went after him but lost him."

"Corvi, how did you know it was the same man?" I inquire gently.

"A car passed, and I saw him in the headlights. It was definitely him," she insists.

"I believe you." I pat her hand. "Archie, could you tell what he looked like?"

"No. As I said, it was dark, and the car had already passed." He leans forward in his chair. "When Ike returned, we discussed what to do next."

"I realized that if Lena went swimming this morning, I'd be all alone." Corvi explains, her voice soft and forlorn.

"Ike and I walked Corvi to her room and woke Lena to tell her about the situation." Archie gestures toward a door on the left side of the room. They must have shared this suite, which makes sense given her role protecting Corvi.

"What did Lena say?"

Archie continues, "She was reluctant to forgo her training. We're supposed to film a big scene at Table Rock tomorrow, so Corvi offered to go with her to the cove this morning." He suddenly rubs the back of his neck. "It just hit me. We'll have to reschedule that shoot. I don't even want to think about finding a replacement."

I close my eyes and shake my head. "Wait. What? One of your cast just died. Will filming continue like nothing's happened?"

He looks at me somberly. "The show must go on."

I roll my eyes. "Back to the matter at hand...I know this will be difficult, Corvi, but can you tell me exactly what happened this morning when you went to the cove?"

She stares at the coffee table as though trying to organize her thoughts. "As I said before, we left here at six forty-five. It took us about twenty minutes to walk there."

"Where was the cove? And can you tell me how Lena seemed during your walk?"

"It was north of here. We had to climb down a steep trail to get to it. I wasn't really paying much attention to Lena. I didn't sleep well last night and was exhausted this morning."

"What did you do once you got to the cove?"

She narrows her eyes, trying to remember. "Well, Lena brought an umbrella for me—I have to be so careful about the sun, even in the morning."

I nod for her to continue.

"I arranged our things on a blanket while she anchored the umbrella in the sand. Then she stripped down to her bathing suit and jogged out to the water."

"Was anyone else there?"

"Not when we got there, but I fell asleep pretty quickly."

"When did you realize that Lena was drowning?" I ask carefully.

She begins rocking in place. "I heard yelling. Kids' voices. I thought they were just playing, so I ignored them. But then a woman said, 'She's dead.'"

"And you looked up at that point."

Tears roll down her cheeks. "Yes."

I dare not ask Corvi to relive any more of this nightmare. "Archie, how did you find out about this?"

"I'd just returned to my room after the meeting with Mr. Lake and Ike, when someone knocked on the door. A police officer was standing there with Corvi. This was around eight thirty."

"Where were Ike and Mr. Lake at this point?"

"I assume Ike was heading back to his hotel—he's staying at the Coast Inn—and Mr. Lake said he was going to pick up something from his room before driving back to the studio in Burbank."

"Do they know what's happened?" I query.

"I was able to catch Mr. Lake—his room is next to mine. He was livid and went on and on about how we've already spent hundreds of thousands on the shoot in Laguna alone."

"Excuse me, Archie, for saying this, but Mr. Lake sounds like a real piece of work," I declare bitterly.

"He's not as bad as all that," he replies defensively. "There's a lot of pressure from the bigwigs at Stardust. They're investing heavily in his films, so he can't risk letting them down."

"Still…"

"And he did offer to contact Lena's family when he gets to the studio," Archie adds.

"That's the least he should do," I remark. "What about Ike?"

"I left a message at his hotel, but we haven't seen him yet."

"Did the policeman say anything specific about Lena's drowning?"

Corvi stands and walks unsteadily toward her bedroom. "If you don't mind, I'd like to lie down."

"Of course," I reply soothingly.

She weakly pulls the door, which doesn't close completely. Archie moves to the couch next to me so we can speak quietly.

"According to the officer, there weren't many people in the cove this morning, but he interviewed everyone who saw what happened," he tells me. "They all said the same thing…Lena got tangled in the kelp and drowned."

That's odd.

The kelp we encountered Friday evening was slimy. I can't imagine it entangling someone. "Did he find that unusual? About the kelp?"

Archie slowly shakes his head. "Not at all. Neither did the lifeguards, apparently."

"There were lifeguards on hand?"

"According to someone on the shore, they arrived after she started drowning," Archie answers.

I furrow my brows. "And no one noticed anything suspicious?"

"Now, I know what you're thinking, Ruby, but there's no way that Corvi's 'stalker,'" he makes quotation marks with his fingers, "had anything to do with it."

I whisper, "Do you doubt she's being followed?"

"I think Corvi believes she's been seeing the same man, but I'm not sure if that's really the case," he confides with a hushed tone. "I mean, what are the odds that a deranged fan has the money to follow her all around the world?"

"I see what you mean. But the letters…"

"Those ARE concerning."

"Nevertheless, you don't think they have anything to do with the stalker," I murmur softly.

Archie taps his nose.

"Hello-o? Corvi?" We hear a knock at Corvi's bedroom door, which creaks as it opens.

"Kit…" Corvi begins.

Archie rises and pushes open the connecting door. "Thanks for stopping by, Kit, but it's really not a good time."

I enter the room as Kit nervously passes a hand through his hair. "I'm sorry Corvi…Archie…it's just that I saw a policeman leave here a little while ago, and I wanted to make sure everything was alright."

"There's been a tragedy, Kit." Archie squeezes Kit's shoulder. "I'm sorry to tell you this, but Lena drowned this morning."

Kit's eyes blink rapidly. "Lena…drowned? Is she…?"

"I'm afraid so," Archie bows his head.

"This is...I mean...I can't believe this," Kit takes a step backward.

"I saw her, Kit. I saw her body," Corvi sobs.

Her colleague rushes to her side and takes her into his arms. "You poor thing!"

A mighty pounding startles us all. Archie barely has time to open the door when Ike pushes forward and stomps inside.

"What's happened to Corvi?" he growls. Before anyone can answer, he spots Kit. "You! What have you done?" he snarls menacingly.

"Ike!" Corvi cries. "He hasn't done a thing. He just stopped by to make sure I was alright."

Her hulking manager grips Kit's arm and forcefully pulls him away.

"Stop!" Corvi bleats frantically.

Archie, much to my surprise, lays a firm hand on Ike's brawny arm. "Easy there. It's not what you think."

Taken aback by Archie's audacity, Ike releases Kit, who flees toward the exit. "Someone tell me what's going on right this minute!"

"It's Lena," Corvi exclaims, as Kit sneaks out with an apologetic wave.

Ike looks around. "Lena? Where is she?"

"She's dead, Ike," Archie morosely reports.

I'm astonished to witness the transformation on Ike's face, which instantaneously fades from crimson to white. "Dead?" he mumbles with a strangled voice.

"She drowned this morning. Corvi was there," Archie says calmly. "As you recall from last night, she agreed to join Lena this morning."

"Corvi?" Ike asks uneasily, "Is that true?"

She silently nods while twisting a handkerchief between her hands.

"Perhaps we can discuss this in the next room, Ike." Archie motions toward the connecting door.

"I'd like to stay with Corvi, if that's alright with her," I comment.

"Sure." She attempts to quell her tears with shallow breaths.

Ike's eyes are round with confusion, as he registers my presence. "Hmm," he grunts and follows Archie into the living room.

"This has all been shocking for you, Corvi," I say with concern.

Lost in her own thoughts, she doesn't respond.

"Why don't you lie back down." I guide her to the bed, whereupon she curls into a ball.

I sit beside her, patting her back. After several minutes, her breathing slows, and her muscles soften.

"Thank you." She stretches out and rolls onto her other side, facing me.

"There's no need to apologize, Corvi." I reach for a clean hankie on the nightstand and notice a neat stack of books.

"Are you an Agatha Christie fan?" I pass her the kerchief.

"What? Oh, those," she shrugs.

I open the cover of the top book, *The Mysterious Mr. Quinn.* "Are they all signed?"

"Yes, Agatha gave them to me after the play. I'm not much of a reader, so I gave them to Lena." Her voice catches, "She must have changed her mind."

"Can I ask you a few questions…about the notes." I tread lightly.

Corvi's eyes widen. "You think Lena's death has something to do with HIM, don't you?"

"It's too soon to jump to conclusions," I say cautiously. "But the timing of the last note is suspicious. The more I know, the better I'll be able to figure out what's going on."

"Top left." She points toward a mahogany dresser with Bakelite drawer pulls.

I retrieve three postcards, all barely legible. The red ink fades at the end of each message. Further, the letters have been formed with a slight backward slant.

The first postcard features a drawing of the Statue of Liberty and reads *"For the moon never beams, without bringing me dreams."*

"This was pushed under your door at the Plaza Hotel?"

"That's right. I found it after dinner the night our ship returned."

"And none of the staff saw anyone?"

"Honestly, I thought it was a joke at the time, so I didn't mention it," she answers.

"But you chose to keep the note," I observe.

"The words seemed familiar, but I couldn't recall where I heard them," she discloses.

A photograph of the Hollywoodland sign is printed on the second postcard, as is an image of the Embassy Club—a popular nightclub among the Hollywood elite—on the third postcard. Like the other two postcards, the messages are incomplete sentences. Nevertheless, I copy them into my notebook, one line at a time, along with the forth line that Archie showed me yesterday.

Together they read:

"For the moon never beams, without bringing me dreams
And the stars never rise, but I feel the bright eyes
And so, all the night-tide, I lie down by the side
Of my darling, my darling, my life and my bride."

"Does Archie still have the last note?" I inquire.

"Yes." She asks earnestly, "What do you think?"

"Well, altogether these phrases resemble a poem—a rather intimate one, at that. Are the other lines familiar to you as well?"

Corvi bites her lower lip. "Sort of…I'm sorry, Ruby. I was never a good student and don't know much about poetry."

"That's alright. Do you think the notes came from the man who's been following you?"

"Definitely! I spotted him before each of the notes appeared," she affirms.

I rise and examine the beach below through a large rectangular window. "Can you tell me about yesterday morning?"

"It was around seven-thirty, and I was looking for dolphins."

I turn back toward her. "Dolphins?"

She nods with a sad smile. "I'd seen them the morning before and hoped they'd come back."

"Was the man was on the beach below?" I wonder how clearly she could have discerned his features. A small, landscaped hill and boardwalk separate the hotel from the sand. "Where was he exactly?"

"He was on the boardwalk. But as soon as I noticed him, he turned his back and walked away."

"I return to my seat next to her on the bed. "Did Lena see him?"

"No, she was swimming." She reaches for a glass of water on the nightstand and takes a sip.

"And you're sure it was him?"

"Of course it was." Water sloshes as she replaces the glass on the nightstand. "A bellboy delivered the note shortly after that. It had been left at the reception desk when the clerk wasn't looking. HE WAS INSIDE THE HOTEL, RUBY! So, I kept my eye out for him all day."

That explains her nervous glances at the ballroom.

"Were you able to notice any new details when you saw him last night?"

"Yes, I realized that he always wears the same hat—a dark brown Homburg with a brim that curls more on one side than the other."

I jot down the details. "Was there a band on the hat?"

"I'm not sure." She bites her nail.

"What kind of coat was he wearing?"

"He didn't have a coat. But he was wearing suspenders. I never noticed that before. And I think his sleeves were rolled up."

"This is very good information, Corvi," I say encouragingly. "With his coat off, were you able to notice his build?"

"His belly was slightly round—but I wouldn't call him fat."

"Did you happen to notice anything else? What about his facial features?"

"His eyes were close together—there wasn't really enough time to see more."

"Are you done? Corvi should rest!" Ike barks. He and Archie have joined us.

"Do you have anything else to add, Corvi?" I close my notebook.

She shakes her head and peeks timidly at Ike.

"I'll stay with her," he asserts.

Archie opens the door to the outside hall. I step through the threshold then pivot back toward Ike. "Archie said you tried to follow the man Corvi saw last night. What happened? Can you describe him?"

He frowns but answers thoughtfully. "It was too dark to see much. By the time I crossed the street, he disappeared. Now, if that will be all..."

"Thank you, Mr. Bronson. Goodbye, Corvi. I'll check in with you later." I close the door.

Bebe emerges from the room on the other side of Lena's. She's wearing a fetching hat that matches her satin bag. "Hello, Archie. What's all the fuss about?"

"Are you heading out? I'll tell you about it on the way down."

CHAPTER 10

A conveniently-located coffee shop on the first floor of the Hotel Laguna gives Archie and me a place to discuss next steps for Corvi's protection. As the hostess places menus in front of us, I gaze through the domed window next to our table and watch Bebe carelessly wiggle past Cafe Las Ondas then disappear among a crowd of beach goers toting picnic baskets, blankets, and small children.

I complain, "You'd think she could have shown some reaction when hearing about the death of a colleague. She was completely indifferent."

Confused, Archie looks away from the hostess and shifts his gaze to the window. "Bebe? I wasn't surprised."

"Why not?"

"It's simple. Lena didn't mean anything to her. Bebe only cares about one thing—herself."

"Well, from what I've heard, she seems to have very strong feelings about Corvi." I tell him about her "just die" comment Friday evening at the beach.

He shakes his head. "She's gonna to take it too far one of these days."

"Is she jealous of Corvi?"

"That's precisely it. Bebe was furious when Mr. Lake cast Corvi as the lead instead of her."

This puzzles me. "But Bebe's hardly an ingénue. On the other hand, I can't really see her as a middle-aged aunt either."

Archie snorts, "You got that right. To be honest, I'm surprised she was cast at all, but Mr. Lake has a soft spot for her."

"I thought that perhaps she's envious of the attention Kit's been paying Corvi? From what I observed last night, she seems smitten with him."

"I think 'smitten' may be overstating things. She's just annoyed that Kit's impervious to her 'charms.'"

"Then there's Lena and Pancho…" I muse.

"You've met Pancho?" he brightens.

"We weren't properly introduced, but I bumped into her at the Art Association Gallery yesterday." I open and close the menu in front of me. I don't have much of an appetite at the moment.

"She's a peach," Archie declares. "Mr. Lake filmed another movie here a couple of years ago, and Pancho let us use her airfield. We hit it off and have stayed in touch ever since."

"Airfield? Here in Laguna?"

"Yeah, she built an airstrip on top of the bluff at Dos Rocas…that's the name of her place." He gestures toward the window. "It's a mile or two past the pier."

"You're kidding? I've got to figure out a way for my cousin Jack to meet her. He'll be here Thursday."

"I'm sure that can be arranged," he grins.

A waitress interrupts our conversation and scowls at us both after giving Archie the once over.

"Coffee?" she grumbles.

"Yes, Winifred, that would be nice," Archie replies with a polite smile.

She glances down at her crisp cotton blouse where her name is neatly embroidered in cursive. Then, with a huff, she fills Archie's cup halfway.

"Perfect!" he exclaims. "Plenty of room for cream."

Turning her back to him, Winifred narrows her eyes and tartly remarks, "I suppose you want coffee too."

I meet her gaze directly and reply, "If it's not too much trouble."

"Hmmm," she snorts and fills my cup.

"Thank you," I respond with affected civility.

Withdrawing an order pad and tiny pencil from the pocket of her apron, Winifred purses her lips. "And to eat?"

"Nothing for me, thanks," I hand her the menu.

"You?" she asks Archie, all the while impatiently tapping the pencil against the pad.

"I'm not hungry." He pushes his menu across the table.

When she's out of earshot, I declare, "How rude! She won't last long!"

"I don't know about that," Archie comments. "She seems friendly with the other customers."

I follow his gaze to the counter, where Winifred smiles at a man and woman before welcoming two businessmen who take a seat alongside them.

"Well, I never!" I protest.

"Wish I could say the same," Archie shakes his head. "This sort of thing happens to me all the time. Honestly, I'd have been surprised if she hadn't reacted that way. A Black man with a White woman…"

"I'm sorry! That didn't even occur to me. On the *Statendam*—"

"On the *Statendam*, I was tolerated because I was part of Mr. Lake's entourage and an assistant director, for good measure. Didn't you notice the disapproving looks when we danced together on the ship?"

"I-I didn't. No one ever said anything."

"They were too well bred for that, but I guarantee you, tongues were wagging behind our backs."

"I'm going to say something to the manager." I rise from my seat.

Archie places a hand on my arm. "Don't bother. Besides, we have more important things to discuss."

"That's true." I sink into my chair and try to shake off my fury.

"You mentioned something about Pancho and Lena. Was Lena at the gallery too?" Archie asks

"Yes. She stopped by but promptly left when she realized Pancho was there."

"Those two are—were—oil and water." His face clouds. "Something must have happened between them."

I ask softly, "What was Lena like?"

"I didn't know her very well, but I've heard that she had a reputation for conflicts with other cast members."

I tentatively sip the coffee then push away the cup. It's bitter as though scalded by the cafe's percolator. "Have there been any issues like that with your current film?"

Archie smells his coffee then slides the cup and saucer to the side of the table. "Not that I've noticed. She's been very professional whenever I'm around. Why do you ask?"

"Something about her death doesn't sit well with me. It sounds like the police and lifeguards considered it a straightforward drowning…but I'm not so sure."

He pauses a moment to process this. "What should we do?"

"I'll talk to the lifeguards if I can figure out who was on duty."

"And the police?" he asks reluctantly.

"Good question." I tilt my head and catch his eye. "Has anyone reported the notes or the stalker to them? Do they know what's been going on?"

Archie winces. "Corvi's wanted to contact the police ever since receiving the note at her house, but without a good description of the man she thinks is responsible…"

"There's not much the police can do at this point," I finish with frustration. "And I imagine that the studio doesn't want to involve law enforcement unless absolutely necessary."

He averts his gaze. "Once the police are involved, word gets out. The press has sources at most stations in the area."

"But Corvi believes that Lena's death had something to do with her stalker. Did she say anything to the officer who brought her to the hotel this morning?"

Archie shakes his head. "He pulled me aside and said that Corvi was incoherent on the ride back, but he didn't mention anything specific."

"I'm sure he'd have followed up with you if she'd said something about a stalker." I roll my head to ease the tension in my neck. "Hopefully a lifeguard can shed light on the circumstances surrounding the drowning."

He smiles wearily. "I'll leave all that to you. I have other fish to fry."

"I can't believe Mr. Lake wants to continue filming immediately," I commiserate.

"It goes with the territory." His shoulders slouch. "But I'm not sure where I'll find a replacement on such short notice. It took months to cast Lena."

"Archie, I don't know a lot about the film industry, but isn't that the producer or casting director's job?"

"Yeah, the production team usually makes casting decisions, but this isn't a typical production."

"How so?" I lean forward with interest.

"Before signing on with Stardust for our last film, Mr. Lake had his own studio—albeit not as large. He was the writer, producer, and director all rolled into one."

"Like Charlie Chaplin."

"Exactly! He's used to having total control over his films."

"And Stardust agreed to that?"

"Sort of," Archie squints one eye and nods. "He had to play by their rules for our most recent film—but that was just to get his foot in the door for *Skin Deep*. After the success of the American release and the European tour for the first film, they agreed to give him full control over *Skin Deep*. If all goes well, they may be open to continuing the arrangement."

"What's so special about *Skin Deep*?"

"It's Mr. Lake's first musical—the studio's as well."

I mull this over and realize it's true. After *The Jazz Singer* was released a few years ago, several other musicals have been made—but none by Stardust.

"Is that why the studio is putting so much pressure on him?"

"You've hit the nail on the head. The brass hats at Stardust know that musicals are the next big thing and want to lead the industry in producing them. Naturally, Mr. Lake wants to get in on the ground floor too, but he needs the studio's money to make the kinds of productions he has in mind. He wrote *Skin Deep* and has several other scripts ready to go if Stardust agrees," Archie enthuses.

"You mentioned last night that Mr. Lake took you under his wing. How did that come about?"

A half-smile tugs at the corner of his mouth. "He cast me in one of his films several years ago. What a mess!"

I chuckle. "A mess? Yet you're still working for him."

"It's strange how these things happen. My role was a small one, and I had no lines. Not exactly what I had in mind when I moved here from Chicago, but it was the only kind of role I could get at the time." Archie shakes his head. "And the production had one problem after another."

"Sounds like your current film."

He winces.

"Sorry, I couldn't resist," I add.

"It hurts because it's true." He shakes his head. "Thankfully, all those problems with my first film led to an internship—you know I'm a chatty person."

I grin remembering the first time we spoke. One sunny day in the middle of the Atlantic when I was curled up on a chaise lounge writing a letter to Uncle Charles, a friendly voice from the chair beside me asked, "Pardon me. Can you think of a four-letter name for a wading bird that starts with an I?"

That question about Archie's crossword puzzle immediately veered into a lengthy conversation about everything from dance marathons to Hollywood tittle-tattle. Days later I figured out the solution to the clue—it was *ibis*—but Archie had completely lost interest by then.

"I've always been chatty. It used to drive my parents bonkers. But behind the scenes of Mr. Lake's production, I was talking to people— everyone in fact—from the lead actors to the grips to the cleaning crew. Before too long, they were confiding in me about their troubles and gripes. Sometimes I was able to help—other times, I just listened."

"And Mr. Lake noticed," I interject.

He nods. "He said I had a knack for smoothing things over with people and figuring out solutions to tough problems. Then, to my amazement, he offered me a position as a production intern. Over time, he gave me more and more responsibility."

"From what I've observed, you're quite indispensable to him."

He laughs. "Oh, everyone is dispensable, especially in show business. But so far, I've been able to work my way up—"

"To assistant director, no less," I cut in with respect. "What next? Director?"

Archie's face clouds. "Have you heard of any Black directors?"

"I suppose not." My stomach clenches at my faux pas. "I'm sorry. I didn't mean to offend you."

His expression softens. "I know you didn't."

"But you could be the first—"

"Ruby, I didn't ask you if there WERE any Black directors. I asked if you've HEARD of any Black directors. Those are two very different questions. It may surprise you to know that there are, in fact, quite a few Black filmmakers, Oscar Micheaux being my favorite. But you won't see their movies in White theaters."

I'm tongue-tied, humbled by my ignorance. As a film enthusiast, how did I not know this?

Winifred approaches our table with a contemptuous expression. "Can I get you anything else?"

"Nothing for me, thanks," Archie replies congenially. "Ruby?"

"No. Thank you, though." I answer quietly, still reeling.

The waitress pulls our check from her pad and leaves it on the table. "You can pay at the cashier counter."

Archie and I reach for the slip of paper at the same time, but he snaps it up before me.

"The studio will cover it," he says and stands. "I should go. I need to call casting about replacing Lena."

An idea springs to mind, and my heart begins to race. "Archie, I may know just the person!"

"I'm listening." He sits back down with interest.

"A close friend of mine is an actress, but she was also a competitive swimmer and lifeguard at the community pool in our hometown. Last

I heard, she had a small role with Warner Brothers, but I think that might have ended."

"While that sounds great…" he hesitates, "she'd need to have the same body type as Corvi."

"Not only is she the same height as Corvi, they have the same shape as well."

His nostrils flare as he inhales deeply, his eyes bright with hope. "What's her name?"

"Eli—Liz. Liz Martin."

I nearly forgot to use her stage name. Her agent felt that she'd land better roles as "Liz Martin"—reasoning that the names of most big stars have three syllables.

"Do you think she'd do it?" Archie asks eagerly.

"Well, there's only one way to find out. Where can I find a phone?" I look around the restaurant. A pay phone is mounted to the wall at the end of the long counter where Winifred is chatting with a few patrons seated on tall swivel seats. "The options here aren't exactly private, and I don't want all and sundry to hear about your predicament. I think I'll ask at the hotel's front desk. I'm sure they can find me a secluded place to make a call."

"In the meantime, I'll take care of the bill," Archie replies.

When I reach the lobby, it's clear that the desk clerk has finally heard the news about Lena. He excuses himself from a couple who are examining tourist brochures and asks me how he can be of assistance. I explain the nature of my task, and he escorts me to a small office behind the reception desk.

"I'll make sure that no one disturbs you." The door closes gently.

I withdraw a small ring-bound address book from my handbag. When I last spoke with Elizabeth, she was staying near Hollywood with a couple of girlfriends. I decide to try that number first.

"You've reached the operator. What's the reason for your call?" The operator answers with an atonal greeting.

"I'd like to place a call to Los Angeles, please. Normandy 382."

After a series of clicks, a perky voice answers, "Hello-o-o. This is Sophie."

"Hi, Sophie. This is Ruby Ray. I'm a friend of Elizabeth's. Is she there by chance?"

"Golly, Liz hasn't been here for a couple of weeks," she informs me. "Have you tried Dean's?"

Dean Larsen, Elizabeth's fiancé, was recently signed by Warner Brothers and lives near the studio.

"No, this is the first place I checked. Could you give me his number?"

"Sure! Just a sec." She muffles the phone to ask someone a question. A few moments later, she apologizes, "Sorry about that. It's Olive 502. Is that all ya need?"

"Yes, thanks so much. Bye." I jiggle the switch hook and ask the operator to dial Dean.

"Olive 502. Dean here," a mellifluous voice greets me.

"Hello, this is Ruby Ray. I'm hoping to speak with Elizabeth. Her roommate gave me your number."

"Ruby! Hello! Elizabeth has told me all about you," he replies amiably.

"She's told me all about you, as well. I hope we can meet soon," I answer sincerely. "It's important that I speak with Elizabeth. Is she there by chance?"

"She's at her folks' house this weekend. Can I take a message?"

"I'll try her there. It's actually rather urgent."

"I hope everything's alright," Dean utters with concern.

"Yes and no. I'll let Elizabeth tell you all about it."

"Of course. I look forward to meeting you in person—hopefully soon," he says warmly.

"Me too. Thanks so much for your help, Dean. Goodbye." I return the receiver to the cradle and flip a page in my address book.

Archie walks in, his eyebrows raised hopefully. "Any luck?"

"Not yet, but now I know where I can reach her."

He crosses his fingers as I place the call.

"Martin residence." Elizabeth's tone is light and musical.

"Finally! You're difficult to track down, my friend," I sigh with relief.

Her laugh tinkles. "After all that time globetrotting, have you lost your skills as an investigator?"

"I hope not," I exclaim earnestly. "It's so good to hear your voice!"

"You too, Ruby! How was your trip? Are you already planning your next sojourn?"

"Hardly," I chuckle. "I have so much to tell you but, unfortunately, now isn't the time. I'm calling about a job for you."

"A job? You know I'd make a terrible detective," she giggles.

"It's for a movie—"

"A role? Oh, you angel!"

My heart sinks. "I'm sorry, Elizabeth. It's not exactly what you're thinking. I've been hired by Stardust Productions to keep an eye out, and their stunt double—"

"Ru-by," she grumbles.

"Hear me out. They need a stunt double for Corvi Styles on Lewis Lake's latest film."

"Corvi Styles?!" Elizabeth shrieks. "Heck, I'd do her hair if they wanted me to. Of course, I'll take the job!"

"Hang on there." I've been so swept up with logistics that the gravity of the situation hasn't hit me until just now, and I'm having second thoughts.

What am I doing? I shouldn't be dragging her into this mess. What if something happens to her as well?

"Elizabeth, when you hear the whole story, you may not feel so enthusiastic. In fact, the more that I think about it, perhaps it's not such a good idea after all."

Archie's eyes widen with panic. Through clenched teeth he hisses, "What are you doing?"

I place a hand over the receiver. "Archie, she's my best friend. I don't want to put her in harm's way."

He buries his head in his hands and blows out a breath.

"Ruby?" Elizabeth sounds concerned. "What's going on?"

I take a deep calming breath and explain the situation to her. She doesn't say a word throughout my monologue, and several seconds pass without a sound. I begin to think that I've lost the connection, when she finally declares, "I'll do it."

"It's not without danger…the notes…the stalker…not to mention the ocean stunts…"

"I can't explain it, Ruby, but I feel as though I'm meant to do this." Her inflection is resolute. "And it couldn't come at a better time. I've been without work since mid-July. I need the money, not to mention the connections…"

"Well, if you're sure—"

"Definitely! Just tell me where I need to be."

A strapping fellow watches the shore through binoculars, the word "GUARD" printed across the chest of his swimsuit. He's perched high above the sand in—what looks like—a white wooden box on stilts with a red cross painted on each side. Below the tower, a young woman, also wearing a lifeguard swimsuit, points out the location of riptides to a family with small children.

"Excuse me," I call out to her as the family wanders closer to the water.

"How can I help you?" She smiles, her pearly white teeth contrasting with a sun-kissed complexion.

"I'd like to speak with the lifeguard involved in the rescue of the woman who drowned this morning."

"That'll be Duke." She jerks her head toward the building beside the tower. "He's getting lunch."

"Thanks so much."

I follow her directions and amble toward a lithe man wearing the requisite red swimsuit. He's chatting with another gentleman while leaning against the sea-facing wall of the Fountain Lunch. Bits of lettuce and tomato fall from Duke's sandwich as he gesticulates wildly with both hands. His buddy laughs and claps him on the shoulder before walking away.

"Pardon me." I approach Duke. "I'm sorry to disturb your meal, but I was wondering if you're the lifeguard who was on duty during the drowning this morning?"

His jovial expression dims, and he asks guardedly, "How can I help you?"

"My name is Ruby Ray." I reach into my handbag and withdraw a business card. "I'm an inquiry agent working for Stardust Productions—they employed Miss Young. Can I ask you a few questions?"

He straightens his posture and tosses the rest of his sandwich into a nearby bin. "I suppose so, but I wasn't 'on duty' as you put it. No one was posted at Shaw's Cove this morning. I just happened to be nearby with my junior lifeguards."

His defensiveness makes me regret my choice of words. "My apologies. I didn't mean to imply that you were in any way responsible. I just wanted to ask you a few questions about what happened. The studio has some concerns about the circumstances of Miss Young's death."

Duke rolls his shoulders and nods for me to continue.

"When did you notice that Miss Young was having difficulty in the water?"

"It's funny you should ask. We were doing training exercises on the bluff above the cove, when a man approached and asked about sharks in the water."

"Sharks?" I blink sharply.

"Yes, ma'am. He said he saw one in the water. Big one too. About ten feet long."

I cast a nervous glance at the waves. "Is that typical?"

"No, not at all. Sure, we see a few leopard sharks here and there, but they're not very big."

They sound terrifying, nonetheless. "Was Lena attacked by a leopard shark?"

"I've never heard of one harming a person—they're more scared of us than we should be of them—and she didn't have any bite marks on her."

"Is that why you went down to the cove? Because of what the man said?"

"That's right. Good thing too. I immediately noticed that Miss Young was struggling."

I jot down a few notes. "Before we go any further, can you tell me what the man looked like?"

"I don't really recall. I was preoccupied with the kids. As soon as they heard 'shark' they made a beeline down the trail."

"You can't remember anything at all? What was he wearing? Any unusual features?"

Duke scratches his head. "Well, he had on a hat. That's about it."

"That's fairly typical for a man out on a stroll," I remark.

"Yeah, but his lid was sort of lopsided."

I look up at him. "Lopsided?"

"Uneven—like it was higher on one side than the other." He motions with his hands above his head.

This brings to mind Corvi's description of the curled brim on her stalker's hat. "Was it a Homburg? What color?"

"Beats me." Duke rubs his jaw. "Look, I'm sorry. That's all I remember."

"That's okay. Back to Lena—how could you tell she was struggling?"

"Oh, there was no mistake about that. She was thrashing around. I immediately told the kids to grab the swim line and the rescue can." He looks out at the water.

"Swim line and rescue can?"

"Yeah, we used the line to help pull the victim to shore. The kids grabbed a hold of one end of the line, while I swam out with the other. The floating rescue can was attached to my end."

"When you reached Lena, was she still alive?"

"Yes, but she was panicking. With all her flailing and twisting, she'd become entangled in the kelp." He shakes his head. "Thank goodness Sal showed up. She cut her loose."

"Sal?" Surprised, I query, "Captain Sal of the *Bonnie Boat?*"

"That's the one. She strapped on her diving knife, jumped from the boat, and fought through strong currents to reach us. I was distracted with Miss Young, but the kids said it was something to see."

I scribble furiously. "Tell me what happened once you brought her to shore."

"We realized she wasn't breathing, so I told the kids to flip her over onto her belly."

My head darts up. "Why is that?"

"We were trying to clear her lungs and restart her breathing. But it was too late. Sal realized before the rest of us that Miss Young had died." He slouches and releases a somber sigh.

"I'm so sorry that you and the children witnessed that."

"It happens," he shrugs while shaking his head. "Never gets any easier, though. Just makes me more determined to prevent it from happening again."

I think about the story Sam shared with me. Rescuers are a unique breed.

"Would you mind if I ask you a few more questions?"

"Sure. I don't know what else I have to add, though."

"This may seem to be an odd question, but are you certain that Miss Young died from drowning?"

He tilts his head. "I don't understand what you're getting at."

"Was there anything out of the ordinary—for a drowning?"

"Well, she seemed…" He searches for the right word. "Rigid. I've heard people say 'scared stiff,' but I never realized it could literally happen."

Hmm…

I don't know what to make of that, so I record his words verbatim. "Were there many others on the shore besides you, Sal, and the kids?"

"A couple of early morning beachcombers—and the actress, of course."

"Corvi Styles."

"Yep. I didn't realize she was there until she started screaming. One of the beachcombers recognized her and shouted her name."

"Did Corvi approach the body?"

"No. She collapsed onto the sand…sobbing. Sal sat with her until the police arrived. Then Miss Styles left with one of the officers."

"Who called the police?"

"I assume that Sal's crew called it in on the radio. An ambulance showed up shortly after we brought her in."

A police officer greets Duke and looks me up and down. I'm surprised to see that he's wearing a beard, which went out of fashion more than a decade ago. The grizzled gray hairs around his mouth are tinted a disagreeable shade of yellow, most likely due to chewing tobacco.

"Everything alright here?" He squints his bloodshot eyes.

"Of course, Officer Jankowski," Duke answers, bewildered. "Why wouldn't it be?"

"Just wanted to make sure she wasn't bugging you." The policeman jerks his head in my direction

"Not at all," Duke replies.

"Just the same, Miss…"

"Ray. Ruby Ray." I smile pleasantly. "Have I done something wrong, officer?"

"You tell me. Why are you interviewing people? Are you a reporter?"

"No, officer. I'm an inquiry agent working for the movie studio. One of their cast, Miss Young, drowned this morning."

"There's no need for all that. As we told Mr. Duval, the victim died from drowning. There's nothing more to discuss."

"I beg to differ."

I jot a name and number on the back of one of my cards and hand it to him.

"Miss Styles has been receiving threatening notes, and she believes someone is stalking her. Miss Young was her stunt double. I'm looking into all of this for the studio. Feel free to contact Sergeant Blockhurst at Fullerton Police if you need a reference. I've worked with his department in the past."

"I'll do just that. If you think someone is stalking Miss Styles here in Laguna Beach, then please urge her to file a report with us. In the meantime, let me make this perfectly clear—Miss Young died of drowning. Case closed." Officer Jankowski tips his cap and walks away.

"Where'd you find that?" I ask Dottie.

She's cramming a towel and thermos into the wooden basket of a shiny red bicycle. I've just returned back to the house, my mind spinning with the implications of my interview.

"There were two bikes in the backyard shed with a bunch of tools and things. Do you think Miss Graham and Miss Holmes would mind if I borrow one?" Her eyebrows furrow with concern.

"I don't think so. But take good care of it. The bike looks new."

"Oh, I will! Trust me!" She gently tucks her Brownie within the folds of the towel.

"Are you leaving? I thought we'd grab a bite to eat." My stomach growls, and I realize I haven't had anything other than coffee today.

"Sorry, Ruby. I had a sandwich while Puck nosed around the yard."

"You let him out again?!" I'm flabbergasted.

"Now, don't worry." Her tone implies that I'm overreacting. "I tied a length of cotton rope to his collar."

"Where is he now?"

"Locked up in the bathroom and—before you ask—yes I removed anything that he could spill, break, or shred."

I nod and pinch the bridge of my nose, my eyes closed. I feel a headache coming on and can't tell if it's due to insomnia, hunger, or the investigation.

"Are you alright?" Dottie rests a hand on my shoulder. "What did you find out about Lena?"

"Would you mind if we go inside? I need food and aspirin and not necessarily in that order."

Dottie parks the bike under the sycamore and follows me inside. Thankfully, the residual stench of last night's debacle has dissipated through the open windows. I don't think I could handle the sensory onslaught right now. While I search for an analgesic, she prepares an avocado sandwich for me. I settle on a headache powder, no doubt containing caffeine as well as aspirin, and join her at the kitchen table while dropping my notebook next to the plate. Between bites, I summarize what I've learned about Lena's drowning thus far.

"But you think it's more than that, don't you?" Dottie steals a few grapes from my plate.

"To be honest, I'm not sure what to think right now. I had a chance to read the rest of the notes, and they're all odd…even disturbing. At first, I wasn't entirely sure that Corvi was being followed—"

"But something changed your mind," Dottie interjects.

I reach for my notebook and flip through the pages. "The timing of Lena's death on the heels of the fourth note, not to mention Corvi's sighting of the stalker last night, and now the lifeguard's description of the hat—my gut tells me that there's a connection."

But what connection? Hats are often lopsided. Further, some people intentionally wear them at a jaunty angle. And what about the shark? It doesn't make sense.

Dottie disrupts my reverie. "Do you regret our stay here?"

"Absolutely not! I'm thrilled to have this time with you." I pat her hand. "And hopefully I can help protect Corvi. However, I do regret involving Elizabeth. I don't know what I was thinking…"

"You'll figure this out, Ruby," she says confidently.

I'm not so sure.

"Enough about me and the investigation. How are you today? What's the latest with the Mystery of the Disappearing Anemone?"

Dottie leans forward and divulges, "Iris called a little while ago and said there were only two specimens left when she visited the tidepool around four-thirty this morning."

"That early?" I was up at that time and, as I recall, the moon was beginning to set. I doubt it provided much light.

"Yeah, she checked the pools with a flashlight. The only other creatures she saw were a hermit crab and a sea snail."

"So, what's your plan for the rest of the day? Where are you heading on the bike?"

She pauses with uncertainty. "I'd like to stop by the pharmacy to drop off some film and buy a few more rolls. Then I want to meet Iris at the lab. We plan to venture further south to visit some tidepools later this afternoon. That's why I need the bicycle. Is that alright with you?"

"Certainly! I'm going to rest here for a while until Elizabeth arrives, then I'll help her settled. Why don't you plan to be back around six-thirty. You and I can grab dinner in town."

"You're the best, Ruby!" She grins and bounces out the front door.

Brrring…brrring…

I awaken from a deep, dreamless sleep, and it takes me a moment to realize that I've fallen asleep on the couch. I massage my tight neck while hastening to answer the telephone.

"Laguna 830. This is Ruby," I answer sluggishly.

Astonished, Archie queries, "Were you asleep?"

"Of course not." I swipe a bit of drool from the side of my mouth.

"Well, I thought you'd want to know that Liz has arrived at the hotel."

"Already?" I check my watch.

Four thirty-eight. I can't believe I napped so long.

"I figured you'd want to stop by." He adds, "Maybe you can fill me in on your interview with the lifeguards, as well."

"Yes, I'll be right over," I assure him.

"Meet us at Lena's old room."

"You're kidding!" I snap.

"Believe me, I feel the same way, but we need a two-bedroom suite so Liz can help keep an eye on things for Corvi, and the hotel is full. This is all they have."

"Okay, I'm on my way."

It takes me less than ten minutes to wash my face, brush my hair, and change into an unwrinkled set of clothes. I drive over to save time and thankfully find parking near the main entrance. Closing the car door, I notice a gleaming Cord phaeton pull directly in front of the hotel. The convertible top is down, and a hotel porter rushes forward to open the back passenger door. Mr. Lake adjusts his ascot before sliding out. He tips the porter, and drifts through the hotel entryway as though he hasn't a care in the world. I *harumph* with disgust and trail him to the elevator.

The attendant asks, "Which floor?"

"Third," commands Mr. Lake.

"The same," I echo.

Noticing me for the first time, Mr. Lake raises an eyebrow.

"Mr. Lake, let me reintroduce myself. I'm Ruby Ray," I hold out my hand.

After a firm but quick handshake, he asks dismissively, "Should I know you?"

"I should think so, sir. We met on the *Statendam*," I remind him.

"Oh, yes—the Cartier necklace. But why are you're here?" He frowns.

"Mr. Duval hired me to assist with Miss Styles' *situation*," I reply vaguely, given the presence of the hotel staff.

His eyes flash with understanding. "I see."

The doors slide open, and without another word, Mr. Lake turns left and tromps away. I thank the attendant and proceed in the opposite direction toward Lena's—Elizabeth's room.

"Ruby!" My gorgeous friend throws her arms around me and, despite her petite frame, pulls me into a fierce embrace.

How I've missed her!

"I took one look at her, and knew she'd be perfect!" Archie praises while shutting the door and leading us into the shared living room.

Elizabeth releases me, her golden eyes shining merrily, and effuses, "I appreciate the opportunity, Mr. Duval."

"Archie...please," he replies kindly.

My friend's smile is infectious, and despite my reservations, I can't help but feel caught up in her jubilation. "Well, I for one am thrilled to see you!"

"I told Liz that she may want to bleach her hair. We could use a wig, but I doubt it'll stay on during the jump," Archie informs me.

Elizabeth pats her titian bob. "I've always wondered what life would be like as a blonde."

"Jump?" I inquire apprehensively.

"At Table Rock. I'm sure I mentioned that to you," Archie pronounces. "Liz assures me that she's a strong swimmer, so we're going to proceed with the scene tomorrow, as planned."

"It's true." Elizabeth takes my hands. "I'm up for it. There's a pool near Dean's apartment where I've been swimming laps every day for weeks."

"It'll be fine," Archie affirms. "And we'll have lifeguards on hand, not to mention a boat just offshore."

I open my mouth to voice my concerns when a brisk knock at the door intrudes upon our conversation.

Elizabeth opens the door, and a young lady—no older than Dottie—waves nervously. "Hello. I'm Poppy. They sent me to see if you want to order anything." She hands Elizabeth a menu.

"Isn't it rather early for dinner?" Elizabeth peruses the glossy bill of fare, while Poppy tries to peek further into the room.

"Maybe Miss Styles wants something..." She tucks a lanky strand of mousy brown hair behind her ear and steps onto her toes to see past Elizabeth.

"I wouldn't mind an iced tea." My friend stands within the door frame to block Poppy's view of the living room. "Can I keep the menu in case I want something later?"

"Of course, ma'am," the girl replies with undisguised disappointment. "I'll be back in a jiffy."

When Elizabeth returns, Archie snickers, "Fans!"

"Where is Corvi anyway?" I'm surprised she hasn't come through to meet her new double.

"She and Ike left a couple of hours ago. I'm not sure where they went, but it's better this way. I was able to brief Liz before you arrived," Archie winks at Elizabeth. "How did it go with the lifeguard, Ruby?"

"Confusing," I admit.

"Care to elaborate?" Archie checks his watch. "Better make it quick. I don't mean to be rude, but I should be leaving soon."

"In a nutshell, the lifeguard believes it was a drowning, just as the police told you."

"But you have doubts," Elizabeth comments then adds, "Archie told me about the notes and the man who's been following Corvi."

I close my eyes and exhale. "Elizabeth, I'm so sorry to involve you in all of this."

"Are you joking? I wouldn't miss this for the world," she beams.

"Ruby, I can tell you're holding back. What did the lifeguard say that makes you suspicious?" Archie asks.

"Honestly, Archie, I'm probably reading too much into it. Give me time to mull things over or—better yet—find additional evidence. We can discuss this later."

He nods, "Alright. I better go. I'm sure Mr. Lake is back from the studio and no doubt wants to speak with me."

"Oh, he's back alright. I rode the elevator with him. Quite the charmer," I say sarcastically.

Archie chuckles on his way out. "Ruby, can you meet us at the hotel tomorrow morning around eight? We'll take buses to Table Rock—it's a few miles south of here."

"Sure thing." I swallow my trepidation.

"If anything comes up before then, you know where to find me." He waves while closing the door.

I follow Elizabeth back into her room where she plops an enormous suitcase upon the bed. "Care to help me unpack?"

"Did you bring your entire closet?" I chuckle.

"Pretty much." She laughs.

While hanging clothes, I learn that despite the hefty cut he takes, Elizabeth's new agent hasn't secured any new auditions—much less work—for her recently. However, she was able to sing a solo in her last role during one of the ensemble numbers. She was even given a speaking part. After that, she'd hoped Warner Brothers would sign her.

"I don't know, Ruby," Elizabeth glances at the chemise in her hands. "Maybe it's for the best. It's not like WB has given Dean any roles lately. He feels like they lost interest once he was on contract."

"Have you two set a date yet?" They announced their engagement a few months earlier.

"Not yet. We'd like to be more stable, as far as work goes." She examines the square cut diamond and sapphires of her engagement ring. "But all it takes is one big break…"

Cautiously, I ask, "This job as a stunt double…isn't it a step backward for you?"

"That's true, but as I said earlier, I feel destined to be here. I can't explain it any better than that." She changes the subject, "How about you? Tell me all about your trip."

After an exhaustive recount, I explain the reason for my stay in Laguna Beach. "Needless to say, with all the ballyhoo over Corvi and Rex during my trip, I was relieved to return home. How ironic that I'm back in the thick of it—even more so."

"These things happen for a reason."

"I suppose so." I hand her a stack of rolled stockings.

"You know, Ruby, you haven't mentioned your delectable doctor. The last time we spoke, you were waiting to hear from him."

My cheeks warm. "Well…"

Elizabeth drops an armful of dresses and pulls me to sit on the bed beside her. "Talk!"

"We had our first date last night."

"And?" she grills impatiently.

"We had a lovely dinner and went dancing. He walked me home. There was a moment…"

"THIS is what I want to hear!"

"That was completely ruined by Norma's kitten." I rise to check the closet for more hangers and explain what happened.

"Oh, boo!" she hisses. "But how perfect that he's here too! I'm telling you, it's destiny!"

CHAPTER 11

"Sorry I'm late. I wasn't expecting to stay so long with Elizabeth," I apologize while using my foot to prevent Puck's escape through the open door. Deterred, he impishly claws my ankle and follows me into the living room.

Already dressed in her pajamas, Dottie is seated on the sofa, furiously scratching her arm. Interpreting her rapid movements as an invitation to play, the frisky kitten wiggles his tail, leaps onto the couch, and pounces upon her hand. Dottie emits an aggravated grunt and places the rambunctious nuisance on the floor.

I collapse next to her. "About dinner—"

"I'm sorry, Ruby. I'm just so itchy. I really don't feel like going out."

"To be honest, I'm not really up for it either," I confess.

"It's been quite a day," she mumbles.

"My sentiments exactly." I rise and head to the bedroom to change. "How does toasted cheese sound for dinner? I saw some cheddar in the fridge."

"Perfect," she calls after me.

I drop my purse onto the bed and notice a pamphlet resting on the pillow. Curious, I quickly undress, don my own nightgown and return to the living room. "What's this?"

"Oh, I thought you might be interested. It's a bird guide they had at the lab," Dottie rises and follows me into the kitchen.

"They didn't mind that you took it?" I retrieve a skillet from the cupboard and find a spatula in a drawer.

She sets the butter and cheese on the counter. "Nah, they have a bunch of copies for the students and people who tour the lab."

"Well, it will come in handy on my morning walks. That was thoughtful of you."

Over dinner, I ask about Dottie's itching.

"I started getting these welts on my arms and legs after I got back." she itches. "We had to climb over some dried kelp to get to the tidepools today. There must have been biting flies," she explains irritably.

"I'm sorry. That must be uncomfortable, but scratching will only make it worse."

"I know," she huffs. "After all, it wasn't that long ago that I had chickenpox."

"Don't remind me."

Both she and I caught it from Jack a few years ago. I'd somehow avoided chickenpox as a child but contracted a rather bad case as an adult that left me with a few scars, including one on my forehead.

"How's Elizabeth?" Dottie inquires before taking a bite.

"Between working with Corvi and sharing a cushy suite, she's in seventh heaven." I place my napkin over the remaining half of my sandwich. I've lost my appetite.

"Then why are you frowning?"

I meet Dottie's perplexed gaze. "I have a bad feeling about bringing her into this mess."

"You don't think the drowning was an accident," she infers.

"No, I don't."

All afternoon I've been ruminating over the lifeguard's report, as well as the mysterious notes and shadowy prowler. There's something there, some connection.

The sharp trill of the telephone interrupts my woolgathering, and I rise from the table. "I'll get it."

The weight of dread dissipates when I hear Sam's cheerful voice. "Hi, Ruby. I'm so glad I caught you. I thought you might be out on the town."

I snicker and glance down at my cotton crepe nightgown. "Hardly. How about you?"

"Oh, you know me...making the big bucks."

"Money laundering again?" I jest.

Sam laughs heartily. "If only—then I wouldn't need a second job."

"Are you at the coroner's tonight?" I cringe at the thought of him surrounded by corpses when it occurs to me that Lena may be there at this very moment.

"As a matter of fact, I am." He pauses. "I'd hoped we could pick up where we left off last night, but I'll be here tonight and tomorrow night."

I sigh with disappointment. I'd assumed we would see each other sometime tomorrow. "That's alright. We'll make up for it Tuesday."

"You can count on it," he replies tenderly. "So how was your day? Did Puck behave himself?"

"Surprisingly, yes for a change." With everything that's happened, he's been the least of my concerns. "Sam, I don't suppose a woman was brought into the morgue today—a drowning?"

Sam is overcome by a fit of loud coughing that continues for several moments.

"Are you alright?"

"Sorry about that, Ruby. Your question took me by surprise just as I was taking a sip of coffee." He clears his throat. "How do you know about that? Don't tell me you saw it happen?"

"No, but the victim was Corvi's stunt double." I brief him on the circumstances surrounding Lena's drowning, as well as my anxiety for Corvi and Elizabeth.

"From everything you've just told me, I share your concern."

I hesitate, then ask, "Has there been an autopsy?"

"Just a sec." Through the receiver I hear a cabinet door close, followed by the sound of shuffling papers. A moment later, Sam comes back on the line. "Found it."

"Sam, I don't want to get you into any trouble…"

"Let me worry about that," he answers, which doesn't exactly quell my fears. "There's been no autopsy. According to the police report, this was an 'unambiguous case of accidental death by asphyxiation due to drowning.' The report cites witness testimony by the lifeguard and bystanders."

"Can nothing further be done?"

"I'll see what I can do about that," he assures me.

Heartened, I reply, "Thank you, Sam."

"Of course. For everyone's safety, including yours—or should I say 'especially yours'—I want to get to the bottom of this."

Warmth spreads through my face and chest, and I feel lighter.

"A burden shared is a burden halved," as Nan likes to say.

"I should let you go…" I murmur.

"Not before I tell you how much I enjoyed your postcards," Sam says gently. "Perhaps I shouldn't admit this, but I read each one a dozen times."

A sense of joyful comfort washes over me. "I'm glad you told me. I may have done the same with your letters."

"I wish we didn't have to wait until Tuesday to see one another," he bemoans.

"Me too. But it sounds like you'll have your hands full tomorrow, and I anticipate that I'll be tied up with Corvi and Elizabeth."

"I'd like to meet your friend at some point."

"Oh, I'm sure you'll meet her this week. I can't wait to introduce you."

"I'd love that. Good night, Ruby," he says softly.

"Good night, Sam." Reluctantly I hang the receiver on the cradle.

MONDAY, AUGUST 25, 1930

The early morning sky is dove gray above the ocean horizon, while the rising sun tinges the fluffy clouds closer to shore a pale pink. A thin blanket provides an adequate barrier against the chill from the damp sand as I sit and watch baby waves roll gently upon the shore like the cream that tops a soda when first poured. A large blue-gray bird with a long s-shaped neck glides above the water, its long spindly legs stretched out behind. Flipping through the illustrations in the bird guide Dottie gave me, I discover that this magnificent creature is a great blue heron. After it passes, I skim the swelling waves, hoping to spot Skipper, but I guess I'm too early. I'd considered walking in a different direction this morning, but I need to speak with Sal before she heads out. Turning my head to glance over my shoulder, I spy her rowboat still resting on the sand next to the lifeguard's dory.

I'm too early for her as well.

I wasn't planning to be up and about so soon, but around five-thirty this morning, screams from Dottie's room jolted me awake from my own dread-tinged nightmares. I rushed to her bedside to find Puck batting her arm as she cried, "Please! No! Don't hurt us!"

"Dottie, wake up." I shook her shoulder with one hand while moving the kitten to the foot of the cot with the other.

Her eyes flew open, and she stared straight at me for a moment before registering who I was. "Ruby?" She looked around with panic. "What's wrong?"

"You were having a nightmare and cried out." I patted her arm soothingly.

Dottie's expression flattened. "Oh, that."

"Do you want to talk about it? You were begging someone not to hurt—"

"I'm fine," she said abruptly. "Just a silly dream. I can hardly remember it now."

"Alright," I yawned. "Since I'm up, I guess I'll make a pot of coffee and take a walk."

"Mm-mm," Dottie muttered and rolled onto her side.

My stomach turns as I replay this scene in my mind. Clearly something is troubling Dottie, but she clams up whenever I broach the subject. In the past, she wouldn't hesitate to share her troubles with me. But all that changed earlier this year when she became involved with Mr. Mains and the Pythagorean Club at her school—a twisted cover for the cult that gradually indoctrinated her and a few other students. She eventually told her father and I everything that had transpired and seemed relieved to have it all out in the open. So, I don't understand her reluctance to confide in me about her nightmares.

As a sixteen-year-old orphan, I suffered many night terrors in the weeks and months following my parent's death. At the time, I wasn't given any specifics. I was merely told that my parents died in a car accident. However, my active imagination filled in all sorts of gruesome details while I was sleeping. Countless times I woke in total confusion—unsure what was real and what was a dream—while my heart pounded, and tears poured down my face. For a while, I was afraid to fall asleep at all, and to this day, I sometimes wake with a general sense of impending doom.

I shake my head and arms to release the tension and watch a couple of long-billed curlews probe the damp sand for tiny crabs and snails. Returning to the bird guide, I skim an entry about these sandpipers, when I suddenly hear, "Ruby!"

"Elizabeth?" I rise to my feet and stride across the sand toward the back of the hotel. "What are you doing out so early?"

She laughs. "I could ask you the same thing."

I wave the pamphlet. "Birdwatching, if you can believe it."

"I never took you for an ornithologist." She points at a long-legged bird, similar to the curlew, but with a straighter beak. "So tell me, what's that fellow called?"

"Oh, him?" I quickly thumb through the guide. "He's a willet."

"Willy! How marvelous!" She drops a colorful straw tote onto a damp lounge chair that's been left out overnight and opens the bag to retrieve a daffodil yellow swimming cap.

With raised eyebrows, I query, "You're taking a dip? The sun's barely up."

She rolls her eyes. "I hadn't planned on it, but when Poppy knocked on the living room door at six, I couldn't go back to sleep."

"The gal from yesterday afternoon?" I recall the young fan craning her neck to sneak a peek at Corvi.

"That's the one," she tucks her newly bleached locks into the cap. "She was delivering something, but it turned out to be a mistake."

"And you believe that?" I smirk.

"Not for a moment." Elizabeth unties the belt of her robe and steps out of her sandals. "I figured that since I was already awake, I might as well come down for a paddle. It's been a while since I swam in the ocean."

"How do you feel about the shoot later this morning at Table Rock?"

"Piece of cake," she waves a hand confidently.

"So, what happened after I left last night?" I perch upon the foot of the lounge while Elizabeth begins a series of graceful stretches.

"Corvi returned with her manager shortly after you left, but you'll never guess who came knocking at the door a little while later!" Elizabeth says excitedly.

"Geez, Elizabeth. I wouldn't know where to begin, but from the look on your face, it must be someone grand. Was it Gary Cooper?" We were both captivated by his magnetism when we saw him in *The Virginian* last year.

"If only!" she exclaims. "I'll tell you—you'll never guess. It was Madame Sylvia!"

"You're right. I would never have guessed," I chuckle. "To be honest, I don't know much about her."

"Sure you do! Remember all that Reduceomania business in *Photoplay* several years ago?"

I recall a series of articles uncovering the unhealthy and sometimes lethal lengths that actresses—as well as ordinary women—would go through to attain the "perfect figure"—that of a twelve-year-old girl. Reduction methods included everything from swallowing the heads of tapeworms to taking medications containing the thyroid glands of sheep, all to attain a slim, angular physique devoid of breasts and hips. Dramatic advertisements for such products filled the back pages of most women's magazines at the time.

"Where does Madame Sylvia fit in with all that?"

"After Barbara La Marr's death from those crash diets and tapeworm treatments, Madame Sylvia said they were flimflam and proposed healthy eating, exercise, and massage. That's why she's such a big deal in Hollywood right now."

"I don't understand. Why did Corvi ask her to come? I'd think that her figure is the last thing she's worried about at the moment."

Elizabeth shrugs. "Corvi likes her. I guess she's worked with her in the past and thought that a massage would help her relax. So, Ike gave Madame Sylvia a call."

"I guess that makes sense." After everything that happened yesterday, I could have used a massage as well.

"She's lucky Madame agreed to see her. Nine out of ten actresses I know make do with emetics from their medicine cabinet."

"Surely it's not as bad as that!"

Elizabeth shrugs and finishes her stretches. "I should get started if I'm going to be ready in time for the shoot."

"I'm really not comfortable with you swimming out there alone. It's not a good idea to go out without a lifeguard nearby, especially after what happened to Lena…"

"I love you, but you sound like my mother. Besides, I know about riptides." She points toward the incoming waves. "See that area where no waves are breaking. It looks like it would be easy to enter the water there, but it's actually a strong current flowing out to sea." She begins to jog toward a rolling wave, calling over her shoulder "I'll be fine."

"Well, I'll be watching from the sand, just in case," I shout after her moments before she dives under the wave.

Once she's cleared the breakers, Elizabeth heads southeast to follow the shoreline at a smooth, even pace. I watch until her yellow cap is no longer visible. Then I return to my blanket and tote where a thermos of coffee is waiting for me. A little while later, I spy a smoke-colored fin surfacing in the water a few hundred yards offshore. My heart skips as a second dolphin leaps, its pectoral fins grazing the surface of the water. Closer to shore, a splash signals Skipper's arrival. The sea lion's sleek form is visible in the curving waves. I breathe deeply with gratitude for this joyful interlude.

"Hey there," a friendly voice shouts behind me.

I turn to see Sal dragging her rowboat toward the water.

"Just the person I wanted to see," I stand to join her.

She runs a hand through her cropped locks. "Didya decide to take me up on that offer? Only, today's probably not a good day for taking you out on the *Bonnie Boat*."

"Are you diving for treasure this morning?"

"Nah. We're gonna visit a site just north of here. Yesterday, a fisherman swore he saw a giant Pacific octopus a couple of miles offshore." She raises her shoulders and hands. "He said it was tangled in his lines, but since it was so big he cut the net and let it go."

I glance at the broad expanse of water. "Isn't that like finding a needle in a haystack?"

She laughs. "Worse than that! But since my crew will be disappointed when I break the news about the filming, I figured I'd make it up to them with the octopus."

"Disappointed?"

"Yeah, we were supposed to take out some cameramen in a couple of hours." She hikes a thumb toward the Hotel Laguna. "Those movie folks wanted to film a scene from the water over at Table Rock."

"I thought they were going ahead with that," I comment.

"You mean after the drowning yesterday?"

She pulls the pail of tuna from her rowboat and waves it in the air. Skipper speeds toward an incoming wave and drifts to shore.

"Exactly."

"I thought so too, but I got a call a few minutes ago that some other emergency came up. Just in the nick of time too—I was headin' out the door. I sure hope they end up goin' through with the filmin'. My guys were really lookin' forward to it."

Sal tosses a chunk of flesh to Skipper, who's waddling toward us.

"Emergency?" I'd wonder if something happened to Corvi, but from Elizabeth's account, she went back to bed after Poppy's early appearance. "Did they say what happened?"

"Not a word," she shrugs. "The fella who hired us just said that he'd be in touch." She chucks another piece of albacore into Skipper's open mouth.

"Sal, I'm actually here to ask you about something related to the movie." I lower my voice as a young couple pass by, both casting curious glances at Sal and me. "I understand that you tried to save Miss Young yesterday morning."

She nods and examines me warily. "Why do you ask?"

"I'm an inquiry agent, and the studio hired me to look into some things for them," I explain. "Miss Young was the stunt double for Miss Corvi Styles."

"So, I was told," she remarks.

"Well, we have reason to believe that Corvi might be in danger. The timing of Lena's drowning seems suspicious. Would you mind telling me what happened at the cove yesterday?"

She covers her mouth and chin with a hand while choosing her words. "I think you're right—about it being suspicious."

"How so?" I retrieve my notebook and pen.

"First off, the way she was thrashing in the water, enough to get herself tangled up in the kelp. I thought she musta been stung by a jellyfish. That or sea nettle—they really pack a punch. But she didn't have any ropey welts on her when we got her to shore. That said, her legs were pretty banged up."

"What could have caused that?" I query.

She squints at the sea. "Well, probably from the fit she was having! There are some huge rocks around the kelp forest. She musta banged up against 'em."

Skipper barks to get our attention, and Sal holds out the pail toward me. "Go ahead."

I dig my fingers into the bucket and grab several pieces of fish then fling the treat toward the eager sea lion.

"Did you notice anything else that seemed odd?"

"Sure did! After I cut her loose, it seemed like she couldn't move her arms and legs." She smiles dolefully. "At the time, I thought she was awfully easy to haul into shore after all that flappin' and kickin'. But once we got her onto the sand, it was clear she was dyin'."

I'd imagine her lungs were full of fluid at that point. "What did you find suspicious about her death?"

Sal's eyes bore into mine. "The smile."

This confuses me. "Smile?"

"She had the most awful grin on her face, even after the light left her eyes." Sal shudders.

Goosebumps prickle my skin. "What happened after that?"

"Well, someone screamed, so I looked up. I saw that actress next to an umbrella, just sobbin' her heart out on the sand. A few other folks were there, but they just stood and gawked."

"Duke, the lifeguard, said that you sat with her until the police arrived."

"That's right," Sal frowns. "Poor girl. She just kept cryin' and sayin' 'It was him. I know it!'"

"I'm not surprised," I reply. That's consistent with what the police told Archie. "The lifeguard mentioned that your crew may have contacted the police from your boat."

"I thought so too. But when I asked the guys about it later, they were embarrassed to admit that none of them thought of calling it in, even though we have a radio phone onboard."

Then who made the call?

"How ghastly!" Elizabeth exclaims after I describe my conversation with Sal. "Do people actually die with a smile on their face?"

"I don't know," I admit. "Thankfully, I haven't had any first-hand experience watching someone die." But given my line of work, that's bound to change at some point.

We walk in silence while ascending the stairs that lead from the sand to the back of the hotel. As we near the interior courtyard, we hear raised voices.

"He's fired, Archie! That's all there is to it!"

We round the corner to see Mr. Lake pacing around the bubbling fountain at the center of the grassy enclosure. Several empty chairs are arranged in clusters around the perimeter. Archie is standing at the edge of the circular walkway, his face lined with worry and his posture uncharacteristically stooped.

"We're sorry to interrupt," I apologize when Mr. Lake scowls at our arrival.

He throws his hands up and marches toward the double doors, but before entering the hotel, he pivots and fixes Archie with a gimlet gaze. "Fire him! And find a replacement, or you're fired as well!"

Archie's eyelids flutter, and his Adam's apple wobbles as he swallows. "I wish you hadn't heard that," he tells us.

I rush to his side. "I'm so sorry! Did our interruption make things worse?"

"Oh, no," he chuckles bitterly. "It was well past 'worse' when you arrived."

I follow him to a group of wicker chairs covered with artfully arranged pillows. He snatches a round tasseled cushion and hugs it to his chest while sinking onto the seat. I drop into the chair beside him, patting his upper back, as Elizabeth continues standing, her face awash with uncertainty.

"It's okay," Archie tells her. "Sit. You need to hear this as well."

Her eyes widen, and she takes a chair across from us, her hands nervously smoothing the wrinkles from her robe. Archie lowers his face into his hands, the tips of his fingers digging into his forehead and temples. Elizabeth casts a bewildered look in my direction, to which I shrug my shoulders.

What now?

The steady tinkle and splash of the fountain, disrupted only by the cheerful chirrup of a red-headed finch, conveys a tranquil mood quite at odds with the tension surrounding us. At another time, under different circumstances, I fancy savoring a glass of iced tea and a good book within the walls of this Mediterranean-style courtyard. But this morning, Elizabeth and I silently wait several minutes for Archie to speak first.

"It's Rex." He lowers his hands, revealing an expression of utter dejection.

My mind whirls with a kaleidoscope of worst-case scenarios before I inquire, "What's happened, Archie?"

"There's been an accident," he replies with a pinched countenance.

My stomach tightens, and Elizabeth gasps, "Another one?!"

"Is he alright?" I place a hand on his shoulder.

He covers his mouth and briefly closes his eyes before responding. "Miraculously, yes. Although, I'm going to kill him when the hospital releases him."

I sigh with relief. Surely, it's not as bad as I expected. "Was he injured?"

Archie presses his lips into a hard thin line. "The fool! He mangled himself surfing, if you can believe it."

"Ah..." I comment with understanding.

"About twenty minutes ago, Pete called the hotel from the emergency room. Mr. Lake spoke with him."

"Pete?" Elizabeth leans forward, elbows on her knees.

"He's a gaffer who's been teaching Rex to surf," Archie explains with a sneer. The words "and other things" go unspoken.

"Did he see what happened?"

"No, he was out in the water himself but saw a crowd gather around Rex on the shore. This was in Corona del Mar. Apparently, he fell off just as a big wave broke, and his board hit him."

I wince with empathy. "How bad?"

"Broken collar bone, concussion, and busted knee," he lists testily. "According to the doctor, he'll be out of commission for at least two months."

Elizabeth bites her lower lip. "And the film?"

"You heard Lake," Archie says wearily. "Rex is out. With all the money that's been dumped into the Laguna location shoot, the studio refuses to postpone. They told Lake to fix it or forget it."

"Would they shut down the film?" I ask.

"That's Hollywood," Elizabeth remarks.

Archie nods. "This picture was meant to capitalize on buzz from the latest publicity tour. Europe wasn't cheap, and the public's chomping at the bit for more Corvi and Rex."

I look up at the row of third-floor windows. "Speaking of Corvi. Does she know about this?"

"Not yet," he says with reticence. "I'll tell her now before I leave for the studio."

"I'm going up too. I need a shower." Elizabeth shakes the sand from her towel onto the grass and makes her way through the doors into the lobby.

Archie begins to follow, but I place a hand on his arm. "How are you doing with all this?"

He forcefully exhales through pursed lips. "This is the last straw. After he and Pete rolled in—both sauced—around two last night, I told him that I've had it and that we're done. He just laughed."

"Oh, Archie." I don't know what else to say.

"Honestly, it's for the best. A big part of my job is to wrangle the talent. That's hard to do when I'm dating one of them." He looks up toward a window that I assume belongs to Rex. "But in Europe, the day-to-day reality of filmmaking couldn't have been further from my mind."

"It was quite romantic," I agree. "Moonlight on the water, champagne on ice, exploring new places…"

"Exactly." He adjusts his cornflower blue bow tie. "Well, that's all in the past. Right now, I have to break the news to Corvi. Then, somehow, I need to find a replacement for that fool."

I open the front door and discover Puck seated directly in my path, one hind leg stretched vertically. Distracted from his grooming, he jumps up and weaves through and around my feet, all the while purring. I bend to pet him when a metallic clang sounds from somewhere down the hall, followed by an exasperated cry.

"Dottie, are you okay?" I drop my bag on the sofa and rush toward the bathroom.

The door swings inward, and I'm thunderstruck by the scene before me. A lumpy beige mush covers Dottie's face, arms, and bare legs, as well as the sink, floor, and base of the cabinets, while an overturned enamel bowl rests against the tub. I suppress a laugh but cannot prevent the corners of my mouth from turning upward. Dottie's narrowed eyes meet mine for a moment, then relax. I'm not sure who giggles first, but before long, we're both in hysterics.

"What on Earth?" I choke out.

Dottie points to the bowl and shrieks, "It slipped!"

Which, for some reason, unleashes another torrent of snort-laughs and side-splitting hoots. At this point, Puck joins us and suspiciously sniffs Dottie's foot. I conclude that he had nothing to do with this mess.

When I'm finally able to control my voice, I clarify, "Not the bowl. I was asking about this slop and why you're covered in it."

Dottie flicks a bit away from her face and licks her index finger. Noticing my disgust, she chuckles at my wrinkled nose. "It's oatmeal."

I smell the contents of the bowl, its nutty odor confirming Dottie's claim. "Okay…"

"It's these bites," she explains. "They were even worse when I woke up this morning, so I called Nan. She told me that oatmeal paste is the best thing for itchiness."

"Is it helping?"

"Not so far," she looks at her legs then rolls her eyes.

"How's everything at home?" I inquire.

"Jack answered and complained again that it's unfair you decided to abandon him," Dottie replies while wetting a hand towel to wipe up the floor.

"He'll be here before he knows it." I pull a washcloth off of the rack and begin tidying the sink area.

"Nan said that Addie and May want to visit. She asked if they could come on Wednesday. Nan promised to bring a picnic lunch, so of course I told her it would be fine," Dottie adds sheepishly.

"She doesn't need to do that. They're more than welcome to join us at the beach, regardless." However, the thought of one of Nan's picnic lunches makes my mouth water. "I hope Nan's coming too."

"She wasn't going to, but I told her we can rent an umbrella and comfortable chair for her. That seemed to change her mind. It sounds like Gabe is coming too."

"Well, that settles it. I'll make sure that I'm not needed on the film set that day."

If there is a film.

Once the bathroom is tidy, Dottie and I retire to the kitchen for breakfast. Over plates of eggs and toast, I examine my cousin thoughtfully. She seems to be in good spirits this morning, despite the irritating bug bites. I hesitate to ask her directly about the nightmare.

"Dottie, I hope you're enjoying yourself here. I'm sorry I'm so caught up in this mess with the film. How are you doing with everything?" I ask vaguely.

"There's no need to apologize," Dottie says earnestly. "I'm thrilled that you're working with Corvi and the others. I'll have a lot to tell Polly when I get back, and I really like helping Iris with her research."

I nod reflectively. "How are you feeling about the move to Berkeley?"

Her smile loses some of its brilliance. "I'm nervous," she says quietly. "But I think I'm ready for it." Dottie pushes at a bit of egg with her fork.

"I have no doubt that you're ready for it. Yes, it'll be a big change for you, but you're brilliant and will have no trouble with the coursework. You're also quite likable and kind, so I know you'll make friends in no time." I smirk, "And you probably won't mind a break from your little brother."

She laughs. "You're right about that."

I seize the opportunity to probe a little deeper. "Is there anything else worrying you?"

Dottie quietly tears half of a slice of toast into smaller and smaller pieces. I eat my own food while waiting for her to respond. I begin to think she's going to ignore my question, when she softly replies, "You're talking about the nightmares, aren't you?"

I slowly nod and give her an encouraging smile. "I am—but only if you feel like talking about it."

An internal battle plays upon her face, as she opens and closes her mouth. "I don't want to dwell on it," she finally admits. "They're just dreams."

"Sometimes it helps to share our dreams with others—even the nightmares."

She squares her shoulders. "Not these dreams." She stands and strides toward the bathroom. "I'm gonna wash off this mush. I feel even itchier than before."

I take my time doing the dishes. The warm water is soothing, and my body relaxes, my thoughts drifting to my interview with Sal. For the most part, her story corroborated Duke's. However, despite mentioning Lena's rigid limbs, he failed to say anything about the smile, which sounded quite gruesome under the circumstances. Hopefully, Sam made some headway last night with an autopsy. Then there's Rex's accident—the timing seems fishy, right on the heels of Lena's drowning. But Rex's intoxication and inexperience surfing are the most likely explanations for his mishap. Still, I can't rule out the possibility that it's somehow connected.

When I finish the dishes, Dottie joins me in the living room. Without the oatmeal poultice covering her skin, I realize that the welts have tripled in number.

"Yikes! Maybe you should stay away from the biting flies today."

"I'll try," she scratches her cheek. "I promised Iris I'd go with her today, but I'll avoid dried kelp. How about you?"

"I expect to hear from Elizabeth soon. The shoot was canceled this morning, so I'm not sure what they'll need me to do."

"Why was it canceled?" Dottie strokes Puck's sleek back as he perches on the arm of the sofa like a small loaf of bread.

"You need to keep this to yourself," I give her a warning glance.

She crosses her heart. "Not a peep. Now tell me what happened."

"Rex was in a surfing accident this morning. He's out of the film."

Her eyes goggle. "Is he okay?"

I describe his injuries and what this will mean for the film. "Archie was breaking the news to Corvi when I left."

The phone rings, and Dottie declares, "That'll be for you." She stretches out onto her back and places Puck on the center of her chest.

CHAPTER 12

"How soon can you come to the hotel?" Elizabeth's voice sounds tense through the phone's earpiece.

I drop my head to examine the slacks and knit blouse I threw on for my morning walk. In another hour or so, it'll be too warm for such an ensemble, and I'm sure my hair is a frizzy mess.

"Can you give me a half an hour? I need to change."

"I suppose," she whines. "But hurry! Corvi's hysterical, and I could really use a hand here."

"I'll be there as soon as I can."

I throw on a dotted Swiss sleeveless dress and run a comb through my tangled curls, which still resemble a bird's nest. Sighing wearily, I swipe my lips with a rose tint and toss the tube, my wallet, and keys into the handbag I carried yesterday, even though it's brown and clashes with the pale lilac of my dress. After sliding my feet into white sandals, I hurry through the living room, blowing a kiss to Dottie, who is still lying on the sofa with Puck.

"Make sure he's locked up when you leave," I shout a reminder over my shoulder.

"Drive carefully," she warns. "You're no good to anyone if you're laid up."

Truer words were never spoken.

"Thank God you're here!"

Elizabeth pulls me into the shared living room where a high-pitched keening carries through Corvi's bedroom door. I cast Elizabeth a bewildered look, to which she shrugs with her palms up.

"I didn't realize that Corvi and Rex were particularly fond of one another," I reflect.

"From what I've heard, they're not." Elizabeth cringes as the wailing becomes louder. "But I don't think that's why she's in a tizzy."

"What did she say?"

Elizabeth looks toward the adjoining wall. "She hasn't said much other than, 'It's him. I know it's him.' After I called you, I left a message at her manager's hotel, but I guess he already left."

I tap on the bedroom door. "Corvi...it's Ruby. Can I come in?"

After a series of audible sniffs, she quietly answers, "O-ka-ay."

The room is dark, but cracks around the edges of the drawn curtains provide enough light for me to discern her delicate frame sitting against the pillows hugging her knees to her chest under the covers. I switch on the desk lamp, illuminating an untouched tray of dry toast, half a grapefruit, and a cup of coffee.

"I heard about Rex." I drag the desk chair next to her bed and add compassionately, "Would you like to talk?"

She slowly nods while delicately wiping away her tears with a silk handkerchief.

"Elizabeth—Liz tells me that you believe the stalker had something to do with Rex's accident," I begin.

She abruptly turns toward me, her red puffy eyes conveying both distress and eagerness. "You believe it too. Don't you?"

"Truthfully, I find the timing suspicious, but I cannot fathom how someone could have orchestrated this."

"But Lena—"

"Lena's situation was different. She was a skilled swimmer, and details of her drowning are highly problematic," I explain. "Rex's accident, on the other hand, can be easily explained. He was an inexperienced surfer and possibly drunk as well."

Brow furrowed, Corvi shakes her head and opens her mouth to speak when someone hammers on her door.

"I'll see who it is."

I've barely opened the door when Ike barrels past me to stand over Corvi.

"Up." He commands, his fists on his hips.

"But—" Corvi bleats.

"No buts! Up!" Ike pulls back the blankets with one meaty paw.

Stunned, it takes me a moment to voice my outrage. "Now see here! There's been another accident. Corvi is—"

He swivels around to face me. "I know what's happened. Lake sent someone with a note. Damn kid woke me up."

I straighten and—unwilling to be cowed by this bully—reply firmly, "Given all that Corvi's been through the last few days, I'm sure you understand why she's upset."

"You're new," he snickers arrogantly. "So, you couldn't possibly understand Corvi's tantrums."

"This is hardly a tantrum!" I wave my hand toward the wide-eyed actress. "She's shocked and terrified by yet another calamity befalling a colleague. Meanwhile, she herself is being stalked and continues to receive distressing notes. Have you no heart?"

Ike quirks the corner of his mouth. "That's cute. But what Corvi needs right now is a distraction. Lying around caterwauling will just make it worse. Trust me. I know."

"He's right, Ruby," Corvi slowly rises and slips on a frilly diaphanous robe. "I need a distraction."

Her manager claps his hands together and flashes an arrogant grin. "See! What did I tell you?"

Forty-five minutes later, Corvi, Elizabeth, and I are blinking at the harsh sunlight while exiting the hotel. Ike left as soon as Corvi agreed to an outing, but not before handing me fifty dollars—roughly equivalent to the weekly earnings of a common laborer.

"Take her shopping. Have a nice lunch. Anything to get her mind off all this," he ordered before plugging a toby into his mouth and taking his leave.

Outside the hotel, I ask, "Where shall we go?"

"Hmm…" Corvi dons a pair of stylish, round-frame sunglasses and slowly scans our surroundings. "You know, this is the first time I've had a whole day off in quite a while."

"Well, I for one need a pair of beach pajamas," Elizabeth comments.

181

"Ooh, good idea, Liz!" Corvi agrees.

We wander up Ocean Avenue where a variety of businesses spread out along the busy street. Pausing at the window of a brightly lit candy shop, we watch automated stainless-steel arms pull and fold a sticky length of fuchsia taffy. An arc of colorful barrels filled with the salt water treat surround the machine. Elizabeth turns toward me and waggles her eyebrows. She and I share a fondness for sweets.

"Need you ask?" I follow her into the store.

Corvi wavers at the door, "Madame Sylvia—"

"Isn't here," Elizabeth interrupts. "And even if she were, I don't think one piece will make a difference."

The starlet's eyes sweep the street behind her before she shuffles into the store. Once inside, she examines the enticing treats with an astonished expression.

"Oh, my." She lays a dainty hand across her upper chest. A school-age boy notices and elbows his buddy, who merely shrugs and continues pawing through a basket of jawbreakers.

"When was the last time you stepped foot in a sweet shop?" I inquire with interest.

"Why...I can't remember," Corvi giggles nervously.

Elizabeth heads directly toward a glass-front display where handcrafted sweets rest in colorful paper cups. She looks over her shoulder. "Ruby...look at these!"

Following her pointed finger, I read a tiny hand-written label. "Penuche fudge?"

"It tastes like the center of a milk Bordeaux from See's—you'll love it!"

"If you say so..." I don't see any chocolate or sprinkles, but I'm willing to give it a try.

When Corvi ventures into the center of the shop, Elizabeth and asks, "Does anything tickle your fancy?"

Corvi pensively chews her lower lip while gazing longingly at—of all things—a display of NECCO wafers. "My brother used to buy a roll for us to share when we'd go to the movies."

"My father used to do the same thing," I recall wistfully.

With a bittersweet smile, she reminisces. "Watching Mary Pickford and Lillian Gish on the muslin screen—that's when I realized I wanted to be up there too. My brother used to say, 'Annabel, that'll be you one day—the brightest star that ever sparkled.'"

"Annabel?" Elizabeth asks as the shopkeeper, a clean-shaven young man in a pristine white apron, hands her a chocolate-dipped strawberry.

Flustered from her reverie, Corvi's cheeks turn crimson. She looks from Elizabeth to the salesman, who just noticed that the boys are shoving fistfuls of gum into their pockets. He rushes toward them, shaking his finger.

"Oops! I don't usually share that." Corvi presses a couple of fingers to her lips, then admits, "Corvi Styles is my stage name."

"Don't worry about it! Liz Martin isn't my real name either."

Corvi relaxes. "I figured as much since Ruby calls you Elizabeth. But at least your stage name isn't all that different."

"Just different enough to hide my heritage,' Elizabeth sullenly remarks. "My father shortened our last name from Martinez to Martin when he and my mama moved here."

Corvi nods sympathetically. "It happens a lot."

"Dean had to anglicize his stage name as well," Elizabeth mentions to me.

"Dean?" Corvi asks.

"He's my fiancé. He took on Larsen—his mother's maiden name—as his stage name because his actual surname is Jiang. His paternal grandfather was from Singapore," Elizabeth explains.

"I didn't realize that," I comment while watching the shopkeeper escort the two boys out of the store.

Corvi interjects, "It's not just the actors and actresses. Archie told me that even Mr. Lake changed his last name, which was Lakos. I guess he thought it was too Hungarian."

I ask Elizabeth, "What are you planning to do when you get married? Will you change your name?"

She nods. "I'll change my legal name, but my stage name will stay the same."

"Corvi, how about you?" I query.

"Oh, I've never been married."

"No—I'm sorry—what I meant to ask was whether you'd change your stage name if you marry someday."

"I know some do, especially if they marry a fellow actor, but I can't imagine changing Styles to anything else." Her eyes glide back toward the NECCO wafers. After a moment's hesitation, she snatches a tube from the pile and walks to the sales counter.

We overhear the salesman telling the boys that, in no uncertain terms, they are never to enter the store again. It's only when he steps behind the counter that he notices Corvi and realizes who she is. I start to pay for our treats, but he waves away the dollar bill I've pulled from the wad Ike handed me.

"For you ladies—it's on the house."

Back out on the boulevard, we pass a bank, a tobacco shop, and a souvenir shop selling postcards and jewelry made from seashells. The display in the window of an arts and crafts emporium showcases attractive earthenware pitchers and serving bowls under a sign reading "Brayton Laguna Pottery."

"My mother would adore that," Elizabeth points at a small figurine of a woman wearing a headscarf and a tasseled shawl around her shoulders. The rich colors remind me of a spring garden. "I'm going to see how much it costs," she informs us.

Corvi and I wait outside. However, after a series of passersby pause to blatantly stare at her, I suggest moving indoors. She wholeheartedly agrees. As soon as we enter the shop, Corvi makes a beeline toward the back of the shop, where a wall of honey gold tableware is artfully arranged on staggered shelves. She carefully reaches for a flower shaped bowl when a saleslady wearing a tan and white smock approaches her.

"These pieces were hand thrown from red clay by Durlin Brayton, a local potter," the elderly woman explains.

"They're lovely," Corvi holds the bowl toward the light. "I like the flecks of orange and dark gold."

"Yes, and if you take a closer look at one of the plates, you'll notice a bit of sparkle here and there, rather like mica in igneous rocks. Excellent glazing."

Corvi taps her lips while making a decision. "I'll take six sets of plates and bowls."

"There are matching cups and saucers as well." The saleswoman is good at her job.

"Ooh, really? I'll take six sets of those," Corvi says decisively.

"Will there be anything else?" The woman smiles with satisfaction.

Corvi looks toward Elizabeth and I. "What do you think?"

"I'm afraid the figurine is out of my price range," Elizabeth admits regretfully.

At the sales counter, the woman tears lengths of brown paper from a large roll then individually wraps each piece before placing them into a cardboard box. "Do you have a car outside? This box will be heavy."

"No, we walked over. Would it be possible to have them delivered to the Hotel Laguna?" Corvi asks.

"Of course, my dear. Not a problem at all."

"Oh, and please add the figurine to the box as well. My treat," Corvi grins at Elizabeth.

"That's so kind," my friend blushes. "Thank you."

As the woman rings up each item on the register, I watch the total climb at an alarming rate. "That'll be twenty-four dollars and seventy-three cents."

That's nearly half of what Ike gave me.

Corvi opens her chic beaded mesh bag and frowns. "All I have is my Bullock's charge plate."

"Don't worry about it, Corvi." I open my wallet. "Ike gave me some cash before he left."

She sighs with relief. "I don't know what I'd do without him. I'm terrible with money and never carry cash myself."

Pleased as punch, the older woman bids us farewell. Back outside, Corvi suggests, "Let's head over to the next street. If I'm not mistaken, there's a dress boutique which may sell beach pajamas, as well."

We no sooner turn onto Forest, when our progress is blocked by cameras and microphones.

"What's all this?" I quiz Corvi. "I thought filming was canceled for today."

"Me too." She looks around. "I only see film crew, so they must be shooting extra footage for staging scenes. Do you see how one camera is trained on the sidewalk across the street, and another is shooting up the avenue?"

"Hi ya, Corvi!" One lean fellow with a pork pie hat nearly drops the boom microphone he's carrying.

Corvi smiles fondly. "Vernon! What are you boys up to today?"

He passes the pole to another crew member and lopes over to us. "You know Mr. Lake. He don't wanna waste any daylight if he can help it, so we're shootin' stock today."

"I thought so," Corvi comments. "Do you boys mind if we scootch through here?"

Vernon's face brightens. "Mind? Course not!" Then he proceeds to clear a path for us.

"Thanks a bunch!" Corvi waves to the crew as we pass. Then, a few shops from the intersection, she points toward a store called Daisy's Dresses.

"I spotted this shop when we were filming a couple of days ago. Only, I never thought I'd have time to stop by."

"This looks promising," Elizabeth says approvingly while gripping the door handle. But before she begins to pull, the door is thrust open, knocking her into Corvi.

"Say! What's the big idea?" Elizabeth snaps.

"Bebe!" Corvi exclaims.

With a self-congratulatory sneer, Bebe purrs, "You should watch where you're going." Then she flips her inky curls and adds, "Or someone might get hurt."

Elizabeth looks at Corvi. "Are you alright?"

Corvi laughs nonchalantly. "Right as rain. She's just jealous."

I watch Bebe slink away, but her spine visibly stiffens when, through the open door, someone shouts, "It's Corvi Styles!"

I don't trust her.

Even though Corvi is convinced that her stalker is somehow responsible for the accidents, I'm beginning to wonder if Bebe had something to do with Lena's demise. I'll ask Elizabeth to help me keep an eye on the bitter actress.

Daisy, the shop owner, is a chic woman of a certain age with dark blonde hair styled into a sleek shingle. She smooths her dress—a printed crepe with a little bertha cape that ties in the front—and graces us with an attentive smile.

"Welcome to Daisy's Dresses. How may I help you today?"

Corvi peers around the uncluttered store, her eyes briefly resting on a rack of swimsuits. When she notices three young ladies—each trying to hide their grins behind their hands—Corvi flashes them a friendly smile, to which they excitedly giggle. Turning back to Daisy, she asks, "Do you have beach pajamas?"

The crow's feet at the corners of Daisy's eyes deepen as her smile broadens. "That I do! A new shipment just arrived from Paris. This way."

"Perfect!" Corvi winks at me as we follow Daisy. Just weeks ago, the two of us were in the City of Light, although I'm sure her shopping exploits were quite different from mine. Unlike Corvi, I—for one— could not secure an appointment at Coco Chanel's atelier.

A wide selection of beach pajamas hangs on a rack along the back wall. Elizabeth grabs a lemon-yellow set with white zig zags and a long pongee cape. Corvi pulls out a backless one-piece halter with extra wide striped trousers in bright green, navy, and white.

"That's my favorite of the bunch," Daisy confides. "However, the pant legs will be quite long on you. I could have them hemmed if you'd like."

"Thank you," Corvi smiles sweetly, "But I'm sure one of the gals in wardrobe won't mind helping me out."

While the two actresses try on their selections, I inquire about bathing suits. When I unpacked a few days ago, Puck hopped up on the bed and snagged the new swimsuit I purchased in Europe. If Sam and I manage to visit the beach together this week, I'd prefer to look my best. My heart flutters at the thought.

"Unfortunately, our selection is restricted because of the bathing suit ordinance," Daisy laments.

"Bathing suit ordinance?" Elizabeth calls through the fitting room curtain.

"Yes, last year one of my customers wore a suit with kidney cutouts along the sides and was issued a three-hundred dollar fine. When she argued with the officer, he told her she could either pay the fine or spend three months in jail."

"That's ridiculous," Corvi declares while walking out of the dressing room in the beach pajamas. She's pulled the legs up at the knees so she doesn't trip.

"I agree, but there's an ordinance for men as well. They're prohibited from going shirtless," Daisy explains while bending to pin up the excess hem on Corvi's trousers.

Elizabeth glides through the curtain, the cape loosely draped over her shoulders. She looks gorgeous.

"This ordinance reminds me of the hullabaloo over painted knees a few years ago," she comments.

"I forgot all about that!" I laugh. Some daring young women rolled their stockings below the knees and painted them with cosmetics. I recall newspaper photos of the more artistic designs, including portraits and detailed flowers.

"It took decades for folks to come to terms with exposed ankles. Drawing attention to the knee—brazen debauchery," Daisy chuckles.

"There are some beaches in Europe where bathers don't wear a stitch of clothing," Corvi mentions impishly.

"Are you speaking from experience?" Elizabeth gives her a sidelong glance.

Corvi lowers her head and bats her eyelashes. "A lady never tells."

We all burst into laughter.

I notice a stunning swimsuit with a flying fish on the leg. A gold sunburst fans out from a hidden ring just above the belt, evoking the Moderne style I saw in Paris.

"Ladies, does this belong to one of you?" I show them the inside label which says, "Worn by the Stars of Hollywood."

"That's a Catalina suit," Elizabeth says. "We carried them, along with a few Jantzens, last summer." Before landing her first film role, my friend managed the local dress shop in Fullerton.

"Try it on," Corvi encourages.

Gazing in the floor length mirror of the fitting room, I'm struck by the flattering fit of the bathing suit, which accentuates my curves. I spin around to see that the suit is nearly backless, save for a narrow strap just above the waist. I'd definitely feel confident wearing this in front of Sam.

"Don't leave us hanging," Elizabeth entreats from the other side of the curtain. "We want to see."

I dramatically parade toward the women and turn in a full circle before posing, hand on hip.

"Well done!" Corvi claps.

"Ooh la la!" Elizabeth declares. "You have to buy it!"

Once we've made our selections, Corvi insists on "paying" for our garments as well. This leaves thirty-seven cents for lunch and any additional purchases. As we depart, Daisy begs us to return Thursday.

"I'll be getting a shipment of evening wear from New York. They're perfect for a night at the Cabrillo Ballroom.

Corvi exclaims when we step outside, "I'm famished!"

"I'm not surprised," I comment. "You didn't eat anything for breakfast. Let's get lunch."

We head toward the hotel, passing the grocery store and Rankin's hanging gate. At the triangular intersection between Forest, Park

Avenue, and Coast Highway, someone whistles loudly. It's noon, and the streets are crowded with summer tourists, as well as locals taking their lunch breaks. I'm about to ask Corvi where she'd like to eat, when the whistle repeats, followed by a masculine voice calling, "Corvi!"

The three of us turn around to see Kit jogging toward us with a couple of other young men.

"Kit!" Corvi exclaims. "I wondered who was whistling so rudely," she jests.

"Hi ya, Corvi." Kit's eyes shine with fondness. "Where are you off to?"

"Lunch," Corvi informs him. "Kit, you remember Ruby?"

He nods in my direction then turns toward Elizabeth with an extended hand. "Kit Morris."

"Liz Martin," she shakes his hand. "Nice to meet you."

"She's replacing Lena," Corvi tells him.

His affable expression dims, "Such a terrible thing to happen. And now Rex…"

Corvi sways as though she's about to lose her balance. Kit shoots out an arm to steady her, and she replies, "Thank you. It's all just too much."

"Tell you what." Kit gestures toward his companions. "We're heading to the White House to grab a bite. Do you ladies want to join us?"

"That would be swell," Corvi agrees softly.

CHAPTER 13

"Are you going to introduce us, or shall I guess their names?" Corvi looks toward Kit's comely companions while we wait for a table.

Kit blushes, "Oh…of course. Where are my manners? This is Edwin. I've known him since the first day we started grammar school."

"Nice to meet you, ma'am," the clean-cut fellow with striped slacks bobs his head.

"Ma'am? You make me sound like somebody's mother," Corvi teases.

"Edwin's a pilot with the Coast Guard," Kit comments.

"A pilot?" I inquire.

"That's right," he grins proudly. "I just graduated from the Coast Guard Academy. I hope to pilot flying boats when I return to the East Coast."

Puzzled, Elizabeth asks, "What's a flying boat?"

"A plane that can land on the water," Edwin explains. "Lately, the Coast Guard has been flying them out of Ten Pound Island in Massachusetts to monitor rumrunners. But if you ask me, the flying lifeboats are the future of Coast Guard aviation."

"Let me guess, a plane that lands on water AND carries the injured," Elizabeth guesses.

"You got it! From what I hear, they're building a prototype as we speak. But you didn't hear that from me." He winks.

"So, what brings you back to Laguna? Visiting family?" I ask.

Edwin tilts his head to one side, "Yes, that…" Then he tilts his head to the other side. "And Pancho's airshow."

"An airshow? That's the absolute berries!" Elizabeth exclaims.

"I haven't seen any posters or flyers. When is it?" I inquire.

"She's keeping it under wraps for now but will make an announcement on Friday. It'll be next Monday on Labor Day."

"Jack will be tickled pink," I tell Elizabeth.

"How do you know Pancho Barnes? Our assistant director knows her, but I've never had the pleasure," Corvi mentions. "He promised me an introduction."

"We met when I trespassed on her airstrip a couple of years ago." Edwin nods toward Coast Highway. "I thought she'd hit the roof, but instead she gave me a tour and told me to visit whenever I was in town."

"Pancho's swell," declares the other young man, a keen looking fellow in coveralls with an oval patch on the chest reading "Pacific Plumbing."

"And who might you be?" Corvi raises one perfectly plucked eyebrow in his direction.

"This is Smitty." Kit hitches his thumb toward the plumber. "He's a newcomer."

"We've been pals since second grade!" Smitty gives Kit a playful thump on the shoulder. "It's nice to meet you ladies," he grins.

Kit looks up at the whitewashed walls of the restaurant and lowers his voice. "You know, this place used to have a speakeasy."

"Really?" Elizabeth grins. "Do you know this firsthand?"

"He wishes," Smitty ribs him.

"You should talk," Kit needles back. "You were a spotty-faced teen. They'd have never let you in."

Just then, a tall, sturdily built man with a ruddy complexion brushes past the hostess at the door and approaches us.

"Miss Styles! I am so sorry to keep you standing out here in the heat. Please, come with me."

He gently rests a hand on Corvi's back to escort her inside while motioning for the rest of us to follow. The air inside the white brick building is cool, and I breathe a sigh of relief. The manager—who has introduced himself as "Mr. Bird"—directs us to a round table with a curved booth seat and a couple of generous, padded chairs. I slide around to the center of the booth and notice a sign across the room that reads "Let the Birds feed you."

Clever.

"Julia will be with you shortly. In the meantime, can I interest you in something cold to drink while you look over the menu?"

Kit and Smitty snicker.

"Yes," the rest of us reply.

Within minutes, Julia arrives with our beverages—non-alcoholic, of course—and takes our order. I glance at Elizabeth when Corvi orders vegetable broth and melba toast. My friend mouths the word "Sylvia," then proceeds to order a garden salad with fish on the side. I opt for a crab cake, but forgo the tartar sauce, as it usually contains pickles, which I loathe.

While waiting for our meal, Kit leans across the table toward Corvi, who's seated next to Elizabeth in the other chair. "What do you think they're going to do about Rex?"

Corvi's face falls, and she scoots out of her seat. "I'm sorry, would you please excuse me for a moment?" She heads for the ladies' room.

Kit passes a hand over his face. "I didn't mean to upset her."

"It's alright," I assure him. "This latest news adds insult to injury—no pun intended."

He nods. "Of course."

Edwin disengages from his conversation with Elizabeth and asks, "Are you talking about the surfing accident this morning?"

"I'm not so sure it was an accident," Smitty remarks.

The back of my neck prickles. "What do you mean by that?"

"He was knocked off his board," Smitty proclaims decidedly. "I saw it myself."

Wide-eyed, Elizabeth asks, "You were there?"

"Yeah, I surf there most mornings before work."

"Can you tell us what happened?" I prompt.

"Well, Rex paddled out at sunup with another guy that I recognized—he shows up every so often. Anyway, it wasn't too crowded—being a Monday and all—and the rest of us were regulars. I don't think Rex knew the rules."

"Rules?" I question.

"Surfing rules. I don't know how it is in other places, but we line up to take turns with the sets. Otherwise, we get in each other's way."

"And Rex wasn't taking turns?"

"Not at all. As soon as he paddled back out after a ride, he'd take the next wave that rolled in." Smitty shakes his head. "This made some of the other guys sore, and they started shouting at him."

"Did he realize his mistake?"

"If he did, he didn't care. He just ignored them. His buddy tried to warn him off, but he ignored him too."

"I think I know where this is going," I mutter.

Smitty continues, "Well, they were fed up, so the next time Rex caught a wave, someone dropped in and cut him off. Both he and the board got tossed around in the shore break."

"Sounds like it served him right," Edwin declares.

"I guess so." Kit mulls this over. "But it could leave a lot of people out of work, including me."

"And me," Elizabeth sighs.

"Archie told me that they'll replace him," I mention.

"I hope so, but I wouldn't be surprised if they cancel the film," Kit says with a hangdog expression.

Corvi's voice carries to our table as she signs an autograph and croons to a baby in the arms of his starstruck mother. "Aren't you the sweetest?!"

Julia approaches our table at the same time as Corvi. The young waitress blushes and shifts her weight to manage the two heavy trays of food while Kit settles Corvi's into her chair.

"What a gentleman!" Corvi smiles sweetly.

As we eat lunch, the conversation bounces from one harmless topic to another before landing on movie genres.

"I, for one, love thrillers," Elizabeth pronounces. "Has anyone seen *The Bat Whispers* yet?"

"Ooh, that one had me on the edge of my seat," Edwin admits. "I never guessed that the killer was—"

"Stop right there!" Corvi commands. "I haven't had time to see it yet."

"You like scary movies?" I ask incredulously.

This seems at odds with her sensitive and vulnerable personality. As for me, they're not my cup of tea. Acquainted with the darker side of humanity in real life, I don't find it entertaining on screen.

"Love them!" She continues, "Especially vampire movies. *Nosferatu, London After Midnight...*"

"That Lon Chaney gives me the heebie-jeebies—especially in *He Who Gets Slapped*. I hate clowns!" Elizabeth squeals with a giggle.

"My brother used to read horror books to me. In fact, the last thing he ever sent me was a story he wrote about the London Necropolis Railway," Corvi says wistfully.

Smitty coughs. "NECROPOLIS Railway?"

Corvi nods, "It was a train that carried bodies and their grieving families from London to a cemetery in the Surrey countryside."

"That can't be real!" he insists.

"Oh, but it was. In fact, you can still visit the station in Waterloo. I've been there."

"Did you go there while we were in London," I ask.

She nods. "I wanted Mr. Lake to set a film there—with me as the femme fatale, of course—based on my brother's story."

"I'm intrigued," Smitty leans forward. "Tell me more about this story."

Corvi straightens her back and begins her soliloquy.

"In the spirit of those great gothic masterpieces from the last century, this film would center on the love story between a specter and an innocent young woman whom he watches while she visits her mother's grave at Brookwood Cemetery each week. He tries to leave her messages scrawled in the dust covering the grave, but to no avail— she never notices them. At night he rides the London Necropolis Railway, pining and planning a way for them to be together, when he finally realizes that the only thing keeping them apart is the one thing that can join them for all eternity."

"Death," Elizabeth murmurs softly.

"Death." Corvi continues, "So, he sets about bringing an end to her time on Earth only to be thwarted by her fiancé—a gallant young officer with the British Army—who one day spies the specter and warns the young woman against visiting the cemetery unaccompanied. Over several romantic scenes, the young couple make plans for their life together and eventually return to the grave to share the news with her deceased mother. However, before they can be married, the officer tragically dies in battle. Devastated, the young woman takes her own life so that she can be with her beloved, but as she draws her last breath, she is met by the specter and realizes that she's doomed to ride the London Necropolis Railway with him—not her love—for all eternity."

No one speaks for several moments. I am immediately struck by the parallels between the specter and Corvi's stalker. I'm also startled by her enthusiastic summary of the morbid narrative—she reminds me of a little girl gleefully sharing a frightening tale while staying overnight with a friend. Then it hits me—she was very young when she first read her brother's story. For her, this is a tale from her youth written by, of all people, her childhood hero. I doubt she sees the connection with her current plight.

"Spooky!" Elizabeth pronounces with delight. "I hope Mr. Lake agreed to make the film."

Corvi shakes her head. "He liked the story but said it would be too expensive." She pouts. "Ike said it's for the best. He was against the idea from the outset."

"Hmph," Kit grunts. "It's none of my business, but it seems to me that Ike holds you back. I don't like the way he treats you."

Corvi waves a hand and laughs, "He's fine. All bark and no bite."

"I'm not kidding, Corvi. You could easily find another agent." His earnestness reveals his deep affection for the actress.

"He's more than that," she looks at him sternly. "I owe him. He made me."

The words "I made you" echo in my mind.

"And he cares for me. Truly he does." It's unclear whether she's trying to convince Kit or herself.

Perhaps both.

Smitty looks at his wristwatch with alarm. "It's after one. I gotta be heading back."

"Don't worry about the check," Kit holds out an arm to stop Smitty from dropping coins onto the table. "I got it."

"Thanks! You're a pal!" Smitty slides out of the booth to leave. "It was nice meeting all of you."

"I'll be just a moment," I tell the group and follow him to the door.

"Say, Smitty. Can I ask you a few questions about Rex? I'll walk you out."

Taken aback, he stammers, "Sure. I guess."

"Is it possible that someone could have put that local surfer up to knocking Rex off of his board?" I query as we head toward the door.

"Well, I suppose one of the other guys could have told him to do it."

"Not one of the surfers—someone else before any of you went in the water."

Smitty scratches the back of his head. "I don't see how. The only other person around was Bebe."

I must have rocked backwards because Smitty lends a hand to steady me. "Bebe Gish?" I spit out. "What was she doing there?"

A roguish grin flashes on Smitty's face which he buries behind a cupped hand. "We sort of…met last night at the Cabrillo."

"Oh?" I immediately put the pieces together. "Oh! I see."

"Yes. Exactly."

"To be honest, I'm surprised she went along with you this morning. I wouldn't have pegged her for an early morning sort of person," I comment.

"Let's just say we were already there before sunup," he smirks.

"I see." I reframe my inquiry. "Was there any way Bebe could have…encouraged…the other surfer to cause Rex's accident?"

He frowns. "Why would she want to? I mean, there's no question that she's nuts, but she doesn't have it in for Rex or anything. Corvi's the one she kept going on about."

"In what way?"

"For one, she kept insisting that Corvi's older than she looks. Can you imagine? I mean, Bebe's gotta be in her forties. Don't get me wrong—Bebe's a looker, that's for sure, and very enthusiastic, if you catch my meaning."

I stare at him blankly. Of course, I catch his meaning. But I detest this sort of masculine braggadocio and refuse to give him the embarrassed blush or conspiratorial snicker that he's hoping for.

"But Corvi's younger than me," he continues, unfazed. "In fact, Corvi could be her daughter," he reasons.

Now, I'm pretty good at judging someone's age, and without all the makeup, I would guess that Bebe is around thirty. But Smitty's right on one count—Corvi can't be any older than twenty. In fact, I'd go so far as to say she's eighteen. Bebe's claim to the contrary sounds like more jealous rhetoric. That being said, just a few months ago two women died in this very town because of jealousy. I wouldn't put anything past Bebe.

"Not that Bebe and I are an item or anything. Just a bit of fun, that's all—"

"Thanks for your help, Smitty. I won't keep you any longer." I'm sure I've gotten what I need from him.

After Smitty trots down Coast Avenue, the rest of the group exit the restaurant. Elizabeth and Edwin walk toward me, but Corvi and Kit appear to be deep in conversation—her brows raised with alarm.

"I can't do that, Kit. I just can't," she insists.

"Can't do what?" A gruff voice demands. Ike has joined the group and is shooting daggers at Kit.

"What? Oh...nothing." Corvi says with a forced smile. "Kit wants us all to drive up the coast."

I'm quite sure their conversation had nothing to do with sightseeing and everything to do with Ike.

The manager wedges his cigar between his lips and says, "Well, I'm glad I caught you, Corvi. I'm heading to LA for a meeting." He then asks me, "Do you still have enough clams?"

I stare at him, perplexed.

"Cash," he enunciates loudly.

"Oh, we're hunky-dory. Don't worry about us," Corvi answers before I have a chance to admit that we've already exhausted the fifty dollars he gave me.

"Well, alright then," Ike says, satisfied. He turns to leave but not before narrowing his eyes at Kit. Looking both ways, Ike hurries across the busy road.

And that's when I spot him—a man of average height with a dark brown Homburg is leaning against a lamppost across the highway, about a quarter of a block from where Ike stepped onto the sidewalk.

And he's watching us.

"Corvi…is that—?" I begin to ask, just as Corvi cries out, "It's him!"

Kit spots him too and narrowly dodges cars as he sprints across the street. A cacophony of ear-splitting honks, beeps, even an *ah-oo-ga*, bounces off of the buildings that line Coast Highway. Meanwhile, the man removes his Homburg and casually walks along the small drive alongside the Hotel Laguna.

"He's over there," Corvi screams while frantically pointing at the retreating stalker.

Distracted by Corvi's shouting, Kit has almost reached the curb when a weathered convertible Ford—easily fifteen years old—swerves around a car that has stopped for Kit to pass. Three teenagers are crowded upon the single bench seat, all wearing the same saucer-eyed expression while their vehicle screeches to a stop mere inches from the young actor. He pounds on the hood with a fist, then races toward the side of the hotel. When the remaining four of us have safely crossed the street and rushed along the front of the building, Kit emerges, his face crestfallen.

"I don't know how he did it," he clenches his jaw. "He just disappeared."

"But you saw him!" Corvi exclaims. "You all saw him!"

I pat her back. "Yes, we saw him, and it was clear that he was watching us."

Edwin claps Kit's back and nods toward the highway, "That was a close call, buddy."

Kit chuckles, "I think I dented their hood."

"What's one more dent on a tin lizzie like that?" Edwin jokes

Corvi's eyes dart left and right scanning the busy sidewalk until finally resting upon a police officer—and not just any policeman. This one happens to be Officer Jankowski. He strolls toward us, recognition in his eyes.

"I should've known I'd find you here," he says to me with an exasperated tone.

"Good afternoon, Officer Jankowski. Did you happen to see a man with a brown Homburg heading alongside the hotel?" I ask hopefully.

He raises his bushy eyebrows. "With all that honking? I didn't notice much beyond the commotion that this young man caused."

Kit gulps. "I'm sorry, officer. I was trying to chase down the man who's been following Corvi."

The petite actress steps in front of him. "It's true. He was trying to catch the stalker."

Recognizing Corvi, Jankowski's expression softens. "Stalker? It seems I heard something about this yesterday."

Corvi's eyes well with tears. "That's right."

"He walked down there. Then he disappeared." Kit gestures toward the diminutive drive.

"The beach is packed." The policeman points toward the boardwalk. "He probably raced down the steps and got lost in the crowd. Did anyone get a good look at him?"

"I did," Kit answers. "He's several inches shorter than me. I'd say he's about five-nine or five-ten."

"And he has ash colored hair," Elizabeth adds.

"Facial features?" The officer jots the descriptions in a small, tattered notebook he's pulled from the breast pocket of his uniform.

"Hooded eyes and a weak chin," I describe. "He was wearing suspenders—they were barely hidden by his unbuttoned coat."

"Anything else?"

Corvi makes a pinching motion with her thumb and forefinger. "His eyes are close together."

When he finishes scribbling, Officer Jankowski looks in my direction. "You mentioned threatening notes yesterday? I don't suppose you can tell me what they said."

With a breathy voice, Corvi recites the puzzling lines, which sound far less threatening when spoken aloud. The red ink renders them more menacing.

Suppressing a smile, the officer peers at her with amusement. "Little lady, they're not threatening. In fact, they sound like love notes from a soppy fan. How do you know that the guy you all described is the one who sent them?"

"Each time I received a note, I saw him sometime that same day— it must be him!" Corvi says fervently.

"Just a coincidence," Officer Jankowski replies dismissively.

"Corvi saw the man in France and New York. The first note arrived when she was in Manhattan. He's followed her around the world. Surely, you can see why all this is concerning," Kit pleads.

"Are you sure it's the same guy?" the officer squints at Corvi.

"I think so," Corvi picks at her thumbnail with her index finger. "It has to be."

I understand Officer Jankowski's suspicion. In fact, Corvi's inability to provide a solid description prior to the sighting Saturday evening makes me doubt whether the man with the Homburg was the same person—or people—she spotted elsewhere. My mind flits to her brother's story about the specter secretly watching a young woman. This idea was planted in her consciousness years ago. For all I know, she may have developed a paranoia, albeit subconsciously, about being stalked. Furthermore, I'm not convinced that the man we just saw is the same person sending her the notes—particularly since no one has witnessed their delivery.

Shaking his head, Officer Jankowski declares, "Doesn't sound like you're in any danger. I'm sure it's a nuisance to be followed around by fans, but as far as I'm concerned, that goes with the business. You can't expect the police to do anything about it. If you don't like it, hire more security."

Corvi gasps, and Kit exclaims, "Now see here…"

Ignoring them both, the officer informs me, "I called Fullerton PD yesterday afternoon and spoke with Sergeant Blockhurst."

Unable to read his flat tone, I ask uneasily, "What did he have to say?"

"He said you won him over."

I relax. "I'm glad to hear it."

"He also said you're a pain in the keister." Jankowski's mouth twitches with the hint of a grin, as he props his billy club on his shoulder and saunters back in the direction of the boardwalk.

Edwin nudges Kit. "Hey pal, I gotta get going. I promised my kid sister that I'd take her pier fishing this afternoon."

The two men exchange farewells, then Kit asks Corvi, "Can I walk you back to the hotel? I know all of this has been very upsetting."

Corvi thoughtfully considers his offer, then replies, "I think I'd like to take a walk, if that's alright with everyone. The fresh air will do me wonders."

After meandering south alongside the highway for about a half of a mile, Kit tentatively wraps an arm around Corvi's back, she leans into him and rests her head on his shoulder. His spine straightens, and he walks proudly—not like a movie star, but like a boy on his first date. It's very sweet and reminds me that, at their core, celebrities are no different from the rest of us.

"Look at this!" Elizabeth stops in front of a narrow, single-story building which, from the front, appears to be windowless. A hand with an eye on its palm is painted upon its indigo door, and a small sign hangs from the knob reading *Come in.*

"Well, that's new," Kit comments.

"What do you think?" Elizabeth asks. "Do you want to give it a go?"

"I've had my fill of psychics for the summer, but I'll go along if the rest of you are interested," I reply.

"It's a great idea!" Corvi declares unexpectedly.

I'm not so sure about that.

Entering the dimly lit parlor, my senses are assaulted by an earthy, musky fragrance, possibly coming from the flickering pillar candles resting on the wall sconces. An assortment of pillows and bolsters with brightly patterned cases cover the perimeter of the floor, where a small circular table—barely knee-high—rests in the center. A spotless glass orb, about the size of a cantaloupe, sits on a dark wood plinth and takes up nearly a third of the table's surface, while a deck of hand-sized cards rests to the side.

"Welcome," greets an ethereal voice from the next room, and a tall, thin woman with wispy blonde hair seems to float through the open door, her footsteps light beneath her long, layered skirts.

"I am Madam Ulyana. Please, make yourselves comfortable." She motions toward the cushions, then seats herself at the table.

Elizabeth plops herself onto a cushion opposite the soothsayer. The rest of us sit behind her on firm pillows.

"What brings you here today? Shall we consult the Tarot? Perhaps a natal chart reading? Or would you like to speak with someone who's crossed over?" The psychic's pitch rises and falls dramatically.

"I'd like to know my future," Elizabeth proclaims.

"Ah," Madam Ulyana's eyes glow, as she waves her hands over the crystal ball. "This Sacred Orb materialized before my grandmother when she visited the ancient Temple of Dola. Only those with the Sight can discover the Temple." She emphasizes the first sound of the words *sacred, temple,* and *sight.* "Place your hands above the Sacred Orb."

Elizabeth lowers her hands within an inch of the ball's surface, when Madam Ulyana suddenly commands, "Do not touch it!"

My friend flinches and raises her hands.

"You do not possess the Sight," the psychic's voice relaxes. "Your earthly body would not tolerate the numinous power of the Sacred Orb."

I roll my eyes. This mystical mumbo jumbo reminds me of the letter I found a few months ago that was written by Dottie's mathematics teacher and, ultimately, helped me locate where she and her friends were trapped.

"Would you like to know about love…money…" Madam Ulyana's perceptive eyes bore into Elizabeth's.

"My career," she replies decisively.

"Are you sure?" The psychic intones. "Because I see white lace…a veil…and rice—a showering of rice."

Elizabeth turns toward me with a look of amazement, until I nod toward the sparkle of her engagement ring. She frowns and refocuses upon Madam Ulyana.

"Yes, I'm sure."

Gazing upon the crystal surface, the medium's eyelids droop, as her torso weaves side to side with a serpentine rhythm. The room is silent. We wait—some more expectantly than others. After what feels like several minutes, Madam Ulyana opens her eyes and, with a shocked expression, announces, "The Sacred Orb wishes to convey a message to someone else. I'm sorry my dear, but I have no answers for you today. Perhaps if you'd like to come back tomorrow."

Disappointed, Elizabeth scoots away from the table and sits between Kit and I.

"Who's the message for?" Corvi eagerly inquires.

"One whose mind is closed to the Empyrean realm." The psychic's eyelids droop once more.

"That'd be me." I raise my hand like a schoolgirl.

"I see a great churning in the depths. Creatures scatter, for they know the danger that is coming." Her eyes fly open and stare directly at me. "Take heed, lest forces beneath the surface carry you away!"

Forces beneath the surface.

I shiver.

"What about me?" Corvi begs and hastens toward the table.

Madam Ulyana gathers the deck of cards in her hands, shuffles, then places the deck before Corvi.

"Cut them," she instructs.

Corvi's tiny hands grasp the upper third of the cards, which she sets to the side. After which, the fortune teller gathers the larger stack and puts them on top of the smaller pile. She turns over the top card and places it face down on the table.

"Past," she utters meaningfully.

She repeats this process with the next two cards—calling "Present" and "Future"—then flips over the Past card. It depicts a man carrying an armful of swords.

"Seven of Swords," Madam Ulyana intones. "Someone has deceived you in your past."

She draws a new card from the deck and places it, face up, above the card with the swords. The card is upside down and features a beautiful woman with a crown and scepter resting against a pile of pillows.

"The Empress reversed…hmm…"

The psychic looks gravely at Corvi but says nothing more. Next, she flips over the card in the middle of the row. It, too, is upside down and shows a different crowned woman sitting on a throne with a black cat at her feet.

"The Queen of Wands reversed. This is your Present."

Above this she places a new card that she has drawn—The Moon.

"The cards show that you are going through a difficult time. There is fear and insecurity."

"Yes," Corvi nods, tears rolling down her face. "Very much so."

Madam Ulyana turns over the last card—the Future—and says dramatically, "The King of Cups reversed. I need more details."

She quickly draws another card from the deck and places it above the King of Cups. Even to someone like me who is unfamiliar with the Tarot, I immediately recognize the card.

"Death!" Corvi shrieks and bolts through the front door with Kit close behind.

CHAPTER 14

"I regret suggesting that we visit the psychic," Elizabeth confesses as we walk back to the hotel.

By the time I paid Madam Ulyana, Corvi and Kit were nowhere to be seen.

"Don't beat yourself up about it," I assure her. "It seemed like a good idea at the time—something to take Corvi's mind off of everything."

"I wish she'd stayed to hear what Madam Ulyana had to say about the Death card," she muses.

The psychic explained that the card most likely pertained to endings and profound changes, not physical death. Given Lena's drowning, however, I can understand why Corvi was so distressed when the card was revealed.

"What do you make of the King of Cups business?" Elizabeth asks.

"Well, since it was reversed, Madam Ulyana predicted emotional instability in Corvi's future."

"I'd say that pretty well describes her present too," my friend comments.

"You're right about that."

Elizabeth says thoughtfully, "I'm curious, though—who deceived her in the past?"

"I'm sure there's a lot of deception in the film industry."

"And how," she agrees. "But when I asked about the other past card, The Empress, Madam Ulyana said it had to do with pregnancy and maternal care."

"I think that card was upside down. What does that mean?"

"Hmm..." She quirks her mouth in thought. "What would be the opposite of pregnancy and maternal care?"

"Miscarriage maybe? Unwanted pregnancy? Maternal abuse or neglect?" I ponder.

"Maybe." She shrugs.

"Sorry that your reading was derailed," I apologize.

"Yours was far more interesting!" Elizabeth declares.

"I'll tell you what's interesting—Madam Ulyana's words were nearly identical to what a psychic told me on Coney Island about a week ago."

"Oh, so that's what you meant when you said you've had your fill of psychics," Elizabeth realizes.

I nod. "She said, 'Beware or forces beneath the surface may sweep you away!'"

"That's a creepy coincidence but still pretty vague," Elizabeth says.

"Perhaps. But Madam Ulyana was a bit more specific. She also mentioned creatures and a 'churning in the depths.'"

"That sounds like forces in the ocean to me," she remarks. "Like riptides."

"Exactly," I concur.

She laughs. "You know, we could get carried away analyzing the predictions of Madam Ulyana, but I think these mediums have a handful of obscure readings that they use over and over because they apply to almost everyone."

"I think you may be right. And it's no surprise that two different seaside psychics referred to the ocean in one way or another."

"Ruby!" A voice calls from across the street.

"Hey ya, Dottie! Long time no see." Elizabeth calls out while Iris and my cousin, both on bicycles, carefully cross the busy highway.

"Hi Elizabeth," Dottie answers. "How exciting that you get to work on the film!"

My friend beams. "Even though I'm a stunt double, I'm thrilled to be working with Corvi and Mr. Lake."

"This is just the beginning." Dottie praises, "We'll see your face on a movie poster in no time."

"From your lips to God's ears." She smiles. "And who is this?"

"Oh, this is Iris—we met a few days ago. She's a student at Pomona College who's studying sea anemones here for the summer at the Marine Lab." Dottie turns toward Iris. "This is Elizabeth. She's a very talented actress and has been Ruby's friend since high school."

"Nice to meet you," Iris waves.

"You as well," Elizabeth returns the greeting. "So, where are you off to this afternoon?"

"We visited a few tidepools down south," Dottie explains, shifting the camera strap away from her shoulder so she can scratch an itch.

"How did it go?" I inquire.

The young women frown at one another before Iris answers, "The numbers were stable at two of the sites, but we didn't find any specimens below the Coast Inn."

"Is that unexpected?" Elizabeth asks.

"This species of anemone don't tend to move around much," Iris explains. "So, their sudden decline is alarming."

"There weren't any crabs or snails either," Dottie reports and claws at her upper arm.

"Still itchy? I hoped the oatmeal would help." I'm concerned that these bites aren't getting any better.

"Me too." She looks deflated. "I'm going to try it again as soon as I get back."

"Well, please don't let us keep you," I urge. "You look quite uncomfortable."

As the girls cycle away, Elizabeth observes, "Look at Dottie, all grown up and leaving the nest."

"I know." I reflect solemnly, "It's like a chapter is ending."

"How do you feel about that?" she asks thoughtfully.

"In truth, I'm worried about her. She's been having night terrors and doesn't want to talk about it."

"That's not too surprising. I'm sure she's nervous about moving away and starting college." She shares, "My brother's having a difficult time as well. He leaves for medical school next week."

"Hopefully, that's all it is," I sigh. "But given everything she went through this spring, I'm not so sure."

"You've seemed a bit out of sorts yourself since I arrived." She grabs my arm and spins me, so we are face to face. "What's really going on with you, Ruby?"

"I don't know." I shake my head. "I've been trying to figure that out myself. Ever since I got back from my trip, I've felt restless—like I want more out of my life—which is, of course, ridiculous. I'm so fortunate to have a stable, loving family, financial independence, and a career I enjoy."

"But…"

"I feel like trying something daring or challenging, but I have no idea what that might be," I admit.

"Do you want to go back to school?" Elizabeth asks. "Perhaps you're a little envious about Dottie's new chapter."

"What? The thought hadn't even crossed my mind," I answer honestly.

However, as our feet shuffle along the sandy sidewalk, I contemplate this possibility. I was never able to complete a four-year degree after studying English and logic at Fullerton Junior College. And since FJC shared the same campus as my high school, I never had the "going away to college" experience. At the time, Uncle Charles needed my help with Dottie and Jack, who were quite young, and I just wasn't emotionally prepared to move away from them.

Elizabeth wipes her brow when we reach the hotel. "It's really heating up out here."

"Let's wait in the lobby for a bit before going upstairs to check on Corvi. After all, Kit's with her."

Elizabeth winks, "Good idea."

A few minutes after we get settled on a cushioned sofa, the desk clerk greets us and asks if we'd like a cold beverage. We enthusiastically accept. The clerk rings a bell for Vinny who—after listening to the clerk's instructions—walks briskly through the lobby toward the formal restaurant at the back of the hotel.

"It'll just be a moment," the desk clerk smiles obsequiously.

After he's walked away, I tell Elizabeth, "That's some service. I've never been offered a drink in a hotel lobby before."

We're discussing our hotel experiences—good and bad—when Elizabeth comments, "Well, look at that. Someone works long hours."

Still in her staff uniform, Poppy walks behind the front desk, past the clerk, and enters the office. Meanwhile, Vinny returns, balancing two glasses of iced tea on a round tray. He cranes his neck to watch Poppy and nearly stumbles over the coffee table centered in front of the couch.

"Easy there," Elizabeth cautions.

"Perhaps you should set down the tray," I suggest.

Vinny blushes and places two round coasters on the coffee table followed by the tall glasses, both dripping with condensation. "Can I get you anything else?"

"No, this is perfect." I fish for a quarter in my coin purse and hand it to the young man.

"Gee!" His face turns a deep red. "Thanks so much!" He rushes to open the front door for Poppy, who has emerged from the office.

"Use the employee exit!" the desk clerk shouts to the pair. "They'll never learn," he mumbles to himself.

"What time did you say she knocked on the living room door this morning?" I reach for my glass.

"Around six. She brought a tonic for Corvi. You should have heard her gushing. I wouldn't have been surprised if she prostrated herself."

I giggle and sip the refreshing drink. "But you said the order was a mistake."

"That's right. I opened my door to see what was going on, but Corvi was already there. She told the girl that the tonic was Lena's. Then Poppy asked if she wanted it anyway. Corvi made a face and told her to take it away," Elizabeth recounts. "I guess Lena drank it each morning before she went for a swim."

My neck tingles. "Did you see the tonic?"

Elizabeth sticks out her tongue. "It was a vile greenish brown color."

"Any idea what it was?"

"Who knows. One of my roommates used to drink all sorts of revolting concoctions for 'health' reasons. Why do you ask?" She squints, as though she's trying to read my thoughts.

"I find it a bit suspect."

"Talk about suspect, Bebe practically threatened Corvi at the dress shop this morning," Elizabeth scowls.

"That wasn't the first time she's taken a swipe at Corvi since I've been here." I tell her about my encounters with Bebe over the weekend and what Archie said about her jealousy.

"Well, if anyone should be sore, it should be me," she fumes.

"Why is that?"

"The racket from her late-night hanky-panky carried through the wall between our rooms." She pretends to gag.

"What time was that?" I extract my notepad and pen from my handbag.

"Around midnight. When they left, she and her fella carried on all the way down the hall."

I look up from my notes. "Did you hear her return?"

"Not a peep. I slept soundly until Poppy's early morning visit."

"What if I told you that her gentleman caller was Smitty," I give her a knowing look and recount the plumber's testimony.

"Well, well, well. So, they were heading to the beach for the rest of the night." Her eyes narrow. "You don't think…"

"I know what you're thinking, but it's unlikely she had anything to do with Rex's accident." I add, "However, I'm not ruling anything out at this point."

"My room is perfectly situated for spying on Bebe," she comments. "I'll keep an eye on things."

"Be careful, for Pete's sake!" I caution.

She flaps her hand dismissively. "You're not the only one who knows how to snoop."

I finish my tea. "Do you have dinner plans later?"

"As a matter of fact, I do," she smirks slyly. "Dean's coming to town and should be here in a couple of hours. He's got nothing going on this week and wants to be on hand in case I have some downtime."

My body relaxes. With Dean here, I'll worry less about Elizabeth's safety. "So…is he staying with you?" I ask her pointedly.

Her eyes widen with mock indignation. "Of course not! I'm a professional!"

I laugh. "Well, I can't wait to meet him."

Her eyes sparkle. "I have a great idea! How about a double date tomorrow night? That ballroom looks swell!"

"I'd love that!" I'm eager to be in Sam's arms on the dance floor once again.

"Thank goodness I found you two," Archie approaches us with a strained expression, his bowtie askew and shirtsleeves rolled.

"How's Rex?" I inquire immediately .

"He's pretty doped up on painkillers, but he'll live," he grimaces. "Damn lucky, though! If the board hit his head…"

"I spoke with someone who was there this morning. It sounds like another surfer deliberately cut him off," I remark.

He nods, "Yeah, that's what Pete said. Fool! Sounds like Rex asked for it."

"I hate to bring this up, but have you had any luck filling his shoes?" Elizabeth queries.

"Nope," Archie clenches his jaw.

I change the topic to one no less troubling but necessary all the same. "I have some concerns about Bebe."

Archie closes his eyes and audibly releases a breath through his nose. "What now?"

I tell him about her veiled threat, as well as her presence this morning during Rex's accident. "Is there any chance that, somehow, she's behind these calamities?"

His eyes crease with amusement. "Are you serious? Bebe is all talk and no cider."

"Okay, let me ask you another question. What type of tonic was Lena drinking each morning?"

He blinks, puzzled. "Tonic?" After a moment's thought, he exclaims, "Oh! Laguna Breeze!"

"Laguna Breeze?"

He laughs. "The hotel wants a celebrity endorsement from Corvi for their 'freshly made, natural restorative.' It's some God-awful brew of kelp, seagrass, coffee, and who knows what else."

"But Corvi said the tonic was for Lena," Elizabeth interjects.

"Corvi agreed to try it, but after one sip, she refused to drink any more. She said it was too bitter. Lena actually liked the stuff, though. The hotel keeps sending it up hoping Corvi will change her mind."

"Ruby, if you don't mind, I'd like to freshen up before Dean gets here," Elizabeth says.

"Of course! Go on upstairs." I make a shooing motion with my hands.

"I should head up to check on Corvi." Archie starts to walk away, but I stop him.

"There are a few more things I want to discuss with you, if that's alright."

He takes Elizabeth's spot on the sofa beside me. "I'm all ears."

I tell him about the stalker, as well as our discussion with Officer Jankowski.

"I'm not surprised he gave Corvi the brush-off." I sense that Archie is relieved the policeman didn't want to get involved.

"I get the impression that he didn't take the situation seriously." I divulge, "I have my own doubts about whether the man we saw was, indeed, the same person Corvi spotted in Europe and New York—or even at her house, for that matter."

"But what about the notes? They've coincided with each sighting," he points out.

"Perhaps. But I'm not convinced that the man we saw is the one sending them." I share my speculation that she may be fixated on this idea of a stalker due to her brother's story.

"The London Necropolis Railway!" Archie spouts. "What a day that was!"

"What happened?" I lean forward.

"Mr. Lake wanted nothing to do with it, but somehow Corvi persuaded him to take a look at the station when we were in England.

I went along but had a touch of a stomach bug and was miserable the whole time."

"Corvi said Mr. Lake liked the idea but that it would be too expensive," I comment.

"That's just what he told her, but the truth is, that story was too sappy for him." Archie lowers his tone. "Plus, Ike pulled Mr. Lake aside and told him it would be a big mistake."

"Really?! Why?"

"He said it would be too upsetting for Corvi." Archie stands and shakes the folds from his trousers. "Anyway, I should check in with her before heading to my room."

"Kit may still be there with her." I rise and realize just how exhausted I am. "I may stay put at the house for the rest of the day, unless you need me."

"Hopefully, there won't be any more drama today," he crosses his fingers.

"I'm back," I shout, trying to block Puck from escaping through the front door.

"In here," she calls from the office.

I find Dottie lying flat on her back in shorts and a sleeveless blouse. Every visible bit of skin is covered with thick oatmeal poultice. Puck hops onto the cot and licks her cheek. I quickly scoop up the furry imp, despite his squirming to be released.

"Is it helping?"

"Not really," Dottie moans. "I must have gotten more bites today at the tidepools—that, or they're spreading somehow."

I examine her neck then lift her shirt to expose her belly. Both are now covered in welts.

"Maybe they're not bites," I suggest. "I wonder if you're allergic to Puck."

She tugs at her shirt. "I don't see how. Polly's had a cat for years, and I've never had a problem."

"Well, just in case, Puck should sleep in the bathroom tonight," I declare.

She sits up. "Are you kidding? He'll cry all night!"

"You have a point." I release the writhing bundle to the floor.

"Before I forget, you had a call a little while ago," Dottie reclines and reaches down to pet the kitten.

"Really? Who was it?"

She flashes a roguish grin. "Guess!"

My heart thumps. "Sam?!"

"Sorry about the oatmeal mush on the receiver!" Dottie shouts as I rush to the phone.

"Good afternoon, Dr. Carroll's office. How can I help you?" a friendly woman answers.

"Hello, I have a message that Dr. Armstrong phoned."

"May I tell him who's calling?" she inquires politely.

"This is Ruby Ray."

"Thank you, Miss Ray." Her amused tone implies a grin. "He's finishing with a patient and will speak with you shortly."

Joining me, Puck weaves between my feet, then jumps upon the desk. When I pull the cord out of his reach, he mews in protest and begins nibbling at the fur on one of his forelegs. I'm sure Dottie is listening from the other room.

"Ruby!" A warm lightness radiates along my spine and outward through my limbs. He sounds delighted to hear from me. "I'm so glad you called back."

"It's great to hear your voice. So much has happened, it feels like weeks, not days, since I last saw you," I reply.

"I feel the same way…" he pauses, "which is why I'd like to stop by before heading off to my night shift. I know we set up a date for tomorrow even—"

"I'd love that!" I interject before he can finish. "I could have dinner ready for you."

He laughs, "I hadn't even thought about dinner, but now that you mention it…"

"What time will you be here?"

"How about five?" He lowers his voice. "I'd make it sooner, but there are still a few patients waiting."

My mind races.

What was I thinking?

I can't cook!

It's 3:30 right now, and all we have are eggs, bread, and sandwich fixings.

I wonder if he likes peanut butter.

I'll need to change and fix my hair.

Oh my gosh, my hair!

I'm sure it looks horrid, and there's no time to set it!

I take a deep belly breath and answer serenely, "Of course. Five would be fine."

"I didn't have time to pick up flowers, but one of my patients brought me these." Sam hands me a sack filled with plums while walking through the front door. "They're from her tree."

I accept the brown paper bag and breathe in the sweet fragrance of the dark purple fruit. "Thank you. They're lovely!"

"One of the perks of GPs," he quips.

"I thought we'd sit under the sycamore in the front yard. It's stuffy indoors," I explain.

"That sounds perfect!" He tugs his collar. "The ceiling fans in Dr. Carroll's office aren't particularly helpful when the office is full of patients."

"Have a seat while I finish dishing the food." I motion toward the couch.

As soon as he's seated, Puck leaps directly onto his lap. "Well, look who we have here. Have you been behaving yourself today?"

"Surprisingly, yes," Dottie answers as she enters the living room. She's wiped away the oatmeal, so the bright pink spots are visible all over her face, neck, and limbs.

Sam does a double take. "What's happened to you?"

"I think it was those biting flies near the tidepools." She scratches her chin.

"How long were you at the beach?" he asks with concern.

"A couple of hours yesterday." She looks down at her legs. "Maybe three hours today. It's gotten worse."

"Would you mind if I take a closer look?" He walks over and positions her under an overhead lamp to carefully examine her arms and face.

"Puck! Stop that!" Dottie's head is still while Sam scrutinizes her forehead, but her eyes are trained on the kitten.

I watch as the tiny feline furiously nibbles at his hip. "How long has he been doing that?"

"He started last night," Dottie answers.

"Look at this," Sam extends Dottie's arm and draws our attention to several bites along her wrist. "See how there are three or four bites in a row?"

"Yes, I see that. And look, there are other rows of bites on her legs," I point.

"What are they," Dottie asks, wide-eyed.

"Flea bites," Sam answers.

"Fleas?!" Dottie and I bellow.

"I'm afraid so. Come here, you little rascal," Sam lifts Puck and begins running two fingers against the direction of the fur around his ears. Suddenly, he pinches and announces, "Gotcha!" while holding up the flattened form of a small brown insect.

I lose my appetite.

"But he's an indoor cat," Dottie exclaims.

"An indoor cat who's been outside a couple of times since we arrived," I remind her.

Sam places Puck on the floor and brushes off his clothes. "Well, the first thing to do is take care of Dottie's lesions. Do you have any calamine lotion?"

"I'll check in the bathroom," Dottie offers.

"How do we get rid of them?" I ask with dismay.

Sam jots down a list of instructions, and my stomach twists as I envision how I'll be spending my evening.

"Found it!" Dottie re-enters the living room with an orange and yellow box in her hand.

"Good! Dab some of that on each of your spots," he directs. "If you stop by the office tomorrow, I can give you a stronger cream that should do the trick. And pick up some alum powder at the drugstore for the rugs, furniture, and anything that can't be washed."

"In the meantime, you belong in the bathroom," I tell Puck.

"You two go eat," Dottie suggests and reaches for the kitten. "I can take care of things here."

"Do you still have time?" I ask Sam hopefully.

He looks at his wristwatch. "I've got about twenty minutes. I'll help you carry the plates outside."

"So, how do you feel about breakfast for dinner?" I ask apprehensively.

CHAPTER 15

~ 🪷 ~

TUESDAY, AUGUST 26, 1930

Even better than I dreamed.

These words float along the tide of my consciousness as I surface from deep sleep. I can still feel his breath upon my ear as he whispered them to me after our first kiss. Light streams in through a crack between the curtains and warms the bed where it lands. I stretch my arms and glance at the bedside clock which, for some reason, isn't ticking. That's when I remember the cotton I shoved into my ears at 2:00 a.m. to block out the woeful caterwauling coming from the bathroom. After a rather brutal bath—brutal for Dottie, not for Puck—we thought it best for Dottie to sleep without the kitten, particularly since her arms and chest were riddled with both flea bites and scratches.

It's nine o'clock, and I really should be getting up, but I'd much rather lie here and relive the brief but memorable dinner I had with Sam. Thankfully, I reached Nan on the phone yesterday afternoon, and she explained how to make French toast. Overall, I was pleased with the results, but not without a burn on my arm from the splattering butter. Sam absolutely loved the meal and told me it reminded him of the breakfasts his grandmother makes for him whenever he visits. Between bites, I filled him in about Rex's injury and our encounter with Corvi's stalker.

"This sounds dangerous, Ruby," he remarked, his voice laden with concern.

"It goes with the job," I replied breezily.

He flinched, probably recalling my attack last spring. "That it does."

"Well, piracy and money laundering aren't exactly tame," I joked, redirecting the conversation. "Speaking of which, how did it go at the morgue?"

"I'm glad you brought that up." He set his empty plate on the grass beside his chair. "I took a look at Miss Young's body and immediately noticed the risus sardonicus and opisthotonus."

"I'm afraid you've lost me. Risus and opistho what?"

"Sorry about that," he apologized. "My grandma's always telling me to 'speak English' when I discuss my work with her. Risus sardonicus is a grin that happens when the facial muscles spasm for a prolonged period, and opisthotonus means that the spine arched backward, and the limbs were rigid. These are all indications that Miss Young was having some sort of convulsion when she died. Then rigor mortis locked those postures into a fixed position," he explained.

"Convulsion? Like a seizure?" I wondered if Lena suffered from some sort of neurological condition.

"Possibly—but the first thing that comes to mind is tetanus. There are other medical conditions that can cause this—such as meningitis or encephalitis—but they don't typically result in sudden death."

"I'd imagine that her lungs filled with fluid while she was having the convulsion. The witnesses said she was thrashing about in the water and got tangled up in the kelp," I commented.

At that point, Sam looked at me evenly. "The coroner conducted a full autopsy today and called me a little while ago. There was very little fluid in the lungs."

My jaw dropped. "She didn't drown?! Did she die from the seizure?"

"Maybe—or whatever caused it. Labs were sent off this afternoon, including toxicology. Hopefully, we'll know more in the next couple of days."

"Do you think something bit her? One of the witnesses said there were cuts and abrasions on her legs. Maybe they were bites," I suggested.

"We'll see. Other than jellyfish and stingrays, I'm not too familiar with venomous sea creatures. However, I do know that bites or stings from some snakes or arachnids can cause opisthotonus. In fact, I saw a mild case due to a scorpion sting when I was in Arizona." Sam checked his watch and jumped up. "Rats! I need to get going."

"Of course," I sighed while standing. "Before you leave, I wanted to ask if you'd mind a double date with Elizabeth and her fiancé tomorrow evening. Dinner then dancing at the Cabrillo?"

"I'd love that." He paused, his gaze intense. "I wish you could see yourself through my eyes at this very moment. You're absolutely breathtaking."

I self-consciously put a hand to my hair which, somehow, I had tamed into smooth waves moments before he arrived. "Thank you," I murmured, my cheeks hot.

He stepped forward so that our toes were touching and extended his right hand. Light as a feather, he traced a line up my neck and rested his palm along my jawbone, his fingertips gently pressing behind my ear. He raised an eyebrow invitingly, and I slowly nodded before he lowered his face toward mine. His lips were full and supple as he kissed me with a tenderness that brought tears to my eyes. I felt my knees weaken as he wrapped both arms around me, pulling me into an embrace that filled me with longing. The devotion and yearning in his kiss mirrored my own emotions. I wished the moment could have lasted forever, but our bliss was interrupted by an amused driver who blasted his horn and whistled out of his open window. Our faces drew apart, but Sam gingerly tightened his arms and embraced me before letting go.

"That was..." Words failed me.

"That was even better than I dreamed." He smiled dizzily.

Thinking back upon that blissful moment, I can't help but compare it with Eddie's hard and demanding kisses. Even his hugs were forceful. I glide the pad of my index finger along my lower lip. I hadn't realized that a man's lips could be so soft and sensuous.

Outside my door, Dottie's feet creak on the wooden floor, and a playful meow indicates that she's released Puck from his overnight detention. I check the clock again. It's 9:17.

I really should get up.

After breakfast, I call Archie to see if they need me anytime soon. I have a few errands to run, such as dropping off piles of bedding and towels with a laundry service in town. Norma and Edith have a Thor washing machine, but I'd rather not spend my morning with a mangle and clothesline.

"Archie Duval here," he answers.

"Hi Archie, it's Ruby. What's the plan for today?"

"We'll be filming at La Casa del Camino from eleven until three. Can you make it?"

"Does this mean you've found a replacement for Rex?" I ask, surprised.

"Don't get me started on that," he grumbles. "No, we're shooting a scene with Corvi and Kit."

"Alright, I can be there around eleven-thirty."

After hanging up, I look for Dottie and find her in the backyard greasing the chain on the bicycle she's been using.

"I'm glad you're feeling better," I tell her. The bites aren't nearly as red, and I haven't seen her scratch all morning.

"The calamine helped, but I want to get my hands on that cream Sam mentioned. I'm heading over there now," she informs me.

"I don't suppose you'd like to join me in a little while—they're filming Corvi and Kit—"

"Yes!" she interrupts. "I've been waiting for this all week!"

"Alrighty then! Be ready to leave by eleven-fifteen."

"That's baloney!" Ike pounds his fist against the Spanish mosaic tile on the lobby's fireplace, causing the hotel manager to wince.

"She can't sing! Plain and simple!" The bellicose director points an index finger dangerously close to Ike's scarlet face.

Archie steps between the two men, his hands raised in a gesture of appeasement. "Sir, Corvi's upset right now. Perhaps if we give her some time to—"

"She sounded this bad during rehearsal too!" Mr. Lake snaps.

"But she's had weeks of practice with a vocal coach." Archie pleads, "Give her time to calm down."

I scan the room and find Corvi huddled with Elizabeth on a rattan loveseat next to a tall potted palm. She's slouched forward, her face buried in a handkerchief.

Dottie nudges me and mouths, "What's going on?"

"No idea," I reply quietly out of the corner of my mouth.

"We don't have a leading man, and our star can't sing a note! This film is a disaster!" Mr. Lake storms through the wide oak front door with Archie close on his heels.

Ike stomps toward Corvi. "Pull yourself together!"

He slams a pair of French doors on his way out to the back patio.

"Oh, my!" exclaims the hotel manager, steadying the painted mica shade of a table lamp—one of several objects that began to topple in Ike's wake.

"Elizabeth, what just happened?" I ask.

"I bungled the scene," Corvi answers while clutching a kerchief stained with mottled reds, blacks, and blues from the thick stage makeup smeared under her eyes and on her cheeks. The starlet looks absolutely defeated.

"It'll be okay," I say feebly.

"That's not the only problem," Elizabeth says gravely. "There's been a theft."

"What's been stolen?"

"Something personal was taken from my room," Corvi sniffles. "I know it was the stalker!"

"What makes you so sure?" I offer her a clean handkerchief from my handbag.

"Who else could it be?" she bleats forlornly.

"What's missing?" Dottie queries.

Flustered, Corvi casts my cousin a sideways glance.

"I'm sorry, Corvi. I don't know if you remember Dottie, my cousin. I told her she could watch the shoot today," I explain.

"I hope that's alright," Dottie adds apologetically.

"Yes, I'm so sorry. Of course, I remember you, Dottie." Corvi slips into her movie star persona. "It's just a small thing that's missing. What's more upsetting is that someone broke into my room and went through my belongings."

"When did this happen?" I inquire.

"I'm not really sure," she replies. "I hadn't looked in that drawer since I settled into the room."

I deliberate whether I should stay and monitor the situation here or head over and search her room for clues. Corvi's next comment settles the matter.

"I turned my room upside down searching for the…the personal item, and it's definitely gone. I asked that housekeeping skip my room today until I've had a chance to put everything away."

Her evasiveness about the stolen object frustrates me, but I respect her privacy and resist the urge to press further—for now. Without more information, I'm uncertain how I'd even begin to investigate. Looks like we'll be staying here for the time being.

Archie returns and looks around the colorfully decorated space, where paintings of Laguna's early years brighten each stucco wall—a marked contrast to the current mood in the lobby.

"Where's Ike?" he asks with annoyance.

"He went through there," Elizabeth gestures toward the sunny doors by the staircase.

"Just as well," he rolls his neck. "Hopefully, he cools off."

"What did Mr. Lake say?" Corvi rises from the loveseat, her hands twisting the handkerchief.

"We'll give it another go." He cautions, "But you'll need to put all those lessons to good use. This is a musical, after all."

She crosses her heart and forces a smile. "I'll do it! I promise!"

Now is probably not the best time, but I ask Archie, "Is it alright if my cousin watches?"

His face softens. "Dottie, isn't it?"

She nods, suddenly tongue-tied. At moments like this, I glimpse the shy little six-year-old who hid behind Nan when I first came to California.

"You're more than welcome to stay and watch."

Dottie and I follow the others outside through the French doors and across an enclosed courtyard. Spanish-style arches and balconies grace the sand-colored walls, and newly planted vines have begun their upward climb along stakes and trellises. We enter another building—closer to the cliff's edge—and ascend a staircase leading to the rooftop lounge, where cameramen, grips, and stylists soak in the glorious sunshine. Noticing Archie's arrival, members of the crew abandon their card games and cigarettes.

Kit lowers a script and—upon spotting Corvi—jumps to his feet. "Corvi, are you alright?" His brows arch with concern.

Her eyes pan dozens of faces, all staring with anticipation. "Okey dokey!" She flashes a carefree grin. "Let's get back to work."

"Kit, while hair and makeup do their thing with Corvi, let's run through your solo," Archie instructs.

In ivory slacks with a sky-blue coat accentuating his height and broad shoulders, Kit cuts quite a figure. While a musician begins softly strumming a guitar, Kit stands on a mark that's been chalked upon the wood plank flooring and faces seaward, one hand in his pocket. I'm unprepared for the power and clarity of his voice as he sings the first notes of a romantic ballad. For an instant, nearly everyone pauses and sighs. Kit shifts his eyes toward Corvi, who's seated on a tall chair under an umbrella surrounded by a posse of young stylists working their magic.

When the music ends and Corvi's makeup has been repaired, Archie shouts through a shiny black cone, "Places."

Dottie and I watch in amazement, as the cast and crew move fluidly to their assigned locations. Two cameras are trained upon Kit while another is focused just off to his right. Strong men carrying boom poles lower the microphones just above Kit's head. A young lady pats powder onto Kit's forehead and cheeks then quickly darts out of the camera shot. Corvi stands on a chalk mark, about twenty feet from Kit's right side. She's fidgeting with the thumb and index finger on her left hand—the only telltale sign that she's nervous. Kit gives her a wink, his dimples deepening, and she returns his smile with a slight nod of her head.

"Okay folks, this first take is a rehearsal," Archie explains through the megaphone.

Elizabeth leans against me and whispers, "That means the cameras and sound are on, but they won't be recording."

"Quiet on the set. Rolling rehearsal and…action," the assistant director orders.

Kit's performance is flawless. After a couple of verses, Corvi glides toward Kit, a camera trained upon her as she walks. The song transitions to the chorus, and everyone collectively holds their breath as Corvi opens her mouth for the duet.

"She's pitchy," Elizabeth murmurs quietly in my ear.

Without losing the melody, Kit's voice shifts to harmonize with Corvi's, and she hits the wrong note—several times.

"Cut!" Archie runs a hand over his face. "Stand by, everyone. Corvi…a word please."

Her eyes brimming with tears, she takes a seat on the stool beside Archie. "I know what you're going to say."

"I don't think you do," he says wearily. "Please help me understand. Both you and Ike said you could do this. I know you've practiced with Kit. What's going on?"

Tears flow down her cheeks. "I can do it," she sniffs. "Give me another chance."

"Kit." Archie gestures for the downcast actor to join them. "Can she do it?"

"Perhaps if we cut out the harmony," Kit suggests.

"We're not cutting the harmony," Archie says sternly. "Can she do it?"

"I don't think she can." Kit looks absolutely despondent.

Clasping a hand to her mouth, Corvi leaps from the chair and runs into the building.

Elizabeth and I start to follow, but Archie yells, "Let her be for now."

"What does this mean?" Dottie asks Elizabeth.

"I'm not sure." She sounds crestfallen.

"Hey ya, pal! Long time no see," Pancho's toothy grin is irresistible. "I heard you were in town."

Archie can't help but return her smile, albeit with less enthusiasm given this afternoon's disaster. "Pancho! I was hoping to run into you."

The upbeat, energetic aviator has caught us just as we're leaving La Casa del Camino. Dottie jabs my rib with her elbow, her mouth open with amazement.

"Hey, I know you!" Pancho tilts her head toward me.

"Yes, we briefly met at the gallery the other day. I believe you stopped by to say hello to Kit."

"That's right, but I didn't catch your name. I'm Pancho," she extends a hand.

"Ruby Ray." Her grip is simultaneously firm and warm. "This is my cousin, Dottie."

"Nice to meet you!" Dottie gives a nervous wave. "My brother watched you break the speed record a couple of weeks ago."

"Is that so?" Thumbs in the belt loops of her slacks, she rocks from heel to toe. "Well, I'm glad he was there to see it." Pancho turns toward me, "So, how do you know my pal, Archie?"

"It's a long story, Pancho…" Archie replies. "But at the moment, Ruby's working with Stardust as an investigator."

"An investigator!" Pancho exclaims with admiration. "Another gal stealin' jobs from the fellas—I knew there was a reason I liked you."

I grin. "And this is my friend, Liz Martin."

Archie clarifies, "She's the stunt double for Corvi's water scenes."

Pancho looks at her appraisingly. "Well, well."

"I take it you heard about Lena?" Archie asks.

228

She replies acidly, "Tough break."

"Come on now. Is that all you have to say? You worked together on a couple of films, as I recall."

"So? That don't mean I had to like her."

"What was it with you two, anyway?" Archie inquires.

I'm wondering the same thing.

Pancho coughs a laugh. "Well, it all started here, if you can believe it."

"Here in Laguna?" Elizabeth asks.

"That's right. Remember that Rin Tin Tin movie several years back? *Lighthouse By the Sea?*"

"We were just talking about it the other day," Dottie remarks.

"Well, they needed a double for the lead actress, Louise Fazenda. Lena thought she had the job, but I knew the director, Malcolm St. Clair. He's a family friend from Pasadena. When he realized I was stayin' at my grandma's place here in town, he offered me the job. Was Lena ever sore!"

"Surely she didn't harbor a grudge." Archie reasons, "Things like that happen all the time."

Pancho shrugs. "All I know is that when I saw her again during the *Hell's Angels* production, I overheard her sayin' she'd bring me down one way or another."

"She threatened you?" I ask.

This adds yet another layer to the mysterious nature of Lena's death.

She chuckles. "A load of bullshit. She couldn't hurt me, but she started snoopin' around. You see, we were trying to unionize the aviators on the film."

"What could she do?" Archie asks. "Tell Hughes?"

"I suppose so. That or the press. It didn't matter. I was able to get our guys five times what Hughes was paying 'em."

"I heard that you and Lena started throwing punches on the set," he recalls.

At that, Pancho bends over laughing. "Not quite! But she backed off after that."

Archie checks the time. "Pancho, I hate to rush off, but we're in a pickle with the film. Is there a chance we can talk later this week?"

"Tell ya what...I'm having a party at Dos Rocas on Friday. The boys will be stayin' over the weekend for the airshow next Monday. You should come."

"Count on it!" Archie grips her hand and claps her shoulder.

"You should come too," she invites the rest of us. "And bring that brother of yours," she tells Dottie. "My son would enjoy having another kid around."

Back at the house a little while later, Dottie berates me, "I can't believe you didn't tell me about the airshow!"

"I only heard about it yesterday, and I didn't want to say anything until I knew for sure." I suggest, "Why don't you call Jack and tell him about it—be sure to mention the party too."

She beams and dashes for the telephone. What a contrast to her mood yesterday!

Preparing for yet another romantic evening in Sam's arms, I sift through my dresses in the closet until I reach a silk georgette gown. Its circular peplum drapes below the hips, and wide straps extend down the back, leaving a generous scoop that nearly reaches my waist. The gown's light moss color sets off the red tones in my hair, and the hemline skirts just above the ankle—perfect for dancing. I open my jewelry case and select a diamond and topaz pendant that belonged to my grandmother. Unlike the decorative setting of most Edwardian pieces, this pendant is simple and won't clash with the modern geometric lines of my gown. I opt for a pair of low-heeled gold D'Orsay pumps and a matching beaded bag. With my ensemble complete, I lie down for a late afternoon nap.

"It was a javelina! And it was charging right toward me!"

"A skunk pig?" Dean laughs with amazement.

"What's a javelina?" Elizabeth asks, absorbed in Sam's tale from his summer in Arizona.

"A type of peccary. They look like a wild boar, tusks and all but, despite their nickname, they're not actually pigs," Sam explains.

"And you call my job dangerous!" I remind him. "What did you do?"

"Well, Jeremiah—he's the reservation doctor who took me to visit the more remote villages—anyway, Jeremiah shouted for me to jump out of the way."

"Didn't the javelina follow you?" Elizabeth's brows furrow with concern.

"That's the best part! Javelinas are nearly blind. This fella just barreled past me."

We all chuckle heartily.

"Speaking of pigs, I don't think I can eat another bite," Dean pushes away the remains of his pork roast and potatoes.

Elizabeth teasingly pokes him in the belly. "I told you to order the halibut. Now you won't want to dance."

He extends an arm around his fiancé and whispers, not so quietly, in her ear, "Nothing could keep me from sweeping you off your feet."

"We'll see about that," she sasses with a wink.

I look around the Hotel Laguna's cliffside patio and realize that I'm not the only one who's enjoying these two and their playful banter. Other diners, as well as restaurant staff, are engrossed with this enchanting couple and their palpable chemistry—and it's no wonder. With russet-colored eyes, sandy brown curls, and a Cupid's bow mouth, Dean Larsen ticks all the right boxes for a glamorous film star. And with Elizabeth's chic style, knockout beauty and—now— platinum blonde hair, the duo could top the list of watchable celebrity couples.

Sam drapes a muscular arm around my shoulders, sending delicious shivers along my spine. "Speaking of dancing, what do you say we tango along to the ballroom," he proposes.

"I see what you did there," I kiss his warm cheek, my lips tingling from the hint of stubble this late in the day. His skin smells woodsy and clean, like a thicket of firs near a swiftly moving river.

"You can do better than that," he stares longingly into my eyes while leaning down until his lips are mere inches from mine. I close the gap and, once again, marvel at how relaxed but utterly alluring a kiss can be.

"Now that's what I'm talking about!" Elizabeth hoots.

"I can't believe it's so crowded at eight on a Tuesday night," Elizabeth scans the ballroom.

"You should have seen it Saturday evening," I remark. "At least there are a few tables free."

"Who needs a table!" she exclaims and tosses her handbag at me before twirling onto the dance floor with Dean.

"Say, there's Archie!" I spot the assistant director sitting alone at a round table for eight. "We can leave our things with him."

"Sam," Archie shakes his hand. "Hey, Ruby, I see your friends have abandoned you."

"Not for long," I drop the handbags on the table. "Do you mind?"

He shakes his head. "Not at all. I'll be here a while."

Sam places a hand on my bare back and leads me to the edge of the swiftly moving bodies. The band is playing a fast-paced "My Baby Just Cares for Me," so Sam suggests, "Balboa?"

I nod, "Perfect!" This dance actually originated just up the road in Newport Beach and is well-suited for tightly packed dance halls.

We join the flow of dancers and, yet again, I'm impressed by Sam's nimble kicks and quick steps. When the song ends, I notice Elizabeth dragging Dean toward the stage.

"What do you suppose that's all about?" Corvi slips an arm through mine and pulls me off to the side of the dance floor.

"Corvi! I didn't expect to see you here this evening." The words are out of my mouth before I've really thought them through.

Diplomatically, Kit ignores my comment and asks, "Who's that with Liz? He looks familiar."

"That's her fiancé, Dean. He has a contract with Warner Brothers," I answer.

"Does he now?" Corvi looks impressed.

"Folks, have I got a treat for you!" the bandleader exclaims into the microphone. "Our singer's under the weather—"

"You mean he's under the table...blotto," someone yells from the crowd.

"You didn't hear it from me," the bandleader jokes. When the laughter dies down, he continues, "As I was sayin', we thought we were down a singer tonight, but these two lookers have offered to croon a tune or two. What do ya say?"

Thunderous applause and howls reverberate throughout the dance hall, as Dean steps up to the microphone. "We thought we'd start with a little number you may have heard before. It's called...'Makin' Whoopee.'"

At that, the dancers unleash shrill whistles and squeals, which die down as the band begins to play the familiar tune. Dean stands at the microphone, singing the first verse in dulcet tones, while Elizabeth poses several feet away, pretending to look disinterested. He sends her lovesick glances, which she ignores—her pert nose raised—until the melody changes and she sidles up to next to him and—with a honeyed, pitch-perfect voice—sings, "Another bride, another groom..." The crowd howls with delight, as the couple take turns with verses and harmonize with effortless finesse during their duets. Throughout their performance, they embody a besotted fellow wooing a young lady who's playing hard to get. As they near the end of the song, someone in the audience tosses Elizabeth a bouquet, and the duo sing the final words as though they're standing at an altar.

Everyone claps and shouts with great enthusiasm—everyone, that is, except Corvi who looks crestfallen. Her face pales and eyes flutter as she watches the crowd shower adulation upon the talented couple for their singing.

When the duo launch into their next song, "You Brought a New Kind of Love to Me," I feel a tug at my elbow. To my surprise, Archie, not Sam, has pulled me aside.

"Can I have this dance?"

Confusion and—if I'm not mistaken—hurt flash upon Sam's face. I'm annoyed with Archie, but I'm sure he has a valid reason.

I ask Sam, "Would you mind? Just for one song. Then I'm all yours for the rest of the evening."

"Of course, Ruby." His smile doesn't quite reach his eyes, and I feel sick to my stomach.

"This had better be good," I declare as the music starts.

"I'm sorry, Ruby! I had to get you alone, so Corvi doesn't hear," he confesses.

My shoulders relax.

Archie's body is abuzz with excitement, "Liz and Dean! They're the answer to this whole mess!"

My eyes snap toward his face. "What do you mean?"

"I spoke with Mr. Lake when I got back to the hotel this afternoon. He told me I had until 8:00 tomorrow morning to find a new lead actor and a voice double for Corvi. I've had no luck and pretty much concluded that the film would be canceled. "

"Wait! Are you saying you want Elizabeth and Dean?" My body lightens with joy for my friend.

"Yes! They're perfect. Since Rex's accident, Liz has not so subtly hinted that Dean is an actor who's had some plum roles. I'll call in a favor with someone I know at Warner Brothers. They should agree to loaning us Dean for the film—it happens all the time. Ruby, this solves everything!"

"How, exactly, are you going to keep this from Corvi?" I'm puzzled.

"I'll have to tell her—but not tonight." He casts a glance toward the stunned actress.

"Dean and Elizabeth's performance really threw her for a loop."

"It's not just that. She was already a wreck when we arrived."

"What else happened today?" That's when I notice Ike brooding in a corner of the hall.

"When Corvi got back to the hotel after the shoot, she found Poppy—that gal from the hotel—inside her bedroom. Poppy claimed she was there to pick up a tray, but Corvi didn't believe her."

"What do you think?" I look at him quizzically.

"I believe the girl. Why would she lie?"

Why indeed.

"After everything that's transpired today, I'm shocked that Corvi wanted to go out tonight?"

"Kit asked her to go dancing. He feels terrible about ratting her out. She was about to say no, but Ike overheard and answered for her. He told Kit that Corvi would be staying in for the evening."

"What did she do?"

"Well, that really annoyed her, so she accepted Kit's invitation. She's peeved at the way Ike handled Mr. Lake earlier, as if he's somehow to blame for her inability to sing."

"So, Ike came along?"

"Not really his scene," Archie chuckles. "When we arrived, some punk called him 'old man.' I thought he was going to slug the guy. Instead he placed his hand inside his coat, as though reaching for a gun, and the kid backed off. Everyone's left him alone since."

"Do you think he's armed?" I ask with concern.

"It wouldn't surprise me, considering the company he keeps."

I file this away to consider later. Back to the matter at hand, I ask, "So, Dean and Elizabeth…what does this mean for the film? Won't Dean need time to learn his lines?"

"I'll feed him lines before each take until he's up to par."

"When will you start filming his scenes?"

"Tomorrow," he says matter of factly.

"That soon?!"

"When we lost Rex, I pushed back the Table Rock shoot by a couple of days, hoping I'd find someone. Everything's already set. I'm assuming Dean can swim, and he won't have many lines."

"Do you need me there?"

"Definitely. Meet us outside the hotel at nine to board the bus. After the shoot at Table Rock, we'll head further north to film at Crystal Cove."

I suddenly recall our plans with Nan and the twins. "How long will it take? I have visitors coming at noon for a beach picnic, and I want to give them my full attention. In other words, I'll be off duty."

"Ooh! We need extras! Would they be interested?" Archie explains. "It'll be a beach scene, so we'll need folks lounging under umbrellas, playing games, etcetera."

"The girls will love it!"

Nan on the other hand...

"But remember, I'll be off duty," I mention.

Archie bobs his head. "Sure, sure, anything you say."

Sam approaches with two glasses of punch as the song ends. "Thirsty?"

"Parched!" I exclaim. "Thank you."

Archie shakes Sam's hand. "Thanks, pal. I'll leave you to it." He makes a beeline toward Elizabeth and Dean, and the trio head to the outdoor patio.

"Sorry about that," I tell Sam with a penitent smile.

"Don't give it a second thought. Clearly you had things to discuss." He adds, "You'll be pleased to know that I'm not the jealous sort."

"In any case, you have nothing to worry about. I'm not interested, nor am I his type."

We return to the table, where Corvi and Kit are gathering their things.

"We're off," says Corvi with a little wave before wandering toward the main exit.

"Corvi's not feeling well this evening..." Kit begins, but when he notices Ike ushering Corvi outside, he apologizes and rushes after them.

After a few minutes, Archie approaches the table—a joyful Elizabeth and Dean hugging fiercely near the stage with enormous grins. Before reaching us, he notices an attractive young man leaning against the wall nearby. He's wearing a polo shirt with snug short sleeves that display his tan muscular arms, and he nods enticingly at Archie.

"That's my cue," Archie removes a lighter from his pocket.

"But you don't smoke," I call after him as he walks away.

"You weren't kidding when you said you're not his type," Sam comments, then draws me into his arms for another spin around the dance floor.

CHAPTER 16

~ ❀ ~

WEDNESDAY, AUGUST 27, 1930
TABLE ROCK, LAGUNA BEACH

"He's dead!" Corvi sobs.

Adrenaline surges through my limbs. "Who's dead? Is it Rex?"

"No. Rex is home from the hospital recuperating for the next couple of months," Archie shakes his head. "Lon Chaney is the person who died. Corvi read about it in the news this morning."

"I adored him! He would have been the perfect specter in my brother's story," she laments.

"But I thought Mr. Lake vetoed that idea." I look at Archie.

"He'll change his mind," Corvi pouts. "If I can just persuade Stardust…"

He throws up his hands and walks away. This morning Archie looks every inch the Hollywood filmmaker, with his plaid plus-fours, tweed flat cap, and megaphone.

"Miss Styles, let's try to fix your mascara," a motherly figure wraps an arm around the frail actress and leads her toward the make-shift hair and cosmetic station in the sandy cove next to Table Rock.

I jog to catch up with Archie since I haven't had an opportunity to check in with him this morning. I arrived at the hotel just before nine but immediately crammed into a Chevrolet bus with Corvi, Dean, Elizabeth, and an assortment of Stardust production employees. The camera operators, sound crew, and grips rode in a separate coach, while a third bus transported the equipment. Thankfully, the cotton balls worked their magic for a second night, so I felt well-rested this morning. Dottie was still asleep when I left, but the kitten was whining in the bathroom. I filled his food and water dishes and left him there.

"Archie, do you have a minute?"

"I suppose," he says coyly. "But let's talk about that dreamy date of yours last night."

"I will if you will," I wink.

"Ah, Monte—what lovely shoulders—but he didn't hold a candle to Rex," he says regretfully.

"At least he wasn't laid up in a hospital bed," I comment.

"Yes, there is that…" Archie agrees happily. "Alright, it's your turn."

"What do you want to know?"

"Maybe start with the skinny dipping." He flashes a salacious smirk.

"SKINNY DIPPING?!" I choke, and a number of heads turn to look in our direction.

Truth be told, the evening ended with a sweet kiss at the door, and that was it. After celebrating with Elizabeth and Dean at the ballroom, Sam walked me home and told me more about growing up in the Sierras, while I described my family home in Manhattan. Eventually, the conversation transitioned to my current investigation. I shared my suspicions regarding the "stalker," Bebe, and Ike, as well as the latest information I gleaned about the conflict between Lena and Pancho, not to mention Poppy's unexpected appearance in Corvi's room yesterday. The weightiness of our discussion quashed any amorous notions we may have had.

"Never mind," Archie grumbles. "Your expression says everything I need to know."

"Sorry to disappoint you," I pretend to take offense. "Perhaps we can discuss Corvi instead. She seems overly distraught about Lon Chaney this morning. How did she take the news about Dean and Elizabeth?"

"How do you think?" He rolls his eyes.

"That bad?"

"I understand the pressure she's under—really I do—but it would be nice to have a conversation with her that doesn't end in tears," he confesses.

"I assume it was Elizabeth's dubbing that set her off," I glance over at Corvi, who's somberly watching Elizabeth and Dean converse with an athletic man gesticulating wildly with his hands.

"Yeah, she was fine with Dean. But she seriously believed that, after yesterday's disaster, she'd still get to sing. She's delusional."

I candidly remark, "Archie, during the brief time I've known Corvi, she's been robbed, stalked, threatened, and witnessed a death. She must feel absolutely raw and vulnerable."

His shoulders drop. "You're right, but she's always so damn melodramatic!" He pauses then laughs to himself. "Okay, now that I think about it, so are many other actresses I've met."

"That's probably why they're so successful onscreen," I reflect.

"Exactly. Anyway, Corvi knows that Dean and Liz have saved the film for everyone and that—in the end—it's her name that will be in lights—not Liz's."

"That may be true for now, but I have no doubts about Elizabeth's future in Hollywood," I defend my dear friend.

He regards the pair thoughtfully. "I have to agree with you. Those two have something special, that's for sure."

My attention shifts to the shore, where a familiar rowboat rides a small breaker and washes up on the sand. A two-masted schooner with a forest green hull appears to be anchored about 500 yards offshore.

"Oh good! Sal's here," Archie claps his hands.

I recall my conversation with the friendly mariner Monday morning. "Is there a film crew aboard the diving boat?"

"I certainly hope so."

We approach the captain as she pulls the rowboat further ashore with a rope.

"Everything alright?" Archie asks Sal.

"Just peachy," she grins. "I wanna make sure your new cast know exactly what's what with the jump and rescue scenes."

"They're talking to the stunt coordinator right now," Archie replies.

"Right! Thanks!" And she tromps through the sand toward the trio.

"What's this about a rescue scene?" I assumed they were just doing the jump.

"We're shooting two scenes today—albeit out of order—as far as the film goes. First, Liz and Dean will jump off Table Rock. This will be the final scene of the movie, as the socialite and skin diver jump into the water, hand-in-hand," he explains.

"Oh, I see. So, the scene will be shot from the onshore cameras, as well as the one on the boat."

"That's right. Then, Dean and Liz will swim toward the *Bonnie Boat*, which will have moved closer by then. At that point, they'll film the drowning scene."

I tense with alarm. Surely, I'm not the only one who's uncomfortable with this. It's only been a few days since Lena drowned.

Archie pragmatically continues, "In this scene, the skin diver rescues the socialite, and they meet for the first time. Once they've got the take, the *Bonnie Boat* will carry everyone onboard back to Newport Harbor."

A young grip suddenly approaches Archie, panting. "Mr. Lake says it's almost time."

Archie shouts through the megaphone, "Places everyone."

Sal pushes her boat into the water and heads back to her ship. Meanwhile, the camera and sound crew gather their equipment. Corvi leaves the hair and makeup station to join Dean and Elizabeth, both women wearing identical ensembles. Their canary yellow slacks stop a couple of inches above the ankle, and a thin band of sunny orange runs vertically along the center of each leg. A hip-length vest in the same orange hue peaks out from a long, loose jacket—also canary with orange trim. Matching sun hats adorn each platinum blonde head. At this distance, it's impossible to tell the two actresses apart. I walk alongside the hair, makeup, and wardrobe crew as they follow the cast toward the film site.

"Why bother with all that color?!" a hairdresser complains. "It's not like the audience will see it."

"Now, hush with you!" the cosmetologist snaps.

"Celanese moiré and Nowitzky, no less!" a costumer moans.

"I still can't believe she's expected to swim in it!" the hairdresser objects.

"Did you say that Liz will be jumping in THAT?" I interrupt.

The costumer nods, infuriated. "Even worse—once she's in the water, she has to strip down to her swimsuit for the rescue scene and discard the garments. They'll never be recovered."

This shocks me for a couple of reasons. First, Mary Nowitzky is a notable designer who ranks right up there with Coco Chanel and Elsa Schiaparelli when it comes to swimsuits and loungewear. Those costumes must have cost a fortune. More importantly, I'm concerned about Elizabeth's safety. "Won't the jacket and pants weigh her down in the water?"

"That's the beauty of Celanese—it's as light in the water as it is on dry land," the costumer explains.

"I may be tempted to jump in after it!" the hairdresser declares.

Several massive rock formations project into the ocean along this stretch of coastline. I've been told that a natural arch leads through the rock toward Thousand Steps Beach at the southern end of the cove but—at the moment—it's inaccessible due to the tide. Table Rock itself is broad and flat on top—hence the name—and rises from the center of the cove. Someone has posted a makeshift sign that reads, "DANGER: No jumping allowed."

I feel a hard lump in my throat.

Oh dear!

The rocks are jagged and irregular, so it's difficult to find a foothold while carefully scrambling to the top of Table Rock. Midway up, I suddenly realize that Ike has been suspiciously absent all morning. I wonder if Mr. Lake banned him from the set after their argument yesterday afternoon. I look over my shoulder to survey the M-shaped inlet—he's nowhere to be seen.

After what feels like a half an hour of discussions with the performers, cameramen, and stunt coordinator, Mr. Lake nods and twirls a finger above his head.

"Okay, folks. This is it. First position," Archie projects through the megaphone.

I find myself adrift as everyone scurries to their assigned location. The costumer motions for me to join her crew about ten yards from where all the action is taking place.

"Roll camera, roll sound, rolling...action," Mr. Lake commands though his own speaking trumpet, while a young man snaps a clapperboard in front of one of the cameras.

Dean and Corvi stand face-to-face at the rock's edge, their hands intertwined. His fitted crab-back suit clings to his muscular form, as the wide legs of Corvi's trousers flap to-and-fro in the breeze. The pair gaze devotedly into one another's eyes, but when an unexpected gust threatens to carry away Corvi's hat, she clamps one hand to the top of her head. With waves crashing below us, it's difficult to hear the performers' lines but—presumably—the microphone dangling above their heads can pick up their voices. The pair turn hand in hand to face the ocean below and swing their arms backwards, as though they will jump, but their feet remain firmly planted.

Mr. Lake calls, "Cut."

The clack of the clapperboard sounds, and Archie shouts, "Moving on. Scene forty-three. Second team. Everyone else, clear off."

The camera and sound crew quickly gather their equipment and head back down toward the beach.

"We gotta go too," the costumer tells me. "We can't be in the scene when that camera on the boat starts rolling."

I look back and watch Elizabeth replace Corvi who, with Archie's assistance, delicately makes her way down the rock onto the sand. Once we've gathered in the cove, we're able to watch the scene without being caught on film. The cameramen set up their tripods at the water's edge to capture the scene from below the massive rock.

At the edge of the promontory, Mr. Lake raises a pair of binoculars and watches the boat, now about a hundred yards away. He rotates his right arm like a windmill.

Archie settles next to me, "He's signaling for the onboard camera to begin filming."

243

"We're rolling," Mr. Lake bellows through his speaking trumpet, then abandons Table Rock to join us on the sand.

Elizabeth slips her hand into Dean's, who leans down and kisses her soundly. Several young women nearby titter.

"We don't have all day," Archie thunders, chastising the pair.

The couple laugh then assume the position that had ended the prior scene. Everyone silently waits for Mr. Lake's next command. Once he's satisfied, he lifts the cone to his mouth and calls, "Action!"

As soon as the clapper snaps, the actors take three rapid steps then jump hand in hand off the cliff's edge. Those of us onshore emit a collective gasp. From our vantage point, we cannot see the pair, nor can we hear their splash over the pounding waves. My heart pounds with terror.

What if the water is too shallow?

What if there are boulders just beneath the surface?

Archie places an arm around my shoulders and gives me a squeeze. "They're fine."

Then he joins Mr. Lake, who is already returning to Table Rock, his arm swinging for the cameramen to keep rolling.

After several tense moments, a cheer erupts nearby. Two heads have surfaced near the *Bonnie Boat.* Unsurprisingly, Elizabeth's hat is missing, but she appears to be struggling with something underwater. A crew member tosses a buoy from the ship, with a length of twine attached. Then a bag of some sort slides down the rope and lands on the buoy.

"They're saving the beach pajamas!" the costumer exclaims joyfully.

I sigh with relief as Elizabeth grabs the floatation device and appears to wrestle the remaining garments off her body and into the bag. She tugs the line, which is pulled back into the boat. Both she and Dean swim several yards away from the schooner, presumably to begin the rescue scene. From the top of Table Rock, Mr. Lake makes a clapping motion with his arms.

"Action."

I wrap my arms around my torso and watch in horror as my best friend appears to drown before my eyes.

"All I'm sayin' is that cats belong outside," Nan huffs while holding the purring kitten against her bosom. "That bein' said, he sure is a cute little feller."

"I'm glad he lives inside," Addie declares. "That street out there looks busy. He could get run over."

"Or lost!" May adds.

"My mama woulda skinned me alive fer bringin' a cat in the house," Gabe interjects. "They're fer catchin' rats and the like on the farm, not cuddlin' and pettin'."

Nan attempts to set Puck onto the floor, but he clings even more tightly to her lightweight cotton frock. Animals adore Nan—I suppose they appreciate her calming presence—but today something seems off. A few minutes ago, when we discussed the twins' new niece, worry lines etched her face. Ordinarily, she'd be the first person to gush about a new baby in the family.

Maybe I'm just projecting my own uneasy feelings upon her after watching Elizabeth pretend to drown earlier. Even though I knew the stunt had been carefully choreographed, I had to remind myself to breathe. To make matters worse, it took five attempts before Mr. Lake signaled "cut" from the rock. Each take looked the same to me, but what do I know about filmmaking? By the end of the morning, my nerves were absolutely frayed.

"Is it true, Ruby? Are we really going to be in a movie?" May asks gleefully.

"Absolutely!" I look at my wristwatch and realize it's later than I thought. "Speaking of which, we should get going."

"But Dottie's not here yet," Nan observes.

"Dottie left a note that she and her friend will meet us at Crystal Cove."

I attempt to pry Puck away from Nan, but he bats at my hands.

"Lemme do it. Where does he need to go?" Nan delicately removes the feline's claws from her dress.

"In the bathroom. His food and water are already there." I point down the hall.

Once Nan leaves the room, I pull Addie aside. "What's wrong with her? She seems upset."

The young woman nods gravely. "My grandma has to move in with my mom and dad."

When Nan's parents passed away nearly thirty years ago, she left Missouri to live with her sister in Fullerton. Over the years, she helped care for her niece and nephew, as well as their children. Now, most of her family have moved out of the area. Addie and May only moved in with their grandmother and Nan because their folks relocated to San Diego a couple of years ago. It never occurred to me that Nan's living arrangement with her sister wasn't permanent.

"Why is she moving? Is Nan planning to go with her?"

Addie lowers her voice further, "My grandma lost her home. She didn't tell any of us that she was behind on her payments. Unfortunately, there's no room at my parents for Nan. As is, I'll be sharing a room with Grandma."

"You're moving too? What about May?"

"She'll stay with my brother and help take care of the baby. My sister-in-law is good at bookkeeping and wants to pitch in at my brother's construction business."

I glance toward her sister, who's holding hands with Gabe. "I'm sure there's another reason May's staying in Fullerton."

"That's for sure," Addie smiles at her twin.

"What will Nan do? Has she mentioned this to my uncle?"

She shakes her head sadly. "You know Nan. She doesn't want to be a burden."

"We'll figure something out," I quickly assure her as Nan returns.

The twins borrowed their brother's car to accommodate everyone, with the provision that Gabe was the driver. Apparently, this suited everyone just fine. As we venture south on Coast Highway, Nan and the girls ooh and aah, but I'm oblivious to the beautiful seascape. Instead, my mind is spinning.

We can't lose Nan!

We'd gladly take care of her for a change. As far as we're concerned, Nan is family and wouldn't have to lift a finger if she didn't want to, but I know she would protest. There must be a way we can persuade her to move in with us.

When we reach Crystal Cove, Gabe parks alongside the highway at the top of a precipitous bluff, where a dusty path snakes its way down to the beach.

"I'm so sorry, Nan. I didn't realize we'd have such a steep trek. I feel just terrible," I say remorsefully.

"Now, dontcha worry none. It may take me a while, but I can do it," she replies proudly and hoists her body—stiff with arthritis—out of the front seat. I watch with concern. We can help her down the trail, but what about climbing back up?

Together the twins remove an oversize picnic basket from the trunk and plunk it on the dusty shoulder of the road.

"Nan, you packed enough for everyone on the set!" Addie exclaims.

"She's afraid we're gonna starve," May remarks while rubbing the arm she used to lift the hamper.

Their great-aunt waves a dismissive hand. "You won't be gripin' none when yer tuckin' into my fried chicken and slaw."

"Let me carry that," Gabe lifts the hefty load.

"I'll take the bags if you two help Nan down the path," I suggest to Addie and May.

When we reach the bottom, Archie greets us. "Our special guests have arrived. And who might this lovely lady be?" He takes Nan's hand and plants a kiss upon her knuckles.

Nan's fair cheeks flame. "Henrietta Fry. But you can call me Nan."

"Thank you, Nan. Please call me Archie." He wraps an arm around her shoulders. "Welcome to our set."

His free hand sweeps toward a collection of makeshift shacks with thatched roofs and reed covered walls. Beneath tall palms waving their fan-shaped fronds in the ocean breeze, studio crew scurry to arrange props and equipment for the afternoon shoot.

"Did you do all this for the movie?" Addie asks with astonishment.

"We added a few touches," Archie winks. "But most of this is from other film productions before us."

"What about those?" May points toward a cluster of tents further down the shore.

"Nah, those belong to friends of the Irvines, who own this stretch of land. Most of those campers will be extras, like you, today."

"Where would you like us?" I ask, aware that the basket in Gabe's hands must be getting heavier by the minute.

"Our crew set up some chairs and umbrellas closer to the water. You should be comfortable there for your picnic. We won't begin filming for a little while, but I'm afraid I'm needed elsewhere at the moment." With that, Archie takes his leave and walks toward a pair of young grips who appear to have nothing to do.

"Nan, let's settle here," I direct her toward a group of teak folding chairs nestled under a pair of umbrellas.

"Oof!" she pronounces while collapsing onto one of the canvas seats. "Can't imagine gettin' back up. I reckon I'll stay put fer a while."

I shake out a beach blanket. "Gabe, why don't you put the food here."

"Ru-u-by-y-y!" a voice calls from the base of the cliff.

I swivel to see Dottie and Iris propping their bicycles against a boulder and wave for them to join us. After introductions are made, we dig into the ample meal Nan has prepared. In addition to the chicken and coleslaw, she's packed a fruit salad, jars of pickles and olives, cheese sandwiches, and an entire cherry pie which somehow made it down the hill intact. Oh, I forgot to mention the large thermos of ice-cold lemonade.

Iris gapes at the spread then looks around. "Are we expecting others?"

Everyone laughs heartily.

Once we've had our fill, Gabe steps behind the umbrella and strips down to a modest and slightly dated swimsuit. The skirt of the belted garment extends to the middle of his thigh, and the neckline reaches up to the base of his Adam's apple. I imagine he borrowed the suit from his boss, Mr. Coleman.

"Ya shouldn't swim right after eatin'. You'll get a cramp," Nan warns.

May casts off her summer dress to reveal a short peach suit with teal stripes. "That's an old wives' tale! Come on, Gabe!" She tags him then races toward the gentle waves.

"They'll be sorry!" Nan rolls her eyes.

"Thanks for inviting me to join you today." Iris rubs her belly. "I haven't eaten this well in weeks."

"I'm glad you could come," I smile. "How'd it go today at the tidepools?"

Iris shoves her glasses up her nose with irritation. "Just awful!"

"Still no specimens below Coast Inn," Dottie elaborates. "And only a couple of mussels. Otherwise...nothing."

"I just don't understand," Iris bemoans. "The populations continue to be stable at the other pools."

"What can you do at this point?" I ask.

"Dottie suggested collecting water samples."

My cousin nods. "That's why we were a little late. We had to drop them off at the Marine Lab on the way here."

"We'll analyze them later today," Iris adds.

I notice that Dottie hasn't been itching as much since they arrived. "How are the bites?"

"Better," she looks over her arms. "And no new ones. I think the flea situation is under control."

"Fleas?!" Nan nearly falls out of her chair. "Don't tell me that little feller has fleas!"

"Not anymore," I assure her and describe the flea treatment process we undertook.

"That's why cats belong outside!" she insists with a frown.

"You'll get no argument from me," I reply.

Dottie stands and adjusts the camera strap around her neck. "Say Ruby, do you think they'll mind if I snap some pictures?" She nods toward the cast and crew.

"Let's ask Archie just to be safe." I stretch out my arm for her to pull me up.

"Hi ya, Dottie," Archie hails as we approach. "Glad you could make it. Hopefully, today's shoot goes better than yesterday afternoon."

"I'm sure it will," my cousin grins. "Ruby told me that Elizabeth will be Corvi's voice double, and I know she's a wonderful singer. I've seen her in a bunch of musicals in Fullerton."

"That she is," Archie returns her smile.

"Speaking of which, where's the cast? I don't see them anywhere," I remark.

"Costume, hair, and makeup are in the shack on the end," he gestures. "They're getting Dean and Corvi ready. Liz will be off-screen, but we want her ready as a stand in, just in case."

"I can't believe he learned his lines so quickly," Dottie comments.

"He's a quick study," Archie folds his arms and nods. "And I doubt he slept a wink last night."

"Archie, would it be okay if I take some photos?" Dottie asks tentatively.

"No pictures of the set or cast, unfortunately. Mr. Lake's rules," he says apologetically.

"That's okay," she shrugs good-naturedly. "There's plenty to photograph down by the water. Starting with THAT!"

Archie and I shift our gaze in the direction of the shore where a teenage girl sits astride a pony-sized floating fish. She attempts to ride a wave but promptly topples from the brightly colored device—to the amusement of her companions.

"A guy in town makes them," Archie shares. "He told me he got the idea from stories about the Gabrielino tribe who lived here for thousands of years. They used to travel to the Channel Islands in wooden vessels made from redwood or pine. Although, I doubt they were shaped like a giant perch."

"Will you include it in the scene?" Dottie inquires.

"Maybe," he replies noncommittally.

When Dottie trots over to the group of young ladies, I bring up this morning's shoot. "Table Rock seemed to go smoothly."

"More than that!" Archie's face glows. "Mr. Lake and I looked over some of the footage, and it's superb!"

"How on Earth did you get it developed so quickly?" I was under the impression that the film was processed at the Burbank studio.

"We set up a lab nearby. On the off chance that we need to reshoot, we don't want to wait for the film to be carted to LA and back," he explains.

"And you liked what you saw?"

"Did I! The jump was flawless, and the footage from the camera on the boat was better than we could have imagined. His eyes sparkle.

"But there were so many takes with the rescue scene."

"That's typical with Mr. Lake. We could've stopped with the first take. It was perfect," Archie says dismissively. "What really impressed us was the chemistry between Liz and Dean. Just before the jump, the onboard camera caught them canoodling. Even at a distance, the magic between them was striking."

I know precisely what he's talking about. "What a shame it will have to be cut."

"Cut? Nothing doing! Mr. Lake insisted we keep the footage. After all, the viewers won't know it's Liz. They'll think it's Corvi."

Right on cue, the charming couple leave the hair and makeup shack and settle under a nearby umbrella. Dean has a ukulele in his hand, which I assume is a prop until he starts playing. After the opening melody, Elizabeth jumps into the first verse of the romantic ballad with a clear and bright timbre. Dean fumbles a bit with the cord transitions but only because his attention is fixed upon his beloved, who returns his gaze with an expression of adoration. A crowd gathers to watch the impromptu rehearsal. This is the song they will soon sing on camera—

albeit with Corvi mouthing the words. As the pair sweetly harmonize on the chorus, several women sigh nearby. A fair number of men remove their hats and—if I'm not mistaken—one wipes away a tear. The love song continues, and nearly everyone wanders closer to bask in their glow. I spot a few couples holding hands, to say nothing of the tender kisses Gabe and May are sharing. At the song's conclusion, I happen to glance at Corvi and Ike—who arrived just after we did. Corvi's wounded expression is at odds with the exuberant clapping and cheering around her.

"Chemistry!" Archie murmurs in my ear, then strides toward Dean and Elizabeth with open arms.

While the crowd disperses, I return to my seat beside Nan and Addie. Dottie and Iris flop down on the beach blanket, whereas May and Gabe return to the water.

"Dean and Elizabeth are so talented!" Dottie exclaims. "By the way, how'd it go at Table Rock this morning?"

"Quite well, according to Archie," I answer.

"Table Rock? Did you jump?" Iris chirps enthusiastically.

"Jump?" Dottie flinches.

"No, I didn't jump, but Elizabeth and Dean took the plunge—literally—during one of the scenes they shot."

"I didn't realize..." Dottie quails uncomfortably.

"It's thrilling!" Iris raves. "The rock is perched high above the water, and during high tide, you can jump from it. A group of us from the Marine Lab did it the week we arrived, and we plan to go back soon. Dottie, do you want to join us?"

My cousin shudders and crosses her arms. "I think I'll pass."

Nan looks at me with a raised eyebrow and shrugs. Dottie's response is unexpected given her adventuresome nature.

What is going on with her?

A little while later, a fastidious woman with a clipboard approaches our little group with hurried instructions. "Avoid looking at the cameras and carry on as you usually would at the beach. You won't be interacting directly with the cast, so do not approach them. And when

Mr. Duval calls 'Quiet on the set,' cease from talking out loud. However, we would like you to pretend as though you're talking to one another. Is that clear?"

Overwhelmed by the rapidity of her directions, we all stare at her blankly and bob our heads.

"Very well." Then she moves on to the next group of unsuspecting extras.

After that, I move my chair into the sun and close my eyes for a bit of tanning. I begin to doze in the bright warm light but nearly jump out of my skin when a persistent finger pokes my shoulder.

"Ruby!" Archie hisses. "I need you right now!"

With a pained expression, I hold my hand above my eyes to block the direct light and slowly regard his frantic expression. "What is it? I'm supposed to be off duty this afternoon."

"I'm so sorry, Ruby, but it's important," he pleads in hushed tones. "Corvi got another note."

I bolt from my chair and visually sweep the beach then look up at the bluff. A man with a pair of binoculars is watching a couple who appear to be arguing several yards away from the set—Corvi and Ike.

"It's him!" I shriek. "Archie, have security race up the trail. He's so distracted, maybe they can catch him."

Archie sprints toward three guards who are lounging under an umbrella. From his gesticulations, I surmise that he's chastising them before sending them on their way. In no time, they are half-way up the bluff. Meanwhile, the stalker registers the pounding footsteps and turns tail, disappearing from view.

The hot sand stings my feet around the edges of my sandals while I scamper toward Corvi. When Ike notices my approach, he grabs Corvi's upper arm, growls something in her ear, then kicks up sand as he stomps away.

"Archie said there's been another note," I pant.

Black streaks extend down Corvi's cheeks from her smudged mascara. She closes her eyes and hands me the postcard.

"Greetings from Laguna Beach" is printed across a crescent shaped cove on the front, while words scrawled in red ink meander across the back.

"It was left in my bag while I was in makeup," she chokes a sob.

This is the briefest note yet and reads:

"In her sepulcher there by the sea."

CHAPTER 17

"Last looks! Places everyone!" Archie booms through the megaphone. "We're behind schedule as is."

A makeup artist hastens alongside Corvi, dabbing her cheeks with a powder puff as the actress meanders toward Dean, who's skimming his lines on one of two rustic stools artfully placed in front of a tropical shack. Pygmy date palms have been arranged on either side of the open door, where a garland of colorful hibiscus flowers drapes the outer frame. A few yards away, a man in wide-legged trousers fiddles with his camera and tripod stand, while a young boom operator assembles two long poles, each with a microphone attached. Meanwhile, as a second camera pans the beach, the extras appear to be following the rules laid out by the no-nonsense production assistant.

"I can't believe Corvi bounced back so quickly," Elizabeth remarks.

My pal won't be needed on the set until the duet, so we're watching from a row of cast chairs under the largest umbrella I've ever seen. I take advantage of the downtime to record my observations of the stalker in my notebook. I didn't notice a jacket or hat, but the man's white shirt was cuffed just below the elbows, and his suspenders appeared to be light gray. Also, a distinct paunch was visible at his waistline, and his hair appeared to be receding at the temples.

"Mr. Lake didn't give her much of a choice," I reply.

When the security guards took off after the stalker, Mr. Lake charged over and categorically insisted that she 'pull it together' and that he had 'no time for her histrionics.' I lean forward to peer at the director, who's perched on a tall folding chair with an air of impatience. I expect him to leap up at any moment and start haranguing the cast and crew.

"Did he know what the note said?" she asks with incredulity.

"I tried to explain, but he didn't want to hear it. He gave her a swat on the behind and sent her to makeup."

My friend cringes. "I've had my fair share of that, even though I'm new to the business."

"This seemed more patronizing than lascivious—like he was reprimanding a child."

"Yeah, I've experienced that too," she sighs. "Tell me again what the note said."

"Why don't I read them all in sequence."

"For the moon never beams, without bringing me dreams
And the stars never rise, but I feel the bright eyes
And so, all the night-tide, I lie down by the side
Of my darling, my darling, my life and my bride
In her sepulcher there by the sea."

"Until that last line, it sounded like a sweet love poem." Elizabeth opens her hand for the notebook so she can read it again for herself.

"Precisely!" I notice that two guards have been stationed near Corvi. "I was so sure they'd catch him this time."

"At least Mr. Lake tightened security."

"That was Archie's doing." I lay a hand on her arm. "Elizabeth, I'm so sorry to get you into all this."

"What are you apologizing for?" She laughs. "This could be my big break. Dean feels the same way."

"The situation is unraveling, and I feel there's nothing I can do to stop it. I don't want you to get hurt. After what happened to Lena—"

"I'm fine! Both Dean and Archie are just down the hall at the hotel, and I'll keep both of my doors locked at night." Elizabeth returns the notebook. "Ike's the one to worry about, but he wouldn't dare lay a finger on me."

"I'm not so sure about that."

"Applesauce!" She flaps a hand. "What did he have to say about the note?"

"Surprisingly, he barked at Corvi then wandered off. I haven't seen him since."

"I don't find that surprising," she whispers. "He was heckling her for hours last night after I got back."

This fits with his earlier behavior when I approached them about the note. "Could you hear what he said?"

"No, he spoke just low enough that I couldn't make out the words, but when he left, I heard Corvi tell him to stay away from her." Elizabeth gives me a meaningful look.

"That may explain his absence this morning at Table Rock."

"First Position," Archie shouts, and Corvi takes the seat beside Dean.

Events unfold much as they did on Table Rock. Corvi and Dean perform a scene where the skindiver tries to persuade the young woman to leave her fiancé and marry him instead. With great skill, Corvi conveys the ambivalence of a lovelorn ingénue who must choose between her head and her heart. Meanwhile, Dean projects a sincerity that will, no doubt, win the affection of many young ladies in the audience. After a few minutes of dialogue, Corvi slowly rises to leave with much hand-wringing and tortured glances.

"Pause right there! Keep rolling!" Mr. Lake cries through his megaphone.

"Liz...take your place, now!" Archie yells.

She jumps from her chair and, alongside a young lady with a ukulele, stands underneath a second boom pole a couple of yards from the set.

"Action!"

I'm in awe as Dean pretends to play his ukulele in perfect sync with the young musician's strumming. Then, with a surprised expression, Corvi turns and approaches him, her mouth open as though singing; however, the bell-like tones we hear belong to Elizabeth. For a split second, Corvi bristles, which Mr. Lake notices and calls for them to restart. The second take is flawless, and the movement of Corvi's mouth perfectly matches Elizabeth's singing. They haven't had much time to work on this, so I'm quite impressed. Mr. Lake has them run through the scene a few more times, much to everyone's dismay, then finally calls, "Cut."

While Archie discusses the next scene with Corvi and Dean, I wander toward the shack for makeup, hair, and costume. Several of the ladies I met this morning are chatting outside the building in the shade.

"Thank goodness we didn't have to hear that caterwauling again," the costumer says.

"They should give Liz the part," the cosmetologist chimes in. "She can sing, act, and do the stunts."

"And when she's with Dean—well, you can't tear your eyes away from those two!" The hairdresser folds her hands against her heart.

"Haven't you got anything better to do?" Ike angrily berates them, shaking his cigar.

None of us noticed his approach. The women's faces blanch, and they disappear into the shack. I—on the other hand—am not intimidated.

"Ike, I need to speak with you."

He grunts something unintelligible and attempts to pass by me, but I step directly in front of him.

"Don't you think the police should be informed about this latest note? Security is supposed to safeguard Corvi while she's on set. I can't—"

"Let me handle this!" he thunders and waves to catch Corvi's attention before she goes in for a costume change.

"What was that all about?" Archie intercepts me as I head back to Nan and our group.

"Oh, you know, just Ike being his charming self."

"I heard something about the police," he persists.

"Can we discuss this in the shade? My feet are starting to burn."

"Oh—yes!" He escorts me to a vacant umbrella. "Sorry about that."

"Don't worry about it. I'm not annoyed with you. I'm irritated with this whole situation. First, the stalker bypasses security, gains access to Corvi's personal belongings and leaves a threatening note. Then, without drawing anyone's attention, he manages to watch her from the cliff. Last, he eludes security when they finally do chase after him. This is absolutely unacceptable!"

"I agree with you wholeheartedly!" Archie shakes his head. "In fact, when we're done here, I'm going to call Stardust and demand that the guards are replaced immediately."

"Well, that's a start, but all this should be reported to the police. I tried to talk to Ike—"

"Hang on…" Archie holds up his hands. "About that—"

"Surely, you're not going to tell me to keep the police out of this!" I'm flabbergasted.

"Well, you're the one who said that the stalker might not have anything to do with the notes," he points out.

"I can confidently say that today's circumstances have changed my mind."

"That may well be, but that officer you spoke with brushed it off," Archie reminds me.

"What's going on here, Archie? Why don't you want to call the police?"

He pauses and stares at me evenly before replying. "I understand where you're coming from—I really do—but a reporter has been snooping around today, and Mr. Lake ordered that we keep this under wraps."

I throw up my hands. "Well, if things continue along the same trajectory, Mr. Lake will soon have no say in the matter—because someone else will get hurt!"

THURSDAY, AUGUST 28, 1930

"How'd you sleep?" I ask Dottie as she joins me at the breakfast table rubbing her eyes.

Her moans and cries woke me around one in the morning. However, I dare not ask about the nightmare directly—I don't want to put her on the defensive again.

"Great! No more itching." Her smile doesn't reach her eyes. "And Puck didn't whine all night long. I think he's getting used to sleeping in the bathroom."

"That's good." I sense she's holding something back but choose to let it go for now.

Unfortunately, I never fell back asleep last night. Little compares with that visceral sense of dread that sometimes overcomes me in the wee hours of the night, particularly when my mind is already brimming with legitimate concerns. Worst case scenarios flash in and out of my awareness like the final frenetic bursts of a firework show on the Fourth of July. Meanwhile, an urgency deep in my stomach compels me to ferret out solutions or—in the very least—prevention tactics for each scenario. Of course, ninety-nine percent of the situations I envision never arise in real life, but during those long angst-ridden hours before the sun rises, this fact brings me no measure of comfort.

Thank goodness for my sunrise walk this morning. The steady slapping of my bare feet on the damp sand was comforting. I followed the shoreline south for nearly a mile before arriving at an enormous rocky outcropping, where I stopped and savored a flask of coffee.

Traces of my nighttime panic still lingered, so I crossed my legs and closed my eyes. With the whirlwind of activity over the past couple of weeks, I'd neglected my meditation practice—never a good choice—so, I slowly inhaled, drawing a breath that filled my lungs. After holding the breath for ten seconds, I exhaled through pursed lips. Eventually, I felt my shoulders loosen while a cool lightness spread throughout my body, and the stream of thoughts slowed in the background of my mind.

I was ready to sort through and prioritize the quandaries that kept me up most of the night, however I realized that I'd forgotten to bring my notebook. Thankfully, I found a small red trowel close to the shore, no doubt overlooked by a young child when it was time to leave. Drawing in the sand, I mapped out the various people and clues related to Corvi and the current threat, starting with Lena's death.

Duke and Sal's interviews were similar enough. Lena appeared to have some sort of fit while swimming in the kelp forest and continued thrashing about when they rescued her. Upon her death, her body was rigid and, according to Sal, she had an unsettling grin on her face. I added Pancho to the diagram, considering Lena's ill will toward her, but when Archie and I chatted with the pilot, she seemed to be an open book. Further, she appeared to be amused by Lena's grudge, not angry or bitter. I concluded that, until Lena's labs are received, nothing further can be accomplished. When Sam called me from the coroner's office last night, he assured me that the results should be available sometime today. Fingers crossed.

Next, I organized what I knew about the stalker and the notes. Until yesterday afternoon, I'd doubted whether he was the person sending the unsettling missives and wondered if he was even a threat to Corvi beyond following her around. He struck me as an ardent fan and nothing more. However, shortly after Corvi discovered the red-inked card yesterday, I spotted him on the cliff. That couldn't have been a coincidence and seemed to implicate him as the author of the notes. Nevertheless, how likely was it that he was aboard the *Statendam* or at the cemetery in France? But what about New York, where the first note was discovered? Perhaps he read about her stay at the Plaza—maybe he was even among the cheering throng on the dock...

I jammed the shovel into the sand with frustration.

Bah!

I've worked on many cases over the years but none as thorny or convoluted as this one. I feared that if we don't catch this man immediately, Corvi may be harmed. Given the menacing nature of the most recent note, the police would surely take the threat seriously. I contemplated calling them myself, however they'd want evidence, and there's no way Mr. Lake would permit Corvi to speak with them or hand over the notes.

Ike seemed determined to keep this quiet as well. I pondered his role in this situation. His relationship with Corvi has seemed volatile, at best. Moreover, his controlling and aggressive behavior toward her made me wonder about his hold over her.

Stumped, I moved on to Bebe and reflected upon her cutting remarks and veiled threats, but I couldn't figure out why she loathes Corvi so intensely beyond bitter jealousy. Further, I questioned whether Bebe had something to do with Lena's death or Rex's accident, for that matter. After all, she was actually on the shore when it happened.

Last, I added Poppy to the diagram. While probably just another starstruck fan, there's something about her that bothered me, so I resolved to speak with the young lady as soon as possible. If nothing else, she may have seen or heard something that could prove useful.

"I wonder if Nan kept the palm frond," Dottie comments.

"Excuse me?" I'm so wrapped up with my thoughts that her comment throws me for a moment.

"You know…Cleopatra?" she laughs.

When it was time to leave yesterday, we realized there was no way Nan would be able to ascend the steep trail. Despite her broad smile and assurance that she was "fit as a fiddle," it was clear that—after sitting in a low-slung chair all afternoon—her arthritis was causing her tremendous pain. Thankfully, one of the prop assistants overheard our dilemma and offered to help. He cleverly assembled a rudimentary litter from a collection of bamboo poles and canvas, to which May added the folded beach blanket as a cushion. When four strong crew members lifted her into the air, one of the costumers handed Nan a fan-shaped frond—presumably plucked from one of the date palms— and told her she looked like Cleopatra. Tickled, Nan hummed the tune "Queen of Egypt" all the way up the hill.

"She still had it in her hand when we said goodbye," I recall.

"I bet she put it in her best vase as soon as she got home," Dottie speculates.

"I wouldn't be at all surprised."

"Are you done with your plate? You've barely touched your food?" She rises from the table.

"I'm not hungry." I give her my plate and utensils. "Thanks for cleaning up."

"No problem! You cooked, after all."

I wander to the bedroom to retrieve my notebook and jot down my thoughts about Corvi's case. This takes a while as I keep flipping through my earlier notes to make sure I haven't overlooked something. Once I've untangled the disparate threads that kept me up last night, I know where to focus my energy this morning and compile a list of tasks. This process settles my nerves and brings me some measure of calm. Then the phone rings.

"Ruby, it's for you," Dottie calls from the other room.

Hopefully that's Sam with the test results.

I no sooner answer when Archie frantically cries, "Ruby, we're at the hospital—it's Liz!"

"How is she?" I grip the arms of an ashen-faced Dean.

"We're not sure yet." He rubs the back of his head, his loose curls standing atop his crown.

"What on earth happened?" I pull him aside as a nun, presumably a nurse, rushes by with a trolley.

"She's not making any sense. Corvi said it all started after breakfast."

His gaze slides toward a short hallway on our right, where Corvi and Archie are seated on a bench. With her eyes closed and head leaning on his shoulder, she resembles a child. As we approach, Archie gives her a shake, and her eyes fly open.

"Oh, Ruby! It's all so frightening!" She leaps to her feet and extends her arms.

My body stiffens involuntarily. Her lower lip quivers, and she sits back down. I didn't mean to offend her, but I'm desperate to know what's happened to Elizabeth. Consoling the petite star isn't my priority right now.

"Corvi, what happened this morning."

She begins to sob. Wrapping an arm around her, Archie suggests, "Perhaps I should explain."

"Well, I wish someone would tell me something," I snap impatiently.

"Of course," Archie nods. "Apparently a half an hour or so after eating breakfast, Corvi heard screams coming from Liz's room. She rushed in and found Liz pointing at a wall and shrieking something about a snake. Corvi immediately ran down the hall and pounded on my door."

"How did a snake get into her room?"

"There was no snake!" Corvi cries out. "She was seeing things that weren't there!"

"That's right," Archie confirms. "When I arrived, Liz insisted that the walls were red."

Dean sinks into a chair and buries his face in his hands. I sit next to him and place a hand on his back.

Archie continues, "The ambulance driver said she was having hallucinations and that her heartbeat was too fast and irregular."

"The doctor said the same thing. He also said that her pupils were dilated. She kept screaming about the sun burning her eyes when they were bringing her in from the ambulance." Dean adds, "And her face was bright red, like she had a sunburn."

"What did she have for breakfast?" I ask Corvi, who's following the conversation with round swollen eyes.

"Coffee, melon, and dry toast—just like mine, only she had two hard-boiled eggs as well."

"So, except for the eggs, you ate and drank exactly the same thing," I clarify.

"Well, no…" She picks at her thumbnail. "I added a little sugar to my coffee. Elizabeth likes hers black."

That's true. She's always teased me about adding a few splashes of cream to mine. "Was there anything amiss with the food or drink?"

Corvi slowly nods her head. "My tray was missing the sugar, and hers was missing the eggs. So, we swapped."

A chill runs down my spine. "Who delivered the trays."

"That Poppy girl," Corvi frowns. "She carried them in when Ike showed up."

"And the trays had your names on them?"

Corvi explains. "No, mine had a little card with my room number. The girl put my tray on my desk and carried Elizabeth's to her room.

After she left, we discovered the mistakes and thought it would be easier to exchange trays."

I look around the waiting room. "Where is Ike? Corvi, you should be back at the hotel with him. This is no place for you."

"I don't know. He stopped by the hotel this morning to tell me he would be gone all day. He had to meet someone but didn't say where he was going." She looks down at her left thumb.

"And you haven't seen him since?"

She shakes her head.

"I thought it best not to leave Corvi alone in her room," Archie interjects.

I release a breath. "I suppose that was wise, under the circumstances."

"Are you Miss Martin's family?" a mature doctor inquires.

We all look up.

Pale-faced Dean raises a shaking hand. "I'm her fiancé."

"You can see her now."

But before Dean can bolt toward Elizabeth's room, the physician stops him with a hand on his arm. "I should tell you that the police will be here soon."

"Why?" Dean asks, alarmed.

"We suspect that Miss Martin ingested poison."

"Hopefully the police intercepted the food tray before the staff threw it all away," I comment during our drive back to the hotel in my car.

Corvi and Archie rode to the hospital with Dean but, understandably, he stayed behind at Elizabeth's bedside when we left.

"Do you think Dean is alright there by himself?" Archie asks. "Maybe we should've hung around."

"Elizabeth's parents were on their way when we left," I assure him. "In fact, they've probably already arrived."

The newly built St Joseph Hospital is the largest medical facility in the county. Driving up, I was impressed by the imposing towers and cypress-lined private road leading to its front doors. This was my first trip to the magnificent campus, and I realized just how much our tiny Fullerton General Hospital pales in comparison. That being said, St. Joseph is quite a drive from Laguna Beach, so it'll take us a while to get back.

"I think the stalker poisoned her!" Corvi insists with panic.

"I've been wrestling with that possibility myself," I confess.

We drive on in silence—lost in our own thoughts—until about twenty minutes later when Corvi falls asleep. Her soft snore assures me that Archie and I can have a candid conversation.

"I blame Mr. Lake for this," I fume.

"What?!" Archie exclaims from the backseat.

"This would never have happened if we called the police yesterday." I glance irritably in the rearview mirror.

"You don't know that." He crosses his arms.

"The police would have caught him as soon as he stepped foot in the hotel."

"We had guards at each entryway, not to mention at the top of the stairs and elevator," Archie waves a hand.

"Yet here we are."

He grumbles, "Even if we had reported it, I doubt the police would have posted anyone at the hotel."

"You don't know that," I throw his words back at him.

His tone softens. "Ruby don't take this the wrong way, but I think your emotions are clouding your judgment. We don't know for certain that Liz has been poisoned, nor do we know that the so-called stalker was involved. There are too many unknowns at the moment to jump to conclusions."

My shoulders sag. "You're right. I'm terrified for Elizabeth, and I'm kicking myself for not protecting her. I should never have brought her into this mess."

"Geez, Ruby, don't blame yourself. I don't know where we'd be without you."

His words do little to placate the swirling maelstrom of thoughts and feelings within me. At least the police are now involved.

"Show me what you put in your pocket!" Corvi demands.

Poppy hangs her head, her stringy hair falling forward. With exaggerated slowness, she retrieves something from the side pocket of her uniform.

The actress takes a step toward her. "Open your hand."

The young woman rotates her fist and releases her tight grip. There, in the center of her palm, rests a small, tangled ball of pale fibers.

"Is that my hair?!" Corvi cries with bewilderment. "I don't know whether to slap you or laugh."

"Please don't slap me," Poppy looks up pitifully.

"She's not going to slap you," Archie reassures.

I'm not so sure about that.

When we returned to the third floor of the hotel, we spotted the teen stuffing something into her pocket while exiting Corvi's bedroom.

"Where did you find this?" I gently remove the clump from her hand.

"I-it was t-tangled around her silver brush." Her voice is tight as she struggles to hold back tears.

"Did you take my brush too?" Corvi reaches toward the girl's uniform. "What else have you stolen?"

"Nothing!" Poppy fervently shakes her head. "I'd never steal from you!"

"Then what do you call THAT?" Corvi wrinkles her nose at the soft tangle.

"I-I didn't think you'd mind. It'll just be thrown away by the housekeepers when they clean your room," Poppy explains.

"This is the second time you've been caught in Miss Styles' room when no one's around," Archie points out. "How did you get in?"

Poppy blinks when she swallows. "Well, Mrs. Gleason—she's in charge of the kitchen staff—she gave me a master key to pick up the tray from room 207."

"So, you decided to pay a little visit to my room, as well," Corvi folds her arms.

"Yes, Miss Styles. I'm so sorry!"

"How many times have you done this?" Archie inquires.

"Just this once." Poppy's eyes shift uncertainly. "I mean…I came to your room on Tuesday, but that was to pick up a tray. I didn't know someone else had already done it. But I swear on the Bible, today is the first and only time I came here to look around."

"And steal!" Corvi rolls her eyes. "One of my belongings disappeared on Tuesday."

"I didn't take anything! I promise!" Poppy crosses her heart.

"Well, I hate to say this, but we need to report you to the manager," Archie motions for Poppy to lead the way.

"Let me take her, Archie," I suggest. I may be able to get more information out of her before turning her over to her supervisor. "But first I need to ask Corvi a question."

Corvi raises her eyebrows as I pull her aside.

"You never specified what was missing on Tuesday."

"It was a bundle of letters tied with ribbon. I always keep it with me." She looks down at the carpet.

"Could you have misplaced it? How do you know it disappeared on Tuesday?" I query.

She sighs. "I suppose it could have been taken before Tuesday. That's when I noticed it was missing—but I didn't misplace it! I remember exactly where I put it when I unpacked and haven't touched it since."

"Did you search your drawers? Maybe it was inadvertently moved by housekeeping."

"They better not be going through my things!" she says indignantly. "But to answer your question—yes, I looked everywhere."

I nod. "Okay. I'm going to take Poppy downstairs, but then I have to be going. My family will be arriving soon at the house. I'll come back later this afternoon."

Heading to the kitchen, Poppy and I are the only ones in the service stairwell. Even though I'm sure of the answer, I ask Poppy, "Why did you take Corvi's hair?"

The teenager blushes. "I love her! I've seen all her movies—even the ones where she didn't talk. She's the best there is! I thought maybe I could just have a little piece of her. I know it sounds weird..." she trails off.

Just as I suspected...I won't press any further about that. "Tell me about this morning. Corvi mentioned that you brought the trays of food."

"Yes, I've been bringing her breakfast all week. The trays get awfully heavy—especially on the stairs—but I don't mind. At least I didn't have to carry them this morning," she remarks.

This catches my attention. "You didn't carry the trays?"

Poppy shakes her head. "No, ma'am. That big man with the cigar carried them up the stairs for me."

"Ike Bronson? Corvi's manager?" I can't imagine him helping anyone.

"Yes, that's him. He saw me in the stairwell and offered to carry the trays."

Why was he using the service stairs?

"Did he take them inside once you got to Corvi and Elizabeth's rooms?" I hold my breath.

"No, I told him I'd carry them in. It's my job. It looked like he may be staying for a while, so I asked him if I could bring him anything, but he said no."

"Do you know what happened to the trays when they were finished?" I ask eagerly.

"Well, a little while later, when I brought up Miss Gish's breakfast, I saw Mr. Bronson put the trays on the floor outside Miss Styles' door. Then he left."

"So, you took down the trays?"

"Yes, but first I knocked on the door because one of the cups was missing."

My neck tingles. "What happened?"

"Miss Styles said she hadn't finished her coffee and that she'd send the cup down later."

"But Miss Martin's cup was on the tray you took down?"

"Yes, ma'am."

Then it was most likely washed right away, along with her plates and utensils.

Rats!

I recall Ike's reaction yesterday when he heard some of the crew suggest that Elizabeth should have the lead role instead of Corvi. His proximity to Elizabeth's food this morning is deeply suspicious and makes me wonder if he had something to do with Lena's death as well. I was under the impression that he had a meeting with Archie and Mr. Lake the morning she died, but maybe he stopped by their rooms beforehand.

But why would he kill her?

Then it hits me—their altercation on Saturday! Of course! Now I'm even more eager to hear about the results from Lena's autopsy. Regardless, I have a hypothesis about what may have happened.

When we reach the basement, I steer Poppy toward an empty corner of the hallway. The kitchen is a hive of activity, and I don't want to be overheard.

"Did you work this past Sunday?"

"Yes, I did a double shift—with all the movie people, we're short-staffed."

"Do you remember bringing a tonic to Miss Styles or Miss Young that morning?"

"Of course, I did. I brought Miss Styles her tonic every morning—that is until Tuesday morning." Her face falls.

"What happened Tuesday morning?"

"Miss Styles told me it was disgusting and to never bring it again."

So much for their celebrity endorsement. "Tell me about Sunday morning—when you brought the tonic."

"I showed up a little earlier than I was supposed to—just before six—and I knocked on Miss Styles' door. I guess it was too early because she didn't answer."

"Did you try Miss Young's door?"

"No, I left the tonic on a tray in the hall."

CHAPTER 18

"He's called four times!" Dottie hands me a scrap of paper. "Here's the number. He said to call as soon as you got in."

I drop my handbag on the floor and head to the phone.

"Dr. Carroll's office, how may I help you?" I recognize the friendly voice from the last time I phoned.

"Hello, this is Ruby Ray. I'm calling for Sam…er…Dr. Armstrong."

Her tone changes to one of urgency, "Of course! He'll be right with you."

Not two seconds later, Sam's on the line. "Ruby! Thank God you called! How's Elizabeth? Dottie told me she's in the hospital."

"Yes, I just got back." I twist the cord nervously with my free hand. "It's not good, Sam. They say she's been poisoned."

"Shoot! It's too late!" Sam wails.

My stomach drops. "What do you mean?"

"The lab results came back a couple of hours ago for Miss Young. She was poisoned with strychnine."

Gulp.

I don't know much about poisons, but strychnine has been in the news lately. A couple of weeks ago, I read an article reporting that strychnine is the most common cause of death by poisoning in children. It's no wonder—nearly every family keeps rodenticide in their home. Just last year, one of my clients told me she'd kill her husband with gopher poison if I couldn't help her escape his abuse. She said she was kidding, but I had a hunch that she may have gone through with it as a last resort. Fortunately, we were able to relocate her to Modesto, where she now lives with a cousin.

"I suspected strychnine, given the risus sardonicus and opisthotonus. Though, I'm surprised she ingested it without knowing. It's quite bitter."

"The health tonic! She probably drank it before swimming, that was her routine. Apparently, the tonic itself is quite bitter—I doubt Lena even noticed."

"That makes sense. I wonder if Elizabeth was also poisoned with strychnine. What were her symptoms?"

"Hallucinations, rapid pulse, dilated eyes, red face—"

"Blind as a bat, mad as a hatter, red as a beet…" Sam interrupts. "I don't think it was strychnine."

"That sounds like a nursery rhyme," I comment.

"It's a mnemonic I learned in medical school to remember the signs of anticholinergic poisoning," he explains.

"Anticholinergic? I've never heard of that."

"There are several types of mediations in that category. They can be deadly if overused," Sam replies somberly.

"Will she be okay?"

The line goes silent for several moments.

"Hello? Did I lose you?"

I start to click the hook on the receiver when Sam's choked voice says, "Ruby, I'm really worried about you. That's TWO poisonings. Wouldn't it be best to let the police handle this?"

I bristle. I know he's concerned—and for that I'm grateful—but this is my job. "I'm fine, Sam. I know what I'm doing. That being said, I'll call the police as soon as we hang up."

"The coroner's office beat you to it. They immediately reported the poisoning when Miss Young's results came back."

"I'm relieved to hear that."

He muffles the phone to speak with someone then returns to our call. "I'm sorry, Ruby. A patient just came in with an asthma attack—but I want to continue this conversation later."

"Let's talk this evening. Can you meet me at the beach below the Coast Inn at six thirty? My family will be staying there, and we have plans for a bonfire."

In fact, Jack and Uncle Charles should be pulling up to the house any minute before heading over to the hotel to check in.

"I don't want to intrude…" Sam protests.

"Nonsense. They'll be thrilled to see you. Plus, Dottie wants to show us the tidepools below the Coast Inn that she and Iris have been investigating. You and I will have plenty of time to take a walk and discuss your concerns."

"I'll be there," Sam replies. "And Ruby…"

"Yes?"

"Remember—less onerous circumstances—alright?" I hear his grin.

"Definitely," I smile.

"I can't believe you're friends with Pancho Barnes!" Jack tugs at the earflaps on his leather aviator hat.

"Who said we were friends?" I laugh and pull the cap off his head.

"She invited you to her party, didn't she?" He asks while scratching his scalp.

"Pancho invited her friend Archie, the assistant director on the film. She only included us to be polite."

Dottie slings an arm around his shoulders. "Pancho told me to bring you specifically, Jack, because she wants you to meet her son."

His eyes light up. "Whoa, that's swell!"

Uncle Charles is standing at the fireplace gazing up at the seascape. I stroll across the living room to join him.

"She loved it here," he says wistfully.

I tuck my arm through his. "I wondered if this would be hard for you…being back after all these years."

He nods thoughtfully. "I don't know why I avoided this for so long. Beatrice and I shared so many wonderful memories in Laguna Beach. By staying away, I feel as though I've robbed Jack and Polka Dot."

"It's not too late, and I'm sure this weekend will be one that they'll never forget," I assure him.

"Jack is in seventh heaven," he chuckles. "A party AND an airshow with Pancho!"

"Despite all the drama, Dottie seems to be enjoying herself, as well." I lower my voice. "But I would like to chat with you about something."

"Sure, Ruby! I'd be glad to check the air pressure on your tires!" he says theatrically.

Shaking my head, I follow him out the front door.

"Do you think they bought that?" he asks.

"Not for a minute," I laugh.

We park ourselves under the sycamore. "You know, I really should check your tires while I'm here."

"They're fine! I have a pressure gauge in my glove box."

"Attagirl!" He beams. "What would you like to talk about? The case you're working on?"

I roll my eyes. "Don't get me started with that!"

"I called Dottie before we left this morning, and she filled me in. How's Elizabeth?"

I close my eyes. "I really don't know. The doctors sedated her, which I take as a good sign. If they thought she might die..."

"She's in great hands. From what I've heard, St. Joseph is the best hospital in the county."

"Thank you for the reassurance...but I'd actually like to speak with you about Dottie."

He nods gravely. "Has she been having nightmares?"

My head twists to look at him. "You know about that?!"

"They started right after graduation."

He removes a pipe from his pocket, and I notice it's the one I brought back from England. As a rule, Uncle Charles only smokes his pipe in the evening, but he fidgets with it at other times, especially when something weighs heavily on his mind.

"Has she spoken with you about them?" I inquire.

He shakes his head. "Clams right up whenever I mention it."

I sigh deeply. "Same here. She's had a few nightmares since we arrived. Each time I bring it up, she becomes defensive."

"Do you think it's just jitters about Berkeley?" he asks hopefully.

"I'm not sure. We chatted about that, and she admitted to feeling nervous, but I wonder if it's something more?"

"That's what concerns me." Uncle Charles' voice is barely a whisper. "Do you think she told us everything that happened with that cult?"

I shrug. "I thought so at the time. Now I'm not so sure." I shudder at the thought of what else may have happened to those kids.

"What should we do?" He sounds baffled.

"You're asking me? I was hoping you'd tell me what to do."

"I guess we continue to let her know that we're here for her. Hopefully she opens up before leaving for Berkeley." He looks at his watch as though it has a calendar. "That's little more than a week away."

"Speaking of opening up, have you talked to Nan?"

He slaps the arm of the chair. "That's another one! What's going on with her? I haven't seen her smile for days."

"I spoke with Addie. Evidently, Nan's sister is losing her house in the next couple of weeks and has to move in with her son and daughter-in-law in San Diego."

His jaw drops. "Why hasn't she said anything?"

"You know Nan—she doesn't want to be a burden."

"Nan could never be a burden!" he pronounces. "Does she have any plans?"

"None. No one has room for her."

I'm sure her family feels terrible about this, but they're all struggling to make ends meet. Investors weren't the only ones who suffered after the stock market crash. From what I've read, the unemployment rate is escalating at an alarming rate, especially among blue-collar workers, and our country's economy continues to worsen.

"WE have room for her!" Uncle Charles exclaims.

"But we only have four bedrooms…"

"I've been thinking about adding on to the back of the house. In the meantime, she can stay in Dottie's room."

My heart swells. I knew Uncle Charles would have a solution.

"You know, I really should look at your tires before we go back in."
He winks while rising from the Adirondack chair.

"They're fine! And I doubt Jack and Dottie are even looking out
the window."

We return to find Jack rolling a yo-yo along the floor. Every time
Puck pounces on the gold disc, Jack yanks the cord, sending the toy
racing in a different direction. He hears our steps and looks up.

"Hey, Dad. Whaddya say we get a kitten?"

"NO!" Uncle Charles, Dottie, and I simultaneously exclaim.

"Strychnine?!" Archie cries out as the elevator door opens.

The attendant inside the elevator jumps, his eyes bulging with
confusion.

"We'll take the stairs," I inform him.

I left the house just after Uncle Charles and Jack drove away. At
Jack's insistence, his father agreed to take him fishing off the pier once
they check into their room.

"That way, we'll have something to eat at the bonfire," he claimed
persuasively.

Dottie asked me to meet her at Rankin's Drugs at four after she and
Iris analyze the samples they collected yesterday. It's a quarter past two
right now, and I just arrived at the Hotel Laguna. Archie intercepted
me in the lobby. Apparently, he had a lunchtime meeting with Mr. Lake
at the hotel restaurant.

"So, both Lena AND Liz were poisoned." Archie thumps up the
steps beside me. "No wonder the police were talking to the hotel
manager just now."

"Yes, but Sam doesn't think it's the same poison," I clarify.

"Does it even matter? Poison is poison." He has a point.

"Archie, when did you meet with Mr. Lake and Ike Sunday
morning? I know it was before breakfast."

"Around six-thirty. Ike was already in the meeting room when Mr.
Lake and I arrived. Why?"

"Poppy told me that she left the tonic in the hall just before six o'clock that morning because Corvi didn't answer her door."

"You think it was the Laguna Breeze?" He gives me an incredulous stare.

"Lena drank the tonic each morning and, according to Corvi, they left for the beach at six forty-five."

"So?"

"So…the tonic was in the hall, unsupervised, for about forty-five minutes. Ike didn't meet you two until six-thirty," I explain.

Archie stops before we reach the third-floor landing. "You think IKE poisoned Lena?!"

"He's definitely a suspect," I clarify.

Archie throws up his hands. "Why would he want to do that?"

"I saw them quarrel Saturday when you all were downtown for a shoot. Ike attempted to speak with Lena, but she wanted nothing to do with him. When she gave him the brush off, he tried to get physical, but she told him to lay off and walked away."

"I have no idea what that was about," he replies, puzzled. "As far as I know, those two were strangers before this film."

"In any case, he's on my list of suspects."

"Do you think he poisoned Liz too?"

"Possibly."

I describe Ike's reaction yesterday when he overheard the women comparing Elizabeth with Corvi. Then I tell him about Poppy's testimony regarding the trays this morning.

He buries his head in his hands. "This is crazy! I thought the stalker was behind all this."

"I'm not sure about any of it right now."

A security guard from the studio nods at us as we reach the top of the stairs. When we get to the suite, Kit opens the door.

"Thank goodness you're here with Corvi!" I declare, having feared that Ike may have come back early and was alone with her.

"I ran into Archie in the hallway when he was heading downstairs, and he told me all about Liz. I'm thunderstruck!" Kit takes a seat beside Corvi on the sofa.

"There's more." I settle into a chair across from them. "I got a call a little while ago that the results from Lena's autopsy came back—she was poisoned too."

Corvi gasps and seizes Kit's arm, all color draining from her cheeks. "That can't be!"

"I'm afraid it's true," I say gently. "Corvi, I need to ask you about that morning—before you went down to the cove. Did Lena eat or drink anything?"

She closes her eyes and shakes her head. "It's so hard to think. I can't believe this has happened!"

Kit strokes her arm. "It's all very shocking."

After a few moments, Corvi opens her eyes and nods resolutely. "I can do this."

I bob my head encouragingly. "Take your time."

"Well…she didn't eat anything that I know of, but she did drink that atrocious tonic," she says with disgust.

"I understand that Poppy knocked on your door around six that morning. She said you didn't answer."

"I suppose I didn't hear her. I wasn't able to fall asleep until around five. After that note Saturday—and seeing that man twice in one day…" She shivers. "I didn't wake up until Lena shook me and said it was time to go."

"Tell me about the tonic. Who brought it in from the hall?"

Corvi raises her brows. "Lena must have. She had it in her hand when she woke me."

"Did you see her drink it?"

"Oh, yes!" Corvi answers emphatically. "She gulped it down without stopping right before we walked out the door."

"I know I asked you this before, but did Lena seem different in any way after drinking the tonic?" I probe.

"Like I said, I was exhausted and didn't pay any attention to her. I barely remember the walk to the cove."

A firm knock on Corvi's bedroom door disrupts our discussion.

"I'll see who it is," Archie jumps up and leaves the room. A moment later we hear him say, "Officers…how can I help you?"

At that, I leap from my chair to join him. An elderly policeman faces Archie. He's fit for a man his age, however he's attempted to style his balding hair in a manner better suited to someone decades younger. The silver pin on his collar—which looks like two parallel vertical bars—indicates his authority. Behind him stand Officer Jankowski and a cadet carrying a duffel bag marked "LBPD."

"I'm Inspector Maggard with the Laguna Beach Police Department. We're here to investigate two poisonings involving women who recently stayed in this suite of rooms."

I lock eyes with Officer Jankowski. He compresses his tobacco-stained lips with chagrin.

"Of course, Inspector. Please come in." Archie holds the door for the three men, who remove their hats before entering.

Corvi quails as they enter the living room, until she spots Officer Jankowski. "We told you about the stalker and the notes, but you said there was no danger! You should have listened!"

Inspector Maggard holds up his neatly manicured hands in appeasement. "Officer Jankowski filed a report after speaking with you. There was no evidence at the time that the gentleman in question was a threat to you or anyone else."

"There's been another note," I interject. "This one IS threatening. Furthermore, I saw the stalker watching Corvi through binoculars just after she found the note."

"When was this?" The inspector opens a black leather notebook and begins to write.

"Yesterday afternoon," I reply and give him specific information about the stalker's appearance, behavior, and the circumstances surrounding the note's discovery.

After jotting down several lines, he looks up. "Are the notes here?"

Corvi nods. "I'll get them for you." She disappears into her bedroom.

"And who are you, young lady?" the inspector asks me, his expression completely flat.

I bristle before extending a hand. "Ruby Ray, inquiry agent. Stardust Productions hired me after Miss Young's death."

When he hears my name, recognition flashes across his face, and he turns to Officer Jankowski.

"Yep. She's the one," Jankowski confirms with a hint of amusement.

Inspector Maggard ignores my proffered hand and scribbles in his notebook. He then asks Archie and Kit each to state their identity and relationship to the victims. The inspector stares uncomfortably at Archie for longer than necessary—his eyebrows furrowed—which makes Archie visibly uneasy. As a Black, homosexual man, I can only imagine the treatment he's received over the years. Thankfully, Corvi returns to the living room and breaks the tension. She hands the notes to the cadet and sits beside Kit. The cadet skims the first couple of postcards and snickers.

"Out loud, Cunningham," the inspector orders.

I watch their expressions as the adolescent reads the notes. At first, they are amused by the romantic lines, but when they hear the words *sepulcher*, their faces fall. Officer Jankowski gives me a sidelong look, while Cadet Cunningham shifts his weight back and forth from one foot to the other.

After a moment, the inspector mutters, "How queer," and locks eyes with Archie.

"Please keep them," Corvi urges. "I only held onto them as proof."

Inspector Maggard clears his throat. "Cunningham, secure them in an evidence bag."

The cadet removes a paper bag from the duffel and fills in several lines on the outside before inserting the notes.

"I'd like to see the rooms Miss Young and Miss Martin stayed in," the inspector demands.

"Miss Martin moved into Miss Young's room after…well, after. It's right through here." Archie motions toward the connecting door.

"If it's alright, inspector, I'd like to have a word with you for a moment outside," I interrupt.

He frowns. "Jankowski and Cunningham, start dusting for prints."

I lead him down the hallway for privacy. After all, Bebe might be in her room, and I'd prefer that she doesn't hear our conversation.

"I don't have a lot of time, Miss Ray. What is it?" Inspector Maggard crosses his arms.

"I have reason to believe that the man stalking Miss Styles may not be the same person who poisoned Miss Young and Miss Martin." I pull out my notebook and flip to my most recent notes.

"Is that so?" He tilts his head with condescension.

In a logical and concise manner, I explain my rationale for suspecting Ike. All the while, the inspector stares at me with a deadpan expression.

"Why aren't you taking notes?"

"I don't see the need." His cheeks dimple as he gives me a smug, close-lipped smile.

"I've laid out all the reasons—"

Inspector Maggard holds up three fingers. "Opportunity…I'll give you that one." He puts down one finger. "But means and motive?" He wiggles the two remaining fingers. "I'm sorry, missy, but your argument is flimsy at best. Leave it with us. We know what we're doing."

"Sure, I saw him," the housekeeper removes a set of sheets from her cart. "A couple of times."

After our discussion, the inspector strongly suggested that I make myself scarce while they collect evidence, so I went to the basement to interview the hotel staff. I've already described the stalker to several people in various departments and asked if they saw him any time since last Friday. The desk clerk reported seeing him Saturday morning in the lobby but asked him to leave when it was clear that he wasn't with

Stardust Productions. None of the kitchen staff recognized the description, but one of the dishwashers claims he saw a man fitting Ike's description in the basement a few days ago. He couldn't be more specific than that.

"Can you tell me when you saw him?" I inquire about the stalker.

"Hmmm…sometime over the weekend. It was the afternoon I was cleaning the third-floor rooms." She squints one eye in thought. "I guess the other time was in the stairwell. I asked him if he was lost. Guests aren't supposed to use the service stairs."

I look up from my notes. "When was that?"

"Monday or Tuesday…sorry, I don't remember which."

"That's okay. Is there anything else you noticed that seemed odd?"

She parts a small curtain on her cart that conceals a shelf of cleaning agents. Pointing at a box on the left-hand side of the space, she says, "My rat poison went missing Saturday, but it was back on my cart Sunday afternoon. I figured one of the other housekeepers borrowed it."

The strychnine!

She adds, "This building may be new, but rats are smart. They know where to find a good meal."

I switch gears. "At any time during the early morning hours, have you seen a big man? He's quite imposing and usually smokes a cigar?"

"I don't get to work until 10:00, but I know who you're talking about. He's here a lot. Someone told me he's Corvi Style's manager. I steer clear of him."

Good idea!

"One last question—do you know Poppy? She delivers trays for the kitchen."

"Of course, I know Poppy!" Her broad smile implies affection. "Sweet girl but a bit bird-brained, if you know what I mean. Why do you ask?"

Not wanting to add grist to the gossip mill, I avoid mentioning the "theft" earlier today. Instead, I ask, "Does she get into any trouble?"

"Not that I know of. She's a good girl," the housekeeper answers with certainty.

Once I've interviewed all the staff who are available, I retrace my steps up the service stairs to leave. I need to meet Dottie soon. When I reach the lobby, I encounter Archie hurrying toward the front door.

"Where are you off to?"

"Believe it or not, Mr. Lake wants to continue with a shoot that was supposed to begin at four."

"That doesn't surprise me one bit. Where's Corvi?"

"In her room. We only need Bebe and Kit for the scene."

"Corvi's by herself?" I start to step toward the elevator, but Archie grabs my arm.

"The police contacted the studio and insisted that they place a security guard outside her door at all times, along with guards to escort her when she leaves the building."

"It's about time!" I exclaim. "Still…maybe I should check on her. What if Ike—"

"She's fine, Ruby. He's not going to try anything with a guard just a few feet away. Besides, didn't you say your family arrived today?"

I blow out a breath. "Yes, you're right. I need to meet Dottie right now, then I'll be with my uncle and cousins this evening. What are the plans for tomorrow? Do you think you'll attend Pancho's party.?"

He winces. "Pancho's party! I forgot about that! We're supposed to film tomorrow morning around eleven. You don't need to be there, by the way."

"Alright, but I'll probably stop by the hotel before that to check in with Corvi."

"See you then," he dashes around the corner to his car.

I cross the street and head for the pharmacy. When I arrive, Dottie is sitting on a bench near the hanging gate licking an ice cream cone.

"Hey, where's mine?" I tease.

"Go get your own," she laughs.

"Nah, I'm alright. Not much of an appetite, to be honest." I sit beside her on the bench. "Remind me—why did you want me to meet you here?"

"I'm out of money, and I need more film," she kicks the ground with the toe of her sandal.

I shove her playfully. "Why didn't you ask your dad for cash?"

"I've used up my monthly allowance," she replies sheepishly. "I thought maybe I could borrow some money from you until September 1st."

"How'd you pay for the ice cream?" I look at her critically.

"I told Mr. Rankin you were on your way," Dottie grins.

I roll my eyes and stand up. "Finish your ice cream."

The air inside is cooler, thanks to three large fans rotating overhead.

"How can I help you," Mr. Rankin asks warmly.

"Can you tell me where I can buy some sticks for roasting marshmallows?"

"I can do better than that. Here's everything you'll need for s'mores."

He points to a display of marshmallows, graham crackers, and chocolate bars. Standing alongside the sweets in a cardboard tube are wooden skewers, nearly three feet in length.

"S'mores? I've never heard of such a thing."

"My daughter told me about them. She's a Girl Scout, and there's a recipe in their handbook." He points to the ingredients. "You sandwich a roasted marshmallow and a piece of chocolate between two graham crackers. It's marvelous!"

Just like Mallomars! "Why's it called s'more?"

"Because you always want 'some more.' Get it? S'more?" He chuckles merrily.

"I love it! I'll need enough for about six people."

"I can get that for you. Have a look around," Mr. Rankin suggests.

Having finished her cone, Dottie strolls inside and collects her developed prints from an older man working at the register.

"That was fast," I remark.

Flipping through the photos, she ignores my comment. "Ruby, wouldn't it be great if you could see your photos right after taking them? That would have saved me all the exposures I wasted on this crab!" she complains.

The blurred images look as though she tried to get a close-up photo of the hermit crab sitting in a shallow pool. "Wouldn't that be something!" I agree.

"Here they are." Mr. Rankin places a sack on the counter, along with six sticks. "Will there be anything else?"

"I need this film developed, and I could use three more rolls." Dottie hands him a small cylinder, which he passes to the other gentleman.

"Arthur, would you mind preparing this for the lab?" Mr. Rankin asks.

The sweet man smiles at Dottie and shuffles to the end of the counter. He withdraws a slip of paper and an envelope from a pair of boxes and asks Dottie, "What's your name, young lady?"

"It's Dottie. Dottie Ray."

He nods and marks the form.

Mr. Rankin tells me, "Arthur's been a pharmacist for decades. He helps me with the dispensary. Good man."

Just then the door flies open and a voice cries out, "Uncle Arthur!"

"Well, hello there, Poppy! I don't think I've seen you in weeks. How was New York City?"

"Good," she replies. "Can I get some ice cream?"

"Help yourself," Arthur looks at Mr. Rankin, who gives him a nod.

"Is that brother of yours behaving himself out there?" Arthur asks.

She nods and walks behind the ice cream counter. "He had to work most of the time, but he took me to see the tallest building in the world."

"Imagine that!" Arthur declares.

Poppy's expression changes when she notices me. "Oh…hello."

"Hi, Poppy," I return her greeting.

"We were in New York too," Dottie exclaims. "When did you get back?"

"A week ago Wednesday."

"Did you start your new job at that fancy hotel?" her uncle inquires. "How's that going?"

Poppy's face reddens, and she shoots me a quick glance. "It's okay."

"Good…good…" Arthur places the envelope with Dottie's film in a shallow box along with a few other envelopes.

I pay Mr. Rankin. "Thank you so much."

"Enjoy the s'mores!" He smiles

"We will!"

We've only just stepped out of the store when I feel a tap on my shoulder. "Miss?"

"Yes, Poppy."

"Thank you for what you said to my boss…about giving me a second chance."

"So, you weren't fired?"

"No, ma'am. And I'm never gonna do nothing like that again."

Walking home, Dottie chatters about her afternoon with Iris, but I'm not really listening.

Poppy was in New York when Corvi was there.

Is she the one sending the notes? That seems improbable. To begin with, the verse seems too sophisticated for anything Poppy would write. Further, how would she have gotten the notes to Corvi in Los Angeles? Still, it makes me wonder. Moreover, Poppy has an uncle who works at a pharmacy. No one would think twice if she was hanging around the drugstore. And not only did she have access to both the food and drink that Lena and Elizabeth consumed, but she was also in a position to wash away the contaminated dishes later. I don't know. It's probably just a series of coincidences, but I should keep a closer eye on her.

"I'm sorry, Dottie. What were you saying?"

"Weren't you listening? We analyzed the samples, and there were high levels of silver among those we took from the tidepool by the Coast Inn. Iris says that silver is toxic to marine animals."

"Silver? I thought silver came from mines, not the ocean."

"Exactly! It shouldn't be in the tidepool, and we found no trace of silver in the samples from the other tidepools. I'm afraid it's all still a mystery."

It's all still a mystery.

CHAPTER 19

"How's Elizabeth?" Uncle Charles asks when Dottie and I arrive at the Coast Inn.

"The doctor says she'll pull through," I mirror the relief I heard in Dean's voice when he called just before we left the house. "They'll keep her overnight, but she may be able to go home as soon as tomorrow. They're just waiting for the lab to confirm the type of poison she ingested."

"Thank goodness for that!" my uncle claps his hands.

We head toward the back of the hotel where a grassy expanse stretches to the top of the bluff. Behind us, the cheerful inn rises up in tiers, each with brightly striped awnings shading the westward facing windows from the late day sun. Wooden decks extend from each level, creating comfortable spaces to enjoy the view from pillow-topped lounge chairs under broad umbrellas, and a steep staircase descends from the lowest deck to the sand below.

"Ruby! Come look at all the fish we caught!" Jack waves his arms and shouts from the shoreline when we reach the bottom steps.

Uncle Charles chuckles. "He didn't believe me when I told him I knew a thing or two about fishing, but after a half an hour, we'd already caught five perch, and he had to concede that I knew what I was doing."

I step upon the stand, still hot from the afternoon heat a few hours earlier, and approach a ring of bricks encircled by half a dozen small canvas chairs. A pile of wood and kindling have been arranged in the center of the ring, and off to the side, a quilt stretches on the sand with a picnic basket and Jack's shoes anchoring three of the corners lest a stiff breeze carry it away. I place the sack from Rankin's onto the blanket and stick the skewers directly into the sand next to the fire pit.

"This is some setup!" Dottie admires.

"We were lucky enough to reserve it when we checked in," her father explains. "The hotel assembled everything for us."

Jack jogs over to us—his feet and ankles encrusted with wet sand—and grabs one of the skewers.

"Neat!" He flings the stick like a fencing foil. "I was wondering how we were gonna cook the perch."

"Exactly how many did you catch?" I examine a galvanized steel tub where a few pinkish gray tails poke out from the ice alongside bottles of soda.

"I insisted we stop with a dozen," my uncle answers.

Jack shrugs. "It's okay. That gave me more time to dig for treasure."

"Treasure?" Dottie tilts her head, her eyebrows raised skeptically.

"Sure! Buried by the French pirate, Captain Hyppolyte Bouchard!" Jack jabs with the skewer.

"A French pirate buried a treasure here—in Southern California!" She rolls her eyes.

"An old guy on the pier told me. He's lived here his whole life, and that's a long time cuz he must've been at least ninety."

"Maybe sixty," Uncle Charles mumbles under his breath.

"He said that Captain Bouchard came ashore in 1818 and buried a metal chest with gold, silver, and all kinds of jewels he stole from the missions," Jack continues excitedly.

"Jack, the man also told you that he supposedly buried it about a mile and a half south of here," his father corrects him.

"So! Maybe it was carried out by a high tide and later washed up here." While irrational at times, Jack's optimism never ceases to impress me.

"Do you plan to dig up this entire beach?" Dottie scoffs.

"It'll give him something to do," Uncle Charles tells her quietly.

Meanwhile, Jack abandons the skewer and retrieves a long shovel from the far side of the fire pit. "Wanna help, Ruby?"

"Aren't we going to cook the fish?" Uncle Charles intercedes.

"Great!" Jack discards the shovel.

I check my wristwatch and realize that it's almost six-thirty.

"I told Sam I'd meet him in front of the hotel," I call over my shoulder while dashing up the stairs.

When I reach the top step, I'm confronted by an enormous watermelon.

"My grandma always says that you should never arrive empty-handed when invited to a dinner party," Sam grins.

"Well, she would be proud. That's quite a melon," I laugh. "Do you need a hand hauling it downstairs?"

"Nah!"

He hoists it upon his shoulder, giving me the opportunity to admire the well-toned biceps peeking out from the short sleeves of his pale blue shantung shirt. His white Bermuda shorts display tanned legs, and I can't help but wonder when he's found time to sunbathe. A few drops of water splash onto the ground next to his canvas sneakers.

"I could use a towel, though," he says. "The grocer pulled this out of the icebox for me, and it's sweating like a pig. There should be one in my bag."

I open the duffel slung around his chest and pull out a terry cloth towel.

"Lift the watermelon a bit, and I'll slide this on your shoulder," I instruct.

Once the green-striped fruit has been secured, we descend to greet my family.

"Sam!" Jack calls. "Dad's gonna let me light the fire with this flint rock!"

Sam shoots me a questioning look as if to say, "Is that such a good idea?"

"You can try," my uncle comments. "But I have a book of matches just in case." Then he formally greets Sam. "Welcome to our Swiss Family Robinson supper."

"Thank you, sir." Sam replies. "I'd shake your hand, but..."

"You should put that down before your fingers turn blue," I gesture to the watermelon. "The blanket would be a good spot for now."

"Hey, Dad! Can I carve it up with the Bowie knife?" Jack pleads.

"Let's see how you do with that fire first," his father reasons.

"Do you want a Coca-Cola, Sam?" Dottie offers.

"Sure! That'd be great. Thanks!" Sam wipes his brow.

"That must've been a bear to carry downstairs," I nod toward the expansive ice tub.

"One of the porters brought it for us," Uncle Charles answers. "I think they're trying to compete with the Hotel Laguna and La Casa del Camino."

"This town is booming," Sam shares. "Some of my patients tell me they hardly recognize this stretch of the highway."

"The same is true in Fullerton," my uncle remarks. "Ruby tells me you're working two jobs while you're here. Have you had any time to enjoy the beach and the weather?"

Sam shakes his head. "Not since I started working at the morgue, but during my first week here, I had my feet in the sand as much as possible."

"Hey, Dottie. Sorry I'm late," Iris strolls up carrying a knapsack and clipboard.

"Dad, this is my friend Iris," Dottie introduces. "Iris, this is my dad."

"Hello, Mr. Ray," Iris politely shakes his hand then pushes up her spectacles. "It's very nice to meet you."

"And you as well," Uncle Charles replies warmly. "Dottie's told me all about the research you're doing and the mystery you both have been trying to solve."

"Yes, sir. That's why I brought my supplies. The tidepool in question is right over there." She points toward a small, craggy outcrop. "High tide was a few hours ago, so this would be a good time to examine the pool."

Jack drops his flint and a sedimentary rock he found near the staircase and jumps to his feet. "I wanna help!"

"Iris, this is my brother, Jack." Dottie winks at her friend.

"Yes, Jack. I've heard all about you. Of course, you can help," Iris says kindly.

Uncle Charles removes a matchbook from his pocket as the three shuffle away through the sand. "Let's get dinner started.

About an hour later, Iris declares, "That's the first time I've seen San Clemente Island this whole summer."

A brilliant, marmalade hue sits just above the horizon and contrasts sharply with the flat, dark outline of Catalina's sister island. My attention, however, is riveted on the horizontal bands of magenta and dark orchid above both islands.

"Fish is ready." Sam holds up two skewers of expertly grilled perch.

"I'll bring over the plates," I rise from my chair.

Jack is quite impressed with Sam's knowledge of cooking over an open fire, particularly since he burned his own fish almost immediately. Sam offered to roast the rest—to which we all agreed.

"The trick is letting the fire go down until it's mostly hot embers," he explains.

"Where'd you learn how to do that?" Jack marvels.

"Growing up in the Sierras, I caught lots of fish in the nearby rivers and lakes. In the summertime, my grandparents would let my friends and me camp out under ponderosa pines and white firs on our property and cook dinner over a campfire. We especially liked this time of evening. My buddy, Victor, call it 'bat-thirty.'"

"Bat-thirty?" Dottie frowns, puzzled.

Sam explains, "Victor noticed that the little brown bats would start flittering around just after sunset. One evening, after spotting the first bat, he looked at his wristwatch and announced, 'Looks like it's bat-thirty.'"

"Crackerjack!" Jack hoots with delight.

"Ugh!" Dottie blurts with disgust.

"They're actually quite helpful to humans," Iris informs us. "A single brown bat can eat thousands of mosquitoes each night."

"It's true!" Sam affirms. "My grandfather built wooden boxes and hung them in some of our trees for the bats to roost in, so they could help manage the mosquito population around our house."

"Brilliant!" Uncle Charles declares. "When I was a kid, we'd stay in the mountains of upstate New York each summer, and we always had problems with biting flies. I wish we knew about bat boxes back then."

"Some of our neighbors think he's off his rocker, but I tell you, it really works."

After we've eaten our fill, I stand and stretch my back. "I don't know about you, Sam, but I could do with a walk."

He leaps from his chair and stacks my plate on top of his.

"Leave the dishes, Sam," my uncle instructs. "We'll take care of it. After all, you cooked."

Sam smiles appreciatively and takes my hand. "Shall we?"

I squeeze his hand in return, and we head south along the shore. I kicked off my sandals earlier at the bonfire and now relish the cool damp sand underfoot. On the cliffs above us, locals begin to switch on lights inside their homes, some no larger than the shacks at Crystal Cove, others palatial.

"How different this is from my rotation on the reservation," Sam murmurs after we've been walking a while. "Don't get me wrong, I loved the beauty of the landscape, and my patients were wonderful. But there was so much poverty, not to mention diseases we just don't see anymore. The Apache people, not two or three generations ago, were free to roam their land. Now, they're trying to eke out an existence on tiny parcels for farming, and there's talk that the newly built Coolidge Dam will rob them of their most fertile farmland."

"That reminds me of the conditions at Bastanchury Ranch."

After my attack, I was rescued by a family who live at one of the labor settlements among the vast orchards in Northern Fullerton. I tell Sam how each family is given a small section of land on which to construct their home from whatever discarded materials they can find. I also mention how a single faucet provides water for an entire village and how disease runs rampant throughout the settlements.

"Yet despite all of that, what strikes me most is the pride the families have for their homes and the strong sense of community. It's so unlike the infighting and self-centeredness I'm witnessing with my current case," I finish.

Sam replies with a single word that encapsulates all that is wondrous and warped about the industry. "Hollywood."

"Exactly!"

"Ruby, I don't mean to pry, but why did you accept the offer from Stardust? Based on what you've told me, it's nothing like your other cases," Sam observes.

"That's a question I keep asking myself," I reply thoughtfully. "Of course, Dottie was thrilled with the whole thing and has loved hobnobbing with Corvi and the other actors."

"So, you did it for Dottie?"

"Not exactly. It's hard to describe, but my heart went out to Corvi during my trip abroad. She's like a child in a forest filled with wolves, and I can't resist the urge to protect her," I admit.

"I can understand that," he concedes. "Are there any other reasons?"

I stop walking and squish my toes into the sand while gathering my thoughts. After a moment, I confess, "The money they're paying me is staggering, but if it was just that, I would have passed. In truth, a part of me feels like I've compromised myself, if that makes sense."

"It does," he says quietly. "I hope you know that there's nothing wrong with appreciating a fat paycheck. That being said, it sounds like there's more to it than that."

I lock eyes with him. "Sam, if I take this sort of contract every once in a while, it financially liberates me to do more pro bono work on the cases that really matter."

He smiles. "I had a feeling you were going to say that."

"So, despite the demands and the infuriating personalities I'm dealing with, I see this as a means to help those who need me most but can't afford to pay."

"Believe me, Ruby, I understand exactly what you're saying." His expression suggests that he's wrestling with something.

"I sense there's a 'but' in there somewhere." I nod for him to continue.

"But…these poisonings have already taken one life and nearly killed your closest friend. I'm just sick about your involvement in all this. As the investigator, there's a huge target on your back." His eyes convey anguish as he wraps his arms around me protectively.

My body relaxes, and I lean my forehead against his chest. His shirt smells of woodsmoke and spice, a pleasing combination that makes me wish we could end this conversation and move on to a more physical way of communicating. However, we really do need to clear the air.

"I'm not going to deny the dangers of this investigation. Had I known this case would involve murder, I'd never have taken it. Nor would I have involved Elizabeth." I pause for a deep breath. "However, I'm not going to back out now, not if I can prevent another tragedy from happening. I owe that to Corvi—"

He holds me at arm's length. "But this isn't the first time you've put yourself in danger. What about this past May? You were assaulted and left unconscious in a burning orchard!"

"My job comes with risks. I accept that. Nevertheless, this is my calling—I save people. For me, that's worth the risk."

Sam takes a step back and bows his head. "Ruby, I respect you so much. Your passion for helping others is one of the things I most admire about you. I just feel so helpless knowing that you're in danger and there's nothing I can do about it. It makes me wonder..."

He turns his face toward the ocean, his eyes closed and lips compressed. I wait for him to collect his thoughts, but after several moments of silence, I ask, "What do you wonder?"

He looks at me with anguish. "I wonder if this is such a good idea."

A lump forms in my throat. "What are you saying, Sam?"

He runs a hand through his caramel blonde waves. "I...I'm not sure that I'm strong enough to live with this anxiety about you, always wondering if you're in danger. And before things get too serious, I need some time to figure all this out."

I feel as though I've been slapped and instinctively step away from him, but my shock swiftly transitions to outrage.

What's there to figure out?

Does he think I'll give up my career for him?

I'd have expected this from Eddie. He treated my work as an adorable hobby and made it clear that if we ever married, I would stay home to raise the family.

"Sam! Ruby! There you are!" In the light of the waning moon, I see Jack racing toward us. He stops and bends forward, panting. "I looked everywhere for you. Dad said we can't start the s'mores until you get back cuz no one else knows how to make 'em."

Sam replies awkwardly, "I really should be going."

Jack's face falls. "What?"

"I need to get back." Sam plants a chaste kiss on my cheek. "Goodnight, Ruby. I'll call you soon." Then he walks to the bottom of the cliff where a dirt path meanders up to the rim.

"Lead the way," I tell Jack.

But as we stroll, I look back and watch Sam's silhouette shuffle up the path, his head down and shoulders slumped.

"They're called grunions," Iris explains while sliding a marshmallow off her skewer.

Jack licks his gooey fingers. "And there are hundreds?"

"Sometimes even thousands." She delicately squishes her marshmallow between two graham crackers.

I can't fathom passing up chocolate, but she says it will keep her up all night.

"Dad, can we stay up and watch for them?" my cousin asks.

"Didn't you hear what Iris told you? It's probably too late in the season," my uncle reminds him.

"Plus, they could show up anywhere along the Southern California coastline," Dottie interjects. "You're about as likely to see them as you are to dig up that treasure. Right, Iris?"

Distracted, Iris squints toward a pair of men on the sand heading north with buckets. "I wonder what they're up to."

We turn and watch as they stop near the small headland that descends to the tidepool. They set their buckets on the sand.

"If they're going crabbing, they're out of luck," Dottie remarks.

"From the way they were walking, I'd say those buckets are full," I comment.

At that moment, one of the men dumps a bucket onto the rocks.

"Mystery solved!" Dottie exclaims.

Iris rises to protest, but I place a hand on her arm to stop her. "You'll need evidence to prove they've been poisoning the tidepool."

"We need one of those buckets," Dottie reasons.

"I have an idea," Jack bolts from the bonfire and races toward the men before anyone can stop him.

Uncle Charles shakes his head. "I better follow him."

Unable to hear their exchange with the men, we're surprised a few minutes later to see Jack and Uncle Charles return with one of the buckets, as the men head back up the stairs.

"Told you!" Jack beams and hands Iris the container.

"What did you say to them?" she inquires.

"He told them we need to borrow a bucket to put out the bonfire," Uncle Charles replies.

"They're staying in room 116, by the way," Jack cackles. "I said we'd return it when we're done with it."

"So, we can identity them as well." Dottie regards Jack with respect. "Well done, little brother."

The unequivocal pride and elation on Jack's face makes me wish I could capture this moment on film.

Iris retrieves a corked test tube and glass rod from her knapsack and squats next to the bucket to collect a sample. Once the tube is wrapped in a roll of cotton and returned to her knapsack, Iris inquires, "Ruby, I don't suppose you could give me a ride to the lab. I'd like to analyze this immediately, but I took the trolly."

"Absolutely!" I reply and gather my belongings.

"I'll come too." Dottie grabs her beach bag then pauses. "Dad, I hate to leave you with all this clean up."

He assures her, "Don't worry about it, Polka Dot. Jack and I have this under control. Plus, the concierge said he'd send someone down to take care of the bonfire, tub, and chairs."

She kisses her father on the cheek. "I'll see you tomorrow."

I fall behind as Dottie and Iris charge up the stairs, my thoughts and feelings in turmoil as I recall the confusing end to what should have been a romantic stroll with Sam.

"I sure wish I could've stayed for the analysis," Dottie bemoans after dropping off Iris.

"I know, but rules are rules," I pat her knee as we pull up to the house.

When we reached the Pomona College Marine Lab a little while ago, Iris told Dottie that no visitors were allowed after ten o'clock. Apparently, a few students snuck some friends in for a party earlier in the summer, resulting in broken lab equipment and an octopus escaping its tank.

"That's okay," Dottie yawns. "I'll head over first thing in the morning."

"How are you doing?" I ask her before she has a chance to open the car door. "This trip was supposed to give us more time together, but I haven't been around much."

"To be honest, I've really enjoyed it. Iris is terrific, and I'm glad I've had something to do. Lying around on the sand isn't really my idea of fun. I like to stay busy."

"You and me both," I chuckle. She's in a good mood, so I dig a little deeper. "The reason I'm asking is because I heard you cry out in your sleep last night."

She sighs. "Ruby, I know you're trying to help, but I'm doing all I can to forget about those nightmares."

"Do they have something to do with Mr. Mains and everything that happened in the spring?"

"Yes, and I really don't want to talk about it," she says firmly. "Dad's been peppering me with questions too."

"Alright, I understand. But we're here for you if you want to talk."

"I know." She deftly changes the subject, "Let's talk about YOU instead. Why didn't Sam come back with you and Jack this evening?"

"He had to get back…"

"But you said he wasn't working tonight. Did something happen?" she probes.

It's my turn to sigh. "Yes, but I really don't want to talk about it."

"Touché." Dottie opens the car door and heads for the house.

I stay in my car for a little while. Now that my initial indignation has passed, I'm left feeling bewildered and dejected. Sam's abrupt departure surprised me. I fully expected that we'd finish our conversation, particularly since I don't really understand what he was trying to say.

Was that a breakup? We've only had a few proper dates. Would you even call it a breakup?

And what exactly does he need to figure out?

His feelings for me?

When will I hear from him again?

The front door flies open, and Dottie jogs back to the car.

"I just got off the phone." She declares, "You'll never guess."

A wave of hope washes over me.

Sam.

"Dad called," Dottie continues. "When he and Jack went to return the bucket, they found out that the men work for Stardust Productions."

"What?!" Not the news I was expecting but important, nonetheless.

"Dad noticed the logo on his shirt. I guess it was too dark to see it on the beach."

"Did they find out what the men were dumping?"

"You know Jack," Dottie laughs. "Of course, he asked, but the man said it was cleaning fluid."

"Cleaning fluid? Then why not dump it down a drain?"

"Right? When Jack asked him that, the guy got nervous and said he had his orders."

"As far as I know, they don't put silver in cleaning fluid. Hopefully the sample Iris collected tonight incriminates them. Then we'll talk to Archie about it tomorrow."

Walking in the door, I brace myself for mewing cries, but Puck is silent. Suspicious, I slowly open the bathroom door for a peek only to find the kitten asleep on the pillow Dottie left for him. To my astonishment, the pillow is intact...no feathers carpeting the floor and no shredded pillowcase dangling from the cabinet knobs. Puck opens one eye and releases a contented squeak before curling up into a ball.

Hopefully, I'm also able to sleep restfully tonight.

Who am I kidding?

CHAPTER 20

FRIDAY, AUGUST 29, 1930

"Dean! I'm surprised to see you here."

I join him in the hotel lobby elevator. When the attendant asks for our floor, Dean holds up three fingers.

"They're releasing Elizabeth today," he smiles with relief.

"That's great news!" The tension I've been carrying since yesterday morning lessens. "I assume she'll stay with her folks."

"Yes, the doctor told her to rest for a few days. Since I'm needed here for filming, I told her I'd pick up a few of her things and bring them by this evening. Thought I'd stop by her room before my fitting with costuming."

After exiting the elevator, I ask him about the results from the toxicology analysis.

"They said it was something called hyoscine—I've never heard of it before," he explains.

Hyoscine. That sounds familiar. I'll ask Sam.

Then my heart sinks. While I've tried to avoid perseverating on our conversation, the sick feeling in the pit of my stomach has been a constant reminder since last night. Thankfully, I was able to slip into a dreamless sleep shortly after going to bed. My body and mind certainly needed the rest.

When we reach the suite, an unfamiliar security guard raises his eyebrows with suspicion.

I introduce myself. "I'm Ruby Ray, the inquiry agent working for Stardust. I'm here to see Miss Styles."

He removes a folded page from his pocket and searches for my name. Satisfied, he then gives Dean a quizzical look.

"Dean Larsen. One of the cast. I'm Elizabeth...er, Liz's fiancé. She asked me to pick up a few of her things."

At once the guard's expression changes to one of adulation. "Mr. Larsen! Of course. Shall I open her door for you?"

"No need." Dean jiggles a key hanging from a tassel. "The desk clerk gave me a copy." He walks down to Elizabeth's room.

I knock on Corvi's door, then ask the guard, "Have you been here long?"

He checks his watch. "A couple of hours. The shift changed at eight-thirty."

"Has anyone visited Miss Styles since yesterday afternoon?" I inquire.

He shrugs. "No idea. All I know is that no one's been here since I came on duty."

I'm appalled. "Didn't your predecessor give you a report?"

"No, ma'am. He just said nothing out of the ordinary happened." He averts his gaze.

This is shocking. Two serious crimes have been committed here. Stardust Productions should be keeping a security log round the clock. I'll talk to Archie about this when I see him.

A few moments pass, and I knock on the door again.

"Have you seen Miss Styles this morning?" I ask.

Maybe she's not even here.

"Yes, ma'am—during the shift change. She heard us talking and opened the door."

"Did she seem alright?"

"She looked okay to me," he answers apathetically.

The door to the living room swings open, and Dean's pokes his head out, a troubled expression on his face.

"Ruby, I think something's wrong."

I rush into the room and follow him to Corvi's bedroom door.

He explains, "I came in to find Elizabeth's fashion magazines and heard Corvi in her room. I thought it would be best for you to check on her instead of me."

At that moment, I discern a muted moan followed by the sound of retching. I jiggle the doorknob, but it's locked. The security guard looks bewildered standing in the middle of the room.

"Can you open this door?" I bark impatiently.

He flinches and reaches into a pocket. "Oh, right."

Once the door is open, I bolt into the bedroom and slide the pocket door attached to the en suite bathroom. Corvi is curled up in a ball on the floor surrounded by vomit. Her skin and hair are soaked with sweat, and she's wincing with pain.

After running cold water over a washcloth, I kneel beside her and place the compress to her forehead. "Corvi, we're going to get you some help."

I jerk my head toward the security guard, who's watching, open-mouthed, at the door. He nods and vacates the bathroom.

Pushing the matted hair away from her face, I ask, "Corvi, can you talk?"

Her head nods limply, and she murmurs a faint, "Yes."

"When did you start feeling sick?"

She licks her lips with a grimace. "Little while ago."

"Did you eat breakfast this morning?"

"Mm-hmm."

I look over my shoulder. Dean is hovering at the door, his eyes wide with distress.

"Find her food tray, and make sure no one touches it," I instruct. "We'll need to send a sample with her to the hospital when the ambulance arrives."

Corvi makes a gagging sound, so I seize the small waste basket nearby and help her to a seated position.

We'll need to send a sample of THAT as well.

When she's finished, I remove a towel from the rack and fold it into a small pillow for her head before helping her lie back on the floor.

"I'm so sorry to make you talk, but I need to ask a few more questions before anyone else shows up."

A tear rolls down her cheek. "Okay."

"Who brought your tray this morning?"

"I dunno," she sniffles. "Didn't see them."

A shiver runs along the length of her body, so I snatch a second towel and drape it over her like a blanket.

"You're doing great, Corvi," I assure her. "Did your food or drink taste bitter or unpleasant?"

"No, but..." She pushes herself up to stare directly into my eyes. "Oh, Ruby! It's just awful!"

"What's awful?"

"I saw it after my bath—that's when I got sick," she cries and points into her bedroom.

"Ruby, you oughta see this," Dean calls from the desk.

As I approach, the desk's surface comes into focus. Sitting on the tray is an empty coffee cup, sugar bowl, and small plate with a few crumbs. The napkin has been neatly folded with the used cutlery lying on top. To the right of the tray is a stack of scripts, and to the left is a bracelet of petite seashells strung on a length of cotton thread. At first glance, the jewelry appears innocuous—something you might pick up at a souvenir shop in the village—but then I notice that it's resting in a pool of something sticky...and red.

"Why did you leave your post this morning?" I grill the security guard, who made himself scarce until the ambulance attendants arrived.

"Nature called," he mumbles, abashed. "It was only for a few minutes."

"Which was long enough for someone to push this under Corvi's door." The carpet still bears a dark red stain.

The guard jerks his head as I offer the bracelet, still covered in goo.

"Is that BLOOD?" His nostrils flare with disgust.

"Cough syrup, from the smell of it," I inform him. "

Shamefaced, the guard pushes open the door to exit, but Archie storms through. The guard sneaks out as Archie booms, "What's going on? I just saw them wheel Corvi out on a gurney. She wasn't making any sense, so I came up to see what happened." His eyes spot the bracelet. "Good God! What's that?!"

The color drains from his face as I tell him what's happened.

"This is just terrible!" He squeezes his forehead. "Do you think she was poisoned too?"

"That was my first thought," I answer. "The ambulance driver has samples of her breakfast, but her symptoms started after she found the bracelet. A part of me wonders if she had a trauma reaction of some kind."

He furrows his brow. "Come again."

"Think about it. The stalker and notes, Lena's death, Elizabeth's poisoning, and now a bracelet dripping with what looks like blood—it's just too much for one person to handle, especially someone as sensitive as Corvi."

He releases a slow breath. "Okay. Here's what we're going to do. Dean…"

"Yes, Archie." Dean steps forward from the corner of Corvi's bedroom.

"We have to get those shots in the ocean—today!" He holds up a hand as I open my mouth to protest. "Ruby, I don't want to hear it. There's too much at stake here, and Mr. Lake will insist we carry on as best we can, especially if Corvi's illness is just some sort of emotional reaction."

"Just some sort of emotional reaction—do you hear yourself right now?" I hiss.

"Yes, and ordinarily I'd be disgusted with myself, but I'm walking a fine line here between meeting the needs of the cast and fulfilling our contract with the studio. There's a great deal of money at stake."

"Lives are stake, Archie." I grit my teeth.

He opens the door to leave. "Dean, meet me on the set in fifteen minutes. Wardrobe shouldn't take long. All you need is a swimsuit."

"And Corvi?" I grab his arm.

"I'll visit the hospital once I'm sure the crew have everything they need." Before closing the door behind him, his face softens. "Look,

Ruby, I hate being the bad guy, and I sure don't want to be at odds with you. Can we talk later?"

I nod.

"Well, I better take this out to my car before changing," Dean lifts a small suitcase.

"Please tell Elizabeth that I'll call her later at her folks." I step up on my toes and peck his cheek. "And give her that from me."

"Ma'am," the security guard pushes open the bedroom door after Dean leaves. "I just got a message from my boss. He told me to follow the ambulance and guard Miss Styles at the hospital. I don't suppose you could wait here until the police arrive. They're sending someone to collect the...um...evidence."

"Yes, of course I'll wait." Hopefully I can get somewhere with Inspector Maggard this time.

I search the floor around Corvi's bedroom, checking for another note that may have been inadvertently pushed under the furniture with all the comings and goings, but I find nothing. Her room is neat and tidy, with the exception of the breakfast tray on her desk alongside the pile of scripts. I wander toward the wide picture window in the living room and gaze out at the ocean. I imagine all the people who will stay in this suite over the years to come and enjoy the view without a care in the world. My eye is caught by a chartreuse kite dipping and swerving above the water. That's when I realize that the color of the Pacific is different every time I look at it—slate gray in the morning when the sun is hiding behind the clouds, dark teal under the midday sun, and turquoise green in the shallows. I lift the sash of one of the smaller windows on the side and listen to the rhythmic crash of the waves. It's already Friday, and I have yet to really enjoy the healing qualities of this beautiful and powerful body of water. How peaceful are the sights and sounds of this inspiring vista, when everything else seems to be falling apart right now.

"Well, well. You're not at all who I expected." Bebe looks me up and down while leaning against her door. A single narrow strap supports her silky black negligee, the other strap having slid down her fleshy shoulder. She flashes a feral smirk.

Much to my disappointment, it was the cadet who stopped by to collect the bracelet and samples from the dishes. I'll call the inspector once we know whether Corvi was poisoned, but it will take a while for the labs to come back. Meanwhile, it's about time I have a little chat with Bebe.

"We need to talk," I inform her.

"Is that so?" she purrs.

I wait for her to invite me into her room, but she doesn't budge. I suggest, "Perhaps it would be better if we take this inside where there's more privacy."

Her shoulders slowly rise up and down. "Why? I have nothing to hide."

I glance into the dimly lit room behind her. The curtains are closed, and several candles in sleek modern candlesticks cast rhythmically moving shapes upon the walls. A floral musky scent wafts into the hallway, and I can't tell if it's coming from Bebe or the room itself. Then I notice a string of shells hanging from a knob on a dresser drawer.

"That looks familiar," I comment. "Mind if I take a closer look?"

Her eyes flash with amusement. "Knock yourself out."

She casually remains at the doorway while I enter her room and lift the necklace for inspection. Unlike the tiny conch shells on Corvi's bracelet, these are smooth and twice the size.

"Cowrie?" I ask.

She shrugs. "Beats me. I pinched it from the costume department. Why do you care so much?"

"Someone pushed a shell bracelet under Corvi's door."

She snickers. "And you think it was me? Sweetie, she isn't worth my time."

"Alright," I adjust my line of questioning. "Then tell me...what's with all the rancor? She couldn't possibly deserve—"

Bebe's mask of haughty indifference slips, and her eyes narrow with fury. "She's not the fresh-faced darling you think she is." She dramatically waves an arm. "I know her better than all of you."

I nod for her to continue. "I'm listening."

"No one believes me, but we started showing up for the same casting calls a decade ago—been extras together in more movies than I can count."

She takes a few steps into the room to retrieve a flashy gold cigarette case and matchbook. I wait while she expertly lights a Camel and takes a deep drag. She closes her eyes and sighs before continuing her narrative.

"Corvi's big break came years after Ike took her on." She uses the thumb and ring finger of the hand holding the cigarette to remove something from the tip of her tongue.

"She couldn't possibly be more than twenty," I comment.

Bebe chokes while inhaling the smoke. "Hardly!" she exclaims when she stops coughing. "She's gotta be thirty, if not older."

"You must be confusing her with someone else." I'm sure Bebe's worked with many actresses over the years, especially extras.

"Snowy locks? Teeth like pearls? Petite figure?" She laughs bitterly, "Don't believe any of it! Ike spent a fortune on beauty operations for her."

"O-kay…but why do you hate her so much?"

"She's stolen every role I really wanted!" Bebe sneers. "Ever since the beginning, when I was sharing a run-down apartment with five other girls, she was living the high life. Before Ike came along, there was a string of stage-door Johnnys outside the studio waiting for her, not to mention the directors and producers who showed up at our dressing room to sweep her away."

That doesn't mean that Corvi's any older twenty-two or so. She could have gotten her start quite young. As I recall, mature-looking girls no older than twelve sometimes stomped the boards in vaudeville, even during the Twenties. The same must be true for movie extras. I'd imagine that some destitute girls lie about their age to casting directors as a way to stay off the streets. The world is a cruel place for children on their own.

"Did you know she's married?" Bebe blurts.

"Corvi has a husband?" I think back to our conversation a few days ago when she said she'd never been married.

She blows a cloud of smoke. "That's what I heard."

Could she be married to Ike? It's certainly a possibility. Still, all this sounds like jealous tittle-tattle.

"Alright, Bebe. I understand your dislike for her, but why the threats?"

She shakes her head. "I never threatened her."

What did she say at the dress shop? "You should watch where you're going or someone might get hurt." The words themselves seem innocuous, but her tone was menacing.

This verbal volley is going nowhere, so I decide to take a more direct approach. "There've been two poisonings so far, and in both cases the victims ingested drinks intended for Corvi."

She shrieks with mirth. "Are you suggesting I tried to kill Corvi?"

I shrug my shoulders for her to continue.

"Honey, I'm a bitch, but I'm no murderess."

At that moment, Smitty walks through the door. "Sorry I'm late."

"It's no bother, sugar. Ruby was just leaving," Bebe sashays over to him and runs a fingernail along the side of his neck then looks back at me. "Unless you'd like to join us."

"Was Corvi poisoned?"

"Who's behind the murder attempts?"

"Have the doctors said anything?"

Stepping out from the hotel lobby into the bright sunlight, I'm surrounded by a dozen reporters, some with cameras. When they realize that I'm not one of the cast or production crew, most turn away, except for one.

The tall, reedy journalist squints through his thick-framed spectacles and shouts, "Say, aren't you the lady dick who found those missing kids in Fullerton?"

I ignore his question and push through the group, but others realize that I may know a thing or two about the current situation.

"Are you investigating the murder of Miss Young?"

"Who is Liz Martin, and why was she poisoned?"

I wave them off and turn the corner. After retreating from Bebe's room a little while ago, I visited the kitchen staff, hoping to glean some information about Corvi's breakfast and any visitors she may have had this morning. Mrs. Gleason, the kitchen supervisor, flipped through a box of cards until she found Corvi's standing breakfast order.

"Dry toast, fruit, and coffee with sugar. Same as always."

"Who delivered her tray this morning?" I inquired and looked around the busy kitchen.

While the employees were going through the motions of cooking and washing dishes, they were clearly eavesdropping, including Poppy who quietly filled saltshakers at one of the counters while sneaking glances in our direction.

"Alma took her breakfast." Mrs. Gleason nodded toward a gray-haired woman with kind eyes, then said under her breath. "Given what happened yesterday, I thought that would be best."

I smiled in agreement then asked Alma to join me in the hallway.

"When I got to the door, no one answered at first. Then a big man with a cigar opened the door and took the tray inside," the employee reported.

I jotted this in my notebook. "What time was that?"

"Just after eight," she twisted her hands together.

"Did you see anyone else inside or outside of Miss Styles' room?"

"Just the security guard outside the door. I didn't try to see into the room. It wasn't any of my business," Alma explained.

"Alright, well thank you so much for your time," I left the basement and returned to the lobby.

Mulling over this interview, I slowly walk to my car. So, Ike was with Corvi this morning, after all. He must have been there during the shift change too. Perhaps when the security guard stepped away and Corvi was in the bathtub, Ike placed the bracelet on his way out the door. I wish I'd asked Bebe if she noticed anything—I'm sure she's been snooping about with all the comings and goings from Corvi's suite—but her proposition threw me for a loop, and I promptly left.

My thoughts drift to Elizabeth, and I wonder how she's doing. I'll telephone her parent's house as soon as I get back. I recall what Dean said about the poison—hyoscine—and suddenly remember that hyoscine hydrobromide was the seasickness medication that everyone took onboard the *Statendam*. When Miss Mabel gave me the small tablets, she cautioned that they were quite potent. Ike would definitely have had access to the drug, but who was the poison meant for? Elizabeth or Corvi?

Approaching my car, I suddenly spot a man with ash-colored hair and suspenders as he rounds the corner behind the hotel. Tossing my keys back into my handbag, I pursue him at a fair clip. My feet pound softly on the dry sand, so he doesn't realize I'm following him until I'm an arm's length away. Instead of running, however, his shoulders sink, and he turns around with a sigh of resignation.

"Hello, Miss Ray."

CHAPTER 21

"You know my name?"

"Of course. It's my job." His amiable tone belies the sinister image I've harbored. Further, his body language conveys congeniality and candor.

"What do you mean it's your 'job?' Who are you, exactly?"

My muscles stiffen as he reaches into the pocket of his trousers, but to my surprise, he removes a flat, scuffed metal case, from which he withdraws a business card that reads:

Tom Nagel
Private Detective
LOrain 8791

Stupefied, I look up from the card. "Private detective? I don't understand."

"Stardust Productions hired me." He adds, "Just like you."

"Why?" This makes no sense.

He chuckles. "I'm surprised you haven't figured it out, Ruby. Is it okay if I call you Ruby?"

I shake my head to clear the confusion. "Figured what out?"

"I've been following Ike Bronson, of course," he pronounces, as though it should be obvious.

"Then why have you been stalking Corvi Styles and sending her disturbing notes?"

"Notes? Psh! I didn't send her any notes, nor have I stalked her. But since Miss Styles is usually with Ike, I can see why you'd draw that conclusion."

One of the grips walks past, his arms loaded with cable. Recognizing me, he says, "We're about to start filming at the shore, if you wanna watch."

"Not today," I tell him.

The young man continues toward the water, where Archie and Dean are conferring with the stunt coordinator, a flurry of activity around them.

"Let's find somewhere else to talk," the detective suggests. "I know a place a few streets over."

He takes several steps before realizing that I'm not following. This is the same man who's been my lead suspect all week. There's been a murder, attempted murder, threatening notes, and now a deranged message in the form of—what appeared to be—a bloodied bracelet. I'm not going off to some backstreet hole-in-the-wall with him. I fold my arms and cock my head to the side.

He holds up his hands, "I get it. Tell you what…let's take a seat on the boardwalk. There are plenty of people around but—with all the activity—we can talk without being overheard."

I nod and tell him, "Follow me." This discussion will happen on MY terms.

Near the lifeguard station, a tanned man with a wide-brimmed straw hat stands beside a bench where an array of photograph postcards are neatly stacked on a blanket. I spot an image of three rocky arches stretched over the tide, as well as a photo of the pier taken from Main Beach. I also notice a postcard of Table Rock—the image now quite familiar to me. A small handwritten sign states:

Share your good time for only a dime.

A second bench is available nearby, but I continue walking, just the same, to ensure that our conversation will be private. When we're halfway between the lifeguard station and the tidepools, I sit at one end of an iron bench and place my handbag beside me.

The detective tugs his trousers at the knees and takes a seat at the opposite end of the bench. He rolls the cuffs of his white long-sleeved shirt. "It's going to be a hot one today."

In the bright sunlight, I get my first good look at him. I'd put him in his late fifties. Deep lines fan from the corners of his hazel eyes, and quite a few gray hairs intermingle with ash brown on the sides of his head. Other than that, his appearance is quite unremarkable. This must be why it was so difficult for Corvi to identify him.

"Mr. Nagel, why were you at the hotel just now if you're following Ike. I was told he's not in town this morning."

"Tom...please. That is an excellent question."

He removes a cigarette from his pocket, lights it with the single match left in a matchbook, and grounds the burnt match under his heel. I expect him to toss the spent matchbook as well, but he replaces it in his pocket with the pack of cigarettes.

Before taking a drag, he asks, "You mind?"

I shake my head.

He sucks on the cigarette then answers my question. "I followed Ike from the hotel when he left around 8:15, but after more than an hour, I lost him somewhere around Norwalk. I decided to backtrack to Laguna to hang around the set. The crew are great sources of information for someone who's not above eavesdropping."

That would mean that Ike had already left when the bracelet was slid under Corvi's door...so much for that theory.

"You claim the studio hired you to investigate Ike. Why?"

"Before I tell you anything more, I want you to know how impressed I've been with your sleuthing skills. Uncovering the young burglars on the cruise—well done. And your work on that cult case several months ago—I applaud your tenacity." He smiles warmly.

"Wait, you were on the *Statendam*?" I lean forward, "Then it WAS you that Corvi spotted at the cemetery in France."

"Yes, after that I had to pull out my disguises—you know...false beard, heavy glasses, cane—I even used rubber cheek inserts to change the shape of my face. But then security caught me breaking into Ike's room. I sat in the brig with those spoiled brats for a few days until the studio wired and confirmed my identity and credentials. After that, I had to lay low until we disembarked."

"If Stardust hired you, does Mr. Lake know about you? What about his assistant, Archie Duval? He hasn't said a thing."

"Only two people at the studio know about my contract, and they're both executives." He takes a puff then knocks ash from his cigarette onto the ground.

"Then why are you telling me this?"

"The men who hired me are aware that you suspect Ike had something to do with the poisonings. I happen to agree. They thought we could help one another," he shrugs.

Archie must be reporting my actions and suppositions to the studio executives. He's the only one who knows the details of my investigation.

"Am I to keep your identity a secret? I work closely with Archie. It'll be hard to—"

Tom looks at me levelly. "Can you trust him?"

Despite his decisions lately, in my heart I know that Archie is an honorable person. "Yes, I believe I can."

The detective blows out a plume of smoke while rolling his head in a circle before arriving at a decision. "Okay. But you have to swear him to secrecy."

"Shall I have him cross his heart as well?" I jest.

He laughs with a snort. "You're funny. I wasn't expecting that."

"Now, will you tell me why the studio hired you?"

After that, Tom launches into a narrative so outlandish that it belongs on the big screen. On top of fleecing his other clients and bribing casting directors to secure parts for Corvi, Ike may have been involved in the death of Corvi's roommate two years ago. At the time, the coroner concluded that it was a case of accidental drowning, but the circumstances were suspicious. First of all, the young woman drowned in less than two feet of water in a freestanding bathtub. Friends of the deceased told Tom that she'd been a client of Ike's but had recently fired him since he wasn't getting roles for her. After her new agent landed her a speaking part in an upcoming film—a role that Corvi was being considered for as well—Ike displayed open hostility toward the young lady and even threatened to inform the studio about an abortion she'd had several months earlier.

The autopsy found evidence of bruising and trauma around both ankles. Ike was arrested but later released without charges when the studio quietly intervened and corroborated his story that the marks were due to the metal bands the young woman wore as part of her servant girl costume in the film she was shooting. In truth, the studio was willing to do whatever necessary to avoid the negative press that would ensue during a murder trial. Both actresses were on contract with Stardust, and Corvi showed great promise as the next "It Girl." However, the studio executives knew Ike was guilty because only the male extras in the film wore ankle shackles.

Following that, Stardust hired a series of private investigators to keep tabs on Ike. He kept his nose clean for a while, and they ended the investigation contracts, but in the spring of 1929, one of their lead actresses was thrown while her horse was galloping at full speed during a shoot. Although, these types of accidents are not unheard of, this particular situation warranted a closer look. When the actress regained consciousness, she reported that a bright flash coming from a clump of bushes along the trail had spooked her horse. As it turns out, Corvi had been originally overlooked for the lead role but was later hired as the replacement since the injured actress would be laid up for several months. This was the role that ultimately catapulted Corvi into superstardom.

"Several months later, plans for the European tour were underway, and the studio wasn't comfortable with Ike's presence on the trip without ongoing surveillance. They were between a rock and hard place. The fans adore Miss Styles and are clamoring for more, but wherever she goes, Ike is there too, and as her private manager, the studio can't fire him. That's why they hired me."

I'm utterly dumbfounded by the story and can't think of anything to say for a moment. It sounds as though Ike would do anything to advance Corvi's career.

"All of this implicates Ike in Lena's death and Elizabeth's poisoning," I finally remark.

Tom slowly nods. "Yep."

"But what about Corvi? She may have been poisoned this morning, as well. Not only that, she received a bracelet that appeared to be coated in blood. Granted, Ike had already left by then…"

He scratches his head. "Is there a reason Ike would want to harm Miss Styles?"

I think back to the altercations I witnessed between them. "I believe she's been trying to cut ties with him."

He exhales a cloud of smoke. "That would do it."

"During the cruise I overheard an argument, and Ike shouted, 'You can't do this! I made you!' But why the notes? They're so odd."

I turn to the page in my notes where I've copied the messages and hand the notebook to Tom.

His eyes swiftly dart across the page. Then he pauses and appears to read each line more carefully. "Bizarre!"

"I'll say—but what purpose could they possibly serve?"

Tom strokes his chin. "Maybe he wanted to put her on edge—prove that she needs his protection."

"That's definitely possible." I reflect, "The intensity of his possessiveness is alarming."

"She's big money for him," Tom comments.

"That's true," I nod.

"When was the first note found?"

"The day we disembarked—at the Plaza Hotel."

"I remember that day. I'd planned to break into Ike's room, but Miss Styles spotted me outside the hotel and alerted the staff. After that, a hotel security guard was posted on their floor."

"So, Corvi did see you…I assume you also showed up at the studio and her house a few days later."

"Yes, I shadowed Ike as best I could, but Miss Styles recognized me on more than one occasion. I figured I'd have better luck here in Laguna, as everyone would be preoccupied with the film. However—as you well know—I was detected more than once."

I recall seeing Tom after our group lunch at the White House when Ike showed up out of nowhere to check on Corvi. Now it makes sense that Tom was there as well.

"Ike was heading to Los Angeles on Monday after we spotted you. Did you follow him?"

"Thanks to all of you, he'd already pulled away before I could follow," Tom laughs ruefully. "I have yet to successfully trail him by car. His other clients say they haven't seen him for months, so I know he's not meeting with them. Between you and me, I suspect he may be involved in some kind of racket—if you catch my meaning."

"The mob?" I lower my voice as a couple of women walk by on the boardwalk.

He nods, casually taking a drag. "I don't have any hard evidence, but all the signs are there."

I stare out at the shore to gather my thoughts and notice Duke, the lifeguard who tried to save Lena. He's chatting with a group of young ladies and pointing toward the water. In the distance, a gray dorsal fin surfaces then quickly disappears. It's obviously a dolphin, but I can see why they're so often mistaken for sharks at this distance. All at once, I remember Duke's testimony regarding Sunday morning.

"It was you, wasn't it. You told the lifeguards there was a shark in the water where Lena was swimming."

His body jolts, and he looks at me with appreciation. "You ARE good. How'd you know?"

"According to the lifeguard, a man with a 'lopsided' hat reported seeing a large shark in the cove. By the way, I haven't seen you wearing the Homburg since Monday."

"Too noticeable. A shame, really. It shadowed my face pretty well."

"So, why were you on the bluff Sunday morning? Ike was at a meeting at that time."

"When I followed him into the hotel that morning, it was very early—around six-fifteen. He used the staff staircase, which seemed fishy. I figured he was heading up to Miss Styles' room, so I snuck up the guest stairs and then watched him approach her suite. A tray with a beverage of some sort was on a rolling cart just outside the door. He grabbed the tray with one hand and reached in his pocket and pulled out a key with the other, but instead of entering Miss Styles' room, he opened the door next to it."

"The living room," I comment. "It connects Corvi's bedroom with the one Lena was using at the time."

He continues, "I waited around the corner, but when one of the serving girls saw me and asked what I was doing, I headed back downstairs. I watched the front door of the hotel from across the highway, but instead of seeing Ike exit, Miss Styles and Miss Young came out. It was around six forty-five, and I was surprised to see Miss Styles out that early."

"That's all to do with you," I inform him. "After seeing you the night before, she wasn't comfortable staying alone in her room while Lena went for her morning swim."

"Well, bottom line, my gut told me that something wasn't right. I watched them from the bluff, thinking that Ike might show up. When I noticed that Miss Young was having trouble, I alerted the lifeguards, then I ran to a nearby house and called for an ambulance."

"I was wondering about that," I comment. Sal said that none of her crew had radioed for help.

"After her death, I tried to get into Miss Young's room to look for evidence that Ike was somehow involved, but between the hotel staff, studio security, and you, Miss Ray, I was never again able to get past the first floor."

"Sorry about that. You were my prime suspect."

He looks at his watch and stands. "I need to have a word with the studio."

I jump to my feet. "Wait, shouldn't we take this information to the police? They should arrest Ike—"

"Now hold on," he raises a hand. "My client is paying big bucks to keep all this under wraps. It's up to them if and when the information is released to law enforcement."

As an investigator, I understand all too well about maintaining client confidentiality, even when crimes have been committed. However, this is a matter of life and death.

"I can't keep this silent, Tom. Corvi's in danger."

"Miss Ray, we don't know for sure that Ike is guilty. This is all speculation," he reasons.

"You do what you need to, but I'm contacting Inspector Maggard."

I start to walk back toward the hotel, but Tom grips my elbow.

"Miss Ray," he chuckles. "I admire your passion and your principles. I was the same way, at one time, but trust me on this. Without my testimony, the police aren't going to do a thing. All you have is gut instinct and circumstantial evidence."

He's right.

"Isn't there anything you can do?" I inquire.

"I'll try to persuade the studio to turn this over to the police, given everything that's happened," he assures me.

"So, where does that leave things with us?"

Tom tosses his cigarette butt on the ground.

"Well, you have my card. If you call that number, the answering service will get a message to me at the guest house where I'm staying."

I remove a business card from my purse and jot down Norma and Edith's phone number on the back.

"You can reach me here, or leave a message at the hotel for Archie. He'll pass it on to me."

He tucks the card into a pocket and offers a hand. "It's a privilege collaborating with you, Miss Ray."

"Ruby," I correct him while shaking his hand.

"Welcome to Dos Rocas," the jovial pilot greets us. I wasn't sure what to expect at a celebrity party, but her knee-length shorts and white T-shirt convey a relaxed tone. "It's Ruby, right?"

"Yes, thank you so much for having us!" I introduce my uncle and Jack.

After leaving the beach several hours ago, I found myself in a quandary about what to do next. Part of me wanted to rush over to the hospital and check on Corvi, but I knew that would take a while, and Jack would never forgive me if we missed Pancho's party. Thankfully, between Kit, Archie, and the security guard—not to mention the nurses and doctors coming and going—Corvi seemed quite safe at St. Joseph Hospital. Now that we're here, I have no doubt I made the right decision and am thrilled to introduce Jack to Pancho.

"Golly! Am I glad to meet you!" Jack energetically pumps her hand with an ear-to-ear grin. "I saw you break Earhart's speed record a few weeks ago!"

"Is that so?" Her cheeks dimple as a smile stretches across her face. "Well, I'm happy you were there!"

"I don't suppose..." He pulls his pilot hat out of his back pocket. "Could I get your autograph?"

"Tell ya what, Jack, I can do you one better."

At that moment, a boy about eight-years-old wanders up. Pancho tousles his dark brown hair.

"Aww, Mom. Cut it out," the boy grumbles with a half-smile.

"Billy, this is Jack. Go find one of my old aviator caps and a fountain pen, so I can give him my autograph."

Her son shoots Jack a friendly smile and motions for him to follow.

"That is so generous," Uncle Charles remarks. "Thank you!"

She waves a hand dismissively. "Aw, it ain't nothin'! I'm glad he's here. Billy gets lonely for other kids when we're in Laguna, especially when I'm throwin' a party."

I look around the grounds above Emerald Bay with views of the ocean—about two-hundred feet below us. Wide porches on both levels at the back of a two-story bungalow overlook the Pacific, while on the western side of the property, a low concrete wall surrounds a seating area with a tile-topped table. Ornate finials resembling bowls of fruit rest on each corner of the structure. Around the other side, an impressive swimming pool bumps up against the house, and dozens of attractive men and women frolic in and out of the water.

"This house used to sit closer to my grandma's mansion, but when she complained about the noise from my parties, I told her to move my house—and that's just what she did!" Pancho cackles. "The pool shares a wall with my basement, so I had the builders install porthole windows down there."

Surprised, I turn to face her. "Why is that?"

"So, folks in my bar can watch the swimmers," she replies matter-of-factly.

That's when I notice the martini glasses and champagne flutes in the hands of the revelers.

Once my stunned uncle stops coughing into his fist, he asks. "Is your grandmother here?"

"Nah, it's Labor Day weekend. She knew to stay away."

"Well, you certainly have a great turnout," I comment, surprised to see at least fifty people—and the party is just getting started.

"Yeah, the boys are stayin' here for Monday's airshow. Most of 'em over there are Short Snorts." She nods toward a dozen or so young men playing volleyball on the lawn.

"Short Snorts?" I laugh at the ironic term. Most of the men look to be at least five feet nine, which is quite average.

"They're my hangar buddies," she proudly explains. "Best bunch of stunt pilots you'll ever meet."

"There's Edwin." I recognize the Coast Guard officer among the group of aviators.

"You know Edwin?" She grins affectionately at the clean-cut young man. "He's a good kid. He'll be flyin' in the airshow."

"Are all of your guests pilots?" my uncle inquires.

"A fair number. But the crowd at the pool are film friends who have places in Laguna." She links her arm through mine. "Lemme introduce you."

I look back at Uncle Charles, who follows closely behind with a look of amusement. We approach several women with cocktail glasses lounging at a table under a fringe-trimmed umbrella.

"Gals, this is Ruby Ray," Pancho wraps an arm around my shoulders and squeezes. "Ruby, that's Ruth and her mom, Tillie," Pancho points at the two ladies on the left.

Despite being immersed in Hollywood culture over the past week, I'm tongue-tied to meet Ruth Chatterton. Her film, *Madame X*, with Lionel Barrymore was one of my favorites last year.

"It's so nice to meet you," I finally reply, to which the actress gracefully nods.

"I'm Ferne," a vivacious woman with silver-blonde hair, introduces herself. "My husband and I live on the next bluff. He's away on business right now."

"Ferne's an aspiring actress," Ruth informs me. "She's hoping I'll help her out."

"Well, it doesn't hurt to ask," Ferne winks.

"And speakin' of aspiring actresses, that's Gigi Parrish," Pancho points to a beautiful young woman who looks to be around Dottie's age. "She and her husband are stayin' in town."

Gigi lowers her drink and waves.

"How do you do," I smile warmly.

"And who's this sheik?" Ferne asks coquettishly while openly admiring my uncle.

"That's Charles Ray," Pancho replies. "Ruby's uncle."

"VERY nice to meet you, Ruby's uncle. Watch out for Gigi, over there," Ferne cautions playfully. "She likes older men."

The young lady blushes.

"Be nice, Ferne," Ruth scolds playfully.

Pancho looks around. "Speaking of which—where is that husband of yours, Gigi?"

"Dillwyn's in the pool with Mary Fisher." Gigi frowns at the duo sitting in the shallow end. From the intensity of their expressions, they appear to be having a serious conversation.

"Makes sense," Pancho says dismissively. "They're both writers."

Gigi relaxes. "Of course. I'm sure that's it."

"I think I'll see what Jack's up to." My uncle politely bows to each woman. "It was delightful meeting all of you."

Everyone—including Pancho—sighs while watching him stroll toward the house. There's no denying that my uncle strikes a handsome figure.

Once he's gone, Tilly asks, "So, what do you do, Ruby?"

"She's an investigator," Pancho answers. "Workin' with the Stardust gang in town."

All three women lean forward with interest.

"Is it true that someone was murdered?" Gigi asks eagerly.

"Unfortunately, I'm not at liberty to discuss—"

"That means 'Yes,'" Ruth remarks. "She's not going to tell us anything." The actress leans back into her chair and lights a cigarette.

Ferne lifts her drink. "Looks like I'm out of giggle water." She rises and heads in my uncle's direction.

"Hey ya, Pancho!" Captain Sal calls, walking up the stairs from the basement with two green glass bottles. "I raided your bar. Figured you wouldn't mind."

"Sal, you salty dog!" Pancho declares and traipses over to the mariner, who hands her one of the bottles. "Considerin' how you've kept my cupboards full from that haul you found on the bottom of the ocean, I'd say you can drink whatever you want."

I excuse myself from the women at the table and join them. "Hi, Sal."

"Ruby Ray! When are ya comin' out for a sail?"

"I'd love to, but with one thing after another—let's just say I'm tied up right now."

She nods somberly. "Archie told me about the poisonings. They were s'posed to film another scene offshore yesterday."

"As a movie fan, I never realized how dangerous the film business can be," I confess.

"Darlin', you can't even imagine," Pancho says candidly.

This conversation brings to mind my talk with Sam last night. I wonder if it's even possible for a married woman to have a career that involves a certain amount of peril. And as far as having children…

"Pancho, can I ask you a personal question?"

"Shoot." Pancho pulls the cork from her bottle and takes a swig.

"How does your husband feel about your flying?"

She bellows a hearty guffaw. "He hates it."

"But you're still married…" I remark.

"Ya gotta understand—I came from a rich family living in a rich neighborhood in San Moreno. I wasn't exactly the proper young lady my folks were hopin' for—especially my mother. They arranged my marriage to Reverend Calvin Barnes when I was nineteen hopin' he would tame me."

"How awful!" I protest.

She laughs. "Don't get me wrong. My husband's a handsome guy—all the women at church are in love with him—but I wasn't cut out to be a wife, much less a pastor's wife."

"What did you do?"

"A few years ago, I told him I wanted a divorce, and he refused. So, I moved here." She elbows Sal, who chuckles knowingly. "Then I barnstormed his church every Sunday mornin' during services."

"Did you really?" I visualize the startled congregation jumping from their seats as her plane nearly clips the steeple.

"Yep. Used to drive him crazy."

I really like this woman!

"Does Billy live here with you?"

"He goes back and forth between us. Why do you ask?"

"I just started seeing someone…"

"Lemme guess—he wants you to give up your job for a safe, predictable life with him," Pancho interjects.

"Not exactly…but he's worried about the inherent danger of my job. It's got me thinking about how it would even work…marriage…motherhood…"

"Dump him!" Pancho advises.

"Here! Here!" Sal raises her bottle and takes a swig.

I squirm. "Don't you worry about what would become of Billy if something happened to you?"

"He's got his dad." Pancho's eyes lose their lighthearted gleam. "I'd rather he knew his mom had the guts to be herself no matter what."

I press my lips together and consider this.

Do I have the guts to be myself no matter what?

She pats my upper arm. "Your wings were made to carry you, not the weight of someone else's expectations."

"Found it, Mom!" Billy shouts, as he and Jack jog over with Uncle Charles in tow.

Jack's smile is infectious. The interruption gives me an opportunity to mull over the pilot's words while Pancho signs the cap. Once accomplished, she squeezes the hat onto Jack's head and pulls the flaps down over his ears.

"Why—it fits you better than me!" she proclaims.

My uncle claps his back, "Looks good, sport!"

"Mom, can one of the Short Snorts take us up for a ride?" Billy begs.

"You know I shut down the runway," she replies solemnly. "All the planes are at Three Arch Bay."

Sal murmurs in my ear, "Her friend Dodds crashed into Crescent Bay last month while trying to land on her airstrip. It took my crew more than a week to find all the wreckage. Just terrible!"

"Well, maybe one of the guys can drive us over and take us up," Billy implores.

"Please, Dad!" Jack whines.

My uncle and I share a glance—he's as concerned as I am. From what I've observed so far, the pilots have all been drinking.

"Well, I for one would love to see the horses stabled here," Uncle Charles tells Billy.

"Yeah! Let's see the horses," Jack urges. "You said one was in *Billy the Kid.*"

They've no sooner dashed away when Dottie and Iris approach, pushing their bicycles.

"Hello, Mrs. Barnes. I hope it's alright that I brought my friend," Dottie says politely.

"Mrs. Barnes?" Pancho looks around with alarm. "Nobody told me my mother-in-law was here."

Dottie's bewildered eyes meet mine, then Pancho bends over laughing.

"I'm just joshin'!!" She waves an arm. "Call me Pancho. Everyone does."

Relieved, Dottie introduces Iris, who asks, "How did you get the name Pancho?"

The pilot places her fists on her hips with pride. "It was a few years back when I was in Mexico. Turned out the boat I was travelin' on was a gun runner for the revolution. A buddy and I jumped ship and ended up in a town overrun by rebels. We traveled our way back to the US with them. One day, I was ridin' my burro next to my buddy on his big horse, and he said I looked like Don Quixote's sidekick, Pancho. I told him it was 'Sancho' not 'Pancho,' but the name stuck, and I've been Pancho ever since."

"Are you telling that same old story again?" a suave voice asks good-naturedly.

CHAPTER 22

Dottie's eyes widen, as she chokes out the words, "Ramon Novarro!"

Pancho pulls the famous actor into a companionable hug. "Mi amigo!"

Ramon's pencil-thin mustache and smoldering dark eyes bring to mind his scanty costumes in *Ben Hur* five years ago, and I find myself blushing. Pancho introduces all of us, and Sal offers to get him a drink.

"Whisky?"

"Gin rickey with extra ice, please."

Ramon's friendly smile reveals perfectly straight teeth. He's wearing a mint green polo shirt which sets off his thick black hair, perfectly slicked with a side part.

"I see that Ruth's here," he comments.

Dottie and Iris follow his gaze, and their mouths drop. Iris whispers, none too quietly, "You weren't kidding about celebrities."

"They didn't wanna miss the show," Pancho replies.

"Ahh...the infamous Pancho Barnes' Mystery Circus of the Air," Ramon pronounces. "Will you be pulling that stunt with the unsuspecting volunteer?"

Pancho chortles. "Nah, we'll be flying over the ocean. Too dangerous."

"Now you're talkin' sense!" Ramon remarks.

"What stunt?" Dottie asks.

Pancho grins at her. "It goes like this...my co-pilot and I choose someone from the crowd—usually a young gal—to go up with us. Then, when we're high enough in the air, we chuck her out of the plane while yanking the rip cord on her parachute."

Dottie's face blanches.

"How appalling!" I despise pranks like this, particularly those involving fear or humiliation.

"I told her the same thing." Ramon rolls his eyes.

Pancho chuckles. "It's all good fun. They always laugh about it later."

Dottie begins to sway on her feet. Pancho and I each grab an arm as she collapses onto the grass.

"Not too fond of heights, I take it," Pancho remarks.

"It never used to be a problem," I smooth Dottie's hair away from her clammy face.

Iris squats beside us. "Gosh, Dottie! Are you okay?"

"I-I'm alright," Dottie mutters and tries to sit up.

Pancho advises, "Put your head between your knees. You'll feel better in no time."

"I'll fetch her something cold to drink," Iris rises and heads for the house.

Ramon and Pancho discuss the airshow while I tend to Dottie.

"Is it the heat?" I ask quietly.

"Maybe," Dottie says faintly.

A couple of minutes later, Iris returns with a glass of ice water, while Sal follows close behind with Ramon's gin rickey.

"Thank you," Dottie takes a sip. "That's much better."

When the color returns to her face, Iris and I help her stand.

"Ya know, the best way to conquer fear is to face it head on," Pancho remarks. "You should go up for a ride with me."

"What? So, you can shove me out of the plane?" Dottie quips.

Pancho throws her head back and laughs heartily. "I like ya, kid. You're a straight shooter!"

"Hey, everyone," Archie walks up.

"I never expected to see you here!" Ramon proclaims with delight. "How've you been, Archie?"

I catch the meaningful glance that passes between them—there's clearly some history there.

"Honestly? I've been better," Archie admits. "I'm sorry, Pancho, but I won't be able to stay long."

Pancho playfully slaps his cheek. "That's what you always say."

"What's up, Archie?" Sal asks. "You canceled on us twice already. The guys are startin' to think you don't like us."

He promises, "Nothing of the sort. We still need to shoot that scene on your ship with Corvi and Dean, but she's indisposed at the moment."

Sal nods. "Well, I'm booked this weekend and fillin' up fast for next week. You lemme know."

"Ramoooon! You-hoooo!" Ferne waves him over.

"Ay, caramba!" the actor exclaims while waving with a fake smile.

"Don't worry," Pancho assures him. "Sal and I will handle her for ya."

The three link arms and ramble toward the women under the umbrella.

"Well, that wasn't at all embarrassing!" Dottie declares sarcastically.

I pat her arm. "It'll be a good story someday."

"Yeah," Iris agrees. "Not everyone can say that they fainted in front of Ramon Novarro and Pancho Barnes."

Archie eyes Dottie with concern. "Fainted?"

"It was nothing," she downplays and abruptly changes the subject. "Ruby, did you tell Archie about the buckets?"

"I haven't had a chance," I confess.

Iris and Dottie recount the story about the tidepools, the mystery, and what they witnessed last night involving the Stardust employees.

"The tests I ran last night on the sample from their bucket showed high levels of silver," Iris concludes.

Archie whistles and buries his forehead in his hand. "Just what we need right now!"

"What were they dumping?" Dottie asks.

"It sounds like they were tossing out the fixer used in developing the film. When silver halides are reduced to silver metal, some silver remains in the solution," Archie explains.

"Silver is toxic to marine life. Why on Earth would they do that?" Iris fumes.

"I don't know, but I can assure you it won't happen again. I'll speak with the director of photography pronto."

"Have you been able to finish your project, Iris?" I ask.

"No, I was so preoccupied with the mystery of the disappearing anemones, I had to abandon my original plan," she replies disappointedly. "But my professor said I could write a paper about all this."

"Speaking of which," Dottie adds, "Iris' professor was beside himself and scheduled a meeting with the Marine Lab's director for tomorrow morning."

"Could you go with us, Ruby?" Iris implores. "You saw the whole thing last night."

"Of course—"

"I'll be there too," Archie interrupts. "What time is the meeting?"

"Eleven," Iris answers. "Gee, I really appreciate it!"

"It's the least I can do," Archie replies.

This entire situation could have been avoided if Mr. Lake sent the film to Burbank for processing instead of setting up a makeshift lab at a hotel. He'll want Archie there to smooth things over and avoid bad press.

"Archie! I'm glad I found you!" Kit approaches with Edwin.

"I thought you had an obligation with your family today," Archie comments.

"I left a couple of hours ago. When I returned to the hotel, Bebe told me about Corvi, so I rushed right over to the hospital." He continues, irritably. "Ike kicked me out of the room."

"We must have just missed each other," Archie comments.

With his shoulders slumped, Kit looks absolutely forlorn, but that doesn't stop Dottie from introducing him to Iris. He smiles politely then introduces the girls to Edwin.

"I think I've seen you two at the tidepools near my folk's house," Edwin comments.

"Probably," Iris answers. "We've been working on my project for the Marine Lab. Dottie will be studying chemistry at Berkeley, so she's been a big help."

Edwin whistles. "Berkeley. Impressive."

I tell him proudly, "She's sharp as a tack and graduated high school at the top of her class."

Dottie blushes. "Ru-by!"

"I'm trying to convince Grumpy Gus over here to take the horses down to the beach for a ride," he nods toward Kit. "Do you wanna join us?"

Dottie squeezes Iris' hand. "Do we ever!"

Finally alone, I can talk to Archie about my conversation with Tom.

"Let's find somewhere quiet. You're not going to believe what I have to tell you."

"The nurse said she's already been released," Archie replaces the receiver, and we walk toward the front door of Pancho's house. "She left with Ike about thirty minutes ago."

"I hope to God he's bringing her back to the hotel." Panic starts to cloud my thinking.

"Corvi told them she was heading back to Laguna."

"He can't be trusted, Archie. According to the hotel staff, Ike answered Corvi's door this morning and brought in her breakfast tray," I tell him. "It proves he had access to her food."

"About that…the toxicity labs came back negative. They diagnosed her with gastritis."

"That's a relief." I forcefully exhale. "Nevertheless, she can't be left alone with him."

"Evidently the guard went with them in the car," Archie says. "You know, Ruby, if we tell the police about this…"

"NOW you want to call the police?" I shake my head. "You promised not to disclose anything Tom shared with me," I remind him.

"But the studio—"

"Somebody at the top already knows what's going on," I laugh bitterly. "The studio has suspected Ike for years—that's why they hired Tom. If they'd turned him over to the police, Lena's death could've been avoided. Instead, they covered up for him. It's deplorable!"

"I agree!" Archie says with disgust.

"In some ways, you're not much better," I condemn. "I can't believe you filmed today, knowing full well that another poisoning may have occurred—and to your lead actress, no less."

"That's not exactly covering up murder!" Archie fumes then throws up his hands. "Ruby, you don't understand the pressure I'm under. Mr. Lake is about to snap. A lot is riding on this film…"

"None of that matters!" I snap. "We're talking about human life!"

We hear voices approaching and stop talking.

"Turn left at the end of the hall. Ya can't miss it," Pancho tells her guest as they walk into the entryway. After the woman heads toward the lavatory, Pancho notices us.

"Don't tell me you're leavin' without saying goodbye," she scolds Archie.

"I'm sorry, Pancho. There's been an emergency." He wraps an arm around her shoulders and kisses her forehead. "I promise to visit again before we leave town."

"I'm holdin' ya to that!" She smacks his bottom and leaves.

"So, where are we right now in terms of protecting Corvi?" I ask calmly. Arguing with him won't accomplish anything. "Security can't control what happens behind closed doors."

"Unfortunately, there's nothing we can do to keep Ike away from her," Archie replies.

I sigh with dread. "Well, we can stay close to her. Hopefully, he won't hurt her with one of us nearby and, if all goes well, Tom will convince the studio executives to hand him over to the police."

"I'll wait for Corvi at the hotel and stay with her all night if I need to," Archie promises.

"I'll stay with her tonight. Why don't I call you in a few hours to iron out the plan." I place a hand on his arm. "And Archie...be careful."

"When that guy dove from the roof into the pool with a bottle of beer in his hand, I knew it was time to leave," Uncle Charles laughs. "I'm surprised the neighbors didn't call the police."

"That guy WAS the police!" I chuckle.

Just after sunset, the afternoon's joviality segued into debauchery, which came as no surprise given the never-ending flow of spirits. Thankfully, Dottie and Iris had left long before the young pilots started removing articles of clothing during a game of strip poker with Ferne. I have to say, though, I was quite surprised to witness Officer Jankowski's diving demonstration following his claim that he competed on the US platform diving team during the 1904 Olympics in St. Louis. When I later asked Pancho about his presence at the party, she cackled and told me that it's always a good idea to make friends with cops when you have a bar in your basement.

"I'm glad Jack was in Billy's room when the hurly-burly started," my uncle comments. "There are certain conversations with Jack that I'd like to postpone for a while longer."

From our seats in the Adirondack chairs out front, we hear Jack trying to persuade Puck to do something clearly at odds with his species.

"Awww! Come on, Puck! It's a toy mouse, for Pete's sake. Fetch!"

"Incidentally, Jack begged to sleep over tonight, so he can spend more time with Puck," I tell him. "Unfortunately, I'll be staying at the hotel to keep an eye on things with Corvi."

I briefly tell him about the latest threat and my suspicions regarding her manager. Of course, I omit my discussion with Tom.

"Why don't I stay here with the kids," he suggests. "I'll feel more comfortable knowing that Dottie isn't alone, what with her nightmares and everything."

"That's a good idea. So far, she hasn't shared much with me, but she nearly fainted today when Pancho was talking about a stunt they pull during her barnstorming show." I lower my voice. "I have a feeling the dreams are related to this newfound fear of heights."

"Fear of heights?" Uncle Charles abruptly stops packing his pipe with tobacco. "She disliked our flights during the trip, but I thought that had to do with the discomforts of air travel."

"I thought the same thing at first."

I tell him about her alarm while climbing down the tree with Puck, as well as her reaction when we discussed Table Rock with Iris.

He lights his pipe and takes three quick puffs. "I don't know what to do."

"Neither do I." I lean forward and rest my chin on my knuckles.

Brrring…

I leap from my chair. "Maybe it's Sam."

Dottie beats me to it. "Laguna 830. This is Dottie Ray… sure, she's right here."

I take the phone. "Hello?"

"Hello there, Ruby! It's Norma!"

Masking my disappointment, I reply cheerily, "Hi, Norma. How did things go in Nebraska?"

"As well as can be expected. Edith was able to settle everything, but it's been hard on her," she says tenderly.

"I understand," I reply sympathetically. "If it's any consolation, please let her know that everything is fine here at the house."

"How's my sweet Puck? I miss him terribly," she intones.

"He's absolutely fine. In fact, he's playing with my cousin, Jack, as we speak."

In truth, Jack is now detangling a length of yarn from his paws. "Hold still!"

"Well, I just wanted to let you know that we'll be back Sunday afternoon."

"That's great! You'll be here just in time for the airshow." I tell her about Pancho's plans and the myriad stunt pilots in town.

"How marvelous!" Norma exclaims. "It sounds like there's been a great deal of excitement since we've been away."

"You have no idea," I say wryly.

I hear a commotion through the earpiece, then Norma comes back on the line. "I have to go, Ruby. We need to board our next train."

"Goodbye, Norma. Have a safe journey."

Wandering back outside, I gaze up at the sky. Just six days ago, Sam and I watched three pelicans fly across the same moon, now waning.

Is this a metaphor for our relationship?

"You're miles away," Uncle Charles observes. "Was that Sam?"

"No." I sag into the chair.

"If you don't mind my asking, what happened last night?"

"I've been wondering the same thing myself."

Pressing two fingers against my lips, I think about his words "I need some time to figure all this out." What did he mean?

"If you don't want to talk about it—"

"Uncle Charles, am I wrong to want both a family and a career?"

"Ah." He removes his pipe and rests his hand on the arm of the chair. "I understand now."

I turn my torso to face him directly. "As we both know, my job can be dangerous at times. Sam's not sure he can live with the constant fear."

"Isn't it rather early to be discussing that? You just started dating," he comments.

"Ordinarily, that would be true but—to be honest—I've already fallen head over heels, and I think he feels the same way too. So, before things go too far…"

He takes my hand in his and gives it a squeeze. "Ruby, I'd be lying if I said I don't worry about you every time you step out the door. I'm concerned about Dottie and Jack too, of course, but it's different. Your work entails threats that most people never have to face."

Disgruntled, I ask, "Are you saying I should quit my job if I decide to get married?"

"Not at all," Uncle Charles replies unflinchingly. "I was going to say that it takes a certain kind of person to marry someone whose career is fraught with danger—a person who can make peace with their fear. Sam may or may not be able to do that."

I consider the women I know whose husbands are firemen, policemen, or soldiers. There's pride among them, knowing that their husbands are heroes. They respect their spouses for putting their lives on the line to help others. There's no reason men can't do the same.

"This work I do…it's who I am. While I'd love to marry and have children someday, I can't see myself giving this up."

"Nor should you." He pats my hand. "Times are changing, Ruby. If the Twenties were anything to go by, the next decade should offer even more opportunities for women like you and Dottie."

"I'd like to think so, but I have my doubts."

It took women more than a hundred years to secure the right to vote in America yet, in some states, Black women still can't vote without passing literacy tests or facing threats of violence. Further, I fear that the progress we've made as women in so many domains, including work, could be hindered, especially with so many men losing their jobs right now.

"Your parents would be incredibly proud of you, particularly your mother," Uncle Charles praises encouragingly. "She was strong, just like you."

I lean my shoulder against his. "And just like Aunt Beatrice."

He takes a puff from his pipe and slowly exhales a cloud of sweet smoke. "I understand Sam's fear of falling in love only to lose you."

"You know better than anyone what that's like."

"To this day, I live my life feeling like half the man I once was. She brought out the best in me."

"Does it ever stop hurting?"

The loss of my parents continues to haunt me. I can't imagine what it would be like to lose your soulmate.

"No, but you come to terms with the pain. It reminds me that not only did I love Beatrice, but I cherished her—and still do, this many years later."

"Do you ever wish you hadn't loved so deeply?"

"As if I had a choice!" He chuckles. "In the end, we can only choose what to do with our feelings. We have no control over how and when they arise."

He must *be lonely.*

"Have you ever thought about another…what I mean to say is…"

"Why, Ruby! Are you asking about my love life?" he teases. "You're no better than Nan."

"I'm sorry to pry," I apologize, recalling how uncomfortable I felt when people brought up dating after my break-up with Eddie. "It's none of my business. I just want you to be happy."

"There's nothing to apologize for," he assures me. "I know you have only the best intentions."

"Ferne was quite captivated by you this afternoon," I jest. "If only she wasn't married."

"I suspect that Ferne is captivated by anyone wearing trousers."

"I think you're right," I giggle. "Not to be nosey, but has there been anyone who's turned your head?"

He quietly draws a breath through his pipe. I think I've overstepped until I notice the grin tugging the corner of his mouth.

"There is someone!" I slap my hand on the armrest of my chair.

"Yes, but it's very new." He stresses the word *new*. "We've only had a couple of dates."

"What?! Okay, now you have to tell me more."

I settle back and listen to the story of how my uncle met Clara O'Ryan, a divorcée whose husband abandoned her and their son, Owen—a new friend Jack met earlier this summer with a shared passion for lizards and snakes.

"I took her out for dinner one evening before leaving for New York, and we attended a matinee at the Fox Theater last weekend."

"What do Dottie and Jack think about this?" I ask.

"Dottie's thrilled for me, but I haven't said anything to Jack yet. For now, Clara's a wonderful companion, and I don't want Jack getting ideas about installing bunk beds in his room anytime soon."

"I look forward to meeting her, whenever you're comfortable," I reply.

"As a matter of fact, Clara and Owen will be joining us for the airshow on Monday. Jack insisted," Uncle Charles informs me.

"Perfect! I can't wait to meet her." I add with a wink, "I suppose the cat will be out of the bag after that."

"You're probably right," he laughs. "Now it's my turn to pry," Uncle Charles raises one eyebrow. "Since you returned, you've seemed preoccupied. I thought it had to do with Sam, but I wonder if there's something more."

"I'm embarrassed to admit this," I sigh heavily. "I've been feeling restless—which is ridiculous. I just traveled abroad, for goodness' sake."

He takes a puff of his pipe and nods for me to continue.

"I feel as though there's something wonderful waiting for me if I rise to the challenge."

"What do you think that is?" he asks thoughtfully.

"Elizabeth asked me the same question, but I don't really know..." My voice trails off.

"There's nothing like traveling the world to show you what may be missing in your life," he remarks sagely.

"True...but I have to admit that I'm feeling a tad envious right now with Dottie spreading her wings," I confess with embarrassment.

This seems to surprise him, and he takes a moment before responding. "Through the years, I've wondered if we held you back, Ruby."

"Please don't say that." I reply with alarm.

"Hear me out," he says firmly. "You didn't go away for college. Furthermore, you've never lived on your own—in your own home. You've stayed with us to help out."

"Those were all my choices," I assure him. "I've never felt that you three held me back. You're my family, and I've gladly stayed exactly where I am because I've needed you too. However, I think it's time for me to consider what the next chapter of my life should look like."

"Finding a place of your own?" he inquires.

In a flash, I have the answer I've been searching for. "Yes, but not in the way you're thinking."

"I'm listening."

"Bear with me because the idea just hit me." I turn sideways in my chair to look him directly in the eye. "I think it's time to expand my business, and I'll need a proper office, maybe somewhere downtown."

"That's wonderful!" he exclaims. "What do you have in mind?"

"Ruby Ray Investigations." I wave an arm through the air as though marking a title on a movie screen.

I explain to him how, up to now, I've been content with maintaining a small practice focused on domestic inquiries, hence my title "inquiry agent." But my recent cases—from grand theft to missing persons to murder—have sparked an interest in accepting more challenging and complex cases as a genuine "private investigator." I would never turn my back on helping women in need, but taking on high paying clients from time to time will better enable me to support my pro bono work. To achieve this, I need to move beyond the cottage and word-of-mouth advertising and open a formal, professionally furnished office where I can actively pursue the types of cases I have in mind. The money I made selling the house in New York would more than cover the start-up costs until the business begins to turn a profit and leave me with a nest egg for when I decide to buy a home of my own someday.

"You've really thought this through," Uncle Charles comments with a grin.

"It's been percolating just below the surface for a while, but now it's crystal clear." I add excitedly, "Not only does this meet my needs— Nan could move into the cottage, as well. "

"This is perfect!" He claps. "And I think she'd agree, especially if I tell her we need a caretaker for the cottage."

The front door swings open.

"Dad…Ruby…come see what Puck can do!" Jack urges.

"Did you come in through the back?" Archie asks while opening the living room door.

"Yes, thanks for the heads up."

When I drove past the front of the hotel, I witnessed a horde of reporters—many more than earlier—accosting hotel guests trying to return to their rooms. I parked alongside the hotel, slinked through the back courtyard and entered the hallway leading to the lobby before a pair of journalists with cameras had time to notice.

"How is she?" I nod toward Corvi's bedroom.

"Exhausted, as you can imagine, but she was able to eat a little dinner," he replies.

I lower my voice to a whisper. "Is Ike still here?"

"No, he left as soon as he brought her up," he says with obvious relief. "I have no idea where he went or when he'll be back, but I told security to alert you if he returns to her room tonight."

The bedroom door opens.

"Oh, Ruby—you're here," Corvi yawns and settles onto the sofa.

"I'm sorry we woke you," I apologize. "I'm going to stay in Elizabeth's room tonight to keep an eye on things."

She leans forward. "There's no need for that. There's a guard right outside the door, and Ike may come back later."

Archie and I share a nervous glance.

"What?" Corvi looks back and forth between us.

"We have some concerns about Ike," I say delicately.

She frowns. "About Ike?"

I tell her vaguely, "We've learned some things about his past that are…troubling."

Her eyes flash with alarm. "What are you talking about?"

I sit next to her and lightly touch her shoulder. "We have reason to believe that he may have poisoned Lena and Elizabeth, and we're concerned that he might harm you...that he's already tried to harm you."

"That's ridiculous!" Corvi jumps to her feet. "He would never—"

Archie interrupts. "Your roommate that drowned? The actress who was thrown from a horse last fall?"

"No! It's not true!" Tears flow down her cheeks. "Those were accidents."

"Like Lena's drowning was an accident?" he continues.

"Archie, that's not helping." I wrap an arm around Corvi's upper back and help her sit back down. "I'm sorry we upset you. Perhaps we shouldn't have brought this up to you, but we are very worried about your safety."

"Ike would never hurt me," she wails.

"Maybe," I comment. "But until we get to the bottom of this, it would be best if you're not alone with him."

"It's not him...it's not..." she repeats over and over while crying.

I pull her into an embrace. "We will keep you safe."

She stiffens. "Then catch the stalker! He's the one! Not Ike!"

"Corvi, I'm so sorry we upset you. We only meant to warn you," I apologize

"Maybe you should turn in for the night," Archie suggests.

"You expect me to sleep after a bombshell like that?" Corvi snaps.

"How about a cup of tea?" Archie looks at me helplessly then glances toward her bedroom door. "Your book! That'll take your mind off things."

"Are you joking?" Corvi stares at him incredulously and stomps into her room, slamming the door behind her.

"I suppose, in hindsight, an Agatha Christie novel wasn't the best suggestion," Archie mutters.

CHAPTER 23

SATURDAY, AUGUST 30, 1930

"Stop!" Dottie shrieks while batting her arms.

I shake her in vain. "You're having a nightmare."

"Get away from me." Her fingernails pierce my cheek.

Reflexively, my hand swings up toward my bleeding face. Dottie's sits bolt upright and reaches for my throat, all the while screeching with fury.

"Wake up!" I bawl with desperation.

"Wake up, Ruby!" a high-pitched shriek pulls me from the terrifying dream.

Disoriented, I raise my arms to project myself.

"Ruby, you have to wake up!" Corvi cries frantically. "He left another note!"

Now I'm fully awake. I remove the postcard from her hands and quickly read:

In her tomb by the sounding sea.

The front of the postcard depicts a pair of fish swimming among a kelp forest.

Leaping from the bed, I grab Corvi's shoulders.

"When did you find this?"

"J-just now!" she weeps. "In the living room."

"Stay here!"

I throw open the door leading outside just as one of the security guards begins to knock. He cranes his neck to look inside.

"Is everything okay, ma'am? We heard a scream."

I'm surprised to notice his partner's hand resting on a holstered pistol. As far as I know, security guards for Stardust Productions have not been carrying firearms up to now.

"There's been an intruder." I hand him the note.

Corvi perches on the sofa, drawing her knees to her chest while sobbing into a handkerchief.

"Did anyone visit you last night?" I ask her.

Corvi's blonde waves bounce as she shakes her head. "No."

"Ma'am, no one entered the suite after you arrived yesterday evening. Where did you find this?"

"On the coffee table," Corvi wrings the handkerchief between her hands. "I came out to see if the breakfast trays had been delivered."

"What time is it?" I ask the security guard. My watch is on the nightstand.

"Five past seven."

The other security guard looks out the living room window. "No one could get in. It's a straight drop down to the sand."

"Not only that, I made sure all the windows were closed before turning in last night," I comment.

Corvi gasps and drops the hankie. "Mine were open. The room was stuffy—"

We rush en masse to Corvi's room where filmy curtains billow back and forth in the breeze. Sticking my head out the leftmost window, I look down. The guard is correct, there's no ledge or balcony for someone to walk on.

Corvi looks out the other window and shouts, "A ladder!"

I swivel my head. "She's right! There's a fire escape alongside that window!"

We step aside for the security guards to take a look.

"Corvi, where was Ike last night?" I inquire.

"I-I don't know," she replies, her eyes round with confusion. "Why do you ask?"

I start to say, "The fire escape goes all the way down to the—"

Corvi's eyes narrow. "Are you suggesting that Ike snuck into my room and left that threatening note?"

"I explained to you last night about my concerns—"

"Why are you going on again about this?!" She stomps her foot with a cry. "He'd never hurt me!"

"Ma'am, no offense to Mr. Bronson," one of the security guards interjects. "But there's no way a guy his size could manage swinging from the ladder into this window."

"He's right," his partner agrees.

"Forget about Ike!" Corvi demands with dismay. "You should be looking for the stalker!"

A knock interrupts our discussion, and I stalk across the room to answer the door.

"I'm so sorry I'm late," Mrs. Gleason apologizes. "Mr. Duval asked that we deliver breakfast no later than seven, but our coffee maker stopped working. Then I couldn't find a percolator anywhere in the new kitchen—had to borrow one from the cafe..."

"It's no trouble." I accept the two trays from the kitchen supervisor and place them on Corvi's bed.

"Please tell Mr. Duval that they're on the house," she backs away from the doorway. "I know Miss Styles will be leaving soon for the film. I hope she still has time to eat."

The shoot!

Before leaving last night, Archie told me they were filming a scene with Corvi and Kit this morning and would leave no later than eight.

"I'm sure it will be fine," I assure Mrs. Gleason while closing the door.

The armed security guard lifts the lids from the trays. One bears a plate with scrambled eggs, a slice of buttered toast, orange marmalade jam, and a cup of coffee—clearly mine. The other carries nothing more than half a grapefruit and a cup of coffee with sugar on the side.

"Where do you want these, Miss Styles?" he asks.

"Forget the food!" Corvi exclaims. "Someone needs to call the police."

A little while later, Archie and Kit stop by to collect Corvi, the police having not yet arrived. I'm inclined to protest, however, Corvi tearfully insists that she cannot stay a minute longer in the suite with everything that's happened. Hopefully, the work will keep her mind off of things. While she's changing, I pull Archie aside to fill him in and show him the latest postcard.

"You there." Archie gestures toward the security guard with the pistol. "I need you to escort us to the shoot."

"Shall I stay outside and guard the suite?" the other fellow asks.

"Yes, please," Archie replies. Before leaving, he tells me, "We'll be done filming before eleven. I still intend to join the meeting at the lab later this morning."

Alone in the suite, I decide to inspect all three rooms before the police arrive, just in case I overlooked something during my search yesterday. I start with Corvi's bedroom. She must have tidied up while I was talking to Archie, for all the surfaces are clear except for a book on the nightstand.

"*The Mysterious Mr. Quinn*," I read the title.

A silver bookmark topped with a filigree heart slips out of a page toward the end. For someone who's not much of a reader, I'm surprised to see that she's gotten this far. However, as I recall, this book—one of Mrs. Christie's latest—contains a collection of separate mini-mysteries, which must be easier for some readers to digest. I picked up a copy myself when I was in London but haven't had a chance to read it yet.

Returning to the living room, I notice that Corvi left her handkerchief on the back of the sofa, but when I reach for it, the hankie slides behind the couch. I peek into the gap between the sofa and the wall and notice something peculiar. A rectangular plate, about a foot wide and two feet tall, is mounted several inches above the baseboard. This reminds me of the wall panel used by the couple on the boat to hide their loot.

It's probably nothing, but I should check, nonetheless.

I move the coffee table to the side, then scoot the couch forward. I'd like to remove the plate, but each corner is secured by a screw with a square-shaped socket. Further, the paint has been scratched on all four screwheads, suggesting that the panel was removed sometime after the room was painted. This strengthens my resolve to see what's behind there. Hopefully, Norma and Edith have a screwdriver back at the house that will do the trick.

Hearing voices outside the hall, I quickly stand up just as the security guard opens the door for Inspector Maggard and Cadet Cunningham.

"They really did a number on the place!" the young man declares.

"No, I just moved the furniture to get at this plate on the wall," I clarify and step away from the couch.

The inspector's eyes droop. "A plate on the wall? Really, Miss Ray?"

"Yes." To my annoyance, I blush. "Something tells me that there may be a clue concealed behind it."

"What's telling you, Miss Ray? Your female intuition?" he mocks and chuckles while nudging the cadet with his elbow.

I raise my chin and gaze steadily into his eyes. "Yes, Inspector. My intuition."

"Well, Miss Ray, before you start prying service panels from the walls, I can assure you that all you'll find is electrical wiring and—perhaps—a pipe or two." His eyes sweep the room. "We were called here about an alleged hostile note. Is that correct?"

"On the end table." I point.

The cadet hands the note to Inspector Maggard.

"Much like the others," the inspector comments indifferently. "Where was it found?"

"On the coffee table."

He tilts his head. "The guard tells me the intruder came in through the bedroom window."

"Yes, he most likely climbed the fire escape." I jerk my head toward Corvi's room.

After a cursory inspection, the two officers return to the living room.

The detective purses his lips. "Let me get this straight. You believe that the intruder climbed up the fire escape, entered Miss Styles bedroom window, left the note on the coffee table in the living room, then left through the same bedroom window…all without harming a hair on Miss Styles' pretty little head or waking her up."

"That's precisely what I think," I cross my arms.

"Why?" He raises his eyebrows.

"Intimidation. I've already told you that I suspect Ike Bronson is behind all this, and you conceded that he had the opportunity." I raise a finger in the air. "Here's the motive—she threatened to fire him. She's big money for him, and he's trying to keep her under his thumb through fear. That's his motivation." I raise a second finger.

"And means?"

"He acquired the strychnine that poisoned Lena Young's health tonic from a housekeeper's cart here at the hotel—rat poison. Then there's the hyoscine that was put in Elizabeth Martin's coffee. Ike was on the *Statendam* a few weeks ago, just like I was. The infirmary was handing out hyoscine hydrobromide tablets like candy to everyone for seasickness. Last, there's the postcards and red ink, all of which could be easily obtained. So, there are your means." I hold up three fingers.

Inspector Maggard slowly claps his hands sarcastically. "It's a plausible theory, I suppose."

"I have records of my interviews. I'm sure we can get the passenger manifest—"

"Tell you what—come down to the station with everything you've jotted down in your little notebook. We'll add that to the file."

I sigh with exasperation. Without Tom's testimony, all I have is circumstantial evidence.

"Polka Dot woke up screaming and crying," Uncle Charles steps aside for me to enter the house.

"Did she say anything to you?" I drop my handbag on a chair.

"Not a word," he sighs heavily. "It was hard to console her, but after a while, she pretended to fall back asleep. I figured she wanted me to leave, so I went back to bed. Granted, I didn't sleep a wink after that."

"This is getting worse."

"I agree." I follow him to the kitchen where he pours a cup of coffee for me. "I tried to talk to her this morning during breakfast, but she excused herself and went back to her room."

"I'll try again. Is she still there?"

"As far as I know. She's waiting for you to pick her up for the meeting with Iris and the lab director." He stops me before I leave. "I owe you one."

"Well, if that's the case, could you find me a screwdriver."

He blinks, puzzled. "Sure, but what kind?"

"It's for a screw with a square-shaped socket." I explain, "I need to remove a service panel in Corvi's suite."

"Oh, a Robertson screwdriver." He pinches his chin with his thumb and forefinger. "I don't have one in the car. Do you suppose Norma and Edith have a toolbox?"

"Yes, Dottie saw some tools in the backyard shed when she found the bike."

"I'll have a look."

I knock on the door to the study before entering. "Dottie?"

"Oh, hi." She sits up on the cot with a book in her hand. "How'd it go at the hotel last night?"

"Another note." I plop down on the bed next to her. "An intruder most likely climbed through the window in Corvi's bedroom."

Her jaw drops. "How scary!"

"It's unsettling, that's for sure, especially with two guards—one armed—just outside her door."

She gulps. "Weren't you petrified?"

"He was already gone when I found out. Honestly, as soon as Corvi showed me the note, my adrenaline kicked in, and I didn't think about the danger. I was too focused on figuring out how and when he got in."

"I don't know how you do it!"

"It's all part of the job," I brush it off. "I'd rather talk about you, Dottie. Your dad told me about the nightmare last night."

She rolls her eyes and sighs wearily. "I wish he hadn't."

"This is important, Dottie. It's disrupting your sleep. Obviously, something serious is troubling you."

"What's troubling me is the idea of having these nightmares when I'm at the boarding house in Berkeley," she admits. "I don't want the other girls to hear me."

"Perhaps, if you talk about the dreams, they'll loose their grip on you," I suggest.

She shakes her head. "I don't know."

"You told me they have to do with Mr. Mains..."

Jack throws open the door. "You won't believe Puck's new trick! Come on." He waves an arm.

So close!

Dottie passes by Jack and heads down the hall, so I follow Jack into the bedroom. I watch as he uses a flake of tuna to persuade Puck to shake hands with him. Then he then runs through Puck's newly learned repertoire of rolling onto his back, fetching the toy mouse, and sitting up on two legs—**all on command**. I have to admit, I'm impressed with the progress he's made in such a short time. There's hope yet for that kitten.

I leave the room and follow the sound of voices to the kitchen, where Uncle Charles and Dottie are cleaning the dishes and pans from breakfast. She avoids eye contact with me, but my uncle points to the kitchen table with a grin.

"You'll be happy to know, I found two different Robertsons. They're over there."

"That's a relief," I confess. "I wasn't sure what sort of tools they'd have."

"I wouldn't be surprised if some of those tools in the shed came with the house. A few look decades old."

I retrieve my handbag from the living room and settle at the table with my notebook, flipping to the page where I've written out all of the lines from the notes, including the most recent one.

For the moon never beams, without bringing me dreams
And the stars never rise, but I feel the bright eyes
And so, all the night-tide, I lie down by the side
Of my darling, my darling, my life and my bride
In her sepulcher there by the sea,
In her tomb by the sounding sea.

Drying his hands with a dish towel, Uncle Charles looks over my shoulder and comments, "Annabel Lee."

"What did you say?" I look up at him.

"Those are lines from 'Annabel Lee,'" he clarifies. "By Edgar Allen Poe. I'm sure you've heard of it. They made us memorize it in high school."

"No," I shake my head. "We covered *The Raven* and *The Fall of the House of Usher* but no poetry."

"I'm not surprised. That type of gothic horror was losing steam by the time I was a teenager, but something about 'Annabel Lee' really resonated with the romantic in me," he muses and takes a seat across from me.

"What's it about?" I lean forward.

"Star-crossed lovers ultimately separated by death—you know the type. It begins sweetly, though."

Dottie pulls out the chair beside me. "Tell us."

He clears his throat and recites,

"*It was many and many a year ago, in a kingdom by the sea, that a maiden there lived whom you may know by the name of Annabel Lee; And this maiden she lived with no other thought than to love and be loved by me.*"

"Quite different from the notes Corvi received," I observe.

"The verses in your notebook came from the end of the poem. Before that, Annabel's well-to-do relatives abducted her, murdered her, and sealed her body in a burial chamber."

"Eww!" Dottie blurts.

"Indeed," my uncle replies. "But it's odd—whoever sent the notes omitted the lines that mention Annabel Lee by name."

I push my notebook across the table. "Could you fill in the lines that are missing?"

With small, neat handwriting, Uncle Charles squeezes the omitted phrases between the written verses, then turns the notebook back around for me to read.

For the moon never beams, without bringing me dreams
Of the beautiful Annabel Lee;
And the stars never rise, but I feel the bright eyes
Of the beautiful Annabel Lee;
And so, all the night-tide, I lie down by the side
Of my darling, my darling, my life and my bride
In her sepulcher there by the sea.
In her tomb by the sounding sea.

A tingle runs down my back.

Annabel.

And I immediately remember the conversation Elizabeth and I had with Corvi about stage names when we were in the candy shop.

"Her real name is Annabel." I pound my fist on the table. "That bastard!"

"Stay in the car," I instruct Dottie. "This won't take long."

"But Ruby, it's already ten forty-five," Dottie shouts out the window, as I jog into the Hotel Laguna. The press have cleared the area—most likely after Archie, Kit, and Corvi left.

The guard outside the suite must have heard my pounding footsteps coming up the stairs, for he takes one look at my determined expression, unlocks the living room door, and holds it open for me.

"Do you need a hand?" he asks, his brows arched above wide eyes.

"I'll let you know." I rush toward the sofa. "Thank you."

I hear the door click behind me as he returns to the hall, and I'm relieved to be alone with the task before me. I have no idea what I will find—if I will find anything. Nevertheless, I remove the tools from my bag and set to work. After fumbling for a minute with the first screwdriver, I realize that it's too large. Frustrated, I toss it aside and reach for the other one which, thankfully, fits. Given my agitation, I'm all thumbs with the tool and struggle to remove each screw. Meanwhile, I continue to fume over the meaning behind the notes.

What a twisted, ruthless trick to play on Corvi!

No doubt, Ike chose that particular poem precisely because it bore her name. He knew exactly how traumatizing Corvi would feel when she realized that the stalker knew her true identity.

I will see him behind bars before anyone else is hurt!

When I extract the final screw, the panel drops to the carpet. Inspector Maggard was correct about the electrical wires. However, a compact parcel wrapped in a paisley scarf rests behind the looped wires in the hollow space. I check my watch and realize that it's ten fifty-five. I need to dash, but I can't resist a peek inside the bundle. On top is a pocket-sized journal covered in textured leather upon which has been stamped *L. Young*.

Lena Young.

My heart races.

By the time I reach the car, it's two minutes until eleven. Dottie is pacing back and forth on the sidewalk but rapidly jumps in the passenger seat when she sees me.

"Finally!" She cries.

I hop in, start the car, and throw the gear stick into reverse. After several cars pass, I turn left onto Coast Highway.

"It's alright, Dottie! They'll wait if we're a few minutes late," I assure her.

The lab is less than a quarter of a mile away, but there are stop signs at both Forest Avenue and Ocean Avenue. Further, these intersections are crowded with weekend traffic.

"We might as well walk," Dottie moans.

When we finally pull into the Pomona College Marine Laboratory parking lot it's seven past eleven. Dottie hops out leaving the door ajar and races between the towering square columns on either side of the main entrance. I lock the paisley-wrapped bundle in the trunk of the car and follow her into the two-story Colonial Revival building.

Archie and Iris are waiting in the foyer with a bespectacled scholar in a white lab coat who appears to be in his forties. He holds out his hand.

"Dr. Christopher Grober. I'm Iris's professor. Thank you so much for joining us today."

"Ruby Ray," I return his greeting. "I'm Dottie's cousin. I'm so sorry we're late."

His kind smile reaches his eyes. "It's no problem. Dr. Campbell is running a few minutes late as well."

Sure enough, about five minutes later Dr. Campbell's secretary asks us to follow her toward the back of the building. Several students openly stare with curiosity, as we pass classrooms and labs down the long hallway. At the very end, double doors open into a spacious room filled with a long table that could easily accommodate two dozen people. A mature, dignified gentleman rises from the chair at the head of the table. Beside him, a man wearing a plaid coat remains seated.

"I'm Dr. Campbell, Director of the Pomona College Marine Laboratory, and this is Mr. Jonathan Hinkle from Laguna Beach City Hall."

Mr. Hinkle nods politely.

"My apologies for the wait. Please sit down." Dr. Campbell gestures toward the chairs closest to him.

After the introductions are made, Dr. Grober briefly describes the troubling disappearance of sea life from the tidepool below the Coast Inn, then turns the floor over to Iris. I'm quite impressed by her articulate, composed presentation—starting with her discovery that the sea anemone population was declining. She then distributes graphs depicting the data she collected and shares the results from the chemical analyses that were performed. Every now and then, Dr. Campbell asks a question, but he seems pleased with Iris' answers. Toward the end, she encourages Dottie to join in as they describe their observations of the Stardust employees Thursday night, at which point Archie shifts uncomfortably in his seat. When the presentation has concluded, Dr. Campbell clasps his hands together—his index fingers pointing upward. We wait for him to speak.

"I applaud your scientific rigor in solving this problem, Miss Lloyd," he smiles benignly at Iris. "I doubt some of our graduate students would have demonstrated the same level of diligence and meticulous thinking if they were in your shoes."

"Thank you, Dr. Campbell," Iris bows her head modestly. "I couldn't have done it without Dottie."

He graciously nods at the two young women. "I have no doubt that both of you will succeed in your academic and professional pursuits."

"Thank you," they reply together.

"I would now like to hear from Mr. Duval."

"Yes, sir," Archie answers. "First, I wish to apologize that our director of photography could not be here today. He is tied up in Burbank at the moment, but he sends his deepest regrets."

"We appreciate your taking the time to be here, Mr. Duval."

Archie continues, "On behalf of Stardust Productions, I would like to express our sincere remorse that members of our crew behaved in such a manner. I assure you that it will not happen again,"

Archie intones the carefully crafted message written, no doubt, by their public relations department. "Furthermore, Stardust Productions will pay the city of Laguna Beach for reparation of the damage our employees have caused and are prepared to make a handsome donation to the Pomona College Marine Laboratory to help support the valuable work you are doing here."

"Thank you, Mr. Duval, for your eloquent apology." Dr. Campbell unfolds his hands and sits back into his chair. "Is this agreeable with you, Mr. Hinkle?"

The city representative speaks for the first time. "Yes, that will do."

"Alright then. It appears that everything is in order." Dr. Campbell then tells Archie, "I assure you that Pomona College has no intention of making this regrettable incident public."

Archie sighs with relief. "Thank you, sir."

Dr. Campbell tilts his head, "I'm curious, though. What reason did your crew give for doing such a thing? There must be a protocol in place for the disposal of toxic materials."

Archie explains how an assistant cameraman had been tasked by the director of photography with transporting the fluids to a local pharmacist each day for proper disposal, along with a cash payment. However, the crew member decided to keep the payment for himself and recruited a colleague to help him dump the developing fluids into the ocean, knowing that if they poured the material down a drain, they may be discovered.

"But why dump the buckets directly onto the tidepool?" I inquire.

"Apparently, the tidepool area was typically dark and isolated at night. On top of that, they wouldn't have to wade out into the water." Archie shakes his head with disgust. "It goes without saying that both men were fired on the spot and will never work in Hollywood again.

As we stand to leave the meeting, Dr. Campbell pulls Dottie aside and tells her, "You're a bright, young chemist. We'd love to have you on board at Pomona College."

357

When she explains her intentions to attend Berkeley, he nods and shakes her hand. "Well, our loss, but we'd be more than happy to offer college credit if you ever wish to attend a summer session with us at the lab."

Before getting into our cars in the parking lot, I ask Archie about Corvi.

"She should be back at the hotel. The security guard promised me he would stick close to her until she got settled in her room."

"How was she?" I bite the corner of my lip with concern.

"Distracted...emotional...just as you'd expect, given the circumstances," he shrugs. "Where are you off to right now?"

I share with him the significance of the poem and tell him about my discovery behind the service panel. Then I add, "I need to drop off Dottie and Iris at the house, so I'll examine the parcel there. After that, I'll head back to the hotel to sit with Corvi for the rest of the day. Hopefully, I hear back from Tom soon."

Archie looks at his watch. "I'll look in on her right now for a few minutes. I have to be back on set with Kit and Bebe very soon."

"We're taking the bikes down to the beach," Dottie calls out, as she and Iris walk through the kitchen door.

"Why didn't you walk there from the lab?" I turn from the counter where I'm slicing an avocado for my sandwich. As much as I'd like to open the bundle immediately, I forgot to eat breakfast and need to get some food in me, or I won't be able to think straight.

"For one thing," Dottie answers, "I didn't have my swimsuit, and for another, we want to cycle down to Three Arch Bay."

"I think there's a runway down there," I mention, recalling Pancho's comment to her son yesterday.

"That's what Edwin told us," Dottie's eyes shift to Iris who grins sheepishly.

"Why don't you just admit that you're going there to meet him?" I try not to smirk.

"I don't know what you're talking about," she says, straight-faced, then winks before closing the door.

Well, good for her.

I sit at the table with my plate and take two bites before unwrapping the paisley scarf. Beneath the journal, I find a stack of cream-colored envelopes tied together with a black ribbon, along with a pair of gold wedding bands tightly secured by the bow. I set the envelopes aside with the journal and turn my attention to the last item in the parcel, a book of poems by Edgar Allen Poe which, under further inspection, appears to belong to someone named "Roland Lowe." A black cord with onyx beads at the ends marks the page containing the poem "Annabel Lee."

My heart thumps wildly.

I push the book aside and carefully loosen the ribbon to remove an envelope from the stack. Inside is a single page of matching cream stationary covered in flowery handwriting, beginning with the words *My darling Roland.*

"Why are you alone?" I pointedly ask the security guard outside Corvi's door.

"Zeke went to pick up lunch from that place across the street," he answers with annoyance. "No one's been here since Mr. Duval left."

"When was that?"

The guard pulls up his sleeve to examine his watch. "Well, it's one now, so it must have been around twelve thirty or so. Mr. Duval answered the door when Miss Styles' lunch tray arrived, and he told the lady that she wasn't hungry. Then he left."

"Did anyone visit Miss Styles before Archie arrived?"

"No, ma'am."

I unlock the door to Elizabeth's room and toss my handbag on the bed.

"Corvi, It's Ruby," I call while passing into the living room, still in disarray.

Even now, the panel lies on the floor behind the couch alongside the two screwdrivers. In my haste earlier, I hadn't bothered to tidy things up.

That's the least of my concerns right now.

"Corvi?" I knock on her door.

No answer.

"I'm coming in."

I turn the knob and push the door to discover a stiff breeze blowing the curtains to and fro through the open windows.

The room is empty.

The security guard enters and surveys the vacant room then rushes to the open window. "She must have gone down the fire escape."

My eyes scan the bedroom for a clue, anything, to tell us where she may have gone. Her bedspread is wrinkled, and there's a head-shaped dent on the lower half of her pillow. The Agatha Christie book is still resting on the surface of her nightstand.

I lift the book to see if anything has been tucked inside and find a tattered envelope addressed to Annabel Lowe. Brown with age, it bears a postmark dated October 12th, 1918 and a bright blue stamp on the lower right-hand corner indicating that the letter has passed censorship. The return address reads:

P.V.T. Roland Lowe, 103 US Inf, A.E.F. France

The fragile letter inside appears to have been read hundreds of times, its edges torn and ink smeared in places. Thick black lines cover various words and phrases, defaced by the censor's pen.

October 9, 1918
Somewhere in France
My beautiful Annabel,

I cannot bear this separation from you. The world is a cruel place, where two souls with a love such as ours must be ripped apart by XXXXXXXX. *The only thing holding me back from the precipice of insanity is the memory of your smile. I wish* XXXXXXXXX

Promise me that, no matter what happens, you never stop performing. You are "Corvi Styles," the brightest star that ever sparkled. I was telling the guys here that you belong on the screen, not stomping the boards at those vaudeville shows. In fact, I've written a script for a movie that will feature you, my beloved, the dazzling actress who steals the show. I'm afraid that XXXXXXXXXXXXXXXX *So, I've enclosed the manuscript.*

For now, I'm also sending you my wedding ring only because I know it will be safer in your loving hands. The conditions here are XXXXXXXXXXXX *No one knows what tomorrow will bring, but one thing is for certain. I will love you no matter where I am.*

Your adoring husband,
Roland

I learned of Corvi's marriage in the letters I found in the wall cavity. The beloved "brother" she mentioned was, in fact, her husband. I can't blame her for keeping this a secret. While she must have been an exceedingly young bride, she's still older than she looks—a fact that could end her career as an ingenue should word get out. I suspect that this was the last message Corvi ever received and confirms some of what I learned from the other letters but, unfortunately, offers no clues about her disappearance. Turning back to the task at hand, I place the letter and envelope on the nightstand and look under the bed.

Nothing.

"I'm gonna call this in," the security guard steps away from the window, his foot uncovering a postcard that was tucked between the curtain and floor.

I pluck the photo, realizing that it's similar to the ones I saw on the boardwalk with Tom yesterday, and instantly recognize the image of Table Rock. I flip over the card to find a single line scrawled with a backward slant in red ink:

1:00. Come alone.

CHAPTER 24

~ 🪷 ~

An exceptionally high tide washes in and covers the sandy stretch of the empty cove, leaving no space for sunbathers to enjoy the shore. Several long-legged sea birds take wing as a furious breaker crashes against Table Rock with a thunderous boom. It's already one-thirty, and as far as I can tell, Corvi is nowhere to be found.

After the security guard called LBPD from Corvi's room, I dialed Tom's answering service and left a message. Then, while rushing out the door, I suggested that the guard stay put in case Corvi returns to the suite. Despite the fact that I broke the speed limit racing over here, I now fear that I'm too late.

Access to Table Rock is tricky. The bluff above the cove is largely private property, and high walls surround the estates, prohibiting views of the stately homes, as well as the beach below. Were it not for the narrow tree-lined trail that steeply descends down rickety wooden steps between a couple of these manors, the cove would be inaccessible from the highway above. Given the twists and turns of the trail, only a sliver of sand and water is visible along the path. Even now, from my vantage point where the trail meets the cove, it's impossible to see the entire surface of Table Rock.

I remove my sandals, tuck them into my bag, and step into the shallow water to wade toward the promontory. To me, the water temperature along the Southern California coastline never feels as warm as the Atlantic, but given that it's already late August, the Pacific shore is at least tolerable. I imagine that, under different circumstances, a swim would prove delightful on a scorching day like today.

A wave rolls in, and the water's depth rises above my knees. Hoisting my skirt, I trudge along, my toes squishing into the coarse sand, occasionally encountering larger bits of broken shells. Every now and then, the sunlight strikes the iridescent scales of small fish darting ahead of me just under the water's surface. As the backwash recedes, my feet sink more deeply into the sand, giving me the heebie-jeebies when I consider the gray, oval-shaped sand crabs that are undoubtedly burrowing beneath my toes. I hurry toward Table Rock.

"Corvi," I call several times, my hands cupped around my mouth. I don't see her, but if she's on top of the promontory, she may be able to hear me. "I'm coming up!"

As I ascend the massive slippery boulders, I'm thankful to be barefoot and cautiously navigate a path to the top, avoiding the slick algae while trying to maintain my balance. However, my foot slips midway, and a jagged fragment scrapes the length of my calf, tearing the hem of my skirt in the process. The wound stings from the salty water not yet dry on my leg, and blood streams to my ankle. Nevertheless, I press on. It's not as though I have a bandage in my bag.

Startled by a splash behind me, I glance over my shoulder, only to witness a seagull flapping about in the shallow water below, no doubt in pursuit of a small fish or crustacean. I shift my attention to the hillside trail, hoping that the police have arrived but, with the exception of local fauna, the cove is still empty.

The desolation of this picturesque beach triggers a sense of foreboding. Corvi should never have come here by herself. Moreover, given her fear of drowning, I can't imagine her wading through the water to climb these slippery rocks. Even so, I spot Corvi as soon as my head rises above the surface of Table Rock. She's at the far end of the broad headland sitting near the edge, her knees drawn up to her chest.

She's alone.

I climb to stand on the flat outcropping just as a wave slams against the rock not ten feet from Corvi. She scrambles to her feet and leaps back to avoid the foamy pool washing over the cliff's edge. Distracted, she doesn't notice me as I carefully tread across the wet surface.

"Corvi! Thank goodness you're alright!"

She spins around. "Ruby!"

"I saw the postcard," I explain.

She nods. "I'm glad you came."

Stopping a few feet in front of her, I ask, "Where's Ike?"

A gust of wind slams into her petite form, and she pulls her long coat tightly around her frame. Puzzled, she gazes behind me for a moment then looks into my eyes with confusion.

"Ike? Why would he be here?"

"But I thought—"

"Wait. Did you think Ike left the postcard? I already told you. Ike would never hurt me."

My mind spins, struggling to make sense of the situation. "If not Ike, then who?"

She shoves her hands into the pockets of her coat. "When I saw the open panel behind the sofa, I assumed you knew."

Flummoxed by her comment, I remark, "Well, I found Lena's journal and your letters. I know you were married, and Lena was trying to sell the story to the press. All those tales about your brother—they were really about your husband."

Between the pages of Lena's journal, I found a telegram from a journalist working for *Variety*, the leading rag for the entertainment industry. He insisted that she provide him with "physical proof" because he didn't want to "poke the Stardust hornet's nest without protection"—hence, the bundle of letters that Corvi wrote to her husband after his death. They'd make front page news if leaked to the press.

The letters in and of themselves didn't surprise me. It's not uncommon for a widow or widower to continue communicating with their deceased spouse in one way or another. I've heard my uncle make comments to Aunt Beatrice when he thinks no one is listening. However, Corvi's missives revealed a disconnect from reality, an unyielding belief that Roland is still alive and will come back to her. The final letter, written while she was on the *Statendam*, described standing above his grave and knowing, with certainty, that the casket was empty, that he was lost somewhere in the world and would one day return.

"Yes, I am married," she readily admits. "It's a tough business. Once you're past a certain age, you might as well throw in the towel. She was trying to ruin me."

"So, you knew Lena was trying to sell your secret?"

"Of course. I overheard her talking to that reporter on the phone. I told Ike all about it," Corvi replies evenly. "At the time, I didn't know where she got her information, but when I discovered that my letters were missing the other day, I considered that she may have taken them. Then I saw the open panel today and figured you'd found them. Thank you, by the way."

"I apologize for reading them, Corvi. I knew they were private, but I hoped they would shed light on whoever is sending you the threatening notes." I step forward and gently reach out, "You believe Roland is still alive."

"He IS alive," she snaps and steps backward toward the cliff's edge.

I take a different tack. "Corvi, who do you think wrote those notes?"

"Need you ask?"

"Corvi, listen to me. There is no stalker. Ike wrote the notes. He used those lines from 'Annabel Lee' to confuse you. Please believe me! He'll stop at nothing to keep you under his thumb."

"I can't do this anymore." She lowers her head, her torso shaking.

My stomach drops, and I place a hand on her shoulder. "Corvi, what do you mean by that?"

Slowly, Corvi raises her head to meet my concerned gaze, and I realize that her eyes are dry—and she's laughing. My hand flies from her shoulder, and I leap backwards. Her expression hardens. Several horizontal lines suddenly crease her forehead, while deep wrinkles emerge around her mouth and eyes.

"Ruby, Ruby," she answers with a deep, harsh tone and steps forward.

No longer the helpless ingénue, she's a shrewd and formidable woman years older than I thought. Dizzy with confusion, countless rationalizations twist and twirl through my mind.

"But…" I mutter feebly.

"I expected more from you," she cackles condescendingly. "The answer's been right in front of you the whole time, but here you are, going on and on about Ike."

In a flash, everything is clear, and I can't believe I didn't realize it sooner.

"You!"

"Bravo! You finally got there." Her mouth twists with mirth.

How did I not see it?

"You ARE a great actress!" I spout with bitter derision.

Corvi takes a bow.

"Tom was getting too close, so you wrote the notes to keep him away," I say vehemently.

"Ah, so the dick's name is Tom." She looks me up and down with a smirk. "I had to ward him off. How better, than to peg him as a stalker."

"But he didn't even suspect you. He was following Ike."

She shrugs. "Well, he wasn't the first."

"But why kill Lena? I'm sure you could have bribed her to keep quiet."

"Where's the fun in that?" Corvi's malevolent tone sends icy chills down my spine.

"Bebe knows your secret, yet you've left her alone," I point out. "She tells anyone who will listen that you're older than you look."

"That coked-up hag?" she snickers with derision. "Who'd believe her? She has too much dirty laundry of her own."

Irate, I point at her, my hand shaking. "You poisoned Elizabeth! Was she really such a threat to you? She didn't know about any of this."

Corvi steps forward, her toes against mine, and leans into my face.

"I heard what they said on the set. They all think she should replace me…ME!" Spittle flies from her ruby-stained lips as she shrieks, "I am the BRIGHTEST STAR!"

I swipe at my face, never taking my eyes off of hers. "She has something you'll never have!"

"So, she can sing...big deal. Songbirds are a dime a dozen," she chuckles dismissively.

"She's real, Corvi! That's why the crew adore her," I exclaim through clenched teeth. Our noses are a mere inch apart. "You're a fake and a flash in the pan. You'll only be remembered as a crook. Nothing more."

Her face flushes, and she raises a flat-palmed hand as though to strike, then drops her arm with a cackle. "We'll see about that."

I wrap my fingers around her left arm and squeeze. "Why did you lure me out here?"

She twists her arm, but I hold fast.

"Let go!" Her pupils are dilated with fury.

"Did you seriously think you could hurt me?" I tighten my hand. She's much smaller than me—I could wrestle her to the ground in an instant.

Corvi's face contorts, her eyes boring into mine. "Sweetheart, you have no idea."

In the blink of an eye, she pulls a small, snub-nosed pistol from her right pocket and points it directly at my head. I drop her wrist and step backward.

A familiar voice behind me demands, "Put down the weapon, young lady."

Swiveling my head, I spot Inspector Maggard and Officer Jankowski approaching and am surprised that Corvi didn't notice them sooner. Now, her eyes dart rapidly between the officers and me—her left thumb and index finger fidgeting nervously.

She wasn't expecting company.

"Corvi, drop it!" I implore. "This will only make things wor—"

"You were supposed to come alone!" she hisses.

"Drop it, or I'll shoot!" the inspector orders.

Corvi looks past me and commands, "Not one step further!"

Nevertheless, the officers continue their approach. Unfortunately, I'm standing directly between Corvi and Inspector Maggard's raised pistol. When they're about five yards away, Corvi shifts her gun from my face and points it over my shoulder.

"Stay back!" she screams.

This gives me the opportunity I need to knock her off balance. I dive at her knees, but she kicks forward before I can tackle her. My body jolts as we both smash onto the rocky surface. With a downward thrust of my forearm, I use my weight to pin her wrist and, after carefully removing the firearm from her hand, push against her to stand back up. However, I'm unprepared when she drives her knuckles into my stomach. Doubling over, I drop the weapon.

Corvi snatches the gun and starts to rise. "I don't think so!"

With a savage yell, I unfold my bent torso and thwack my fist against her chin. Her head rocks backward, and a crimson spray splatters the rock. Nevertheless, she maintains her grip on the pistol.

In the mere seconds that Corvi is distracted, I look around and realize that we are standing at the edge of the precipice. Further, Inspector Maggard's firearm is still pointed in our direction. I try to back away, but Corvi reaches forward with her free hand and latches onto my blouse.

"And so, the curtains fall!" she spews theatrically.

CRACK!

A pistol's blast deafens me, as Corvi sends us both careening off the cliff.

My lungs burn when my head surfaces above the water. Reflexively, I inhale through both my mouth and nose, the air stinging as it flows down my throat. The salty taste triggers a fit of convulsive coughs, while my legs and arms bend and circle frantically to tread water. I blink several times to clear my eyes and get my bearings. I must be nearly fifty yards away from Table Rock.

When we hit the water, Corvi clung to me with both arms. I expected to begin surfacing after the initial drop but quickly realized that a powerful current was dragging us along the seabed. In response, Corvi clamped her legs around my waist and held fast, which I assumed was a desperate attempt to avoid drowning. However, through the turbulent water I caught a glimpse of her face—and she was smiling.

I wrestled to free myself, yet no amount of twisting or squirming loosened her hold on me. Gripping her skull, I pressed my thumbs against her eyelids and jerked her head to one side, but she only squeezed my waist more tightly with her thighs. As the tide drew us out to sea, we spiraled like a stunt plane in a barrel roll, and at that moment, I realized with horror that I was not only fighting Corvi but also wrestling with my body's impulse to inhale. I dug my fingernails into her throat, prompting her to release one hand and grab a fistful of my hair.

Pressure that had been steadily building in my ears and throat became unbearable. My head felt as though it would implode at any moment, while peripheral darkness expanded to obscure my visual field. I let go of Corvi's throat and violently thrashed my arms and legs to carry us both to the surface. Nevertheless, the force of the current—coupled with her sodden weight—hindered any upward movement.

Visions of my loved ones filled my thoughts, unleashing a deep anguish within me. My eyes, already bathed in saltwater, swelled with tears. All those moments of uncertainty about my future were for naught. No plans to be made. No career change to consider. No budding romance. With poignant resignation and regret, three words surfaced in my mind:

This is it.

I succumbed to the growing blackness when, with great suddenness, Corvi and I collided with a huge underwater boulder. Let me rephrase that…CORVI collided with a huge underwater boulder. By some miracle, I was above her and—while feeling the impact—was not injured by the collision. In fact, the strike compelled Corvi to release me, at which point I kicked as hard as I could to reach the surface.

Now, still caught in the same current, I paddle my arms in a windmill motion and scissor kick with all my might to reach the shoreline. I've never been a strong swimmer, despite spending summers on a lake in upstate New York throughout my youth. Most of the time, my friends and I just floated around on inner tubes. Now, my movements are irregular and ineffective, and the cold doesn't help—my body shivers and my teeth chatter. At times, I feel I have no control over my limbs.

After a little while, I lift my head to check my progress. Table Rock appears farther away…and empty. Hopefully, that means Inspector Maggard and Officer Jankowski have called for help. On the other hand, maybe they assumed that both Corvi and I drowned when they didn't see us resurface.

The beaches around Table Rock also appear to be empty. In fact, I have yet to spot a boat anywhere, which is shocking considering that it's Saturday and Labor Day weekend. Where are all the weekend mariners? For that matter, where's Corvi? She must have drowned, unless her inability to swim was also a lie.

Despite my best effort, I drift farther from shore. Worry gnaws at my mind, but I continue paddling furiously until my arms and legs weaken, my strokes becoming increasingly feeble. To top it off, I'm out of breath, my lungs still recovering from my underwater struggle.. Were it not for the breath work I do as part of my mediation practice, I most certainly would have drowned.

I stop paddling to—once again—orient myself to the shoreline and discover that I'm twice as far away from Table Rock as when I last checked. Further, the water's frigid temperature is more noticeable when I'm stationary.

I must press on.

However, as I resume paddling, my right foot suddenly arches with an intense cramp, and my toes point at an improbable angle. I stop swimming to clasp my leg and release a scream, but my mouth fills with saltwater, unleashing waves of choking gags that ripple with each spasm of my diaphragm, sending me underwater again and again.

Incapable of logical thought, my mind reels with terror, and I flail desperately. My entire being is completely out of control. After successfully fighting Corvi and the tide for my life, death looms yet again.

Is this my fate? Cycling through hope and despair until oblivion consumes me?

For a brief instance, certain that I'm going to drown no matter what, I consider letting go and sinking to the ocean floor. By giving up, I can end this on my own terms. However, the compulsion fades as quickly as it surfaces. One thing I've learned over the years is that when I'm overcome with fear, the best thing to do is control what I can.

So, as challenging as it is to do, I focus my awareness on what my body is doing and allow the sensation of pain to direct my attention. My immediate danger is aspirating water, so I observe the contractions of my diaphragm to avoid breathing at the wrong moment. Between each gag, I raise my head above the water and inhale deeply. Not only does this intentional breathing slow the retching, it also releases the tension in my body. Once my breathing is under control, I turn my attention to the foot.

For some reason, my right foot tends to cramp when I least expect it, both at night and during the day. Prior experience has taught me that the cramp will usually last no longer than several minutes as long as I focus on relaxing my mind and body. I gently rotate my arms and left leg to stay afloat while slowly flexing my right foot over and over again. Before too long, my foot relaxes and, although sore, I can slowly kick it to tread water as long as I keep the foot flexed. For the moment, I need to conserve energy and stay afloat.

I have no idea how long I've been in the water, so I check my watch, only to discover that the crystal is cracked, the case filled with water.

Figures.

Who knows how long I'll be out here. One thing I do know…time moves differently when you're in the middle of a crisis.

Bobbing up and down, I remember the psychics' warnings about "forces beneath the surface." I've never put stock in fortune-telling or séances, but I now have to wonder. The current is, quite literally, a force beneath the surface, as was Corvi when she was trying to drown me. But the expression also applies, metaphorically, to the actress once known as Annabel Lowe. There was so much beneath the surface that she kept hidden, far more than her perennial youth—which brings to mind my discussions with Miss Mabel and Elizabeth about *The Picture of Dorian Gray.*

"All art is at once surface and symbol. Those who go beneath the surface do so at their peril," I recite Oscar Wilde's words.

I consider myself to be an excellent judge of character and would berate my inability to see through Corvi's facade—but what an actress! The intensity and believability of her emotional responses and fragility over the past week are astounding when, all the while, she was methodically eliminating those she viewed as a threat.

About twenty yards to my left, a brown pelican dives headfirst, its maw open and wings tucked as it hits the water. When it resurfaces, a fish writhes within the fleshy sack below its beak. The prehistoric bird floats for a few seconds then pounds its webbed feet on the water while energetically beating its mighty wings to lift off. Two other pelicans dive several yards from the first but remain floating on the water with their meals.

Until this moment, I hadn't considered the countless sea creatures going about their business below my kicking feet. During my morning walks, I've seen dolphins leaping and splashing, but as charming as they appear from the shore, I quail at the thought of such large, intelligent creatures suddenly surfacing beside me.

Then there are the sharks…Despite Duke's assurance about leopard sharks the other day, I assume that there are great whites out here as well. I shudder and recall the series of attacks along the Jersey Shore during the summer I was fourteen. Over a twelve-day period, four people were killed, including an eleven-year-old boy near Keyport Harbor and the young man who swam out to recover the boy's body.

With a shiver, I remember the leg wound I suffered while climbing Table Rock. The scrape stings as I paddle my legs, and I wonder if it's still bleeding. Didn't someone tell me that a shark can detect blood in the water from miles away?

Think of something else, Ruby.

Without hesitation, my thoughts drift to Sam, and my breath catches. This is precisely the type of "onerous circumstance" he's always referring to. Adrift out here with no help in sight, I'm reminded of being seriously injured and lost among burning orange trees. Sam was aghast when he learned about that perilous incident—and we barely knew each other then.

He'll want nothing to do with me after this.

I can't say that I blame him. I'm not so sure that I'd be able to tolerate the constant worry if I were in his shoes. Yet my heart aches at the thought of the relationship ending before it really began. Unlike Eddie, Sam really saw beneath the surface and admired what he found there. Given our chemistry and ease with one another, I never anticipated such an insurmountable obstacle—and definitely not so early in our relationship.

Perhaps it would be best to break it off regardless of what he decides.

The devastation I experienced when Eddie dumped me was excruciating, and my feelings for him paled in comparison to those I already have for Sam. That being said, I have no intention of giving up my life's purpose to appease him, despite the danger—which, at the moment, seems like a ridiculous statement to make. Any normal person would quit in a heartbeat after going through something like this, but I've never considered myself to be normal—nor would I want to be. So, if I must choose between Sam and my career, I choose my career, and it would be best to make that choice now, before he has an opportunity to break my heart.

Or is that fear talking?

I shake my head and let go of these musings. Right now, I need to focus on staying afloat—and alive. The shore continues to recede from view and, with the glare of the sun glinting off of the small pools in the sandstone, I can't tell if anyone has returned to Table Rock. I'm not even sure that someone onshore would spot me at this distance. I look northwest toward Main Beach and realize that a white boat with four people is rowing away from me. They appear to be men, all wearing red-tank style shirts—perhaps swimsuits.

The lifeguard dory!

They must have been heading my way but turned around. Now, they're too far away to hear my shouts, and no one is looking in my direction. My heart sinks. Have they given up? Here I am, mooning about Sam, and I completely missed an opportunity to be rescued. They probably concluded that I drowned and are heading back to file a report.

But surely the search isn't over.

When Uncle Charles finds out, he'll call in the entire Coast Guard if he has to, and Archie won't stop looking either. Once he tells Pancho, she and her aviator friends should be able to spot me from the air. I only hope I can bob along until someone sees me.

Thankfully, the swells aren't too choppy; otherwise, I'd have trouble keeping my head above water. I notice that I'm starting to drift parallel to the shore instead of further away from it.

Maybe I'm out of the riptide.

Be that as it may, I no longer have the strength to attempt swimming to shore again. The top of my head burns from the beating sun, so I lean back and wet my hair in the chilly water. This instantly provides some relief. In the distance, Catalina Island is a dark gray streak on the horizon, barely discernible. Closer, yet still far away, a couple of sailboats are visible, but I have no way of signaling them. My heart races, but as hysteria threatens seize control, yet again, I take a deep breath.

Help must be on the way.

Fear gives way to anger, and I'm vexed to find myself in this treacherous plight. One thing's for certain…I must learn from my mistakes to avoid such situations in the future. So, what were my mistakes with this case? Well, that's simple—I didn't even consider Corvi as a suspect. And if there's one thing I should have learned from Agatha Christie's novels, it's that the guilty party is often the one who seems the most harmless.

This brings to mind the play I saw in England—*Black Coffee*. The murderer turned out to be the victim's polite young secretary—a most unassuming character. I stop paddling, struck by the memory that the young man poisoned his employer's coffee…with hyoscine. Moreover, strychnine has been mentioned in a few of Mrs. Christie's stories over the years, starting with her first novel, *The Mysterious Affair at Styles*.

"Not much of a reader, my foot!"

After a while, I find it difficult to tread water. My shoulders burn, and my thighs ache. Moreover, I feel as though the harsh sun and numbing water are further depleting my energy. While I refuse to give up mentally, it's clear that my body has other plans, so I stretch out onto my back and simply float—a task made far easier by my buoyant chest and legs. This is less taxing than paddling in place, and I'm easier to spot from the air. Closing my eyes against the harsh sunlight, I watch shapes and lines meander across the brick red background of my eyelids. The steady up and down of the ocean lulls me into a state of calm reflection. Every so often, I raise my head to survey the sea for boats which, thus far, have been nothing more than tiny specks in the distance.

Splash!

With a lurch, my eyes fly open and I drop my legs beneath the water. Not three feet away, a dark fin breaks the surface and disappears before I can get a good look. My heart races as I scan my surroundings for anyone who can help. I resist the urge to panic and maintain a slow, even motion with my arms and legs. There's no way I can outswim whatever has joined me. All I can do is remain calm, so I don't look like prey. Which is fine and dandy, until the beast nudges me on my lower back.

Splish! Plop!

My arms and legs flap and kick in a frenzied uncoordinated fashion, while my mind flashes with image after image of razor-sharp teeth and mangled flesh. To top it off, I'm unable to keep my head above the water.

Then, something brushes against my hand, but it doesn't have the rough, sandpapery texture I would have expected. Instead, it feels slick and spongy, like wet velvet. I slow my frenetic motion, enabling my body to float and my lungs to fill with air. Directly ahead of me, an adorable face pops up out of the water. Its upturned nose, wide-set chocolate brown eyes, and white whiskers remind me of a boxer puppy. Even its curious, playful expression is doglike. However, this grayish brown beauty has tiny flat flaps covering the opening of its ears—and a crescent shaped scar on its forehead.

"Skipper!" I exclaim joyfully.

She raises one flipper and slaps the water, splattering me in the process. Delighted, I splash her back. Skipper dives beneath the surface.

"Hey! Don't go!"

Several yards away, she leaps out of the water, her fins pressed against her arched body, then descends nose-first into the sea. She repeats this process several times before bobbing up beside me.

"Nicely done!" I compliment. "I don't suppose you'd mind keeping me company for a while. What do you think?"

I stretch out onto my back, and she extends her body to float alongside me. Before long, I start to feel drowsy, but each time I drift off, Skipper splashes about or leaps out of the water to catch my attention. Fully awake, I then search the area for boats and, finding none, stretch back onto my back. This cycle repeats over and over as the sun begins its descent in the western sky.

After what feels like hours, fear rears its ugly head yet again, and I wonder if anyone will ever find me. The sailboats have all disappeared, and I haven't seen or heard an airplane. I contemplate whether Skipper could tow me ashore, but she's a wild animal and may bite if I grab hold of her. Not only that, I have no way of knowing what direction she'd take me. For all I know, she could carry me further out to sea.

As if reading my thoughts, Skipper suddenly dives beneath me and bumps my back with her snout. I twist around to face her and spot a familiar green two-masted schooner between us and the shoreline.

"The *Bonnie Boat*! Skipper, you're brilliant!"

Unfortunately, Sal and her crew are moving at a fair clip and don't appear to be slowing down. With hard kicks, I lift my body above the surface of the water, waving my outstretched arms to get their attention, but to my alarm, they don't appear to see me.

"If only I had a flag!" I tell Skipper, then realize that my blouse is cherry red.

After slipping off the sleeveless garment, I grip it in one hand and wave it back and forth over my head. Skipper dives underwater and disappears for several long moments. She then propels herself out of the water about ten yards from the ship. One of the crewmen notices her and, spotting me in the water, begins waving and shouting something I'm unable to hear.

"Thank the stars you wore red!" Sal declares.

As soon as her ship was close enough, she jumped into the water with a life jacket in tow. Now behind me, she helps me climb the rope ladder.

"I didn't know how else to get your attention," I explain, gripping the wooden bars with slippery fingers, which is tricky to manage given my weakened state.

When I reach the top rung of the ladder, several pairs of arms grab hold of me and lift me onto the deck. One crewman wraps a blanket around my bare shoulders and hands me a cup of water.

"Little sips," the elderly man advises.

"Thank you!" I follow his counsel but yearn to chug it down in one go.

Sal squats down beside me on the bench and pats my knee. "I told ya I'd take ya out for a sail, but this isn't what I had in mind."

"Yeah, me neither," I chuckle wryly. "How'd you know I was out here?"

"The harbormaster got a call from the lifeguard station—good timing too. We'd been out all day chasing the tuna run with some fishermen and had just docked."

"I don't know how long I was out there."

"Two hours, I reckon. I was startin' to think we wouldn't find ya. The lifeguard launched their dory as soon as they got the call from the police. We passed 'em on the way, but it looks like they were too far north."

Two hours!

I'm astounded. I didn't think I had it in me to tread water for that long.

"I see that Skipper kept ya company." She rises to her feet. "Speakin' of which...I owe that gal some fish."

CHAPTER 25

"I thought you were a goner!"

I try not to flinch as Jack flings his arms around me, my skin already tender from the sun's scorching rays.

"You and me both!" I blink away a tear.

Jack steps aside for his father who's hovering behind him.

"Thank God you're alright!" Uncle Charles exhales, holding me gingerly.

Safe in his arms, tears spill from my eyes. My body quakes so forcefully, I find it difficult to draw a breath. Ordinarily, I'd feel deeply embarrassed to cry so openly in front of others, but at this moment I could care less about the ship's crew, marina staff, and ambulance attendants watching me on the deck of the *Bonnie Boat*. With each sob, I release the terror, helplessness, and doubt that plagued me over the past few hours. Fury rises as well, but this is not the moment to tackle my feelings for Corvi and the trail of wreckage she's left in her wake. Over time, my tears begin to slow, and I find it easier to breathe.

As my distress lessens, Uncle Charles releases me and gazes into my eyes, his eyebrows raised with the unspoken question, "Are you okay?"

I nod and accept his proffered handkerchief.

"Can you walk, ma'am?" The piercing blue eyes of an ambulance attendant examine my slumped posture. "If not, we can carry you on a stretcher."

I scan the docks where dozens of bystanders, including a pair of reporters with cameras, watch with nosey fascination. When I read the newspapers tomorrow morning, I'd prefer not to see a photograph of myself sprawled out on a stretcher.

"I'd prefer to walk…" I reply timorously.

"Are you sure, Ruby?" Uncle Charles frowns with concern. "You're not even wearing shoes."

I gaze down at my bare feet. "Huh. I forgot about that."

"Try these." Sal drops a pair of woven leather sandals on my lap. "They're probably too big for ya, but they should do the job."

"Oh, I couldn't take your shoes," I protest.

"Why not? They're older than dirt. Besides, I'm not even sure that they're mine," she snorts.

I slide my feet into the weathered sandals—which actually fit quite well—and tighten the blanket around my body, all too aware that I'm shirtless.

Nodding to Uncle Charles, I declare, "I'd like to give this a try."

"Alrighty then." He wraps an arm around my back while the ambulance attendant takes the other side.

"On the count of three," the young man says. "One-two—"

"Three," I finish, slowly rising to my feet.

Lightheaded, I take a moment to find my balance—the rocking motion of the ship doesn't help. To my relief, a police officer clears the gangway and escorts us to the back of a waiting ambulance, where an older attendant seats me on the side of a gurney and asks me a few questions.

Jotting notes on a form, he summarizes my condition. "Exposure, mild hypothermia, dehydration, and exhaustion, but you're clearly oriented and alert. Still, it would be a good idea to visit St. Joseph for a full examination."

The thought of hours spent in an emergency room fills me with panic. I slowly stand and tell Uncle Charles, "I'd rather go back to the house."

The attendant and police officer open their mouths in protest, but Uncle Charles assures them, "Trust me. I'll keep a watchful eye on her and will immediately take her to a doctor if anything changes."

With my uncle's help, I walk around to the front of the ambulance where Jack is waiting, along with Archie and Sal.

"Sal!" I exclaim. "How do I even begin to thank you? Were it not for you—"

"Nah!" She waves a hand. "There's no need for that! Besides, Skipper's the one who saved ya."

"That she did!"

During our trip to the marina, Skipper swam alongside the ship and gobbled three bucketfuls of fish that Sal and her crew tossed into the sea along the way. When we reached Newport Harbor, she disappeared—presumably heading back out to sea. I hope to see those chocolate brown eyes again before leaving Laguna Beach.

"We're forever in your debt," Uncle Charles adds. "If you ever need anything—"

"Yer too kind," Sal replies with an awkward grin. "I best be gettin' back to the ship."

Sal starts to pat my inflamed shoulder but registers my alarmed expression.

"So long, Sal," I take her hand and give it a squeeze. "I promise to stay in touch."

"Ya better! I still owe ya a proper ride on the *Bonnie Boat*. Gettin' rescued don't count," she laughs. "And put some aloe vera sap on that sunburn. You'll thank me later," she calls over her shoulder and strides back to her schooner.

"Ruby, I can't begin to tell you how sorry I am to get you into this mess." Archie's voice cracks, his eyes misty.

"How could you have possibly known?" I take his hands in mine. "But how did you find out what happened?"

"We'll tell you the whole story when we get you to the car," Uncle Charles suggests. "You need to sit."

A few hours later, cosseted on Edith and Norma's bed with a plate of spaghetti, warm crusty bread, and a glass of iced tea, I reflect upon the tale Uncle Charles and Archie shared with me.

Evidently, Tom got my message and arrived at Table Rock just as Corvi fired the gun and pulled me over the cliff. Detective Maggard collapsed while Officer Jankowski rushed toward the edge of the rock to look over, not realizing that his fellow officer was injured. Tom raced to the detective but immediately knew that he was dead, given the amount of blood pooling on the rock, his vacant stare, and the round entry wound above his left eyebrow. Officer Jankowski—still peering into the dark water below Table Rock—called back to Maggard, saying that neither Miss Styles nor Miss Ray were anywhere to be seen. When there was no reply, he turned and noticed the detective, supine on the gravelly surface. Jankowski darted back and instructed Tom to call police headquarters from one of the clifftop homes.

After that, Tom returned to Table Rock and searched the water for any sign of Corvi and I, to no avail. The police chief, along with a sizable squad, arrived not long after receiving Tom's call. Tom gave his testimony, then returned to the nearby house and called the number on the back of the business card I'd given him.

"The timing was perfect," Uncle Charles told me. "Dottie was away with Iris, and we only stopped by the house because Jack left his harmonica on the kitchen counter."

"You must have been frantic!" I exclaimed. "What did you do?"

"I called the police station, but the cadet answering the phone couldn't tell me anything specific. So, Jack and I drove over to the lifeguard station."

"That was my idea," Jack piped in.

"When we got there, Archie introduced me to Tom. They'd just arrived themselves," he added. "Tom told us everything he knew and then left."

"He went looking for Ike," Archie apprised me with a knowing expression.

"How did you find out about all this, Archie?" I asked. "I thought you were filming this afternoon."

"Tom found me on set behind the Hotel Laguna with Kit and Bebe." Archie grimaced. "I'm in utter shock! Corvi—CORVI—why didn't we realize it sooner?"

"Trust me, I've been asking myself the same question for hours." I shook my head bitterly. "There's so much to tell you, but I'm just not feeling up to it right now."

"Of course!" His eyes were round with apprehension. "You should get some rest. We'll talk later."

During our ride to the house, Jack described their torturous wait at the lifeguard station. While the lifeguard dory searched for Corvi and I, calls were made to the Coast Guard and the local harbormasters. However, coordinating a rescue effort took time, which was why I didn't see any boats along the shore. Meanwhile, Archie called around town to track down Pancho, hoping she and some of the other pilots could search from the air. He had just reached the aviator, when Sal flagged down the lifeguard dory with me onboard.

Jack added hesitantly, "They never found that Corvi lady. Did she really try to kill you?"

I nodded solemnly.

He gulped. "Golly."

I asked Uncle Charles, "Does the lifeguard believe she drowned?"

"That's what they're saying."

"What do you think, Ruby?" Jack inquired.

"At this point, I don't know what to think." I closed my eyes for the remainder of the trip.

Uncle Charles found an Italian restaurant in the village and picked up dinner, leaving me to bathe. Meanwhile, Jack went door-to-door asking the neighbors if they had aloe vera in their gardens. Most had never heard of the plant, but after a half an hour, he secured a sizable length of the succulent from a man he described as "an old guy who smelled like liniment." After bathing, I rubbed the gelatinous sap all over my face, neck, arms, and legs, its slimy coolness providing some relief for the blisters that had already begun to surface.

"Knock, knock," Dottie calls while pushing open the door with her elbow, her hands holding two small bowls of ice cream. "It's chocolate. I hope that's okay."

I set my plate, now empty, on the nightstand. "That's more than okay!"

We devour the tasty treat in companionable silence—Dottie sitting cross-legged next to me, careful not to lean against my tender shoulder.

She arrived home in time for dinner and was staggered by the news, which hadn't reached Three Arch Bay, where she and Iris were enjoying a game of volleyball with Edwin and his friends at the time.

After a while, Dottie stacks her empty dish next to the plate and reclines on one side, propped on her elbow so she can look at me. I carefully lie back, the cotton sheet feeling abrasive against my skin.

"Why are the heroes in books and movies always men?" She pouts her rose-colored lips.

"I beg your pardon?" Her unexpected question catches me off guard.

"It's always the prince, knight, handsome stranger—you know what I mean—that saves the day."

"I don't know about 'always.' Surely there are exceptions." I yawn, unable to think of any specific examples.

"They should make a movie about you," she says earnestly. "You're a hero…you're my hero."

My throat tightens with emotion. "What a sweet thing to say."

"It's true! You're brave and daring. You put yourself in harm's way to help others, and you rescue people, including yourself." Her violet eyes shine with admiration.

"It's my job, Dottie."

"Yeah, but you could have any job you want—you're smart and capable. But you picked one that requires courage and selflessness. Most people never do that."

"You're brave and selfless. Need I remind you how you kept Polly alive when you were trapped?"

"It wasn't just me. In fact, Leo and Earl did more, and you're the one who rescued all of us," she replies emphatically.

"I appreciate your compliment—I really do—but I happen to know that you're far more courageous than you think." I pat her arm.

"If that's true…" She sits up and declares decisively, "I need to tell you about my nightmares."

I push myself up to face her directly. "I'm all ears."

Dottie closes her eyes and takes three deep breaths, her eyes shifting beneath her eyelids as though she's visualizing the night terrors. "It's about that tower—the one Mr. Mains and the others jumped from."

I had a feeling it was something like that, but my heart clenches, nonetheless. About a week after Dottie and her friends were found, their teacher and the other cult members jumped to their deaths off of a water tower in Sunset Beach. Within hours, reporters discovered the identity of the students in Wallace Mains' "club" and snooped around our house for almost a week. At the time, Dottie and her friends seemed to take the news remarkably well, but ever since, I've wondered if the gruesome tragedy left a mark on her. How could it not?

When Dottie opens her eyes to gauge my reaction, I nod encouragingly for her to continue.

"In my dreams, Mr. Mains and the others force us to climb the tower and threaten to push us off if we don't jump. They tell us it's the only way to bring the Divine Quaternity into our realm." She scowls with disgust, her nose scrunched.

I take her hand. "Oh, Dottie. I'm so sorry! How horrifying."

"I've tried to banish it from my mind, but the harder I try, the more terrifying the dreams become."

"I understand. You must have felt so helpless and alone." I smooth her silky hair.

"That's exactly how I've felt. And when Dad and Jack started hearing me shout and cry at night, it made me scared that the others at the boarding house will hear me too." Her eyes widen with panic. "What if they find out I was mixed up in that crazy cult—it was in all the papers."

"Oh, Dottie," I wrap my arm around her and pull her into a hug.

She cries into my hair. "I didn't want to talk about it because I thought it would make things worse. But I just have to, or I'll burst."

"I'm glad you told me," I assure her.

She settles next to me, and we listen to the radio together, and in no time, I sink into a deep sleep.

SUNDAY, AUGUST 31, 1930

A disk of bright light sweeps across the hallway, just ahead of my bare feet, then swings up the wall, followed by a shadowy wraith. I nearly stumble, my thoughts foggy and confused.

Am I still asleep?

"Gee whiz, Ruby! Did we wake you?" Shining a flashlight under his chin, Jack's features are distorted and grotesque.

"No, but I almost tripped." Puck rubs his back and tail along my shin. "What time is it?"

"Beats me." He shrugs with a lopsided smirk. "Puck wouldn't let me sleep, so I invented a new game for him. He goes bananas chasing the light. Why are you up?"

"Bathroom." I shuffle forward in the dark. "I don't suppose you could light the way for me?"

"Sure thing, Ruby."

Once inside the restroom, I flip the light switch, only to catch a glimpse of my scarlet reflection in the mirror. Every muscle in my body aches, and my skin is tender. Two long chunks of aloe rest alongside the soap dish. Jack must have returned to the neighbor's yard for more. At this moment, however, I'm just too exhausted to deal with applying more goo to my sunburn.

When I return to the hallway, I find the office door closed, Jack and Puck having abandoned their game. My throat is parched, so I tiptoe toward the kitchen for a sip of water. Passing through the living room, I notice a dim light shining through the front windows—the waning moon, perhaps—and I realize that, apart from a crumpled throw blanket, the sofa is empty. I wonder where Uncle Charles has gone. That's when I detect the irresistible aroma of fresh-brewed coffee. I make a beeline for the kitchen and find the percolator sitting on the stove, and it's still hot. I fill a mug and trudge outside.

"I thought I might find you here." I cautiously sink into the Adirondack chair next to my uncle.

"Ruby!" He leaps to his feet and helps me get settled. "I wasn't expecting to see you for hours."

Were it not for the faint moonlight and a few stars, the sky would be pitch black. Nevertheless, house sparrows and mourning doves have begun their morning chorus, suggesting that the sun will soon rise.

"Nature called," I reply. "How about you? Did the feline shenanigans wake you?"

"To be honest, I didn't sleep a wink," he admits.

I nod and wrap my hands around the warm mug. "That doesn't surprise me."

We sit in silence for several moments. An orange glow brightens Uncle Charles' face each time he puffs his pipe. He must have replayed yesterday's events over and over in his mind all night long. My stomach twists. Despite his mask of calm strength yesterday after my rescue, I could not help but notice the anguish lying just beneath the surface.

"Uncle Charles, I cannot begin to express my remorse for putting you through—"

He lowers his pipe and straightens his back with astonishment. "Are you...apologizing?"

"I'm sure you're upset—"

"Ruby, you have absolutely nothing to apologize for." He takes my hand. "What happened to you..." His eyes narrow and nostrils flare. "That was not your fault, nor was it your choice! There's no way you could have known."

I close my eyes to fight back the tears. "But that's just it. I should have known. I should have figured it out sooner."

"How? You're not a mind reader. Archie told me everything while we were waiting. That monster fooled everyone. If you hadn't put all the pieces together, more would have died, Ruby."

My throat tightens, and I find it difficult to draw a deep breath. "Then why do I feel as though I've failed?" I lean forward and rest my face in my palms.

Uncle Charles delicately extends his arm across my shoulders, mindful of my blistered skin. "You're too hard on yourself, Ruby. According to Archie, the studio hired other detectives over the years. None were able to do what you've done."

I sit back forcefully and wince as my back slams against his arm. "He told you about that? I swore him to secrecy."

"He didn't go into any detail. Nevertheless, he made me promise not to say anything." He pats my hand reassuringly. "I think the young man felt out of his depth and really needed to confide in someone. We were all so worried about you."

"After everything you went through when Dottie disappeared—I'm so sorry to put you through it again."

"Sweetheart, what I endured was nothing compared to what you suffered out there." He assures me, "You handled the situation as best you could. You made sure the police were notified, as well as Tom."

"I suppose."

"And YOU solved the case—not those other detectives who've had far more training and experience than you."

"I thought you were going to berate me for going to Table Rock alone," I confess.

He's taken aback. "When have I ever berated you?"

"Alright, perhaps 'berate' is too harsh. How about 'admonish?'"

"I wasn't going to admonish you either. But you have to admit, you were in over your head—no pun intended."

I cringe. "Go on."

"This situation—along with Dottie's disappearance—were unlike any cases you've ever taken."

"That's true."

"When we last spoke—right here in fact—you mentioned expanding your business and working as a 'genuine' private investigator. This may be too soon to ask, but have you changed your mind about that?"

"Should I?" With everything that's happened since then, I haven't had time to think about it.

"That's up to you. But I'd like to make a suggestion."

I take a sip of coffee. "I'm listening."

"Self-defense training would be a good start."

"You're absolutely right!" With training, I could have pinned Corvi in a heartbeat and avoided my struggle at sea, not to mention Maggard's death.

"You know, I recently read about jiu-jitsu training in Fullerton. I'll find the article for you when we get home."

"Perfect." I yawn.

"Why don't you go back to bed. You need more rest."

"Good idea."

Uncle Charles stands and takes my hands to pull me up.

"Oh, before I go, I should tell you about my conversation last night with Dottie," I comment.

He gives me a gentle hug. "She came to me last night after you fell asleep and told me everything."

My body softens. "I'm so glad."

"I know Edith and Norma are returning later today. The kids and I will take care of getting the house ready. I want you to get some rest."

"I won't argue with that." I kiss his cheek.

"Now, scoot…and sleep till noon."

"How does he look?" My hands feel like stiff paws as I struggle to tie the sash of my sundress.

"Devastated!" Dottie hands me a comb.

"Devastated because of my near drowning? Or devastated because he's come to end things once and for all? It could go either way." I ineffectively hack at my knotted curls.

Dottie removes the comb from my hand, sets it aside, and smooths pomade through my unruly locks. Unused to being pampered and filled with nervous energy, I fidget with the jar's lid.

"Sit still!" She forcefully turns my head forward and resumes her coifing. With a softer tone, she soothes, "There's no way Sam is here to end it. He's not that kind of guy."

"You're right," I sigh. While my mind feels less jittery, my body is a coiled spring. "I'm on pins and needles and need to do something useful."

"Can you manage lipstick?" She places a tube in my palm.

I reach back with my other hand and give hers a squeeze. "I really appreciate this."

Thanks to Dottie, I'm presentable and calmer several minutes later when I greet Sam in the living room. Jack and Puck have presumably relocated to the office, while Dottie and Uncle Charles meander to the front yard.

"What happened to less onerous circumstances?" One corner of Sam's mouth quirks with uncertainty.

I smile politely. "I'm surprised to see you." Whether intentional or not, his greeting cuts right to the heart of the matter.

He flinches but recovers a split second later when, after taking three quick strides, he envelops me with his long, solid arms. Relief floods every cell in my body, and despite the pressure of his arms and chest against my burned skin, I return his embrace.

"I should have been there," he mutters, his lips pressed against the crown of my head.

I lean back to examine his face and find an expression there that I hope never to see again. Forlorn eyebrows arc above doleful eyes, while his mouth and nose twitch uncontrollably. His countenance conveys sorrow and regret, and I cannot help but wonder if his contrition has to do with my misadventure or his own mishandling of our disagreement the other day—or perhaps both.

As though reading my thoughts, he gushes, "I should never have left things like that Thursday night! You've been on my mind every minute since. I started to call you countless times and walked past this house on several occasions to talk—"

"Why didn't you?" I interrupt.

Sam averts his gaze nervously. "I was afraid."

"Afraid of me?" I chuckle with disbelief.

His eyes meet mine. "Of course, I was afraid of you! Ruby, you have no idea how strong your hold is over me. If you were to meet my apology with fury—and you have every right to do so if that's how you feel—I'm not sure I'd be able to recover from that."

"So...are you apologizing?"

The hard line of his lips relaxes. "I'm trying to...maybe not very well...but that's the general idea."

"Well, I'll make it easy for you. I forgive you for abruptly ending a very important conversation—one that we still need to have, by the way. I forgive you for leaving me in a state of utter confusion and self-doubt for days on end. And I forgive you for cowardly staying away," I utter the last words with a playful smile. "Now promise me you'll never do that again."

"I promise." He gathers my hands in his and draws them to his mouth, his breath warm on my skin. "I know how tenuous life is. We can't take anything for granted. Which makes my feelings for you all the more precious...and terrifying."

My eyes widen. "Terrifying?"

"That didn't come out right."

I tilt my head. "Terrifying?"

"See what you do to me?" he laughs. "I'm usually a gregarious guy, but here I am stumbling over my words."

"Take your time. I'm not going anywhere," I encourage him.

"Ruby, the thought of losing you—that's what's terrifying," he replies, his head lowered but his eyes gazing into mine.

I pause to consider how best to respond. This is important, and I want to make sure we both say what we mean, so there are no misunderstandings. Less than twenty-four hours ago, while drifting farther and farther from the shore, I wrestled with my feelings for Sam and resolved that—given the choice between my career and a relationship with him—I would choose my career.

"Sam, I understand your fear. Like you, I've suffered losses in my life and know just how precious and unpredictable life is."

He nods hopefully.

"But I cannot deny my purpose in life—to do whatever I can to prevent catastrophe from befalling others. I admit, at times it feels as though some power is working against me. Yesterday was a very good example. But I feel an even stronger protective force guiding my intuition and keeping me safe. I don't know how else to explain it, and if I have to choose between my work and—"

His face brightens with understanding. "But I'm not asking you to choose—is that what you thought?"

"Well," I reply uncertainly. "Yeah, that's exactly what I thought."

"No! When I said I needed time to figure things out, I didn't mean you and I—this relationship. What I meant to say was that I needed time to work through my own anxiety about your work. I felt it was important to do that now, early in our relationship—not at some future date after numerous spats because I couldn't handle my fear. I wouldn't want that to tear us apart."

"So, you're not opposed to my work?"

"Quite the contrary. I'm proud as hell—pardon my French." He pulls me closer, his hands at my waist.

"And you think you can handle the risks?" I smile broadly.

"Ruby Ray, I can't imagine my life without you—risks and all."

"Oh, Sam! I feel exactly the same way!"

Our kiss is both gentle and demanding, a balm for the tender heartaches we've endured for days.

"What I don't understand is why he didn't come to see you sooner—like last night?" Dottie sits at the foot of the bed watching me pack my suitcase.

"He was tied up at the morgue last night. As soon as he heard about Corvi's death on the radio this morning, he ran out for a newspaper and saw a photo of me on the deck of Sal's ship. Then he rushed right over."

Uncle Charles raps on the door. "Everyone decent?"

"Yeah, Dad!" Dottie calls. "Come on in."

"Here's the burn cream Sam prescribed." He tosses a small paper bag on the bed.

"Thanks for running over to Rankin's." I unscrew the top of the metal tube and sniff the ointment. "I'll put some on after I finish up here."

"Are you sure you want to stay for the airshow tomorrow? We could all head home after Norma and Edith return," he suggests.

"We're not staying for the airshow?" Alarmed, Jack bounds into the room with Puck on his shoulder.

"Don't worry, Jack! I wouldn't miss it for the world," I reassure him.

My uncle nods. "Alright. I've arranged a room for you and Dottie over at the Coast Inn. Jack and I will head over there now to get out of your way. Dottie, do you want to come along?"

"I'm going over to the Marine Lab to see Iris. Would you mind taking my bags?" she asks.

"Lead the way," he waves her through the door and down the hall.

"I don't wanna say goodbye to Puck." Jack plops on the bed and buries his face in the kitten's fur.

"I'm sure you can come and visit." I snap the clasp on my case.

"Well…just in case." He leans forward and places an unevenly folded page on the bedspread. "I made a list of the tricks I taught him along with the new games he likes to play."

"I'll be sure to pass that on." I scratch between the kitten's ears. "I have to admit—he's kind of grown on me."

"Then you'll help me talk Dad into getting a kitten?" Jack pleads hopefully.

I tap Puck's spongy nose. "I wouldn't go that far…"

About an hour later, Norma and Edith return home to a mewling welcome from the little beast.

"There's my angel!" Norma croons to Puck. "Did you miss Mama?"

Puck emits a joyful *meow* and scurries toward Norma, who is squatting with her arms extended and fingers wiggling playfully. Little does she know that moments before they arrived, the rascal knocked over his terracotta pot of alfalfa. I'd barely returned the dustpan to the cupboard when they walked through the door.

Edith lumbers into the living room with a suitcase in each hand and unceremoniously drops them on the floor with a thud.

"I can't believe what you've been through!" she plants a maternal kiss on my forehead.

"How did you hear about it?"

"Front page news at every newsstand from Arizona to the train station in Santa Ana today! You're famous!" Norma leans in for a hug.

"They were all talking about it at the grocers. We picked up a few things on the way home," Edith adds.

"Oh my." My stomach drops as I consider the repercussions of all this.

"How can we ever thank you for taking care of our dear Puck?" Norma asks. "This was meant to be a respite for you."

"Things may not have turned out as we planned, but I'm glad Dottie and I could help out," I assure her.

"Any time you fancy a weekend at the beach, you've got a warm bed waiting for you here," Norma continues.

"Thank you." I retrieve Jack's detailed notes and hand them to Norma. "You'll find that Puck learned a great deal while you were away."

Edith reads over her shoulder. "He can sit on command? That'll come in handy."

Brrring…brrring…

"Not home five minutes," Edith mutters. "Laguna 830. Yes, she's still here." She puts a hand over the mouthpiece. "Ruby, it's for you."

I accept the receiver. "This is Ruby."

"We need to talk…"

CHAPTER 26

The cheap parasol I picked up on my way to the boardwalk casts a wide shadow; nevertheless, the late afternoon sun stings my arms. I adjust the sunshade as best I can. It will have to do for now, but I'll need something more substantial for the airshow tomorrow. Up ahead the vendor selling photograph postcards tidies the stacks on the bench. My eyes scan the collection until they land upon the photo of Table Rock. I hasten my steps.

Further on, I notice Duke standing on the platform of the lifeguard tower, a broad straw hat shading his face and a pair of binoculars slung around his neck. Closer to the shore, a group of industrious children dig a trench in the damp sand with their tiny metal shovels. Each time a foamy wave rolls in, water and loose sand fill the ditch, prompting them to excavate with renewed enthusiasm. I look beyond the tykes, just past the shorebreak, hoping for a glimpse of dark brown fins and a whiskered face amidst the bobbing swimmers, but that's wishful thinking. It's far too late in the day for the pup to venture this close to shore.

Ten or so yards further down the boardwalk, I spot the lopsided brim of the detective's Homburg before he notices my approach.

"Hi, Tom." I perch beside him on the riveted iron bench and shift the parasol to block the sun's glare.

"Ruby." He tilts his head, hazel eyes taking in my weathered appearance. "Some case."

"Some case."

"I wish I could give you more time to recuperate before having this conversation, but I have a lot to tell you, and the studio wants me back in LA immediately." He leans toward me and murmurs. "They don't know I'm speaking with you."

"Should we move?" I nonchalantly survey the passersby.

"I've been sitting here a while. I think we're alright." He leans back and crosses his ankles.

"Thank you for your help yesterday—showing up so quickly, calling the house, and finding Archie. It meant a great deal to my family and me."

"I should be thanking you for putting an end to all this." Tom pauses to light a cigarette. "You mind?"

"Not at all."

He takes a drag and grinds the match under his loafer. "I owe you an explanation about Miss Styles, Ike, all of it. But you didn't hear it from me."

"O-kay." I'm intrigued.

Tom gives me a hard stare, wrinkles deepening around his eyes. "You can't share this with anyone, including Archie. Consider this a professional courtesy."

"Duly noted," I reply.

"I visited Miss Style's suite at the hotel yesterday, as well as her house in Hamilton Park—figured I'd get a jump on the cops."

"Officer Jankowski said they'd sealed everything off."

He nods. "Yeah, the police pulled up as I was walking out. When did you speak with him?"

I check the watch I borrowed from Dottie since mine was filled with sea water. "A couple of hours ago. He stopped by to take my statement."

Officer Jankowski knocked on the front door a little while after Uncle Charles, Jack, and Dottie left the house. Given his involvement with the case, the police chief agreed that the aged officer was best suited for the interview. Jankowski was incredibly kind and told me how worried he'd been yesterday when I was missing. Sensing that he was still rattled by the death of his comrade, I expressed my condolences. Despite my dislike for Detective Maggard, I was dismayed to hear that he died.

"What did you tell him?" Tom asks.

"I didn't mention the studio coverup, if that's what you're worried about," I reply pointedly. "Other than that, I told him everything I knew about Corvi and the crimes she committed over the last week."

"Sorry about that. I shouldn't have doubted your word."

"Don't give it another thought," I reply dismissively and change the subject. "Did you find anything of interest in Corvi's suite?"

"When I arrived, it looked like someone had already sacked the place."

"The open panel behind the sofa?"

"Yeah, that, and the breeze blowing in through the bedroom windows had scattered things across the carpet."

"Did one of the security guards let you in?"

"No, I didn't see anyone." He adds, "I jimmied the lock."

"The panel was my doing." I describe Lena's journal, the book of poems, and the envelopes—all wrapped in the paisley scarf. "When I went back later, I found a letter Corvi's husband wrote to her from the front. It was tucked inside a book—one of Agatha Christie's. That's when we found the postcard and realized Corvi had climbed out the window and was headed for Table Rock."

"I saw the postcard on the bed." He nods. "The message you left for me said that Ike had lured Corvi to Table Rock."

My cheeks flush. "I still thought Ike was behind all of this. In hindsight, I should have realized..."

"She fooled us all. If you'd had time to dig a little deeper, you'd have found the incriminating evidence in her bedroom."

"What evidence?"

"Well, for starters, I found several postcards in a dresser drawer under Miss Style's undergarments, all showing various local vistas. But most damning, I discovered a paper bag from a stationery shop in Germany. It was shoved under the head of the bed."

"Let me guess...it contained a bottle of red ink."

"Yep. That and a glass pen. She must have picked them up on the cruise."

"Did you find anything in the bathroom? Maybe an envelope of white tablets?" She must have stashed the packet of hyoscine somewhere.

"No tablets, but I found ipecac syrup in the medicine cabinet."

"That explains her vomiting Friday morning," I reply. "Anything else?"

"A bottle of Goff's cough syrup. I thought it was strange, since ipecac can be used as a cough suppressant. Why have both?"

"I think the Goff's served another purpose." I recall the shell bracelet "bloodied" with the sticky syrup.

"To be honest, as soon as I realized that she'd written the notes, I left to search her house. Boy, was I in for a surprise."

"What happened?" I ask a bit too intensely. A pair of teenage girls look back over their shoulders after passing us.

"Ike was already there!" He blows out a plume of smoke.

"I wondered when he'd turn up. He vanished Friday afternoon and, to my knowledge, hasn't been seen since."

"He told me he was making arrangements for Miss Styles to enter treatment. He didn't want anyone to find out and spoke with several psychologists until he found one he could trust. In fact, as he was leaving the doctor's office, he heard about Miss Styles from the receptionist who was glued to the radio."

"I'm surprised he told you that."

"So was I." He tosses the cigarette butt into the sand a few feet away. "But that's not all. He spilled the beans about everything."

"Why didn't he just bolt?"

"I asked him that very question. He said he was leaving the country and would never be back, but he wanted me to know the truth before he left."

"That doesn't sound like him."

"I sensed a grudging respect. I think he enjoyed our little cat and mouse game."

"Hmm…or he wanted someone to hear his side of the story. Does the studio know he split?"

"That they do. After he left the psychologist, he went straight over to bargain with them. He knew the police would be looking for him and told the studio bosses that he was willing to keep mum about their coverups over the years if they'd fund his exit and send him off with enough money to keep him comfortable."

"Ugh! This whole thing disgusts me."

"That's how it works." Tom shrugs.

"Why did Ike stop by Corvi's house? I'm surprised he didn't make haste for a boat dock as soon as the studio paid him off."

"I think he was looting the place for things he could quickly and quietly pawn. Although, I doubt he got much for the stuffed raven," he chuckles.

"Stuffed raven?"

"Weird, huh? I figured the home of a Hollywood starlet would be light and feminine, but this place was eerie. The walls were covered in dark wood, and there were old-fashioned candlesticks everywhere. I half expected Dracula to swoop in at any moment."

"I can't say that I'm surprised." I shiver thinking about the Necropolis Railway.

Tom looks at his wristwatch. "Damn! Look, I don't have much time, and I have a lot to tell you."

According to Tom, Ike's story unfolded over a shared bottle of bootleg gin that Ike kept at the house. He reported meeting Corvi years ago through one of his clients, an actress who told him that her pal was in a "tight jam" with a thug she'd been dating and could use Ike's help. Her agent was hopeless, and she didn't want to get the police involved.

Used to that sort of thing, Ike reluctantly agreed to meet Corvi, but as he watched her perform on the set, he was pleasantly surprised by how the delicate yet talented young extra captured the hearts of the crew with a single wistful sigh. Realizing her potential to go all the way, he agreed to—not only serve as her agent— but to manage her career, as well.

"Through his 'connections,'" Tom gives me a knowing wink, "Ike made sure that the bully never bothered Miss Styles again."

"Sounds like he invested heavily in her career. Bebe told me that Ike paid for Corvi's beauty procedures when he took her on. Given her youthful appearance, he must have hired a top-notch surgeon."

"He knew a gold mine when he saw one, that's for sure."

"Did Ike mention her marriage?"

"She didn't say much to him, early on, about her history. But one day, Ike heard some of the girls gossiping about her dead husband. When he asked her about it, Miss Styles confessed that she had lost her husband during the war."

"'Lost' is an interesting choice of words. Corvi believed he was still alive and would return to her one day." I tell him about the content of her letters.

"Nah, Ike said he was definitely dead. He found the telegram from the War Office while helping her move into her house."

Interesting…despite the telegram and the grave in France, Corvi still believed that her husband was alive. "I wonder what was behind such delusional thinking."

"I think I have an explanation for that," Tom says uncomfortably. "Ike told me that Miss Styles' mother was also an actress. She had bit parts in vaudeville but found greater success using her theatrical skills as a grifter."

"You're kidding!"

"Not only that—Miss Styles' mother involved her in the scams as soon as she was born. *My baby Annabel is sick, and we have no money for medicine. My husband left us, and we have no place to stay…*that sort of thing. However, one con went completely south, and a man ended up dead. Her mother claimed it was self-defense, but little Annabel witnessed the whole thing. According to Ike, Annabel's mother convinced her that the lie was true so she wouldn't blab what really happened."

"That's terrible!"

In spite of my fury at Corvi, a part of me feels empathy for the little girl who was raised on lies. No wonder she was able to convince herself that Roland was still alive, despite solid evidence to the contrary.

"After a while, Annabel joined her mother on the vaudeville circuit as a child actress and dancer. Of course, she eventually grew up and grew wise to her mother's schemes. Then, in 1917 when she was eighteen, Annabel met her husband, a stagehand for the light opera company where Annabel and her mom worked. The young couple bonded over their shared passion for gothic horror—if you can believe it—and quietly eloped. For the first time in her life, Annabel was free from her mother. Ike said she referred to Roland as the knight who rescued her."

"How tragic to lose him just a year later!" The letters…Edgar Allen Poe's "Annabel Lee"….it all makes sense.

"Annabel tried to get by on her widow's pension but eventually resorted to the scams she'd learned from her mother. In fact, she was far more successful at grifting than her mother had ever been. There was no end to the line of rich, married men who waited for her backstage at the theater and a few years later outside the studio."

"Bebe mentioned that Corvi was living the high life off stage-door Johnnys—as she put it."

"Well, eventually she fleeced the wrong Johnny. Were it not for Ike, Miss Styles would have died years ago, just like her mother."

"What happened to her mother?"

"Strangled by one of her cons in 1920," he answers bluntly. "Still, Miss Styles learned from the best. However, Ike saw right through her. It didn't take him long to realize that Miss Styles could 'lie to a priest without breaking a sweat.' He made sure she knew he was on to her and threatened to ruin her career if she ever lied to him."

"Did he say anything about the roommate or the actress who was injured during the horse stunt?"

"He readily admitted to covering up for Corvi. 'Why beat around the bush? I'm sure you already know all about that,' he said to me." Tom lights another cigarette.

"Did Corvi tell him what really happened?"

"At the time, she claimed her roommate was having a seizure in the tub and that she grabbed her ankles to pull her out."

"That doesn't even make sense," I comment. "Surely, if someone is having a seizure in a tub, you'd try to prop up their torso to keep their head above water."

"Ike told her as much and threatened to turn her in, but—in the end—he didn't want to lose his cash cow. So, he concocted the story about the ankle cuffs and, to his relief, the studio corroborated it."

"What about the horse?" I ask

"He knew Corvi wanted the part and accused her of using a mirror to spook the horse. Of course, she insisted she had nothing to do with it. That's when he realized that she was out of control."

"Last Saturday I witnessed the two of them having an intense conversation, and he stormed off when I approached."

"He mentioned that conversation. Miss Styles told him she'd overheard Lena talking on the phone with a reporter. He was livid but also concerned that she'd do something rash."

"As in poison her?" I huff.

"He urged Lena to back off, but when she rejected his warning, he concluded that she could fend for herself. However, after she drowned, he knew Miss Styles had something to do with it."

"So, Ike didn't believe her about the 'stalker?'"

"No, when he spotted me last Saturday night, he recognized me from a club in LA where he plays cards. I'd been showing up there since we got back from Europe to keep an eye on him. So, when he saw me near the hotel, he realized that the studio had hired another dick to trail him and that Miss Styles mistakenly assumed I was stalking her."

"And the notes?"

"At first, Ike thought they were from an adoring fan. That sort of thing happened all the time. But after Lena's death, he asked Miss Styles pointblank if she was writing the notes."

"Did she admit it?"

"She told him that she knew I was a PI and that she had to keep me away."

"Did Ike set her straight about who you were following?"

"He tried, but she didn't believe him. Meanwhile, Ike was up to his ears struggling to keep her career afloat. Mr. Lake was pressuring Ike to change Miss Styles' contract since she couldn't actually sing or do her own stunts, and the studio threatened to drop her after they finish *Skin Deep*."

"His meeting with Archie and Mr. Lake on Thursday morning! But why did Ike sneak up the service stairs just before the meeting? Why was he using the service stairs at all? You said he did the same thing Sunday morning."

"Beats me. Maybe he didn't want to run into Lake without having Archie around as a buffer. That kid's pretty good at keeping Lake from blowing a gasket."

Maybe Ike helped Poppy with the trays so she wouldn't make a fuss about him using the service stairs. "Corvi must have poisoned Elizabeth's coffee just after Ike brought up the trays Thursday morning."

"That's exactly what happened. Ike panicked knowing that if he didn't quietly get her into treatment, the truth would come out—and he'd go down with her."

"What about Rex's accident?"

"She had nothing to do with that. For once, it was just a coincidence," Tom remarks

I think back to Corvi's mocking cackle and malicious grin on the cliff. "Where on earth did she get the gun? She certainly knew how to use it."

"Believe it or not, it was hers. Ike told me she bought it years ago after her mother was murdered. Apparently, she carried it with her everywhere."

"The fragile victim who couldn't protect herself," I laugh bitterly. "The tears…the frailty…the hysteria…not once did she break character."

"She duped us all," he reflects calmly. "That being said, it's Ike's opinion that—to some extent—she believed the lies she told. That's what made her so convincing."

"You know, for the past twenty-four hours I've struggled to keep my rage in check, telling myself I'll deal with it later. But now, all I feel is confusion. Why? Why did she do it?"

"I asked Ike that same question." Tom inhales through his cigarette.

"And?" I growl impatiently.

"Fame. What else?" Tom checks the time. "Oh, I should be leaving."

"Thank you for sharing all this with me. Ike's testimony answers so many questions."

"It's important that you don't repeat anything we discussed—not to the police, nor anyone else for that matter," he warns. "If the studio executives find out we spoke, they won't hesitate to aggressively end both our careers."

I gulp. "You have my word."

"Good." He grounds his cigarette underfoot. "Incidentally, they asked me what I thought about retaining your services for future cases."

I blink with surprise. "Whatever for?"

"Background checks…keeping tabs on misbehaving actors…investigating folks who are trying to extort the studio—that sort of thing. They'd pay handsomely. Two or three cases could keep your business afloat for a whole year. Not many people these days can count on a steady income," he points out. "I told them they should make you an offer."

I bark a hearty laugh. "You're kidding?"

He persists, "Ruby, you're really good. I've seen you in action now on two cases. You're a keen observer with a dependable gut instinct. You're analytical, and you don't rush to conclusions too soon."

Taken aback by his compliment, I choke, "Thank you."

"And you can wear a skirt." He adds with a smirk.

"Excuse me?" I'm not sure whether to be amused or offended.

"Trust me—you'll find the skirt helps with undercover work. No one would ever suspect that you're a private investigator."

"Private investigator…" I echo.

"That's another thing…what's with this 'inquiry agent' business? You need to change that business card of yours. You're a detective."

"Funny you should mention that."

After explaining my tentative plans to expand my practice, Tom offers to teach me the ins and outs of the "PI business" and connect me with sources for clients.

"Can you shoot?" he asks matter-of-factly.

Taken aback, I admit, "Until yesterday, I'd never touched a firearm."

"Well, that's gotta change—for your safety and the safety of your clients."

I promise to think about his offer and give him a call in the next few weeks. We say goodbye, and as I'm gathering my handbag, he disappears into the crowd of beachgoers.

"You're the last person I expected to see here today," Archie closes the door behind us.

I stroll into the living room of the hotel suite. "I have to say, I'm surprised to see you as well. I thought I'd have to sweet talk a police officer to let me inside. I left a few things here yesterday after my overnight stay."

"The police swept through here this morning," he explains. "The housekeeper just let me in to pack up Corvi's things. I guess the hotel needs the room for other guests."

I'm sorely tempted to tell Archie everything I just learned from Tom—for no other reason than to help me digest the information myself. However, I don't want to jeopardize my career...it's too dear to me. I tried mulling things over during my walk to the hotel, but my mind was preoccupied with Tom's offer to mentor me. On the one hand, I could learn a great deal from him and, potentially, avoid some of the pitfalls I may encounter if I go it alone. However, there's something shady about Tom, and I have serious doubts about his ethics. Further, I'm not looking to become someone's protégé. I'm a competent investigator who merely wishes to expand my practice.

Archie snaps his fingers. "Did you hear me, Ruby? I asked how you're feeling."

I shake my head to clear my muddled thoughts. "Sorry about that. I have a lot on my mind."

He lowers his eyebrows with concern. "Maybe you should sit down for a bit."

"That's not such a bad idea." The walk in the summer heat has left me lightheaded, so I drop onto the sofa—now returned to its usual position against the wall.

"How are you, Ruby? Really?" Archie takes a seat across from me in an armchair.

"Physically, I'm recovering. Sam prescribed something for the sunburn, which has helped. My muscles are sore, and I'm still exhausted, but on the whole, I'm feeling better than I expected."

"And mentally?" he probes.

"That's a work in progress," I confess.

He nods compassionately. "Can I get you anything? I could call for a pitcher of something cold."

"I'd like that. Thank you."

Archie rings the front desk from Corvi's bedroom. When he returns, he drops a stack of books on the couch next to me. "Do you have any use for these?"

My first instinct is to reject the collection of autographed Agatha Christie books—not wanting to keep anything that belonged to Corvi. But then I remember the ladies who attend my reading parlor. "Sure. Why not? I know several women who'd be thrilled to read them."

"Great! Keep them. Corvi didn't have any next of kin and—from what I understand—Ike's flown the coop."

"Really?" I feign surprise.

"Yep. Mr. Lake heard it from one of the studio executives."

Well, that didn't take long.

Archie ventures back into the bedroom then returns several minutes later with an armful of clothing which he unceremoniously plops beside a wooden trunk.

I ask, "What does all this mean for you?"

"Me?" He folds a flimsy dressing gown and tosses it into the trunk. "I'm sure you can guess."

"The show must go on?"

"Bingo." Archie flings a pair of feather-toed boudoir slippers on top of the gown.

"What about—" I'm interrupted by a knock at the door.

"I'll get that. You stay there," Archie instructs and opens the door.

"I have the lemonade you ordered," Poppy enters, mumbling dejectedly. "Do you want it on the table?"

"Yes, thank you, Poppy," Archie says kindly.

Her lank locks frame a desolate expression until she spots me. "Oh! Miss Ray!"

"How are you doing, Poppy?" I ask. "This must be very hard for you. I know how fond you were of Corvi."

Tears well in the teenager's eyes, and she sniffs. "Not as hard as it is for you—I heard what happened."

"I'll be alright, but right now, I'm concerned about you. Would you like to sit down?" I pat the sofa cushion next to me.

Poppy quickly shakes her head. "Oh, no, ma'am. I couldn't—I'm supposed to be working."

Archie comments. "It's a shame they didn't give you the day off."

"My mama wouldn't let me stay home. She said actors are just like the rest of us and that there's no need to carry on about what happened."

"Nevertheless, it can't be easy." I reach out to take her hand. "It's dreadful when our heroes fail us."

"How could she do those terrible things?" Poppy wails.

"She tricked all of us. None of us knew what she was really like."

"I understand why she was mad at me—I should never have stolen her hair—but to kill someone! And after being so nice to Vinny…"

"Vinny?" Archie blinks.

Poppy pulls a handkerchief from her apron pocket and dabs her tears. "Yes, sir. Vinny said her tips were more than he earned in almost a week…but he'd have run her errands for nothin'."

"Poppy, what errands are your talking about?" I inquire with keen interest.

A look of panic washes over her face. "Um…well…I shouldn't…"

I stand up and look into her eyes. "This is important. I promise that Vinny will not get into any trouble. What did Miss Styles ask Vinny to do."

"He picked up things for her in town…you know…like medicine and souvenirs," she explains.

Ipecac…cough syrup…postcards…the bracelet…that's how she did it!

Poppy continues, "But it was all on the up and up. She couldn't do it herself because people would hound her for autographs."

"How in the world did she pay him? Ike managed her money," I reflect.

"To my knowledge, she never carried a dime," Archie concurs.

"Oh, Vinny said that was easy," Poppy remarks. "She gave him checks to cash at the bank—all with enough for a fat tip."

"Thank you for sharing this with us. You have my word that we won't repeat this information to anyone," I assure her.

At this point there's no need.

"Thank you, ma'am…sir…I should get back to work. They'll wonder where I am." She backs up.

"Thank YOU, Poppy. You've been most helpful." Archie hands her two dollars.

Awestruck, she heads for the door muttering, "Golly!"

Archie closes the door behind her.

"There are probably thousands of fans just like her," I remark

"I'd wager there are millions," Archie comments. "Stardust is still preparing an official statement for the press."

"Speaking of Stardust, I was about to ask about *Skin Deep* when Poppy knocked on the door. Is Mr. Lake pulling his hair out?"

"On the contrary, you can't buy this sort of press," he laughs ironically.

"What?!" I sputter, flummoxed.

"The public is obsessed with the saga of Corvi Styles. Heck, I wouldn't be surprised if someone makes a movie about it. Who should play your part?" He drums his fingers on his chin. "I know! How about Marion Davies?"

I laugh, "Well, you're not the first person to notice the similarity."

"You think I'm joking?" He raises his eyebrows.

"The truth is stranger than anything you'd see on the screen," I reply. "But what's going to happen with *Skin Deep*?"

"It'll be Stardust's biggest film yet."

"How? You'll have to cast a new lead," I remark.

"You should give Liz a call," Archie grins.

My dear friend answers the telephone at her parents' house on the second ring. "Martin residence."

"Elizabeth, this is Ruby!"

"Ye gods and little fishes! Where have you been? I called your house and cottage, but no one answered," she exclaims.

"I'm still in Laguna Beach. I left Norma and Edith's place a little while ago and will be staying at the Coast Inn tonight with my family," I explain.

"After what you went through? If it was me, I'd refuse to leave the comfort of my own bed for a week!" she insists.

"Uncle Charles' offered to take me home straightaway after my rescue, but I declined. Tempting as it sounded, there are still some loose ends I need to tie up here."

"Only you, Ruby Ray! I for one have been relishing bowlfuls of Mama's albondigas soup and boxes of coconut brittle from Taylor's Chocolate Shop while listening to 'The Shadow' on the radio," Elizabeth states without a trace of guilt.

"How are you feeling?" I ask with concern. "Hyoscine poisoning is nothing to sneeze at."

"Much better. To be honest, I don't remember much about Thursday."

"That's probably just as well. You were having some horrible hallucinations. Archie said you were carrying on about a snake and red walls," I inform her.

"Red!" she shrieks. "Ruby, I forgot to tell you! I found a bottle of red ink Thursday morning inside Corvi's desk! It had completely slipped my mind until just now when you mentioned the red walls! I was looking for a stamp and pulled open one of the side drawers. There, sitting on top of a paper bag, was the ink alongside a glass pen. I thought it was odd, considering the red ink on the postcards Corvi received, and I wondered if Ike had stashed them in the desk drawer."

"Did Corvi see you at the desk?" I'm willing to bet she did and then hid the pen and ink under the bed, where Tom found them.

"I'm not sure. I think that's when our food arrived." She pauses. "Ruby, I'm so, so sorry!"

"Why are you apologizing?"

"I should have called you immediately. Then none of this would have happened—"

"Stop, Elizabeth!" I insist. "You have nothing to apologize for. You had no way of knowing that Corvi was behind all of it."

"Do you think that's why she poisoned me?" Elizabeth asks uneasily.

"That was probably the nail in the coffin, so to speak. When she and I were on the cliff, she said she'd overheard the crew talking about replacing her with you as the lead."

She chuckles bitterly.

"What's so funny?" I ask, confused.

"Despite her devious schemes, I've been asked to replace her after all."

"Oh, Elizabeth, that's wonderful!" I squeal.

"Thank you!" she cries. "Archie phoned a little while ago with the news. Costuming won't be an issue since we're the same size, and now they don't have to worry about voiceovers for the musical numbers."

"This is it, Elizabeth! You and Dean will be superstars!" I gush.

"Do you really think so?" she giggles.

"I know so!" I gaze through the partially open door into the living room where Archie continues packing. "I hope they're not planning to put you up in this suite."

"Egad, I hope not!" she chokes.

"We're moving the cast over to La Casa del Camino," Archie shouts from the other room.

"Did you hear that?" I ask Elizabeth.

"Yes! Thank goodness!" she says with relief. "What about you? What's next?"

"Well, in the short-term, my family and I plan to attend the airshow tomorrow. Do you feel up to joining us?" I inquire.

"I wish I could, Ruby, but I'm not quite up to snuff. Plus, I have to learn my lines. Dean's here right now, and we plan to work all day tomorrow. I'm expected back in Laguna Beach on Tuesday."

"How exciting!"

"It is! Mama told me to stop pinching myself or my arm will be covered in bruises," she laughs. "Enough about me. How are things with Sam?"

I blush. "Things have proven to be more challenging than I expected, that's for sure, but hopefully we're past the rough waters."

"Well, we need a face-to-face chinwag soon so you can fill me in on all the details," she demands.

"Deal," I reply. "I do have some other exciting news, though." I briefly share my plans for expanding the business.

"Ruby Ray, PI. It has a nice ring to it," she pronounces enthusiastically.

We hang up, and I gather the few belongings I left here yesterday. A conversation in the next room tells me that Archie has company.

"Honestly, where would I be without you?" Mr. Lake's voice carries.

"You're too kind, sir," Archie replies humbly.

The director snickers, "Well, I've never been accused of that before."

As I enter the living room, Mr. Lake's congenial expression hardens.

"I'm sorry to interrupt," I say politely.

"No need for that," Mr. Lake replies uncomfortably. "I'm actually here to see you, Miss Ray."

"Me?" For the life of me, I can't imagine what this is about. Mr. Lake has pretty much ignored me over the past week.

"Archie has kept me abreast of your investigation." He clears his throat. "I'd like to apologize for the dangerous position we put you in and any suffering you may have experienced."

I quickly close my mouth, which had reflexively dropped when I heard the word "apologize."

Mr. Lake continues, "On behalf of myself and Stardust Productions, I'd like to offer you an extended stay in Laguna Beach— all expenses paid, of course—for next week. Archie tells me you were originally here on vacation."

"Thank you, Mr. Lake. I sincerely appreciate the offer, but I must return home after the airshow tomorrow. I've neglected my business for far too long already," I reply.

"Well, the offer stands, whenever you'd like to schedule a stay. Archie will fill you in on the details." The director nods toward his assistant, who winks at me with a grin.

"That will be lovely." As far as I know, Sam will be in Laguna Beach a while longer.

"Stardust asked me to mention that they're interested in retaining your service for future cases." Mr. Lake roots around inside a trouser pocket then hands me a business card. "Give this number a call to make the arrangements."

"Thank you, Mr. Lake. I'll give it some thought."

He nods and reaches into his blazer, withdrawing an envelope embossed with the production's logo on the top left corner. "Compensation for your assistance."

I accept the envelope. "Thank you."

"You might want to look inside," Archie suggests with a meaningful glance.

I withdraw a neatly typed check for an amount that exceeds my annual income and look up at Mr. Lake. "Oh, my!"

"I hope this will cover your services, any costs you may have incurred and, of course, your discretion regarding the details of the case," Mr. Lake says unambiguously.

Compensation is one thing. This feels like hush money.

"Sir, discretion is part and parcel of my work as an inquiry agent." I try to return the check. "This is entirely unnecessary."

Mr. Lake gapes at my outstretched hand. "Are you refusing payment?"

"I'll provide the studio with an invoice of my fees—" I begin.

He relaxes. "Miss Ray, let me give you a piece of advice. Don't look a gift horse in the mouth—especially in this business."

CHAPTER 27

~ 🪷 ~

MONDAY, SEPTEMBER 1, 1930
LABOR DAY AIRSHOW, LAGUNA BEACH

"And I told him, 'Howard, ya gotta pay the guys better wages. You're asking them to work long hours doing crazy stunts, and there's nothing for their loved ones if they crash. One pilot has died, for Pete's sake! How many more have to perish before you do something? And ya know what Mr. Hughes said?'" Pancho's voice rumbles through the speakers on either side of the podium in front of Rankin's shop, the hanging gate suspended over her head.

Hundreds of onlookers lining Coast, Forest, and Park Avenues hang on her every word, while thousands more frolic and picnic on the beaches from Crystal Cove down to Three Arch Bay. I even heard that the auto camp at Aliso Beach is packed with vehicles and tents. Jack commented that there are so many picnic blankets on Main Beach, you can walk barefoot from the boardwalk to the water without scorching your feet on the hot sand. The airshow and Labor Day festivities have attracted crowds from all over Orange County, despite coming together at the last minute.

"He told me to go to hell! Which is funny considering that he ended up calling the film *Hell's Angels,*" Pancho hoots.

Nan *tsks* beside me at the aviator's colorful language. Gabe brought her and the twins to the show, along with a trunk load of picnic baskets and thermoses. On the other side of Nan, Uncle Charles shares an affectionate grin with Clara, while Jack and Owen argue over the pilot's cap that Pancho gave Jack.

"I only wanna wear it for five minutes." Owen extends his hand. "Then I'll give it back—I swear!"

"Shh!" Clara gently admonishes. "You'll be sorry later that you missed Pancho's speech with all this squabbling."

Jack's towheaded friend abandons his plea for the moment and turns his attention back to the pilot's animated narrative, while his mother only has eyes for my uncle.

"You know what we did?" Pancho shakes a fist in the air. "We unionized!"

Behind us, a group of laborers chant "Union! Union! Union!" to the dismay of several hoity-toity men and women nearby.

Despite the fact that Labor Day has been a federal holiday for over thirty years, many employers still refuse to give their workers the day off. And while communities gather across the country to celebrate Labor Day with parades and picnics, conflicts between labor and business continue to mount—including recent strikes in the textile industry. I've even heard rumors that farm workers in California have started to discuss organizing to improve worker safety, living conditions, and wages.

When the chanting dies down, Pancho carries on with her speech. "That's right! We formed the AMPP—the Associated Motion Picture Pilots. There's still a lot of work to be done to make this thing official, but we were able to get $50 a day for the pilots on Hughes' film. Right now we're fighting for insurance. God knows we need it."

"What did we miss?" Dottie sidles up with Iris at her side.

"One of the performers with the Community Playhouse sang the national anthem, then the mayor introduced the dignitaries sitting in those chairs by the podium. The police chief stepped up and gave a brief eulogy for Detective Maggard. It sounds like his funeral will be later this week." I nod toward the chief, who—like the other officers I've seen today—is wearing a black armband.

"And Pancho?" Dottie asks.

"She's been at it for quite a while, but I think she's wrapping things up now." I ask, "Where've you been? Nan's been worried about you for the past hour and a half."

"Sorry we're late. I wanted to say goodbye to the other students at the Marine Lab, and then it took eons to find you all."

"How on earth did you spot us?" I query.

"Your parasol." She flicks a finger at one of the ribs on my sunshade. "It's bright pink."

"It is rather gaudy," I laugh.

Daisy at the dress shop persuaded me to buy it, along with the matching coral-and-pink-striped beach pajamas I'm currently wearing. In hindsight, I'm glad I purchased the Crepe de Chine set yesterday after leaving the Hotel Laguna. Its lightweight fabric is cool but also covers my sunburned skin.

Dottie looks down the row at our group. "Where's Sam?"

"He's at the Red Cross tent across the street. Between the airshow and the Hillclimb today, they needed all the help they could get at the first aid booths." I sigh, disappointed that he can't join us.

The Laguna Beach Hillclimb—a dirt track race where riders on motorbikes zoom up and down the hills surrounding Laguna Beach— has been a popular sporting event for the past five years or so. When Sam called the hotel this morning, he said he was relieved to work the Main Beach booth instead of the Hillclimb, where he knew the temperatures would be insufferable and the injuries far more severe.

"Who's ready for some barnstorming?" Pancho bellows from the podium.

Loud hoots and hollers erupt from the eager throng, while Jack and Owen spin tin noisemakers that Jack picked up in town yesterday with Uncle Charles. After a little while, the tightly packed mob begins to disperse—most heading for the sand. When we visited Pancho at Dos Rocas Friday afternoon, she mentioned that they'll fly a mile or so offshore along the coastline, which should be visible to everyone on the beach. When I asked how high they'll have to fly, she explained that, if it's a relatively calm day, they could fly as low as two hundred feet, but she didn't want to take any risks. Given the recent death of her friend, Dodds, I can understand why.

"Shall we find our umbrellas?" Uncle Charles holds out an elbow for Clara.

"Great idea!" she slides a svelte arm through his.

Early this morning, Uncle Charles and Jack scouted out the "perfect spot"—as Jack put it—and arranged several picnic blankets and two navy and white striped umbrellas borrowed from the Coast Inn.

"Not too close to the water—we don't wanna wash away at high tide," he reasoned. "But close enough that someone else's umbrella won't block our view.

"I think I'll stop by the Red Cross tent to see Sam and meet you at our spot in a little while," I announce once we've crossed Coast Highway.

"We'll go with you," Dottie declares. "Iris wants to visit the Marine Lab booth."

"You'll find us straight out from the Union Oil filling station," my uncle informs us. "Look for the hexagonal tower."

Before entering the warren of food and game booths haphazardly situated alongside the boardwalk, Dottie pulls me aside.

"You go ahead, Iris. I need to talk to Ruby for a minute." My cousin waves to her friend.

"Is everything alright, Dottie?" I inquire.

"Better than alright!" she exclaims brightly. "I told Iris everything, and she was so sympathetic."

"That's wonderful!" I enthuse. "The more you talk about it with people you trust, the less it'll haunt you in your dreams."

"I'm starting to understand that." Dottie nods thoughtfully. "Still, I told Iris that I'm nervous about the girls at the boarding house finding out. They might not be so understanding."

"I'm sure it will work out. You didn't have any bad dreams last night after talking to your dad and me," I point out. "And the other boarders may surprise you."

"True. But Iris had a solution to the whole thing!" she declares excitedly.

"Tell me everything!"

"Well, her aunt is a psychology professor at Berkeley and just bought a house. She was talking to Iris' mom about taking in a student boarder for extra income—if you can believe it. Iris is going to call her after the airshow to see if the room is still available!"

"Oh, Dottie! How marvelous!" I give her an enthusiastic hug.

"Come on, you two!" Iris motions for us to follow.

She leads us to the Marine Lab booth, where Professor Grober and another student are supervising four young children handling the fragile remains of several tidepool creatures, including a purple striped sea urchin and a dried starfish.

"Miss Ray," the bespectacled professor holds up a hand. "So good to see you!"

"You too," I return his smile. "What do we have here?"

A little girl with two missing incisors dangles an exoskeleton alarmingly close to my face. "A crab sheded it!"

"*Shed* it, Shirley," her older brother corrects her.

"Thank you for showing it to me." I take a step backward.

"Perhaps you can help me persuade your cousin to attend Pomona College instead of Berkeley," Professor Grober pleads. "I've been telling her all week that we could use a chemistry student at the Marine Lab—our students are largely biology majors."

"I doubt I could change her mind." I grin proudly at Dottie. "She's had her heart set on Berkeley for years."

"But I plan to accept Dr. Campbell's offer of enrolling in the summer term at the lab next year," she promises Dr. Grober.

He claps his hands. "Excellent!"

"I don't suppose you can direct me to the first aid tent," I question Dr. Grober.

"Oh, my. Are you alright? You do look rather burned," he observes, wide-eyed.

"I'm fine," I assure him. "Thank you for your concern, but I need to meet someone working the booth."

He scratches his head. "My apologies. I'm not sure where it is."

"That's alright," I smile. "I'm sure I'll find it."

"We'll help you," Iris comments.

Dottie and Iris follow me through the maze of tents. We nearly pass a large open-sided marquee when I recognize Lillian from the Art Association Gallery.

She notices me as well. "Hey, I remember you! Ruby Ray, right?"

"Yes. Hello, Lillian," I return her greeting. "How nice to see you again."

She leans forward and lowers her voice. "I saw your photograph in the newspaper yesterday. What a horrific thing to happen! How are you feeling?"

"I'm still recovering, as you can imagine," I reply. "Thank you for asking."

"You know, I got the chills when I read the article. Such a coincidence after telling you about the Dresden China Doll business." She raises her brows.

"Dresden China Doll?" Dottie inquires.

"I'll tell you about it later," I reply out of the corner of my mouth.

"What is it with these actresses?" Lillian huffs.

Wishing to change the subject, I look past her into the booth. "Is this for the Art Association?"

"Yes," she affirms. "In fact, Edith stopped by a little while ago. I heard she was back yesterday, so I called and asked if she wanted to show a couple of her pieces."

Toward the back of the tent, I recognize Edith's watercolor painting of a woman gazing out a window. She's watching a lady and gentleman walk past arm in arm—her face shadowed and arm hanging loosely at her side, a letter enfolded in her grasp.

Lillian notices my gaze. "So poignant," she comments.

"It is." I nod. "I saw it at their home in Fullerton before they moved."

Dottie, Iris, and I take our time perusing the artwork, including many plein air paintings of local coastlines, as well as several modern sculptures—all geometric forms and unrecognizable figures. I'm deeply moved by the emotion conveyed with simple lines and brushstrokes and vow to begin collecting art once I have a place of my own.

As we begin to leave, I ask Lillian, "Do you happen to know where the Red Cross booth is located? I need to speak with someone there."

She shakes her head. "I don't, unfortunately. Set-up was rather disorganized this morning."

We say goodbye to Lillian and continue on our way. A crowd is gathered around a ring toss game where the prizes consist of handheld pinwheels, small chalkware figurines, and a wide-eyed Kewpie doll. A clown wearing a ruffled Elizabethan collar and a tiny cone-shaped hat entertains the waiting patrons with his antics. At one point, he matches his steps with those of a very serious looking man who doesn't realize he's being followed. Dottie and Iris begin to giggle, but the clown holds a finger to his mouth and winks. The surly fellow suddenly stops at a booth, and the clown crashes into his back. Startled, the unassuming victim turns with a glower but bursts out laughing when he glimpses the sheepish jester.

We turn left at a ceramics stand and pass a stall selling popcorn and lemonade. Further down the zigzagging row, the Laguna Beach Garden Club booth appears to be well-staffed with volunteers helping folks plant seeds in small ceramic pots.

"Yoo-hoo," one aproned matron calls out to us. "Would you like to plant some columbine?"

As much as I love the delicately complex blossoms, I don't want to tote around a flowerpot all day. "Maybe later."

"How about an envelope of poppy seeds? You can plant them this fall," she offers.

"That would be lovely." I accept the tiny packet. "Can you tell me where I can find the first aid tent?"

"You're almost there." She points. "It's between the boardwalk and the lifeguard tower."

"Thank you."

Once we reach the lifeguard station, the expansive white tent with its oversized red cross is hard to miss. I step into its shady interior—

the girls close behind me—and witness a flurry of activity. A dozen or so cots, several occupied, are arranged in a neat line. A young woman wearing a pristine white pinafore takes one look at my scarlet arms and face and shouts over her shoulder.

"Another sunburn."

"Oh, no." I hold up a hand. "I already have ointment for the burn. I'm here to see Dr. Armstrong."

At the sound of my voice, Sam stands up from the cot where he's been sitting and turns around.

"Ruby!" His delight is contagious, and the fresh-faced nurse grins too.

I walk over to him and notice a wincing youth outstretched on the cot, a length of thread dangling from his bare foot.

"Oh, no. I've caught you at a bad time," I apologize.

"Not at all. I'm almost done stitching up this brave youngster," Sam pats the boy on the shoulder. "He's not the first to step on broken glass today, but— if I do say so myself—his stitches are my finest work yet."

"Take your time," I reply woozily. I've never been one for blood and needles. "We'll wait over there."

"Busy day?" Dottie asks the nurse near the front of the tent.

"Crazy day," she replies. "Besides the usual sunburns, cuts, and water-related problems, one guy burned himself roasting weenies and another broke his arm diving for a football, but the wackiest thing was the stingray attack."

"Stingray attack?" Iris pushes up her glasses. "Does that happen often?"

"No, from what I hear, it's pretty rare. One of the lifeguards said that fishermen occasionally catch them from the pier, but he hadn't heard of any swimmers getting stung here in recent years," the young lady replies.

"I read an article about five years ago where a man caught a stingray while shore fishing in Huntington Beach," I recall. "When he pulled the creature onto the sand, five babies squirmed out. The reporter said that stingrays carry their babies in pockets like opossums."

Iris dissolves into peals of laughter. "That's ridiculous! Stingrays give birth live. The pups probably left her body because of all the stress."

"What's this about stingray pups?" Sam walks toward us while drying his hands with a clean white towel.

Iris blushes. "I was just explaining about stingray live birth."

"We heard that someone was stung today," I clarify.

"Yeah, poor kid. That was an ugly flesh wound," he remarks "We sent him to the hospital."

"Ruby, now that you've found Sam, Iris and I are going to meet up with Edwin," Dottie interjects.

"Aren't you hungry? We're supposed to eat pretty soon," I remind her. "Nan will be disappointed if she can't stuff you full of ham sandwiches and potato salad."

"I'm not hungry right now, but I'm sure I will be later," she says cryptically.

"Well, try to be back for the airshow. Jack wants us all to watch it together."

She waves, and the duo leave the tent.

I look past Sam to make sure no one's watching and slide my arms around his torso. He kisses the top of my head.

"I wish you could watch the airshow with us." I playfully bat my eyelashes.

"If you give me that look, I'll lose my resolve and follow you." He wraps his arms around me.

"Are you refusing to answer my siren's call to abandon your patients?" I tease.

"I'm afraid so." He raises my chin with his index finger and soundly kisses my lips.

I sigh blissfully, so thankful that we worked things out. "I should be going. Jack will be doubly disappointed if I'm not there to watch the stunts with him."

"Before you do, let's make plans for later today," he suggests. "When can you leave?"

He looks around the booth. "Hopefully by six."

"That late?" Missing the comfort of my own bed, I'd planned to drive home no later than early evening.

"Afraid so. Will that work for you?" he asks with concern.

"I'll make it work. What do you have in mind?" I raise an eyebrow.

"Archie stopped by a little while ago," he replies. "He was looking for you, but with all the people—"

"Archie?" I ask, confused.

"Pancho's having a party this evening and wanted Archie to extend an invitation to you and a guest—I hoped that would be me," he grins.

"How do you feel about that?" I gaze at him seriously.

"I'd love to go. This may be my only chance to visit Dos Rocas. From what I hear, it shouldn't be missed. How about you? Do you think you'll feel up to it this evening?"

"Once I leave here, I'll plant myself on the sand and won't get back up until it's time to meet you."

"Well, I'm glad to see you've brought this." Sam hands me my eye-catching parasol. "But it won't offer much shade if you're stretched out on a blanket."

"Then it's a good thing Uncle Charles brought two beach umbrellas." I kiss his cheek.

We decide to meet back here at six. I'll need to call the Coast Inn at some point to extend my stay and forgo sleeping in my own bed for one more night—not too high a price to pay for spending the evening with Sam.

Thankfully, the Red Cross tent is a stone's throw from the boardwalk, so there's no danger I'll be distracted by booths and stalls while finding the way to my family. Once clear of the bustling bazaar, a sea of colorful umbrellas nearly blocks my view of the shore. Just ahead, a court has been marked off with ropes and stakes for a volleyball game, where several barefoot players hop from one foot to the other to avoid the blistering sand while waiting for the serve. After passing through a covered walkway that runs alongside the Cabrillo Ballroom, I continue up the boardwalk until I reach the corner of Broadway and Coast Highway. There I glimpse Union Oil's six-sided tower adorned with small portholes and a lantern perched atop the uppermost tile shingles. The gasoline pumps next to the tower remind me that I should fill my tank before heading home tomorrow—my windows could use a swipe as well.

To my left, the picnicking horde readily awaits the airshow on blankets and beach chairs all the way down to the tide line. My heart sinks as I notice dozens of navy and white umbrellas straight out from the tower. Finding my family could prove more challenging than locating the first aid booth—at least I had some help with that. I hop off the side of the boardwalk onto the sand and immediately hear my name.

"Ruby!" Jack bustles toward me, carelessly kicking a spray of sand on the blanket behind him.

"Do ya mind?!" a man in a straw boater growls.

"Sorry, mister!" Jack calls over his shoulder.

I wave an apology as well.

"Nan was getting worried and told me to wait at the boardwalk for ya," Jack explains.

"Well, your timing is impeccable!" I declare with relief

"Follow me!"

Like a salmon swimming upstream, Jack weaves his way through umbrellas, kicking sand along the way, until we're about ten feet from the damp sand.

"Wow!" I exclaim. "There's no one blocking our view!"

"The tide's still going out, so we should be good for a while," my uncle rises from one of the blankets. "How'd things go?"

"It took a while to find Sam, but we had a couple of minutes to talk before he had to tend to another patient."

Nan leans forward in her canvas chair to look past the edge of the umbrella. "Where's Dottie and her friend?"

"They went to find someone, but I reminded them to be back in time for the show," I assure her.

Nan motions toward the empty chair next to her. "Now, you get under this shade so those blisters don't get any worse."

When we all met up a couple of hours ago in front of the White House Restaurant, Nan lamented my tribulation on Saturday and refused to release her embrace until I assured her that I was alright, just a bit red. Later, while waiting for the speeches to begin, Uncle Charles and I explained our plan to convert the cottage into a home for Nan. She nearly fainted with relief and gratitude but only after putting up a fuss for a little while.

"Don't sit down, Ruby," Jack insists. "Come out in the water with me and Owen."

"I think Ruby's had enough water for a while," my uncle intercedes.

"Your dad's right," I nod.

"Race you!" Owen challenges Jack, and the two sprint across the sand into the whitewash—Jack winning by nary a foot.

Clara tucks her wavy dark hair beneath a bathing cap and extends her arm for Uncle Charles to pull her up from the blanket. The look of fondness that passes between them warms my heart. I couldn't be happier for Uncle Charles.

"They make a handsome couple," Nan observes as the pair join Addie, May, and Gabe at the water's edge, while the boys splash their way past the breakers.

"That they do," I agree.

"It's starting!"

Jack's energetic shout—not to mention the rumbling drone of a biplane—rouse me from my postprandial nap. I consumed far too much food from Nan's bountiful picnic baskets and drifted off a while ago. Standing to leave the shady comfort of the canvas chair, I join the rest of our group at the edge of our blankets, then realize we're missing a couple of people.

"Where are Dottie and Iris?" I scan behind us.

"They're gonna miss it!" Jack replies irritably.

"They probably couldn't find us," Uncle Charles points out. "I'm sure they're still watching it."

The biplane ascends into a broad loop over the water, and a deafening roar explodes from the crowd gathered onshore. Further south, a seemingly endless line of planes barrel roll, spin, and dive while following the shoreline northwest. Jack and Owen share a pair of binoculars and enthusiastically comment about the stunts.

I—on the other hand—hold my breath throughout each exploit, while Nan mumbles, "If God meant for us to fly, he'd have given us wings."

Over the next hour, over twenty planes pass by, and my skin begins to sting from the intense sunrays bouncing off the water. Yet, I dare not open my parasol, lest I block someone's view. Thus, despite the heat, I wrap a towel around my shoulders and borrow a broad-brimmed hat from Addie.

Nan encourages me to pour myself a glass of cool lemonade so I don't overheat. Consequently, my back is turned when Jack whoops, "It's Pancho and her Mystery Ship!"

I swing around, spilling the icy liquid in the process, just in time to witness the low-wing monoplane—deep scarlet with a sleek design—streaking past. Pancho raises her arm to wave from the cockpit, and I find myself waving back, along with everyone else onshore.

"Dad and I saw her break the women's speed record in THAT PLANE last month!" Jack boasts to anyone who will listen. "You know, they only built four of 'em."

Pancho disappears from view, and we conclude that the airshow is over. Families begin to shake the sand out of their blankets and pack up their belongings. But minutes later, Pancho returns…traveling in the opposite direction.

"She must have done a U-turn over Corona del Mar," someone next to us comments as the Mystery Ship approaches the pier.

Without warning, the aircraft shoots skyward in a tight spiral. Our necks ache as we watch the plane climb until it's a tiny speck against the thin, wispy clouds so high in the sky. Then, unexpectedly, Pancho begins a dive so perilous that a child nearby begins to cry.

"She's cwashing!" the child wails.

"Nah, it's a stunt. She'll be right as rain," the child's father comforts.

Sure enough, Pancho levels out well before she reaches the water and wags her wings while continuing her southward journey. Below her, thousands of pairs of hands clap furiously.

"What a finale!" Gabe exclaims with a wide grin.

"I can't believe Dottie didn't make it!" Jack complains with a surly frown. "She promised."

"I'm sure she has a good reason," I drape an arm around his lanky shoulders.

"It's not over!" May pronounces a split second later.

While the Mystery Ship shrinks from view, a biplane sedately approaches from the south at a much lower altitude.

Jack presses the binoculars to his eyes and yelps, "Dad! IT'S DOTTIE!"

Uncle Charles snatches the binoculars from his son's hands. "Polka Dot…" he utters with anxious wonder.

Even without the field glasses, I can easily discern Dottie's face…and she's beaming.

Nan prays, "Dear Lord, please protect Dottie and bring her back to us safe and sound."

"Who's the pilot?" Jack asks, tugging at the binoculars.

"It's Edwin." My uncle resists his grabbing hands. "The young Coast Guard pilot we met at Pancho's party." It's difficult to infer from his tone how he feels about this.

"She sees us!" Owen exclaims.

Dottie points directly at our group and waves exuberantly, as the boys race along the seashore, their arms flying. Nan, on the other hand, continues her prayerful plea, while Uncle Charles drapes an arm around my shoulders.

Together we watch our dear Dottie conquer her fears.

"Have I told you how ravishing you look tonight?" Sam glances at me admiringly while driving my car to Dos Rocas.

Able to secure an extra night at the Coast Inn, I had time to shower and change into something presentable before heading over to the Red Cross booth. After walking to my car, Sam insisted upon driving the rest of the way, which—I must confess—I didn't mind one bit.

From the passenger seat, I'm able to watch the hive of activity along Main Beach as vendors break down their booths, and stylish couples meander toward the ballroom for the final night of the Cabrillo's summer season before going back to their weekend only schedule.

"You're kind to say that Sam, but I feel like one of Jack's lizards molting its skin."

While dressing for the evening, my arms and chest felt itchy, and I realized that my skin had started to peel. So, after covering my burns with the cream Sam prescribed, I settled on a loose sleeveless evening gown that wouldn't further irritate my skin.

Sam laughs then takes my hand and kisses my knuckles—his eyes shifting back to the highway. "My dear, there is nothing reptilian about you!"

During the drive, we chat about our day. Sam regales me with amusing stories about patients suffering the consequences of poor choices, and I recount the aftermath of Dottie's aerial adventure.

"She didn't mention this to anyone ahead of time?" he asks with amazement.

I shake my head. "Only Iris."

I reflect upon my conversation with Dottie after she, Iris, and Edwin found us on the beach about an hour after the flight.

"I knew it was something I had to do, but I was afraid I'd chicken out if I told any of you ahead of time," Dottie disclosed.

"Well, you nearly gave us a heart attack." Nan patted Dottie as though confirming she was still alive and in one piece.

"Edwin was great! He explained everything to me ahead of time." Dottie smiled at the young pilot. "It was so different from our flights a couple of weeks ago, Ruby. Out in the open with the air rushing past, I felt free."

I tell Sam, "She's been struggling with nightmares after everything that happened."

"I can only imagine," he sympathizes, while pulling through the gates of Dos Rocas.

"Dottie told me that during the flight, she felt more like herself than she had for nearly a year."

"She seems like a remarkable young lady," Sam comments. "When does she leave for Berkeley?"

"Uncle Charles will drive her up this Friday," I reply.

At the end of the long drive, Sam releases a whistle while parking behind a dark green Bugatti Coupe. On the other side of the drive sits the Duesenberg I spotted outside the Hotel Laguna when Dottie and I first arrived.

"Some crowd!" he declares.

"And how!" I agree.

The rhythmic beats and brassy tones of a live band become louder as we follow a path of candle-lit luminarias to the back of the house. There we find dozens of revelers surrounding a makeshift stage next to the pool. Pancho steps up to join the band during the final intense notes of the song, and—once the applause dies down—she pops the cork on a bottle of champagne and takes a swig.

A pilot I recognize from the party Friday afternoon foists a couple of overfilled glasses at Sam and I, then claps him on the shoulder.

"Bottoms up!" the aviator grins.

Pancho lowers her bottle and ballyhoos, "That was some show!"

Shouts and cheers erupt as her guests express their agreement.

Sam discreetly sets his glass on a small table, and I follow suit. He leans over to speak into my ear, "I don't mind a drink now and again, but as the doctor for some of these folks…"

"You don't have to explain," I assure him. "I had my fill of champagne in Europe. Besides, I'd like to keep a clear head this evening."

"To Pancho!" someone cries out from the pool, and the air rings with clinking glasses and a chorus of toasts to their beloved friend.

With a broad toothy smile and gleaming eyes, Pancho raises the bottle. "To my flyboys! That was some top-notch barnstorming today, fellas!"

A series of whoops arise among a group of pilots next to us.

"That's all the yappin' I'm gonna do. Now, let's hear some more music!" She sweeps an arm toward the band and steps down to join her guests.

The drummer slaps a few jazzy beats, and the cornet begins to wail.

"Let's dance later. I'm starving!" Sam declares.

The food tables are laden with everything from oysters on the half shell to stuffed cannelloni. There's even a carving station with an impressively pink prime rib. Sam loads his plate then gives me a quizzical look when he notices my selection of a single small cup of shrimp cocktail.

"I'm still stuffed from Nan's picnic," I explain.

"Well, I could eat a horse! All we had today were warm egg salad sandwiches, so I passed."

"Smart choice," I grimace.

We find a small wrought iron table with two chairs slightly removed from the hubbub, and Sam dives into his meal.

"We forgot our drinks," I rise and place my napkin on the chair. "I'll find us something a bit less toxic."

Just then, Ferne—the silver blonde who fancied my uncle—passes our table and pauses when she notices Sam.

"Watch out for that one," I caution under my breath.

"Don't I know it," he says while grinning politely at Ferne.

"Doctor," she greets flirtatiously but continues toward the pool.

"Whew," Sam exhales.

"How do you know her?" I inquire.

"Let's just say that she's been a frequent visitor to Dr. Carroll's office since I arrived," he replies meaningfully.

I laugh. "Dare I leave you alone to fetch some sodas?"

"I think I'm safe," he chuckles. "For now…"

I walk past the pool and descend a set of stairs, nearly colliding with Bebe who's exiting the bar inside Pancho's basement. "Whoops! I'm sorry!"

"Ru-by," she slurs. "Washn't eshpecting to shee you here."

"I might say the same to you." I step aside for someone else to enter. "I didn't realize that you know Pancho."

She shushes me, her breath heavy with gin. "I don't know Pansho. I'm here with Kitty who'sh here with Shmit." She narrows her eyes and looks up. "Wait! That'sh not right. I'm here with SHMITTY who'sh here with KIT. Kitty…" she giggles.

"Well, either way, I was hoping to see you before I left town," I comment.

"Reeeally," she says coyly.

"I wanted to apologize," I clarify. "I'm sorry I didn't believe you about Corvi."

She waves a hand. "Shmall potatoesh. No one ever believed me."

"Honestly, I wish I had. I was barking up the wrong tree the whole time," I admit.

"Well, she got what she desherved," Bebe says dismissively. "But YOU…you know, I washn't kidding with my offer the other day." Her gaze travels up and down my body. "I like a gal with curvsh."

Luckily, Smitty walks up at that moment and wraps an arm around her shoulders. "There you are, doll face."

"Kitty!" she purrs.

"Honey, let's find a place for you to sit down for a while," Smitty says. While leading her up the stairs, he mutters so only I can hear him, "She's zozzled."

Once inside, I push my way through the densely packed crowd toward the bar. One of the pilots appears to be playing bartender, so I ask, "Is there any soda back there?"

He looks around for a minute or so. "Nah, just hooch. Unless you want noodle juice." He holds up a tea bag.

"How about a couple of glasses of water?"

He nods. "That I can do. Ice?"

"Sure. Thanks," I shout over the din.

Back outside I notice Kit leaning against a eucalyptus tree, his shoulders drooping with melancholy.

"Hi, Kit," I greet him with concern. "How are you this evening?"

"Ruby!" The actor straightens. "How are YOU doing? I can't believe what you went through!"

"A bit pink…a bit sore…but I'm alright." I give a lopsided smile. "Kit, I know you were very fond of Corvi—"

"She lied to me—to all of us!" He runs a hand through his thick hair. "Ike told me to back off, but I thought he was just jealous. Then Bebe told me these ridiculous things about Corvi's past. I figured she was jealous too."

More likely, Ike didn't want Kit to get too close and figure out what was happening. "We were all taken in by her," I console him.

"Just as well she kept me at arm's length," he reflects. "I never really got my hopes up."

"Hey ya, kids," Archie greets while pushing Rex over the well-manicured grass in a wood-framed wheelchair.

"Archie," I lean in for a hug. "And Rex, it's so good to see you," I pat his shoulder. "How are you feeling?"

One of Rex's pant legs has been shortened to accommodate a Plaster of Paris cast extending above his knee. Otherwise, he looks quite good.

"Just swell," he flashes that striking smile—so familiar from his movies and photos.

"It's good to see you," Kit extends a hand to his fellow thespian. "I appreciate you showing me the ropes when we started filming."

While the pair of actors chat, I pull Archie aside and lower my voice. "So, you and Rex…"

"We'll see," he shrugs. "He claims the accident knocked some sense into him, but you know these actors…"

"Yes, I do," I reply soberly.

"How about you?" He looks around. "Where's that dreamy doctor of yours?"

"Over there, past the food station," I point. "I just went for drinks."

He sniffs one of the glasses. "You call those drinks?" he laughs.

I chuckle along with him. "So, does filming begin tomorrow?"

"Logistics mostly. We'll start in earnest on Thursday. How about you? Will you stay another week? I can make the arrangements."

"No, I need to leave in the morning. There's lots to do, including finding a new office." I smile warmly. "But I'm so glad to have the opportunity to say goodbye to you."

"You talk as though we'll never see each other again," he laughs. "Ruby, after everything we've been through, we're friends—good friends—so, you're not getting rid of me that easily."

I draw him into a hug. "I wouldn't dream of it."

After bidding farewell to the three dashing fellows, I return to the one man who has captured my heart.

"You were gone so long I considered sending out a search party." He chuckles then scrunches his face when he realizes his blunder. "Oh! Sorry! That was poorly timed."

Just then, a couple stumbles past in differing stages of undress.

"What do you say we get away from the shenanigans?" I suggest. "There's a path down to the beach."

He stands and lightly places a hand on my back. "Lead the way."

We find a cozy spot at the base of the cliff and sit against a smooth, straight rock. I snuggle close, my head on his strong shoulder, and gaze out at the water. The dim light from the crescent moon doesn't quite reach the rolling waves, yet—despite the darkness—I feel safer than I have in quite some time. As much as I treasured my trip abroad, traveling alone as a woman required keeping my guard up at all times. And since returning home, I've been swept up in a maelstrom of apprehension and uneasiness due to Dottie's struggle…the case with

Corvi…my misunderstanding with Sam…and my own feelings of restlessness.

"This is nice," he kisses the top of my head.

"Mm-hmm," I agree contentedly.

Several minutes later he says, "We should talk about our plans for the next few months."

I raise my head to look at him. "OUR plans…I like the sound of that."

"I'd hoped to secure a placement in Fullerton starting in November, but there was nothing available. So, I've extended my rotation here with Dr. Carroll through the end of the year," he explains gingerly. In the semi-darkness, I sense that he's watching me closely.

"Well then, I'll need to take Mr. Lake up on that offer of a weeklong stay here." I place my palm against his warm cheek. "I promise not to work next time."

"I'm so glad you're alright with this," Sam sighs with relief.

"Of course, I am. We'll make the best of it." I stroke his stubbly face.

At that moment, a high-pitched whistle rises up from the cliff above us, followed by an explosion of bright color in the sky over the water. We barely have time to register the first display before three more flashes dazzle the sky in quick succession.

"Pancho sure knows how to throw a party," Sam chuckles, his face illuminated by the glittering pyrotechnics.

"That she does." I lean my head back against his shoulder to watch the show.

A little while later—after the frenzied roar of the spectacular finale abruptly ends—the band strikes up a slow, romantic tune.

Sam rises and takes my hand, "Would you like to dance?"

"I would love that," I reply as he pulls me up from the sand.

We attempt to box step through the first couple of verses but laugh as we find ourselves tripping over the sand. After that, we settle into a comfortable sway while standing in one place.

When the song ends, Sam leans down to whisper in my ear, his breath warm and his voice husky, "It may be too soon to tell you how I feel, but I can't keep it to myself any longer."

I nod, my ear pressed against his mouth, my body tingling with anticipation.

"Ruby Ray, not only do I love you...I cherish you."

EPILOGUE

WEDNESDAY, DECEMBER 24, 1930
FULLERTON, CALIFORNIA

"The snowflakes arrived." I swivel back and forth in my new cherry wood desk chair, the latest addition to my office in downtown Fullerton.

"Snowflakes? It's sunny here in Laguna," Sam's tenor carries along the thirty miles or so of telephone wire.

"The SNOWFLAKES. Surely you remember your grandma talking about them when we visited Twain Harte for Thanksgiving."

Over the past few months, my time with Sam has been quite limited. Sure, I was able to spend a week in Laguna in early October—thanks to Stardust Productions—and Sam made a couple of weekend trips to Fullerton. But until our visit to Northern California several weeks ago, our time together has mainly consisted of evening telephone "dates" when Sam isn't working at the morgue.

Just thinking about the trip to Twain Harte brings a giddy smile to my face. Sam was eager for me to meet his grandparents and invited me to join him during the holiday. We could have taken the Southern Pacific Railroad to Sacramento and then caught a bus to Sonora from there, but Sam suggested making the journey by car, as I'd never visited Northern California and would appreciate seeing the sights in a more leisurely fashion. We broke up the drive over two days—both ways—which required overnight stays at a hotel in Fresno where, in keeping with social decorum, Sam reserved two rooms…we only needed one.

Sam laughs. "I know what you meant. She told me she was rushing to finish them all in time for Christmas. How many snowflakes did she send?"

I lift one of the delicately crocheted ornaments out of the parcel I picked up at the post office a little while ago and dangle it from my index finger.

"Six," I reply. "She even included one for Nan."

"That accounts for five. Who's the sixth one for?"

"You, silly," I chuckle. "Your grandma is so thoughtful. By the way, Nan's trying out the mincemeat pie recipe she sent her."

"I hope she's not going to all this trouble on my account. I'll eat anything for Christmas Eve dinner."

"Between you and me, Nan's over the moon about the new kitchen Uncle Charles installed in the cottage," I confide. "She told me, 'Now I have an extra oven, I might as well cook a few different pies.'"

A few months ago, Nan comfortably settled into the cottage where—for the first time in her life—she has her own space. When she moved in, her nephew and Gabe delivered her well-tended cedar chest containing all of her most treasured possessions. Over time, Nan brought out the Delft cake plate I bought her in Holland and the patchwork quilt her grandmother made from scraps of clothing that she and her siblings wore as children. She also hung a shadow box displaying the Civil War campaign medals awarded to her father and uncle, both of whom fought for the Union when she was a small child. And I couldn't help but notice a small bookcase next to her bed that contained dozens of dime romance novels. Now that Uncle Charles hired Penny—Gabe's younger sister who recently arrived from Kansas—Nan has had more time to read. Of course, Nan insists that she continue cooking dinner and holiday meals, but we hope that, in time, she'll let Penny take over the kitchen entirely.

Speaking of books, we moved the reading parlor to the local library, which has given us more space to welcome newcomers and has allowed other women in the group to take on leadership roles which—I must admit—is a relief now that my business is keeping me so busy. The head librarian even offered a locked glass-fronted cabinet to house the signed Agatha Christie novels that Archie gave us. However, since so many of our members continue to borrow them, the cabinet sits empty most of the time.

"I'm looking forward to seeing you soon," Sam croons. "I plan to leave for Fullerton within the hour."

"In that case, I better finish my work here and go home." I consider the pile of mail on my desk waiting to be opened.

"You know," he lowers his voice. "Not only do I love you…"

"I cherish you," I finish with a smile.

Hanging up the phone, I glance around my office and still can't believe that it's mine. Shortly after returning from Laguna Beach, I found a single room office on the second floor above Alpha Beta Market, of all places. Today, tinseled garland frames the wide window looking out onto Spadra Road, and a foot-high crepe paper Christmas tree decorated with red and white pom poms sits on my filing cabinet. Most importantly, just outside—mounted to my door—the nameplate reads *Ruby Ray Investigations*.

When news of my involvement with Corvi's case hit the national press, I began receiving inquiries from as far away as Boston. Consequently, I've wrestled with the types of cases I'm willing to accept. While continuing my pro bono work helping and protecting women in need, I have found it necessary to take on assignments that I wouldn't have considered when my operating expenses were far less. For example, a recent referral from Tom involved trailing the spouse of a well-known actress in order to prove that he was cheating on her, so she could serve him with divorce papers.

Thankfully, my most recent case was far more fulfilling. In fact, just yesterday I unmasked the vandals who defaced the meager homes of field laborers at their settlement on Bastanchury Ranch. Meanwhile, some women from the reading parlor enlisted their husbands to repair the damage while the ladies brought Christmas treats for the children.

That being said, my training continues, so that I'm better able to defend myself and others, should the need arise. For the past few months, I've attended jiu-jitsu classes at a studio a few blocks away. Further, Sam and his grandfather taught me how to fire a pistol during our time in Twain Harte. When we returned home, I bought a small Colt Vest Pocket weighing less than a pound with a barrel length of only two inches—small enough to conceal in a handbag. I'm still not entirely comfortable firing it, but with practice, I hope to increase my confidence.

After more than three months, Corvi's deception still plagues me. I'd like to think that—given years of dealing with Eddie's lies and betrayals—I could easily see through a prevaricator. But Corvi's neediness and feigned weakness triggered my protective instincts. She presented herself as the very sort of person I'm most driven to defend. Yet, in spite of everything that she did, my heart aches for the little girl who was so misused by her mother.

At the moment, I have to wonder if my difficulty moving past this case stems from the fact that Corvi's body was never recovered. Last month, a femur washed ashore a couple of miles south of Table Rock. However, the forensic scientist who analyzed the bone reported inconclusive results. The bone could have belonged to a very small adult female or a young teenager. It was difficult to tell.

I shake my shoulders to release a sudden wave of melancholy and shove the unopened envelopes into the top drawer of my desk. I'll deal with them another day. It's Christmas Eve, after all, and I have better things to do than mope around here.

"Thank you?" Uncle Charles blinks sharply while accepting the pair of champagne bottles from Sam.

"Hey, stranger," I stand on my toes and peck Sam's cheek as he walks through our front door.

Sam wraps his arm around me and nods toward his buddy, who has followed him inside, "You remember Clark, don't you?"

I shake his friend's hand. "Dr. Collins. I'm so glad you could join us tonight."

Dr. Clark Collins was the ER resident who treated Dottie and I last May. Sam and Clark bonded during their time together at Fullerton General Hospital, where Clark now works as a permanent staff physician. He was kind enough to invite Sam to stay with him for Christmas, since our house is full to the rafters with Dottie home. Uncle Charles insisted that we invite him for dinner, as well.

"Please, call me Clark," the friendly physician smiles warmly and adjusts the strap of his guitar case. "Thank you so much for inviting me."

We follow Uncle Charles into the living room, where Clara and Dottie are seated in armchairs near the fireplace. "Please make yourselves comfortable while I put these on ice," he tells Sam and Clark.

Once settled on the love seat with Sam, he murmurs, "I hope I didn't offend your uncle with the bubbly."

"Not all. You just surprised him," I reply. "But where on earth did you get them?"

Sam grins sheepishly. "Sal claims she 'found' them while diving."

I laugh, "Of course she did. I'm surprised she shared them with you, though."

"She owed me after I removed a fishing hook from her shoulder."

Clara startles. "How awful!"

Sam chuckles and shares the story of Sal's misadventure with a fisherman who refused to follow her rules. "He decided to cast from the boat, even though she told him in no uncertain terms that only trolling was permitted on deck."

"I don't like where this is going," I gulp.

"Then it will come as no surprise what happened when she inadvertently walked behind him just as he began casting his line overhead."

"Oh, no!" Dottie closes her eyes.

"Exactly. After chewing him out, she clipped the line, rowed herself to shore in the dinghy, and walked to Dr. Carroll's office," he says with an amused chuckle.

"That had to hurt," Clark winces.

"That sounds just like her!" I declare fondly. "How is she otherwise?"

"You know Sal," Sam smirks. "Incidentally, she wanted me to tell you that she still owes you a sail."

I'd hoped to go out for a brief cruise with her during my stay in October, but her ship was in drydock for maintenance. Thankfully, however, I spotted Skipper a few times from the shore during my morning walks.

Uncle Charles returns and announces, "Nan says that supper's on. Dottie, please go upstairs to round up Jack and Owen."

I don't think we've ever entertained so many people around our dining room table. When Nan moved into the cottage, she began joining us for dinner, but tonight, we had to borrow the chair from the telephone desk so that all nine of us could eat together. Before leaving for work this morning, I set the table with our best china and silverware, including a gravy boat and platter that belonged to my mother. Now, accompanied by orchestral Christmas music from the radio in the next room, we load our plates with turkey and all the trimmings.

After an initial bout of enthusiastic feasting, conversation begins in earnest, and Uncle Charles asks Sam about his next rotation.

Sam's jovial expression becomes downcast. "I'd hoped for another assignment here in Fullerton, but I'll be transferring to St. Mary Hospital in Long Beach."

My heart sank when he broke the news a few days ago. We'd both hoped to finally have more time together in person. Nevertheless, the placement makes sense. St. Mary Hospital will give him more opportunities to deliver babies—something that didn't happen as often at Fullerton General.

While the others chat, I lean against Dottie, who is seated on my right. "How are you feeling with everything? Your letters described your schoolwork but not much else," I comment.

Uncle Charles picked her up from the train station this morning after I left for work. She didn't sleep well on the sleeper car from Oakland and napped most of the afternoon, so this is the first opportunity we've had to talk.

"I know what you're getting at," she smirks. "Dad asked me the same thing on the way home. Everything's been fine since I moved in with Iris' aunt. Dr. Hoffman is very kind, and she introduced me to a colleague of hers who worked with shell-shocked soldiers after the war. He's been helpful, and I haven't had a nightmare about Mr. Mains for several weeks."

"I'm so relieved to hear that," I pat her hand. "Have you heard from Iris...or Edwin?"

Dottie gives me a sideways glance. "I've spoken with Iris on the phone a few times...and I've been writing to Edwin regularly."

"Regularly?" I tease.

"Regularly," she says firmly and leaves it at that.

"Speaking of Long Beach, did anyone hear the report on the radio today about the murder suspect the police caught there?" Clark inquires.

"Does this have to do with that couple who were kidnapped?" I ask.

I've been following the case in the newspaper for a couple of days. Zeke Caress—the head of a large gambling ring in Los Angeles—and his wife were leaving for a Mexican resort when they were kidnapped, presumably by gangsters.

"Yeah, two witnesses contacted the Long Beach police after noticing a motorist who'd pulled off the road to burn bloodied clothing."

"Did they catch the guy?" Owen asks.

"Only after a gun fight that seriously wounded an officer. But get this...the suspect had checks in his pocket that had been written by Mr. Caress for large sums of money," Clark remarks.

Jack whistles. "He's gonna hang."

"There's more," Clark declares. "The suspect's name is Ralph Sheldon—bootlegger and former lieutenant of Scarface Capone!"

"What?!" we all exclaim.

"To think...Chicago gangsters here in Southern California!" Dottie remarks.

"Oh, you'd be surprised," I comment.

"Ruby, how's Elizabeth?" Nan—visibly uncomfortable with the discussion—changes the topic.

"And when can we see *Skin Deep* at the theater?" Dottie adds.

"Well, according to Archie, it's scheduled to premiere at the Egyptian Theatre in Hollywood sometime in January. They're rushing production to capitalize on the press from Corvi's death," I explain. "The public is clamoring to see the film."

"Do ya reckon we'll see ourselves up there on the big screen? Those film fellers sure were nice," Nan recalls with a grin.

"I don't know," I admit. "Wouldn't that be something, though!"

"What's next for Elizabeth and Dean? Surely, they'll have their pick of films after *Skin Deep*," Dottie fancies.

"I do know that as soon as Warner Brothers released Dean from his contract, Stardust signed them both. The rest has been rather hush hush, but Elizabeth promised there will be a big announcement at the premiere."

She gave me no hints, but I had the impression that the news would involve more than their next film.

After dinner, Dottie, Clara, and I insist that Nan join the others in the living room while we tidy up and put away the leftovers. Uncle Charles rolls up his sleeves to help, but Clara asks him to keep an eye on the boys while they decorate the tree.

"Otherwise, they'll fling the popcorn at one another instead of stringing it," Clara shakes her head.

"Good point," my uncle agrees and lights his pipe while strolling toward the front of the house.

As Nan likes to say, "Many hands make light work," for in no time, we join the others for carols while Clark strums his guitar. Dottie and the boys continue hanging colorful glass ornaments and beaded baubles, while the rest of us try to recall the verses to "Up on the Housetop" and "Jolly Old St. Nicholas."

Jack shouts, "Do you know 'Marshmallow World?'"

"Give me a second, and I'll figure out the cords," Clark replies.

During the intermission, Nan points to a side table. "Another card arrived fer ya, Ruby. It's got a New York postmark."

I retrieve the card and slide a nail under the corner of the envelope. "It's from Miss Mabel and Miss Violet," I tell everyone.

The card depicts a Victorian Christmas scene with the greeting "May all Happiness be yours at Christmas and throughout the Coming Year" printed in black script. I flip open the card to find a note in Violet's handwriting.

Our Dear Ruby,

We hope this card finds you well. Sister and I plan to visit California soon and hope to see you. The last time we traveled west was before the big earthquake in San Francisco. I told Mabel that we shouldn't visit the Bay Area, in case that happens again. Speaking of calamities, Sister and I were most alarmed to read in the newspaper about your perilous mishap in Laguna Beach. She reminded me of our conversation with you at L'Aiglon regarding that fortune teller's prediction. If ever there was a real-life Dorian Gray, it had to be that wicked actress, Miss Styles. Please keep yourself safe.

Affectionately yours,

Violet and Mabel Tenbrook

"Let's play wink murder!" Jack announces, already distracted from his request to sing "Marshmallow World."

"Absolutely not!" his father objects.

"How about Consequences?" Clara suggests.

"I love that one!" Dottie exclaims.

Knock, knock, knock

"That might be Polly," Dottie jumps up to answer the door. "She was gonna try to slip away from her parent's party."

She returns a moment later wearing a puzzled expression.

"Who was it?" Uncle Charles asks.

"I have no idea. No one was there." Dottie shrugs. "But they left this on the porch. It has your name on it, Ruby."

She hands me a plain brown parcel, about ten inches in length and tied with string. Sure enough, "Ruby Ray" is handwritten in blocky letters on the front.

"Strange." I comment. "There's no address or return address—just my name."

"Well, go ahead—open it!" Jack urges.

The string is unknotted, so the bow slips loose quite easily. I unfold the brown parcel paper only to find a plain cardboard box bearing no marks whatsoever. Something about the simplicity of the packaging fills me with uneasiness. My neck tingles as I slowly remove the shallow-sided lid and discover that the box is empty...

...except for a single black feather.

AUTHOR'S NOTE

I have long treasured Laguna Beach as a retreat for inspiration and relaxation. Shortly after arriving at the University of California, Irvine in 1986, I was thrilled to discover this idyllic beach town nearby with enchanting coves, tidepools, and dozens of art galleries. Through the years, as I learned more about the town's history, I would often experience what is best described as time slips, where vistas of decades past opened before me—when the Hotel Laguna and La Casa del Camino were new, and the glorious Cabrillo Ballroom rose high above the Main Beach boardwalk. So, it should come as no surprise that I selected Laguna Beach as the setting for the second Ruby Ray Mystery.

As with *Felony in Fullerton*, I endeavored to achieve historical accuracy when describing places and events. However, it was necessary at times to take liberties in the interest of the story. That said, references to state and national events, newspaper articles, fashions, entertainment, even automobiles, are largely based on true events reported in digital archives and books. The information that follows is included for folks who, like me, adore Laguna Beach and wish to take a deeper dive into its rich history.

Several books and online sources were instrumental in my research on Laguna Beach in 1930, including: *Images of America: Laguna Beach* by Clarie Marie Vogel; *Then & Now: Laguna Beach* by Foster J. Eubank and Gene Felder; *Laguna Beach, California: An Illustrated, Narrative History* by Roger W. Jones; *Orange County: Postcard History Series* by the Orange County Historical Society; *The First 100 Years in Laguna Beach: 1876-1976* by Merle and Mabel Ramsey; *California Light: 1900-1930* by Patricia Trenton and William H. Gerdts; and *Early Artists in Laguna Beach: The Impressionists* by Janet Blake Dominik. I also found *A is for Arsenic: The Poisons of Agatha Christie* by Kathryn Markup to be particularly useful, for obvious reasons. And I highly recommend *From Sleepwear to Sportswear: How Beach Pajamas Reshaped Women's Fashion* by Janine D'Agati and Hannah Schiff for readers interested in the history of fashion. Of course, *The Happy Bottom Riding Club: The Life and Times of Pancho Barnes* by Lauren Kessler was my most enjoyable read, as Pancho Barnes' life story is fascinating.

Digital archives for the *New York Times*, *Times Herald*, *Los Angeles Times*, and the Center for Bibliographical Studies and Research at UC Riverside were most helpful when tracking down information about many elements of this story. In addition, the website for the Laguna Beach Historical Society included photographs, videos, and a highly detailed chronology. Finally, a YouTube video of Kai Weisser's presentation to the Laguna Beach Historical Society on October 27, 2015 was highly informative regarding the history of Laguna Beach lifeguards.

LOCATIONS

Most buildings and businesses mentioned in the book did exist in 1930, with the exception of Daisy's Dresses, Madam Ulyana's parlor, the candy shop, and the souvenir store, although businesses such as these would have existed in town at that time.

Beaches

All of the beaches and coves in the story were real; however, I took narrative liberties in a couple of cases to suit the story. First, there are currently no tidepools below the Coast Inn, nor could I find evidence that they ever existed there. Further, I depicted Table Rock as rising out of the center of the cove, but it is actually a bluff above the north end of the cove. That being said, the trail down to the beach is as described in the book, and videos are available on YouTube of people jumping from Table Rock. Nevertheless, given the submerged rocks and strong currents below the bluff, I would not recommend this.

Main Beach looked quite different in 1930, as many more buildings sat along the boardwalk. Further, above the north end of Main Beach, a pier extended from a gazebo at what is now Heisler Park to the top of Bird Rock. Built in 1926, the pier was ultimately destroyed by a major tropical storm in 1939.

Crystal Cove was owned by the Irvine family from the mid-1800s until they sold it to the State of California in 1979. During the early 1900s, James Irvine allowed people to tent camp on the beach during summers. Beginning in the 1920s, movie studios used the cove as a tropical setting for films. Producers planted palm trees and assembled grass huts, while locals added scavenged materials to create the shacks and cottages that the cove has become known for. Presently, some cottages have been restored and are available for rental.

Businesses

Laguna Beach witnessed the opening of three large hotels from 1929 through 1930. La Casa del Camino was the first to welcome guests in January 1929 as a Spanish Revival gem offering luxurious accommodations. While the Coast Inn, which opened in May 1929, could not boast the grandeur of La Casa del Camino, the panoramic views of their cliffside rooms could not be beat. Perhaps the most visible of the three, the Hotel Laguna opened its doors during the summer of 1930 and replaced the original Hotel Laguna which was condemned and razed in the 1920s. The Early California Mission-style building of the "new" Hotel Laguna included a bell tower and graceful Spanish arches. While this hotel was fully booked during Ruby's visit to Laguna Beach, in truth, the owners struggled until they launched a marketing campaign to attract guests from Hollywood. Over the years, the Hotel Laguna has welcomed many celebrity guests, including Lauren Bacall, Rosalind Russell, and John Barrymore. On a personal note, I have many fond memories of staying and dining at the Hotel Laguna with my family, as well as frequenting their beach club. The rich history of each of these hotels can be found on their respective websites, but unfortunately, both the Hotel Laguna and the Coast Inn are currently closed for lodging.

All of the restaurants where Ruby and friends dined actually existed in 1930. Café Las Ondas sat on the boardwalk next to the Hotel Laguna, and the Sandwich Mill stretched out along Forest Avenue where the Vladimir Kush Gallery now resides. In the 1920s, the

Sandwich Mill became the setting for the Round Table, where local writers and authors would gather for meetings (think Algonquin Round Table). The White House Café opened its doors in 1918 and was managed by Jennings Bird in 1930. There were signs inside and outside of the restaurant that read "Let the Birds feed you" and "Eat with the Birds." Further, a speakeasy entrance from the Twenties was reportedly located in the back alley. Of the three restaurants, the White House survived the longest until 2022 when it was replaced by Finney's Crafthouse.

The Gate has been a prominent feature of Laguna's downtown area since 1915, when it was stationed above Carl Hofer's ice cream parlor. As described in this book, a little girl won a contest to name his store, and her submission was painted on the hanging gate. Eventually the gate was moved to the corner of Park and Forest just outside of Rankin's drugstore and soda fountain. After Mr. Rankin's death, his wife donated the soda fountain to the Laguna Beach Boys Club. However, an ice cream parlor has occupied that location for as long as I can remember.

Given the park and open space that stretches along Main Beach today, it's hard to imagine the ocean view from Pacific Coast Highway obstructed by a massive building with a huge domed roof, but that's precisely how it looked in 1930. Opened in 1926, the Cabrillo Ballroom was a popular dance hall in Laguna Beach with an enormous dance floor reported to be 7,500 square feet. Over the years, many celebrities danced under its arched roof, including Douglas Fairbanks, Judy Garland, and Mickey Rooney—who was said to play the drums onstage from time to time. During the Depression, the ballroom was converted to a bowling alley but was eventually torn down.

A Union Pacific Oil filling station sat at the corner of Broadway and Coast Highway in 1930 and featured a tall hexagonal tower that served as the cashier's office. Several years later, the tower was moved across the street and installed as the now infamous Laguna Beach Lifeguard Tower. Over the years it's had many upgrades, and the tower is frequently depicted in art and photographs of Laguna Beach.

Arts Scene

By 1918, the growing beachside town of Laguna Beach had become a thriving art community, particularly attracting Impressionist and plein air painters. At that time, the Laguna Beach Art Association Gallery was located where the Hotel Laguna now stands. A decade later in 1929, thanks to the efforts of Anna Althea Hills, a more spacious custom-built gallery was opened at the location that is currently the Laguna Art Museum. Tragically, the art community lost their beloved friend just a year later, who suffered a heart attack at age 48.

The original Gallery building was moved about half a mile south in 1929 and was used by the Community Players, the local community theater group, for play rehearsals. Other community performances during the 1920s included two "Indian" Pageants in Laguna Canyon. In the early 1930s, the Community Players collaborated with other arts groups to launch the Festival of the Arts and the Pageant of the Masters, both of which continue to run each summer in Laguna Canyon.

Pomona College Marine Lab

Construction of the Pomona College Marine Laboratory began in 1913, however students did not live on campus, as depicted in this book. Instead, they lived with Laguna locals or rented tents next to the beach. Incidentally, the lab was transformed in 1934 into what was called a "Serpentarium" which studied snakes, and the last classes were held at the lab in 1944.

Dos Rocas

In 1915, Caroline Dobbins, Pancho Barnes' maternal grandmother, bought a 20-acre estate, then known as Dos Rocas—a reference to the Seal Rocks nearby. Resting on a two-hundred-foot bluff at the south end of Emerald Bay in Laguna Beach, Mrs. Dobbins built homes for herself and her daughter, Florence Mae—Pancho's mother—the latter of which was inherited by Pancho when her mother died in 1924. At one point, due to the chaos and noise from her granddaughter's parties, Mrs. Dobbins hired an architect to dismantle and reconstruct Pancho's house elsewhere on the estate. Of course, Pancho added additional bedrooms, the swimming pool, and the basement bar. In 1927, Pancho built her infamous airstrip at Dos Rocas so that her pilot friends could visit. Tragically, as mentioned in this book, the airstrip was closed in 1930 after her friend, Dick Dodds, crashed while trying to land. Today, the property is known as the Smithcliffs Community consisting of twenty multi-million-dollar homes with breathtaking views of the ocean.

EVENTS

While most of the events in this novel are entirely fictitious— including the Labor Day festivities and airshow—some were, in fact, true, and a few were just too ludicrous to leave out of the book.

Dresden China Doll Murder/Suicide

I stumbled upon an article about what was coined "The Tragedy of the Dresden China Doll" in a digital archive of the *Times Herald*, dated September 30, 1930. Additional articles published in the *New York Times* reported the gruesome news just after it occurred in April, 1930. The details unfolded just as Lillian told Ruby and shocked the Laguna Beach Community Players who never suspected that Adele Ritchie was capable of such violence.

Rumrunners and Other Smugglers

Many of the books and online articles I read about Laguna's history mentioned rumrunners using the coves to unload their contraband, particularly during the 1920s. In fact, the story about the bogus filmmakers was true. The dummy ship actually contained liquor, which some locals transferred to a truck onshore. The men were furious they'd been had, but from what I can tell, the story was told and retold for many years in Laguna Beach.

However, more than alcohol was trafficked through the coves. The French pirate, Captain Hippolyte Bouchard, was thought to have come ashore in Laguna Beach to bury treasure he had stolen from California missions during the early 1800s. Additionally, one book I read described how smugglers carried male Chinese slaves from Mexico on ships and transported them to land via Laguna Beach. The slave traders hid the men in nearby eucalyptus groves by day and then drove them to Los Angeles at night. I was horrified to learn that when the boats were spotted by law enforcement, they tied weights to the slaves' ankles and tossed them overboard to drown.

Bathing Suit Ordinance

The book *The First 100 Years in Laguna Beach: 1876-1976* by Merle and Mabel Ramsey mentioned the bathing suit ordinance of 1929. Language from the ordinance is quoted on page 71 of the book: "For women, all bathing suits must be suspended from the shoulders and cover the front of the body from the nipples to the thighs. Must not be transparent"—I chuckled at that last part. Violators faced a penalty of $300, three months in jail, or both.

PEOPLE

References to authors, famous actors and actresses, artists (including Anna Althea Hills and photographer George Hurrell), personalities (such as Madame Sylvia) and criminals were based on information found in newspapers, books, or online sources. Further, some of the Laguna locals mentioned by name were also real people. However, all of these individuals were used fictitiously as characters in this book to meet the needs of the narrative.

But what about legendary "aviatrix" (she really did hate that term) Pancho Barnes? Believe it or not, I first learned of Florence "Pancho" Barnes while standing in line for the Soaring Over California ride at Disney California Adventure. Years later, when I read that Pancho was once a Laguna Beach resident, I was thrilled to research this barnstorming, cursing, larger than life debutante. References in this book to her accomplishments and antics with her Mystery Ship were based on true stories. Further, she was the first female stunt pilot and organized the Association of Motion Picture Pilots—a fact that fit in nicely with my Labor Day event. All of the celebrities at the parties Ruby attended were real-life friends of Pancho's who also had homes in Laguna Beach or frequently visited. If you enjoyed Pancho's character in this novel and would like to learn more, I highly recommend both the documentary *The Legend of Pancho Barnes and the Happy Bottom Riding Club* and the book *The Happy Bottom Riding Club: the Life and Times of Pancho Barnes* by Lauren Kessler.

MOVIES

Given its tropical beaches and proximity to motion picture studios in Los Angeles, dozens of movies have been filmed in Laguna Beach over more than a hundred year period. From what I can tell, *False Colors* was the first of several movies filmed in Laguna during the 1910s and 1920s, including those mentioned in this book. While writing scenes that involved shooting *Skin Deep*, I drew inspiration from *Tanned Legs*, a Pre-Code musical comedy released in 1929 that was shot in Laguna and can be viewed on YouTube. A few of the most well-known movies with scenes filmed in Laguna Beach over the years include *All Quiet on the Western Front* (1930), *Lassie Come Home* (1943), *A Star is Born* (1954), *Beaches* (1988), *A Few Good Men* (1992), and *Mamma Mia!* (2008).

Still curious?

Links to additional information and other sources related to this book can be found online by scanning the following code.

Coral Cloche Press

sites.google.com

ACKNOWLEDGEMENTS

I cannot possibly list all of the family, friends, co-workers, and readers who have encouraged and supported me while writing this novel, but you know who you are, and I am profoundly grateful to you. I would like to specifically thank Nelda Stone and Karen Lagrew, along with the Laguna Beach Historical Society for answering my obscure questions and providing a wealth of information on your organization's website. As with *Felony in Fullerton*, I owe a debt of gratitude to historian Jesse La Tour, archivist Cheri Pape, and Fullerton Heritage for your assistance regarding Fullerton's history in 1930.

My heartfelt thanks to advance readers, Lesley, Amanda, Christine, Jennifer, Julie, and Monika. I greatly appreciate your insightful feedback which helped me improve the final narrative. Loving thanks to Ziyah for your kind words of encouragement and warm, gentle presence. Special thanks to Kim for your support and insightful suggestions as I navigated quite serious health challenges while writing this book. And thank you to my fantastic team of physicians for keeping me alive and thriving as best I can.

To my son, Charles, I am so thankful for the love and encouragement you've given me throughout this writing journey. Some of my favorite memories with you involve chatting about our creative projects and brainstorming together. Your dedication to your art, your students, and your commitment to building a career focused on helping others continues to inspire me. I love you with all my heart.

My dearest Lance, thank you for filling my life with joy, comfort, and love. Thank you for not calling the police when books about poisons started showing up in the mail. Thank you for answering my cryptic medical inquiries regarding things like risus sardonicus and opisthotonus. And thank you for being the first person to read this novel. Without a doubt, you are my favorite human. I say it all the time, not only do I love you—I cherish you.

ABOUT THE AUTHOR

Photo by Katie Ann O'Keefe

Southern California native Debra Brunner writes historical mysteries and has co-authored several published academic articles. She also works as a school-based speech-language pathologist. Debra began writing mysteries in 2019 when Ruby Ray introduced herself as an opportunity to dig into the rich history of Fullerton, her beloved hometown. However, she had barely completed the first few chapters when her plans were derailed by a breast cancer diagnosis and serious complications related to her treatment. Following a brush with death, Debra vowed to embrace joy whenever possible and resumed crafting her first Ruby Ray Mystery while still confined to her home. Today, when not writing novels or working with children, Debra enjoys sartorial adventures with her husband, some involving swing dancing at local Art Deco venues.

Debra L. Brunner

www.ingramcontent.com/pod-product-compliance
Lightning Source LLC
Chambersburg PA
CBHW022023110726
47901CB00006B/1637